MW00641346

Forgive or Forget Me

a novel

ANN EINERSON

Copyright © 2023 by Ann Einerson

All rights reserved.

No part of this book may be reproduced, distributed, or transmitted in any form or by any electronic or mechanical means, including information storage and retrieval systems, without written permission from the author, except for the use of brief quotations in a book review.

This book is a work of fiction. Names, characters, businesses, places, and events are the products of the author's imagination or are used in a fictitious manner. Any resemblance to actual persons, living or dead, or actual events is coincidental.

ISBN: 978-1-960325-01-3

Credits:

Developmental Editor: Sam Chavez, Samwise Reads Editing

Editors: Brooke Crites, Proofreading by Brooke | Jovana Shirley, Unforeseen Editing

Proofreader: Brooke Crites, Proofreading by Brooke

Cover Designer: Nicole Hower

To those who have suffered a miscarriage, battled cancer, lost a loved one, or endured a broken heart. I admire your bravery, strength, and resolve.

Playlist

"You Could Be Happy" by Snow Patrol

"Someone You Loved" by Lewis Capaldi

"Play This When I'm Gone" by Machine Gun Kelly

"Fingers Crossed" by Trevor Daniel, featuring Julia Michaels

"Paris" by The Chainsmokers

"Somewhere Only We Know" by Keane

"Issues" by Julia Michaels

"Faded" by Alan Walker

"So Good" by Halsey

"If You're Going Through Hell" by Rodney Atkins

"Home" by Edward Sharpe and The Magnetic Zeros

"Until I Found You" by Stephen Sanchez

Author's Note

I WROTE THIS BOOK WITH you, the reader, in mind. I want you to experience the events taking place right alongside Milo and Olivia, and there are several scenes that might be a trigger to some.

For a detailed list of content warnings for this book, scan the code below or visit AnnEinerson.com.

Chapter One

OLIVIA
Present Day—October

LOVE, LOSS, PASSION, AND RESENTMENT.

On the surface, these four little words don't appear to have much in common. Yet, if you examine them up close, you'll find that you can't experience one without the others.

With great love comes grave loss, and with unbridled passion comes all-consuming resentment that brands your soul.

My name is Olivia Rae Dunham, and I know firsthand the havoc these four little words can cause. I know all too well what it feels like to love a person more than I love myself. To cripple over in pain from a loss so great I didn't think I would survive it. To feel immense pleasure while in the throes of ecstasy. To let resentment fill my soul when the person I care about most betrays me.

A fifth little word has my entire life hanging in the balance: *forgiveness.*

The action of forgiving. The willingness to put aside the betrayal you feel when another person has wronged you.

How does a person wholeheartedly forgive someone when both parties have hurt each other? When the offense is so egregious, it costs someone else their life? What happens when the truth a person has believed their entire life isn't the truth at all?

If you don't choose to forgive, the bitterness will consume you whole, gradually stripping away your ability to achieve true happiness, until you're left with nothing but your thirst for revenge.

Which begs the question, which is easier: to *forgive* or to *forget?*

My body is weighed down with bone-deep exhaustion, and I instinctively want to wrap myself in warmth. Reaching down to pull my organic cotton duvet over my head, I'm vaguely aware of my hands grasping thin air.

I scrunch my nose, trying to recall where I fell asleep last night. Did I fall from my bed after another anxiety-ridden night terror, or pass out on one of the cots in the on-call room after a long shift?

I slowly pry my eyelids open and blink rapidly as I try to reorient myself. The fluorescent light overhead flickers as the potent smell of antiseptic and bleach invades my nostrils. I scan the stark white hospital room as the walls close in around me and I struggle to gulp in fresh air.

The sterile, cramped space brings back a flood of unwanted memories from my past, taking me back to when I was sitting in a similar room all those years ago, listening to a young man break apart after he received the tragic news that altered life as he knew it. To the distant smell of vomit while I held my mom's head in my hands, her prized chestnut locks thinning from the failed round of chemo. To the far-off sound of my own sobs as I lay alone, curled up in a hospital bed, grieving a loss so devastating that I thought I would never recover.

Taking my therapist's advice, I inhale slowly for five seconds and exhale for another five, counting as I go.

Breathe in for one, two, three, four, five.

Breathe out for one, two, three, four, five.

I squeeze my eyes shut, solely focused on the gradual rise and fall of my chest as I repeat the breathing exercise several times over, pushing back the impending panic attack trying to find its way to the surface. I can't help the humorless laugh that escapes my lips as I think about the severity of my situation.

I'm a pediatric oncologist who practically lives at the hospital most days. Yet, in times like this, ghosts of my past return, rendering me unable to control the residual trauma of being surrounded by death and sickness.

Over the years, I've strived to build an impenetrable wall around my consciousness, searching for creative ways to disassociate my past experience as a patient's family member from my present role as a care provider.

Pediatric cancer ruthlessly robs children of their independence and youthful innocence, often requiring them to take on the role of the comforter as they put on a brave face for their loved ones.

I fight tooth and nail to keep my young patients alive, and I have been fortunate to watch countless families come together in a united front to help a sick child live to adulthood. It's an honor to do everything in my power to ensure families don't have to go through the gut-wrenching pain of losing a loved one to cancer like I did. I know firsthand that there is no peace in the aftermath of their death, and many people find themselves living a lonely existence, one without purpose, unable to move on, trapped in an endless loop of solitude and torment with no escape.

Like me.

I find it difficult at times to shut off the overwhelming emotions swirling inside of me when I remember what it was like to watch my mom lose her life to an inoperable glioblastoma. I had known from a young age that I wanted to be a doctor, but the day she died, I vowed to dedicate the rest of my life to fighting cancer.

And now, years later, it's ironic that I'm being forced to watch yet another person I love lose their fight against the same unforgiving disease.

I often ask myself what I must have done in a previous life to deserve so much heartache and loss. It seems that the universe has been against me all along, taking away the people responsible for my happiness one by one until I'm left completely alone.

"Olivia." I hear my name hoarsely being called out. "Kiddo, are you alright?" Mac's strained voice shakes me out of my dismal thoughts.

In this particular hospital room on the fourth floor, I'm not Dr. Dunham, the pediatric oncologist who helps children fight cancer.

Here, I'm just Olivia.

A helpless family member, watching Mac Covell—the man who's been my father figure for the past fifteen years—wasting away from terminal pancreatic cancer, unable to control the outcome of his diagnosis.

I take one more deep breath before opening my eyes, finding Mac staring back at me with a concerned expression. He reaches his trembling hand up to tenderly wipe away a tear that must have snuck past my eyelid without permission.

I shift my focus to Mac, who is being swallowed whole by the twin-sized hospital bed.

Once a burly man with muscular arms, he is now nothing more than skin and bones. His cheeks are sunken in from extreme weight loss, his bald head is a reminder of the failed chemotherapy, and his ocean blue eyes are hazy from the cocktail of drugs flowing through his system. The most unfortunate side effect is a near-constant, groggy-like state, leaving a mere shell of the man I knew in its wake.

Until three days ago, he refused a single dose of pain medication.

As a recovering alcoholic who is nineteen years sober, he insisted on waiting until the pain was unbearable before he accepted any drugs. I sighed in relief when he finally asked the nurse for morphine the other night, knowing that I no longer had to watch him suffer unnecessarily.

"Good morning, Mac," I say, plastering on an over-the-top smile and gently grabbing his hand, still resting on my cheek, keeping it in place. I inhale the citrus and clove—Mac's signature smell—adding this moment to the ever-growing list of memories I want to file away to revisit when he's gone.

"You stayed the night again?" Mac's brow furrows in concentration as he scowls down at my crumpled navy-blue scrubs and the metal folding chair I slept on.

I came straight to his room after my shift last night, confused when I found the green recliner that had once resided in the corner of the room missing. It turned out, the patient next door—a woman battling liver disease—had her two daughters stay the night. Mac had heard the nurses talking and insisted they roll the chair from his room to hers so the girls could both sleep comfortably next to their mom.

Leave it to Mac to be thinking of others even while he's at his worst.

"Kiddo, you look like absolute shit," he says frankly. "You haven't slept in a real bed in over a week, and you've barely eaten since I was admitted. It's about damn time you put yourself first. I might not be around much longer, but that doesn't give you an excuse to let yourself go." His eyes bore into mine, silently daring me to try a rebuttal.

I gape at him, pleasantly surprised that his unfiltered opinions are in full force today. His good days are rapidly dwindling, and I'm filled with gratitude each time I get a rare sighting of his brash side.

"Thanks for the boost of confidence. I appreciate being told that my appearance is subpar—that's what every girl wants to hear." My voice drips with sarcasm as Mac gives me a smug smile, appearing very pleased with his joke until his expression slowly shifts to a serious one.

"All I want is what's best for you, and spending every waking moment caring for a dying old man isn't it."

I release a sigh, frustrated he doesn't understand. "Mac, from the moment we met, you've always put me first. Even from inside a prison cell, you did everything possible to take care of me. It's my turn to look after you now, okay?" I say with sincerity. "In full transparency, you should know my primary reasons for doing this are purely selfish. For starters, I get extended time off work, and as a bonus, I don't have to socialize with anyone else while I'm away. It's a win-win if you ask me." I give a forced smile, hoping he doesn't hear the crack in my voice.

After Mac was hospitalized last week and the diagnosis was that he wasn't going to get better, it was a no-brainer for me to take an extended leave of absence from work. I know our time together is limited, and I refuse to miss a single minute.

"You're the only family I have left. Please let me do this for you," I beg, taking hold of his hands and clasping them tightly in mine.

"That's bullshit, and we both know it," he says sternly. "I'm not the only family you have left. Milo might not be my biggest fan, but I know he'd come for you."

His words cause the unhealed bruise on my heart to ache.

"Mac, he left me behind. He could have come back at any point over the past fifteen years, but he never did," I say, my voice dripping with venom. "That's not how family treats each other. Besides, he'd want an explanation for why you're in my life, and I don't owe him that. I don't owe him anything, not after what he did to me. Can we please drop it now? I'd like to get you discharged so we can get you out of here. What do you say?"

Mac nods, sensing it's best to move on to another subject. "I got confirmation last night that my parents' brownstone is ready. Jane is going to meet us there. I'll sleep comfortably tonight in a giant, king-sized bed and wake up feeling refreshed in the morning," I promise.

That's a lie.

There's a good chance I'll continue to spend the night by his side, fixated on the unsteady rise and fall of his chest to ensure he's still breathing.

As if Mac can sense my unease, he squeezes both my hands. "You know I appreciate everything you're doing for me, right? I would do anything to take away your grief."

"I'm a big girl. I can handle this."

"I know you can. I just wish you didn't have to."

"Thank you," I whisper softly.

"I've been thinking…my days are numbered, and I might not have another chance to tell you this," he starts. "You're the daughter Jada and I always wanted, and if things had played out differently, you would have been my daughter-in-law. I couldn't be more proud of the beautiful, brave, and dedicated woman you've become. Everything good I've experienced in the past fifteen years is because you had the courage to walk into my life." His eyes shine with sincerity. "I mean it when I say that you deserve the whole wide world served to you on a silver platter. I don't want you to spend the rest of your life mourning me. It's high time you learned to live again, my beautiful Olivia. Don't be a prisoner to your past any longer.

You deserve better. Take life by the horns and show it who's boss."

His words feel like poison coursing through my veins. How can I live happily ever after when everyone who's ever meant anything to me has passed away or left me behind?

"Mac, I—"

"I'm not finished," he interrupts. "Promise me, Olivia…promise me you'll live a life of infinite happiness, no matter what it takes. Don't let the grief debilitate you like last time. Take it from a man who's spent the last two decades living in the past…it won't do you any good. Promise me that you'll try…please?" He stares at me, pleading.

I'm speechless, and I can't help the tears streaming down my face this time.

Once upon a time, I was surrounded by a loving family and a boy who promised me forever, a future of immeasurable joy on the horizon. Unfortunately, those things slipped through my fingers one by one until I lost all hope, left only with agonizing pain and suffering filling the corners of my soul.

The day I met Mac, he sat shackled to a rusted metal table at the New Jersey State Prison, and he saved my life—in more ways than one.

The big, muscular, tattooed man with a scar slashed across his left eyebrow gave me a quizzical look when he found me waiting for him in the prison visiting area. I remember staring up at him, watching him with uncertainty as he walked toward me. Tears pooled in my eyes as I realized that, aside from his skin tone, Milo was the spitting image of Mac.

He skeptically eyed the guards as if silently asking them what to do with the emotional teenage girl standing before him, the one he had never officially met and had no familial ties to.

He must have smelled my desperation for a parental figure because he slowly approached me, the steel limiting his movements as he hesitantly accepted my impromptu hug— despite the no-contact rule. He awkwardly wrapped his arms around me before lightly patting me on the head like you would a puppy.

Despite our unconventional circumstances, a rare bond was formed inside the walls of a dark, dank, prison visiting room. In the most unlikely place, we both found a renewed purpose.

When Mac was given the chance at parole eight years ago, I did everything I could to ensure it was granted. It was nothing short of a miracle that he was released when he was, and I thank God every day for the time we've had together since. At my insistence, he moved in with me after he was a free man.

He was diagnosed with pancreatic cancer for the first time three years ago. Thankfully, we caught it early, and after several rounds of chemotherapy and radiation, he was declared to be in remission. Unfortunately, six months ago, during a routine checkup, we discovered the cancer was back with a vengeance, and no amount of treatment could cure the disease this time.

We'd both been pretending everything is fine, until last week, when Mac collapsed in our kitchen while preparing his morning coffee. I had just gotten home from a graveyard shift and immediately called 911, lucky to have found him in time. We were forced to face the stark reality of Mac's terminal diagnosis, unable to ignore it any longer.

I refused to let Mac spend his last days surrounded by a revolving door of nurses and nursing aides who consider him just another job, and I am looking forward to finally getting him released from the hospital today.

"I'm going to go see about getting you discharged so we can head home," I say into Mac's hair.

My parents' empty brownstone isn't really a home. It hasn't been in a long time, but I'll pretend for Mac's sake. I know he'll be more comfortable once we can get him out of the crowded hospital and remove all the tubes and monitors hooked up to his body.

I let go of his hands and get up out of my chair. Once I get to the door, I make sure to close it behind me so that Mac isn't disturbed by any commotion from fellow patients or staff.

I turn around, bumping into what feels like a solid brick wall. As I stumble backward, a firm hand grips my forearm to keep me from falling over. I slowly look up to see long legs, finding that the brick wall I bumped into is actually a person.

"Oh my gosh, I am so sorry. I need to look where I'm going next—" I'm cut off from my rambling when I lift my gaze further and see the man standing before me is none other than Milo Covell. The boy who left me behind all those years ago without so much as a goodbye.

His jet-black hair is styled with the top in natural curls and the sides trimmed into a tapered fade. His flawless, bronzed skin complements his arctic blue eyes perfectly as he stares daggers at me, void of emotion.

I can feel his animosity immediately. The man might look like he stepped straight off the red carpet, an angel in disguise, but there's no doubt in my mind that he's here to play the role of the devil.

I stare up at him, frozen in place. My mouth feels like it's stuffed with cotton, making it impossible to form a coherent sentence, let alone a single word. My heart is about to beat out of my chest, and I've suddenly reverted back to the lovestruck teenager I used to be.

Milo Covell was once my best friend, soulmate, and kindred spirit. We were inseparable, and he vowed to never leave me, promising it would always be us against the world.

He lied.

When things got hard, he left in the blink of an eye, disappearing without a word.

Seeing him standing before me right now, I almost forget the past, wishing he would wrap his strong arms around me and embrace me in a hug like he used to when I needed his comfort. However, based on his facial expression, it appears that, after all these years, he'd rather hug a porcupine.

I'm at a loss as to why he's here, trying to march into Mac's hospital room like he owns the place.

Who does he think he is?

He hasn't contacted Mac or me a single time in the past fifteen years. Mac's lawyer made it clear that Milo had done everything possible to keep Mac from being granted parole, and that he was outraged when Mac was released.

As I observe Milo, the scent of his resentment permeates the air when he registers that I'm here with his father. The man he believes to be responsible for his mom's death.

To his credit, before he left New York, I had never met Mac. I had only heard from Milo how much he hated the man and why he had chosen to disown his father.

I refuse to let Milo intimidate me. He made the decision to abandon me, leaving me to my own devices, so it's his burden to deal with the rippling repercussions of his past choices. Mac is my family now, and anyone who tries to mess with my family will have to go through me.

I draw in a deep breath, straighten my spine, and stare straight into Milo's emotionless eyes. He made his bed, and now, after all these years, it's finally time for him to lie in it.

"Hi, Milo," I say, my voice steely with confidence even though I'm shaking like a leaf caught in a windstorm.

Chapter Two

MILO
Present Day—October

I STAND FROZEN OUTSIDE MAC'S hospital room—he lost the right to be called Dad the day he made the decision to drive drunk, resulting in Ma's death.

I find myself staring down at the alluring ghost from my past: my beautiful Stardust.

Olivia has haunted my dreams every night of the past fifteen years. I've been back to New York plenty of times since then for work, but I've resisted the temptation to reach out. If I heard her voice, I would need to see her, touch her, taste her.

From the moment I saw her for the first time, it was as if an invisible tether had bound our souls, shackling us together, for better or worse. The pull I feel toward her is undeniable, even after all these years. I wish more than anything there were a way to permanently sever our connection, to rip the cord linking us so I could leave her behind once and for all.

When I left my old life behind a week after my eighteenth birthday, I thought it was for good. I didn't think my past would ever catch up to me.

Until eight years ago, when my then-assistant, Julie, timidly entered my office. She had a message from the New Jersey State Parole Board, notifying me that my estranged father, Mac Arthur Covell, was up for parole. I was enraged at the injustice of the situation.

Ma didn't get a second chance at life, so why should he?

I felt much better after unceremoniously launching my laptop across the room, shattering the frosted glass wall separating my office from the reception area, and then getting rip-roaring drunk, courtesy of Jack Daniels.

I stewed in my resentment for over a week, and then Mac's bastard of an attorney had the audacity to reach out to me. He asked if I would speak to the parole board—*on Mac's behalf*—which showed how little Mac had told him about our relationship. He claimed they had "new information" regarding the case that would persuade the board to grant Mac parole.

I didn't give a damn what information they had; I knew the truth.

I told the hotshot lawyer to go to hell before hitting end on our conversation.

After hanging up, it occurred to me that Mac no longer had a public defender representing him. I wondered who was footing the bill, as I knew he didn't have the money to afford legal counsel, but I never investigated it further.

Now that I see Olivia standing in front of me, it's clear that she's the one who helped him, though I still have no idea why she would do that.

I flew to New Jersey the day of Mac's hearing to provide in-person testimony, begging the board not to grant him parole. I wove the tale of an emotionally damaged kid who would never recover from losing his mother so tragically, pleading with them not to release Mac early.

It wasn't a lie. I am emotionally damaged, and anyone who knows me can attest to that.

The truth of the matter is, Mac was a devoted father and husband. He loved Mom and me unconditionally, and at one time, I thought he hung the moon, worshipping his every word. Unfortunately, in the end, he loved alcohol more, and he let it destroy our family beyond repair.

The day I found out he had been set free despite my best efforts, I drowned myself in a bottle of whiskey and chain-smoked four packs of cigarettes.

Over the years, I almost managed to forget Mac was a free man. He knew better than to try and reach out to me. Until six months ago.

A single letter showed up on my desk, Mac's handwritten name mocking me in the upper-left corner, no return address included. I ripped it to shreds and notified Richard, my assistant, to throw away any subsequent letters.

Pike, my predecessor as CEO of Lawson Co., my mentor, and my dear friend, insisted I take Richard on a few years back, saying that I needed someone who would refuse to entertain my childish behavior. Richard had worked for Pike for several years at that point, and he is still resentful that he got stuck with me.

Yesterday, while Richard was out for lunch, a call came through that I sent straight to voicemail, but I couldn't resist listening to it when I didn't recognize the caller. Later that night, I paced back and forth in my living room, playing it on repeat, the words consuming my mind.

"Milo, this is Jane Roberts. I'm a nurse at Jameson Memorial Hospital in New York City and a friend of Olivia's. I'm calling regarding your father, Mac Covell. He's been hospitalized, and I'm sorry to say, it doesn't look good. He's been put on hospice. I'm concerned about Olivia and thought you might be able to help. She's been beside herself with grief and could really use a support system right now. From what she's told me, you lived with her family during high school but haven't seen each other in a while. I wouldn't be calling if she didn't need you here. They should be releasing Mac sometime tomorrow, so hopefully you get this message in time. If you're anything like your father, you must be a great man, and I know you'll do the right thing."

At first, I was stunned, but that quickly turned to rage.

Olivia had never met Mac—at least not when I was around. I only visited him in prison once, and she didn't come with me. She knew I hated the man, and she should have been celebrating right alongside me that he was finally getting what he deserved. Instead, she was apparently spending her days and nights at his bedside. Not to mention, this Jane person must not know Mac very well if she thinks he's a great man.

Just when I was ready to go to the nearest bar and get hammered, my phone rang, Pike's name flashing across the screen.

"What do you need, old man? I'm busy," I said, impatiently tapping my foot.

"Let me guess. You're about to head out to a bar or strip club. Those appear to be your only coping mechanisms as of late," he countered.

"What makes you think I need to cope with anything? Why can't I enjoy some good booze and hot sex after work?" I snapped back.

"It's never made you happy before, yet you keep doing it, hoping for a different result. Richard called me after he saw you storm out of the office."

Of course he had, the sneaky bastard.

"He mentioned a voicemail regarding Mac and thought I might be able to talk some sense into you. Milo, it's okay if you're struggling with this news...you know that, right?"

I blatantly ignored his comment about Mac, not ready to discuss it.

"What the hell, Pike? Richard's my assistant, not my babysitter. You made the decision to give him up, and he shouldn't be reporting back to you anymore. Especially not when you're retired. I'm the CEO now, shouldn't his loyalty be to me?" I questioned. "You know what? Since you're his pal, tell him not to bother showing his face at work on Monday. He's fired."

Pike let out an exasperated sigh, not impressed with my antics. "First off, I'm semi-retired—there's a difference, and don't you forget it," he stated, leaving no room for argument.

"I started this company from the ground up, so you can bet your ass I'm getting regular updates to guarantee you don't burn the place down. You might have proved yourself as CEO, but you're a shit boss and an even worse team player. Someone's got to keep you under control." He paused for effect before continuing, "Second, we both know Richard is the best employee we've ever had. You're not firing him. In fact, he's getting a raise for calling me so quickly."

I rolled my eyes at Pike's theatrics, thankful he couldn't see me. "Fine, you win. Richard stays. Can I hang up now?"

"No, Milo, you can't. You know why I called, so stop stalling. Eloisa and I talked about it, and we think you should visit Mac. This might be your last opportunity. Besides, you were heading to New York next week for the Bushwick project anyway. It wouldn't hurt if you went a few days early."

I groaned loudly into the phone, making my annoyance known.

Of course Pike had discussed it with Eloisa. You'd think being married would be enough. Oh no, those two gossiped like old ladies at the hair salon. They couldn't go more than five minutes without making another decision related to *my* personal life. I was a grown man, for Christ's sake. I should be allowed to handle my own problems without them meddling.

They only want what's best for you. Is that so bad?

"Milo, you are part of our family first and foremost, CEO of my company second, so it's well within my rights to tell you that you've taken this too far."

I hated when he made valid points.

"Son, you've never grieved properly. You didn't only lose your mom when she died; you lost your dad too. I know from personal experience that type of loss changes a person. If you choose not to see Mac before he passes, that's on you, but trust me when I say you'll regret that decision for the rest of your life. You don't have to forgive him, but you should find the closure you need to move forward. You've let the animosity you feel for him consume you for far too long. No amount of booze, sex, or drugs will take away the pain you feel."

There was a sudden silence on Pike's end of the phone before he sighed.

"Milo, clearly you don't want to hear what I have to say. I'm going to hang up now. Eloisa and I are here if you need us."

True to his word, he didn't wait for a reply before he hung up. That was the thing I liked most about Pike—he knew me well enough to give me space after speaking his mind.

I would never forgive Mac for what he did. He took Ma away from me, and that wasn't something I'd *ever* get over. However, Pike was right: I needed closure. I had to figure out why Olivia had gotten involved with Mac in the first place and how she could betray me.

Which was how I found myself throwing together an overnight bag after finding a first-class ticket in my inbox, courtesy of Richard. He knew I detested crowds and needed personal space that economy wouldn't provide.

That brings me back to the here and now, where I'm staring back at the enchanting goddess in front of me. She peers up at me with dazzling, emerald-green eyes. Her shoulder-length caramel hair falls gently around her face. Her signature scent of vanilla, jasmine, and orchid wafts through the air. I'm not surprised she still uses the same perfume after all this time. She's always been a creature of habit. Once she finds something she likes, she sticks with it.

Like you—until you left.

Her rumpled navy-blue scrubs mold perfectly to her body, doing nothing to hide her flawless hourglass figure.

She's all grown up.

We're suspended in time, immersed in a moment meant for the two of us, where I never left her behind and she didn't welcome my estranged father into her life with open arms.

"Hello, Stardust." The former nickname passes through my lips without permission.

I absentmindedly reach out to tuck a stray piece of hair behind her ear, and a slight shudder ripples through her body at my touch. Despite the time that has passed since we've seen each other, our chemistry is still as explosive as ever.

The slight movement snaps me back to reality, and I snatch my hand back, placing it at my side. Olivia betrayed me, and I don't think I can forgive her.

"Milo, wh-what are you doing here?" she stutters.

Given how shaken up Olivia seems by my surprise appearance, I assume Jane must not have given her a heads-up that she called me.

Unfortunately for Olivia, I didn't come here for pleasantries. As far as I'm concerned, our history was null and void the moment she befriended Mac. My outrage starts to bubble up, and I can't contain it anymore. Turns out a lifetime of emotional damage means also having a slight anger management problem.

"What are *you* doing here, O-liv-i-a?" I punctuate each syllable of her name, making sure she knows I'm purposefully using her full name.

She's always been Liv to me, and soon after that, she became my Stardust. My charismatic, beautiful, source-of-sunlight Stardust.

Not now, though. Not after what she's done.

"Is it safe to assume it's not a coincidence that you're walking out of Mac's hospital room? You know, the man responsible for killing my mother?" I say with a sneer. "I was hoping he would be dead by the time I got here, but I guess that was too much to ask."

She flinches at my cruel and insensitive words.

"How could you do this to me? You know better than anyone the devastation he caused. He deserves to die alone, not to have someone like you at his beck and call."

Liv glares at me, refusing to give me the courtesy of a reply.

There I go again, using one of her damn nicknames. At least I didn't say it out loud this time.

"Answer me, dammit! How could you do this to me? I want the truth!" I realize too late that I'm shouting. My hand is wrapped around her wrist, prepared to drag her out of this damn hospital, away from the monster behind the door she's blocking with her body, as if Mac's the one who needs to be shielded from me.

"That is quite enough of your bull...crap." Olivia's eyes are lit with fury as she yanks her wrist from my firm grip.

I guess she's never gotten over her aversion to swearing—another habit she must have held on to after all these years. Too bad I don't have the same problem.

"You lost the right to an opinion regarding my life choices the moment you abandoned me the morning after my own mother's funeral. You have absolutely no idea what I've been through since you left. If you think you can march into this hospital making demands, you're wrong. This is my place of work, my territory." She jabs her finger into my chest for emphasis. "You don't get to charge back into my life like this. I won't allow it. You want the truth? The truth is that I consider Mac my family, so get used to it. Nothing you say or do will change that, and I refuse to let you ruin the limited time he has left. He deserves so much more than that, Milo, despite what you think."

I let out a snarled growl. I'm furious watching Olivia stand firmly in front of Mac's door, barring me from entering as if she were a knight protecting her king. She folds her arms against her chest, daring me to make my next move. I forgot how stubborn she could be, but I won't make that mistake again. I came for answers, and I'll get them one way or another.

"Olivia, I'm telling you to move aside. I've come a long way, and there is a whole lot that I've waited too long to say to that bastard. I deserve to tell him off before he finally bites the—"

"Dr. Dunham, are you okay?"

I'm interrupted by a soft voice coming from behind me. I turn around to find a petite woman with a pixie cut and oversized square glasses dwarfing her small face pushing a girl in a wheelchair.

The woman narrows her eyes at me suspiciously, seemingly concerned that I'm going to hurt Liv. Even in my unstable emotional state, I would never physically hurt her. It doesn't seem like I have a problem with causing her emotional pain, though.

We're the only ones in the hallway, and I quickly deduce that the woman is addressing Liv, since I'm sure as hell not Dr. Dunham.

That means...*she really did it.* Liv became a doctor.

Despite my best efforts to tamp down the unwanted reaction, I can't help but feel a sense of pride that she fulfilled her dream. I shouldn't care about her anymore, but I've also never learned how to stop.

Liv's face immediately lights up with a genuine smile. "Stella, Grace, I'm so glad you stopped by. I've missed you both so much." She embraces Stella before bending down to envelop Grace in a hug.

The little girl is dressed in a fluorescent-pink jogger set, pastel tennis shoes with a heart pattern that light up every time she moves, and a tie-dye scarf covering her bald head. Her bright hazel eyes shine with excitement, and she seems full of life.

"Dr. Dunham, you're silly. I saw you yesterday, so you couldn't have missed me *that* much!" Grace bursts into a fit of giggles before forcing a serious expression back on her face. "Is Mac awake? I have the biggest, most bestest news, and I can't wait to tell you both." Grace is practically bouncing out of her chair, her shoes lighting up like a Christmas tree from all the movement.

She's far too bright and cheery for my taste and those damn shoes are giving me a headache. Despite her sunny disposition, she's a little nuisance in my opinion.

"Let's go check, why don't we? He'll be delighted to see you. I wonder what on earth this exciting news could be." Liv gives Grace a knowing grin with a twinkle in her eye. She ignores me as she opens the door to Mac's hospital room, pushing Grace's wheelchair inside.

I'm ready to follow behind Liv, refusing to miss my chance to observe this interaction, when I hear a quiet, "Excuse me, sir."

I glance back to see Stella, who I can only assume is Grace's mom, standing firmly in place with her hands clasped tightly in fists and a scowl on her face.

"I have something I'd like to share with you before I go inside." She points toward Mac's room. "My Grace was only six years old when she was diagnosed with leukemia. Dr. Dunham has been an absolute godsend this past year, supporting us at every turn," she says with adoration. "On the day of Grace's first round of chemo, Mac stopped by with a stuffed elephant adorned with a rainbow-colored, polka-dot bow on its head, somehow knowing that had been Grace's favorite accessory. He didn't know us, but he was there for Grace because she was important to Dr. Dunham. During every round of chemo, he showed up with a book, puzzle, or another stuffed animal to add to Grace's ever-growing collection, and he stayed by her side during every treatment. Once he was diagnosed with cancer a second time, Dr. Dunham made it possible for him and Grace to get their treatments together."

Stella lets out a long breath before going on. "I lost my husband to an unexplained case of cardiac arrhythmia three years ago. I woke up one morning, and he was gone." She pauses, a flicker of pain flashing in her eyes. "A week after his funeral, I had a miscarriage, losing our second child. Grace is all I have left, and without Dr. Dunham and Mac, I wouldn't have gotten through her cancer diagnosis."

Stella shuffles from side to side, obviously uncomfortable sharing these painful memories with a total stranger, but she doesn't let that deter her from finishing her thought.

"I might not know Dr. Dunham's life story, but I know what tremendous loss looks like. I see a familiar haunted expression lingering in her eyes, similar to mine. She saved my baby girl and has become a good friend to me. She deserves nothing but the best. I don't know who you are, but I won't tolerate you coming here to bully Dr. Dunham or Mac. So, if you mean them any harm, you can turn around and go back to where you came from."

The brazen woman doesn't give me a chance to respond before brushing right past me while I stand, dumbstruck, in the middle of the hall, unable to fully process what just happened.

I'm shaken out of my thoughts by another round of giggles coming from Mac's room. I hesitantly take a couple of steps toward a curtain separating me from the room, giving me partial visibility while keeping me out of view.

I can see that Grace's wheelchair has been pushed up close to Mac's hospital bed, and the little girl is grinning from ear to ear. "Can you believe it, Mac? I'm not sick anymore!" she exclaims. "I can finally go back to school and play with all my friends. I am so excited!"

She leaps out of her wheelchair, launching herself onto the bed, wrapping her small hands around Mac's neck as she nuzzles her head into the crook of his shoulder. Mac lets out a small grunt of discomfort, but he doesn't outwardly show any signs of pain.

"They even let me ring the bell this morning," Grace declares.

Mac gives her a droopy, lopsided grin. "I'm so happy for you, Peanut." He gingerly leans into her embrace.

It's obvious this little girl thinks the world of this man, and it rubs me the wrong way. He cut my childhood short without remorse, yet here he is, giving another kid the love stolen right out from underneath me.

"I wish Dr. Dunham had been the one to give me the news, but I know you needed her more than I did. I just want you to get better too. I'm not ready for you to go to heaven," Grace whispers. Her smile dims, and she drops her head down in defeat.

"Hey there, Peanut. It's going to be okay, you'll see." With great effort, Mac reaches out to lift her chin with his thumb so she's looking up at him. "Remember what we talked about a few weeks ago? Heaven is a beautiful place. They've got unlimited ice cream, unicorn rides, and ice skating. Besides, I'll finally be with my Jada again. I miss her very much," Mac says solemnly.

I'm angry that he would even dare to bring up Ma, especially after what he did to her.

Suddenly, Liv jerks her head in my direction, somehow sensing my presence. Her eyes are wide with horror, and there's no question she's nervous that I might storm in and destroy this perfect moment after Mac's comment.

I'm not that coldhearted. Grace didn't do anything wrong, and she deserves this moment of victory for kicking cancer's ass.

"It makes me happy to know you'll be here to take care of Olivia when I'm gone. She's going to be really sad, and she'll need you to be her friend. Can you do that for me?" Mac asks.

Grace enthusiastically nods her head before turning to Liv. "Don't worry, Dr. Dunham! You won't be alone. Mom and I would *never* let that happen. You can be part of our family now."

Liv walks over and scoops Grace off the bed. She twirls her around as she gives her a giant bear hug. "Thanks, Little Miss Grace. You have been an exemplary patient, and I'm so glad you're finally in remission."

I continue to watch from my place near the door as Stella and Grace say their goodbyes to Mac and Olivia. As the mother-daughter duo passes me, Grace crooks her finger, beckoning me to lean down so she can talk to me. I arch my eyebrow in surprise but figure it's best not to infuriate the kid with the obnoxious light-up shoes.

I slowly bend down so I'm at her level. "What do you want, little girl?"

"Hi there, mister. Are you Dr. Dunham's friend?" she asks inquisitively.

That's a loaded question.

"We used to be friends. Why do you ask?"

"She's brave like me, but I know she's really sad that Mac is sick," Grace says with a solemn expression. "I was hoping that if you were her friend, you could take care of her until I can visit her again. That way, between the two of us, she'd never have to be lonely. Isn't that a great plan?"

I pause for a moment, unsure of how to respond. I don't want to complicate things by giving her an answer she won't understand.

"Sure, kid, I'll keep an eye on her."

"You really mean it? Promise?" Smart kid to question my motives.

"Yes, I promise that Dr. Dunham won't be lonely, okay?"

Technically, it's not a lie—at least until I get the answers I'm looking for. That doesn't mean that I'll be good company, but she never specified that part.

"Thank you!" She claps her hands with glee as she kicks her feet on the wheelchair's footrests, her shoes flashing on impact.

As Stella starts to push Grace down the hall, she gives me a warning look as she passes.

Her threats don't scare me, though.

No matter the cost, I'm here to get the answers I came for, and no one can stop me.

Chapter Three

OLIVIA
Past—Ninth Grade

I TRUDGE DOWN THE STREET, the scorching sun beating down on my face as sweat trickles from my forehead. My clammy hands keep sticking to the copy of *Bastien Piano Basics: Primer Level* that I'm holding.

I should have brought my backpack. I'm sure Mom will say she told me so when I complain about the sheets sticking together the next time I have to practice.

Now that we're back in New York after spending the summer in Paris, Father insisted I start taking piano lessons again. "The idle mind knows not what it wants"—his favorite quote from Quintus Ennius—was said on repeat over the past three months. He thinks that because I'm starting high school this fall, my education needs to be taken more seriously.

My mind might not know exactly what it wants, but it knows for certain that it isn't piano lessons. Besides, Father barely spends any time in the city with Mom and me, but for some reason, he still thinks he's entitled to try to dictate my life. Most of the time, when he demands I do something, Mom flat-out tells him no. Unfortunately, this is the rare occasion that she agrees with him.

She loves playing the piano, finding peace in running her hands across the keys and creating music. I think she secretly hopes that if I take enough lessons, I'll find a way to love it too.

I won't. I have no patience for it. I skip out on practicing whenever possible, which is most likely the reason this is my third year taking a beginner's course.

The only reason Mr. Salazar tolerates me coming back each year is because Father pays him a fortune to put up with my testy attitude. The plus side is that the man refuses to take house calls. He insists that all his pupils learn better without the distractions of their daily life. Lucky for me, his apartment is in Lincoln Square, so I get to cut through Central Park on my way home. It's one of my favorite places in New York City, even in the scorching summer heat.

The moment I step inside, I'm transported to another dimension—an idyllic version of the city where people go to take a break from their mundane lives.

Every time I walk by Turtle Pond, I longingly look at the ducks, vowing to someday remember to bring breadcrumbs to feed them. I always steer clear of the shady lone goose that always seems to hang around, though. I'm not sure what his problem is, but he can't be trusted.

As of late, I've reached what Mom calls my "hormonal teenage years."

I'm obsessed with watching the endless streams of couples gazing into each other's eyes, both young and old, as they stroll through the park holding hands, making out on a bench, or rowing across the pond. I'm mesmerized by the passion and electric spark that flows through two people in love. I've never experienced it firsthand, but I hope I will someday soon.

I usually take a leisurely stroll through the park on my way home, but today is an exception.

My mouth is parched, and I can't wait to chug a freshly squeezed glass of lemonade. Mom always keeps an ice-cold batch in the fridge, displayed in a Queen Lace crystal pitcher filled to the brim, waiting just for me. When Father is around, he likes to remind her that the pitcher was a wedding gift from a New York senator and isn't meant for everyday use.

If he had it his way, our entire house would be decorated with priceless antiques, purely for show when the occasional influential acquaintance comes for a visit.

Luckily for me, Mom disagrees, insisting that beautiful things should be cherished and used to make lasting memories.

Needless to say, my parents' marriage is one of convenience.

My grandfather built the world's most prestigious international business law firm, Kingsman & Reed, from the ground up, known for its ruthless business practices and lack of ethics. My mom—an only child—had never shown an interest in law, instead getting what my grandfather deemed a "useless" astronomy degree, giving him no hope of her carrying on his legacy.

When Grandfather took my father on as a first-year associate, he knew within a week he had found his successor.

My father married my mother, and eventually inherited the business when my grandfather passed away.

Over the years, my parents have developed a mutual respect while living separate lives. However, my father's career and image will always come first.

Most of his time is spent traveling for work while mistresses from across the globe discreetly warm his bed. He has spent the better part of his adult life being groomed for greatness, and he would never let a tarnished reputation damage the outward appearance of his perfect family.

Some would say my parents have more money than God, although that's of little importance to me. All I've ever needed is love.

I was conceived to be an heir to my father's empire. The day I was born, he had a nanny flown in from Paris, insisting that she take over my care immediately. Mom called him and straight up told him to—and I quote—"fuck off." She said that she would be the one who raised me, that no one else had earned that privilege—not even him as he sat on his throne in Paris, refusing to return home even for his only daughter's birth. Mom kicked the poor woman to the curb less than five minutes after she arrived.

Mom single-handedly woke up multiple times throughout the night when I was teething, chased me through the sandbox as a toddler, and now spends countless evenings teaching me about the constellations.

Marie Dunham is my North Star, teaching me to stand up for what I believe in and to fiercely love and protect those who matter most in my life. She's the most stubborn and unwavering person I know, and Father blames her for my strong-headed nature. He's not wrong, but I think it's a gift, and I use it to my advantage any chance I get.

Much to Father's dismay, I announced while in Paris over the summer that I don't want to go to law school when the time comes. I want to save lives, not destroy them. I told him I plan to attend medical school someday, although I haven't yet decided what my specialty will be.

Most parents would be thrilled at my chosen career path—Mom sure is—but Father, not so much.

He spent three days brooding around the Paris apartment, refusing to leave for his next business trip until I agreed to reconsider. On the third day, Mom kicked him out, insisting I should enjoy my time in high school without the looming decision of what I wanted to study in college.

That's fine. I know I won't change my mind, but there's no need to rock the boat any more than I already have.

Our New York brownstone is my safe haven, and I cherish the one-on-one time I get to spend with Mom whenever I'm not in school. The only time she has to spend with Father is when he's in town and needs to wine and dine an important client, demanding that she play the part of the perfect socialite, which she does with finesse.

I'm beaming as I approach our idyllic house, remembering Father is out of town for three more weeks and Mom promised we could order pizza and eat it up on the roof tonight. The sky should be clear, perfect for stargazing—at least as good as it gets in the middle of the city.

I race up the stairs and yank open the front door. I kick off my dirt-stained white sneakers, not looking to see where they land. Thankfully, our housekeeper has left for the day, so she can't scold me for my lack of discipline.

I listen for the sound of music coming from the parlor, but when I don't hear my mother playing the piano, I bound down the hall to the kitchen. I open the fridge to find the Queen Lace crystal pitcher on the top shelf, full of fresh lemonade, just as I expected. I get up on my tippy-toes and carefully pull the pitcher down before pouring myself a tall glass. I gulp down the contents in less than a minute before racing to the stairs.

"Mom, I'm home!" I shout as I take the steps two at a time, heading straight for the master bedroom on the second floor.

The double doors leading to my parents' room are wide open. The custom-canopy, king-sized bed in the middle of the room dominates the space, with a disproportionate number of throw pillows piled on top of the crisp white sheets. My mom's favorite painting—*Starry Night Over the Rhône* by Vincent van Gogh—hangs centered above the bed.

I hear the shower running and make my way toward the bathroom. When I peek inside, I don't see her in there, which is odd because Mom has always been conscientious about water conservation and constantly reminds me not to waste water.

"Mom?" I call out again.

After a few seconds, I can vaguely hear muffled noises coming from her walk-in closet that is fit for a queen. As I walk to the threshold, I come to a halt.

Mom is curled up in a ball at the foot of the alabaster-upholstered bench set against the island in the middle of the room. Mascara lines stain her cheeks, and her hair is haphazardly falling across her face.

Something is terribly wrong.

I've never seen her in this condition before. She's a strong, confident, well-put-together woman, always ready to battle with my father or anyone else who is causing injustice in the world. She's made it her mission to stand up for those who can't fight for themselves, and she never allows herself to break down.

She startles when she hears my voice, looking up at me with a vacant expression. I rush to her side, dropping down to lie next to her. I reach out and grasp her hands tightly in mine.

"Mom, it's Olivia. Are you okay?" Clearly, she's not, but I have no idea what to do in this situation.

"Hi, Livvy." She finally *sees* me and pulls me into her arms. After a while, she finally speaks. "I'm sorry. I didn't mean to scare you. I just…I got some devastating news and needed some time to process it, that's all."

"What is it?" I abruptly sit up. "Did something happen to Father?" Despite the indifference he feels toward me, I still care about his well-being for some reason.

"Your father is fine." She climbs up off the floor to sit next to me as she presses a kiss to my forehead. "My best friend Jada was in a terrible car accident."

"Your best friend? Mom, no offense, but you don't have any friends."

She lets out a little chuckle at my blatant honesty. "You're right, Livvy," she admits. "Jada is the only person I've ever considered a true friend. We met on the playground in elementary school. I heard one of our classmates calling her names. The day before, the same kid approached me, telling me I was so ugly that even my own mother couldn't love me.

He was nothing but a bully, preying on those he deemed weaker than himself." Fury laces Mom's voice, and she pauses to compose herself.

"So, when I heard the punk insulting Jada, I did what any self-respecting schoolgirl wearing a plaid skirt would do: I punched him square in the face and laughed as blood dripped from his nose," she says proudly. "I spent a week in detention, but it was worth it. Jada and I were inseparable from that point forward, and I couldn't have asked for a better friend.

"She grew up in foster care most her life, and unfortunately, she had to move to a new foster home the year after we met. We wrote each other letters often, and as we got older, we started talking on the phone nearly every day. She's been living in New Jersey with her husband and son. Last week, we finally made plans to meet up…"

"Mom, Jada didn't make it, did she?" I say with hesitation.

"No, Livvy, she didn't make it." Tears fall silently down my mom's cheeks as she stares off into the distance. "I never took the chance to tell her how much she meant to me," she says with downcast eyes. "Jada was the only person who never judged me for my social standing, who I married, or where I lived. It was nice to have someone who was genuinely my friend for the right reasons."

Most of the women in Mom's social circle are stuck-up snobs who detest her because of her unpopular opinions and unwillingness to accept their privileged views. I can't imagine what she must feel, losing the one person she could trust implicitly—other than me.

"Apparently her husband Mac was driving under the influence." She takes a deep breath before focusing her attention back on me. "He's been arrested, and her son Milo doesn't have any other family—at least, none that I know of." She reaches out to clasp my hands tightly in hers as she looks me directly in the eye. "I want him to come stay with us. At least until we can track down his extended family or find him somewhere safe to go. I owe it to Jada to take him in. I know she would have done the same for you." She patiently waits for me to process what she's asking.

I bite my lip, unsure of how to react.

It's not a surprise that my mom wants to help Milo. She has a heart of gold and would give the shirt off her back if the situation called for it. However, I know my opinion matters, and she won't bring him back here if I ask her not to.

I've never had to share my space before. Our guest bedroom is down the hall from mine, a bathroom connecting the two rooms. That would mean I'd have to share my safe haven with a total stranger—a boy, no less.

Like Mom, I mostly keep to myself, and the few friends that I do have are all girls.

What if Milo doesn't like me?

I take a deep breath, willing myself to calm down for my mom's sake. I don't want her to see my internal panic. She wants to do this—I can see it in her eyes. No matter what happens, I know that we'll be okay.

"I think it's a great idea. Yes, let's have Milo come stay with us," I say confidently.

"You mean that, Livvy?" she says. "The doctor said Milo's in a medically induced coma due to some swelling on his brain. I want to be there when he wakes up. Will you come with me?"

"I…you're sure I won't be intruding?"

"Milo will be grieving when he hears the news about his mom. I think it would help him to have someone his age in the room when he wakes up, especially since he won't know anyone there."

"Okay, I'll come," I say hesitantly, hoping I've made the right decision.

Mom presses a kiss against my forehead. "Thanks for doing this, Livvy. I couldn't get through this without you."

I slump against the window, staring into the hospital parking lot, watching the rain fall from the sky.

Aside from going to the hotel across the street after visiting hours have ended, Mom and I have barely left Milo's side since we arrived three days ago.

They took Milo off the ventilator early this morning, and the doctor said it's just a waiting game now for when he will wake up.

The gossip about Milo's family has spread like wildfire throughout the hospital. I heard one of the nurses say his dad was driving drunk and wrapped the car around a tree, both his parents were thrown from the car, and Jada died on the scene. One of the lab techs said they think Milo was asleep in the backseat at the time of the accident and remained unconscious throughout the whole ordeal.

I turn to face Milo, surprised when I find his eyelids starting to flutter open as he shifts to his side, groaning in pain.

My mom is sitting in a chair a few feet away, absorbed in her paperback copy of *A Brief History of Time* by Stephen Hawking. I walk over and tap her lightly on the shoulder. "Mom, I think Milo's waking up," I whisper, afraid that I'll frighten him if I talk too loudly.

She walks over and slowly caresses his tousled black hair. "Milo, sweetheart, I'm glad you're finally awake." Her angelic voice creates a calming effect that seems to settle Milo.

Marie Dunham is a classic beauty, a modern-day Elizabeth Taylor. Her glossy chestnut-brown hair is pulled back into a sleek, high ponytail. A fresh manicure adorns her hands, and her clothes appear freshly pressed even though she's been sitting in the same spot for hours. That's my father's doing. He insists she keep up with appearances to symbolize our wealth and status anytime she's out in public.

She is definitely out of place here in Camden, New Jersey.

"Where am I? Where's Ma?" Milo's voice is raw and raspy—a side effect of the tube they removed from his throat earlier this morning.

"Milo, my name is Marie. I'm a friend of your mom's." She gently brings her hand down to clasp his hand in hers.

"Ma doesn't have any friends, except if you count Ms. Kilpatrick down the street, but she only tolerates us because we do her grocery shopping. I want to see Ma...where is she?" He does his best to hide the rising inflection in his voice.

My mom drops her eyes, doing her best to compose her emotions before responding, "Milo, there was an accident. What do you remember last?"

"What kind of accident?" he asks. "We went to pick up my dad from Lucky's. Ma was arguing with Dad about who was going to drive home. I fell asleep…"

Milo suddenly becomes agitated and goes to yank the IV out of his arm. Mom intervenes at the last moment, seizing hold of his hands.

"Milo, please don't hurt yourself. I need you to take a deep breath and look at me."

He pauses, and his haunted eyes speak volumes.

He knows his mom is gone.

"Sweetheart, your mom…she didn't make it," my mom says, trying to keep her voice from cracking. "They tried to resuscitate her at the scene of the accident, but it was too late. Luckily, the paramedics got you to the hospital in time to save your life."

"What about…what about my dad? Where is he? Does he know about what happened?" Milo asks.

"Your dad knows. He's the one who called me. He's…he has to sort some things out, that's why he can't be here with you right now."

"What do you mean, sort some things out?" Milo demands. "Wait…we went to pick him up at the bar. He was drunk that night. He was driving, wasn't he? If he was driving…I don't understand. Why would Ma have let him get behind the wheel?" He starts to become agitated again.

"The social worker can give you more information later, but Milo, it was an accident. Once you're feeling better, you can come stay with me and my daughter, Olivia. We'll figure this all out, I promise. Everything will be okay. You don't have to go through this alone," Mom says in a soothing voice.

"No, I don't want to stay with you. I want to go home. I want to see Ma!" Milo starts to scream at the top of his lungs as he clasps his hands over his ears, shaking back and forth. "She's not dead. You're lying, you're lying, you're lying!"

He reaches for his IV again, this time successfully ripping it right out of his arm, and blood gushes down his arm. He swats his hand out, accidently hitting my mom on her forearm in the process.

"No, no, no, no! You're lying!" he repeats over and over.

My mom has her arms banded around his waist, keeping his arms pinned so he can't cause any more damage. I'm frozen in my chair, unable to process what I'm watching.

Suddenly, two nurses come barging into the room, rushing over to the bed to help my mom.

The closest nurse turns to look at me before pointing at the door. "You need to leave. Right now!"

I blink rapidly before rushing into the hall as additional medical staff comes running into Milo's room. I take one backward glance as I see a nurse jabbing a needle into Milo's arm.

A single tear slips down my cheek as I watch this lonely boy suffer.

I make a silent promise that he will never be alone again. He doesn't know me yet, but he will, and one day, we will be the best of friends.

Chapter Four

MILO
Present Day—October

I WATCH STELLA WHEEL GRACE into the elevator at the end of the hall before peering back into Mac's hospital room. Liv is lying down next to him, her head resting against his shoulder, having forgotten my presence entirely.

"I can't believe Grace is finally in remission. I'm so happy for her," Liv says with a smile. "That right there is why I became a doctor. It gives me purpose, knowing that I'm saving young lives from a vicious and uncaring disease. If only I could save you…"

Anger rolls off me in waves, and I refuse to stay silent in the shadows any longer. Without a second thought, I charge into the middle of the room. I come to a sudden stop, overcome with hate when I'm face-to-face with Mac for the first time in nearly twenty years.

I only visited him in prison once a couple months after Ma died. I disowned him that day, refusing to see him again. He deserved to suffer a life of solitude and loneliness as penance for the life he took.

I don't recognize the frail, ailing man lying in the hospital bed. His face is gaunt, his eyes sunken, and he looks malnourished. His strained breathing is a clear sign of his poor health. I see a faint scar running across his left eyebrow that wasn't there the last time I saw him.

The man I knew was a formidable force to be reckoned with.

The man in front of me is anything but.

Aside from my bronzed skin and lack of tattoos, I'm the spitting image of Mac back in his prime. The one thing I didn't inherit was his talent for baseball. He was the starting pitcher on his high school team and had a full-ride baseball scholarship to a college in Florida. Until an accident during his sophomore year caused irreparable damage to his shoulder, and his dreams were shattered.

I was a preschooler then, and due to financial constraints, we were forced to move back to Camden where he had a job waiting for him at the local mechanic shop. Ma said his problem with drinking started shortly after that, though he did an excellent job of hiding his addiction for a while.

Every night after a twelve-hour shift, he'd come home with a smile on his face and cook dinner for us. He always told me a real man helped his woman with household chores. On the fourteenth of every month, no matter how little money we had, he'd bring a bouquet of two dozen red and white roses home for Mom in honor of their monthly anniversary, because he said that celebrating once a year wasn't nearly enough.

We might have been as poor as church mice, but the love in our home more than made up for our lack of money.

Little did I know there were demons knocking on Mac's door. It wasn't until I was older that I realized Ma spent most nights fishing him out of Lucky's—our local dive bar—always forgiving him the next day after he promised that things would get better.

They never did.

As I look at Mac now, I realize this was a mistake. I thought nearly twenty years would be enough time to prepare myself to face the man who single-handedly dismantled my life.

It wasn't.

I turn to walk out the way I came until I hear a vaguely familiar voice say my name.

"Milo...son...is that you? You're all grown up," Mac calls out with great effort.

I spin around as the frail old man fumbles with the remote for his bed, raising it up so he can see me better. He grimaces in pain as Liv jumps up to add a couple of pillows behind his back to help him stay upright. His eyes are filled with hope and a silent plea.

He'll get no mercy from me.

Ma died alone in the street that fateful night, covered in third-degree burns, more than half the bones in her body broken. The least Mac can do in return for her suffering is spend the time he has left on this earth in complete and utter misery.

"I'm no son of yours. You sure as hell made certain of that," I snarl. "Was taking Ma away from me not enough for you? Oh, no, you had to go ahead and take away the only other person I've ever cared for more than myself." I point angrily at Liv. "You deserve to be rotting in a prison cell, and yet somehow, you not only managed to get released early, but you also have an angel catering to your every need until your last dying breath."

Mac's expression is blank, and Liv sits next to him, gaping at me in shock.

I get up close and personal. "Is your moral compass so far gone that you don't have any qualms about taking advantage of a traumatized woman who's stuck in the past, so desperate for affection that she'd befriend a convict, a mere replica of the man she loved?"

He doesn't budge, remorse shimmering in his eyes.

Two decades' worth of pent-up rage roars inside of me like a caged beast and I can hardly contain it. I have to physically force my hands to remain at my sides to avoid slamming my fist into Mac's jaw.

"Enough!" Liv shouts, her voice filled with disgust as she jumps from the bed. "For heaven's sake, Milo, grow up. When you left me, Mac was the only person I had to turn to." She briefly pauses, glancing over at Mac. "Instead of punishing him, you should thank him for giving my life purpose again. I don't care that you're hurt by the fact that Mac and I are close. You can shove your outrage and resentment up your…butt!" Even when she's angry, she can't bring herself to swear. "Next time you decide to make petty comments about my past, get your facts straight. You give yourself too much credit. I moved on from you years ago. The only trauma I'm suffering now is the reality that I'm about to lose the man who's been my best friend for the past fifteen years, and that sure as heck isn't you."

Her voice rings with conviction, yet I can sense that my earlier words hurt her deeply.

I draw in a deep breath as I force the animosity pumping through my veins to dissipate. I can see now that coming to confront Mac was a mistake. I'm not ready to face my past, let alone unravel the feelings I have for Liv. It never crossed my mind before yesterday that she could be the one who fought to get Mac out on parole or the one to become his sole caregiver.

Before anyone can say anything else, a security guard comes rushing into the room, pointing in my direction. "Sir, I'm going to need to escort you off the property. This is a place of healing, and you're disturbing the peace."

"No need to escort me out. I was just leaving. Goodbye, Liv." I ignore both Mac and the security guard as I step out of the room.

As I storm down the hallway, I shove past a couple who appear to be clutching each other in comfort.

Damn them.

There was a time Liv and I were in a similar position, huddled together as I whispered words of comfort as we waited for the news that would destroy our lives. I had painted a picture of a happy life for us. One with marriage, kids, and a house outside of the city with an atrium that we could use for stargazing. Months later, I went back on my word with no explanation.

Yanking open the door to the stairwell, I race down three flights of stairs to the ground level. Before I leave, I find myself slamming my fist into the wall once, and then a second time, feeling the rush of adrenaline that I tried to keep bottled up while I was in Mac's presence. I shake out my hand, slowly opening and closing it to ensure it's not broken.

Finally, I move toward the exit, anxious for a smoke. As I step outside, I inhale the crisp autumn air. I reach my good hand into my back pocket and pull out my pack of cigs. I'm about to light one up when I notice the *No Smoking Within 25 Feet* signs posted around the hospital's perimeter.

Seriously? It should be a crime to make people wait longer than necessary to relieve their stress, even if their vice of choice might cause lung damage.

I scan my surroundings and locate a park right across the street. The perfect place for a quick smoke break before I get the hell out of here. It's mid-afternoon and the park is deserted, so I sit at the closest picnic table.

I light the cigarette and take my first hit, inhaling the smooth and rich flavor, providing the slow burn I crave. I flick the ash off the tip and take another long drag.

Ironically, the source of my relaxed state will probably kill me one of these days, but I don't give a shit. Aside from Eloisa and Pike, who else would miss me when I'm gone?

Liv would miss you.

She needs you now more than ever.

The unwelcome voice in my head needs to shut up before I have another outburst.

I bring my cigarette to my lips for another puff but stop midway to my mouth when an obnoxious ringtone starts coming from my pocket. I throw the cigarette butt on the ground, snuffing it out with my shoe while fumbling to pull out my phone.

Eloisa's name flashes brightly on the screen, and I can only assume she must have changed her ringtone so I'd know better than to ignore her.

"Hi, Els. What, you and Pike miss me already?" I say with a cheery disposition.

"Milo, honey! Thank goodness you answered," Eloisa says with relief. "Did you make it okay? You didn't call this morning, and I was worried sick when I didn't hear from you."

"I'm so sorry, Els," I reply. "After landing, I stopped by the apartment to drop off my things and came straight to the hospital. There's no need to worry, I promise."

The sound of something sizzling in a pan in the background catches my attention, and I can picture it now. Eloisa anxiously pacing up and down her industrial-grade kitchen, wearing her signature pinstriped apron. Every so often rushing back to the stovetop to turn over the veal shanks she's preparing for her world-famous osso buco. Pike sitting at the island, reviewing another budget report for the upcoming Bushwick project while asking Eloisa for a play-by-play of what I'm saying. He might be semi-retired on paper, but you wouldn't know it based on the amount of time he spends managing CEO-related tasks that he can't bring himself to pass on to me.

"How did it go? Did you talk to Mac? Was Olivia there with him? What does she look like? Were you on your best behavior?"

If anyone else peppered me with that many questions at once, I would tell them to mind their own damn business. Eloisa knows she's the exception, though, and she milks it for all it's worth.

"Yeah, Liv is here," I say hesitantly. "I might have gone a bit unhinged when I saw her, and I didn't talk to Mac so much as I shouted at him, but he deserved it."

She lets out a sigh. "Oh, Milo, what am I going to do with you? You have no idea what that sweet girl has been through. I'm sure there is a good explanation for why Olivia and Mac are friends; you just refused to take the time to get the facts straight. Don't forget that you walked away from her first. The way I see it, she has just as much of a right to be infuriated with you," she states matter-of-factly.

Damn Eloisa for being right. She is most of the time, but I can't tell her that or it'll go straight to her head.

I did hurt Liv first, and based on what I saw in the hospital earlier, I don't think she befriended Mac out of spite. She genuinely cares for him.

Not that it makes a difference to me.

I still detest the man, and I disapprove of Liv showing him compassion.

"I appreciate your insight, but coming here was a mistake. I'm heading back to the apartment in Brooklyn to finish up the Bushwick project, and then I'm coming back to Vegas as soon as I can. You know how much I hate New York City."

"Whatever you think is best, dear. You know that Pike and I are here if you need anything. We just want you to be happy."

"Thanks, Els. I'll call you later tonight, okay?"

"I'll be waiting for your call. I love you."

"Talk to you soon."

The words "I love you" are on the tip of my tongue before I hang up, but even after all these years, I've never been able to vocalize my feelings for Eloisa and Pike.

I remember the day I left New York. I was hungry, homeless, and wholly alone. I ended up in Las Vegas on a whim, taking shelter in the cab of an excavator sitting on a construction site in the middle of the night. Pike had been the one to find me the following morning. Instead of calling the cops or telling me to get lost, he silently drove me to his ranch-style home, where I was introduced to Eloisa. His eccentric, carefree wife who had a flair for wearing bright red lipstick and black dresses under her chef's apron. Her Italian heritage was apparent from her outward affection, the way she spoke with her hands, and her passion for cooking. She welcomed me into her home with open arms and a freshly prepared breakfast. It was no surprise when I later learned that she owned a three-Michelin-starred flagship Italian restaurant—Eloisa's Place.

The next day, Pike dropped me off at the same construction site he had found me at the day prior, assigned me to one of the foremen, and told me to get to work.

Despite my near-constant bitter attitude, Eloisa and Pike helped me adjust to adulthood and the real world. They insisted that I get my GED, cheering me on every step of the way. And when I decided to get my Bachelor's degree, Pike helped me adjust my work schedule to accommodate my classes. My hard work and dedication paid off when he appointed me CEO of Lawson Co. Although, some days, he forgets I'm the one in charge now.

Movement from across the parking lot catches my attention, and I glance over to find Liv stepping out of a white Toyota RAV4 parked at the hospital's front entrance. I shake my head as I watch her from afar. I'm not surprised to see her driving a basic model that is several years old. She's just like her mom, refusing to conform to society's expectations, always erring on the side of practicality. It's one of the reasons I fell so hard for her in the first place. Her love for me was genuine, and she never thought less of me because of my status as the poor kid from Camden, New Jersey.

An orderly appears, pushing Mac in a wheelchair with one hand and firmly clutching her phone in the other, her eyes glued to whatever social media site she's more than likely perusing. She smacks her lips as she chomps on a bright pink piece of bubble gum. I swear I can hear the obnoxious pop from here as she blows a giant bubble in Mac's ear.

As she gets closer to the SUV, she lets go of the handle of the chair, not once lifting her eyes from her phone. I cringe as I watch the chair veer to the side due to her lack of attention. Mac is slumped over, having been haphazardly dumped into the seat without any care for his comfort.

No one deserves to be treated this way. Not even him.

Seriously, what is with this nice guy act my conscience is trying to pull today?

I grit my teeth as I watch Liv rush over to grab hold of the wheelchair to keep Mac from rolling off. She pushes it next to the car and struggles to lift Mac into the vehicle's passenger side by herself. Mac appears to be mostly dead weight, and I continue to watch, waiting for the orderly to get the memo that it's about damn time to start doing her job before Liv hurts herself.

"Fuck this," I mutter under my breath.

Before I can stop myself, my feet are moving, jogging in Liv's direction. As soon as I get close, I gently push Liv aside. "Here, let me help," I say.

I cup Mac's elbow and wrap my other arm around his waist as I hoist him up into the SUV, watching carefully to ensure he doesn't bump his head getting in.

"Thank you," he slurs.

Mac doesn't seem to comprehend that it's me who's helping him. He must have been given another dose of pain meds before he was released. If he was fully alert, I'm certain he would have told the useless orderly off, especially for the way she disrespected Liv.

"I didn't realize you were still here," Liv says coldly.

Her icy stare holds no gratitude for my act of kindness. She should be kissing the ground I walk on for putting my feelings aside and helping Mac. Instead, she looks ready to kick me in the balls, disgust written all over her face.

"I heard you caused some serious damage in the stairwell on your way out of the building. Don't worry, I made sure the hospital administrator knows who to send the bill to," she says with a smile.

I grin right back at her snarky comment. I couldn't care less about paying for the damage.

"Can I go now?"

I spin around to face the worthless orderly who has a bored expression on her face.

"Yes." Liv and I both scoff at the same time.

The orderly rolls her eyes and walks off, slowly dragging the wheelchair behind her with one hand, focusing back on her phone screen.

"Thanks for your help, Tiffany!" Liv shouts after her, no doubt trying to get under my skin.

"You meant to thank me, right?" I say to her. "Since I'm the one who did the heavy lifting?"

"Thanks…for making an already crummy day even more unbearable," she mumbles under her breath as she buckles Mac into his seat, laying a blanket over his lap.

Liv jogs around to the driver's side, prepared to leave without saying goodbye. I follow after her, not ready for our conversation to end.

"Wait." I grab her shoulder, forcing her to turn back to face me.

"What do you want, Milo?" Her voice is weary as she stares up at me. "Haven't you done enough damage for one day? It's time for you to leave now. You don't want to be here, so go. Mac knows you still hate him, so you should be satisfied with the outcome of your visit."

I miss you, Liv.

I'm so close to voicing my thought. I really need to get my conscience under control or else one of these days, I'm going to say something that I regret. Not that I don't already do that more often than not.

"Liv, I won't apologize for my behavior back in Mac's hospital room. I can't turn a blind eye to what he did to my ma…what he did to me."

Liv looks up at me, a slight frown on her face. "Goodbye, Milo," she says as she gets into the SUV and closes the door behind her. The engine starts, and without a backward glance, she leaves me behind, standing alone in the hospital parking lot.

As I watch the car merge into the flow of traffic, I come to the startling realization that I'm not ready to say goodbye to her yet. My feelings toward Mac be damned. I still haven't gotten the answers I came here for, and she owes me those at the very least.

"Shit!" I squeeze my hand into a fist, hitting it against my forehead. I was so absorbed in my own agenda that I never thought to ask where she lived or where she was taking Mac.

Then it hits me: *Jane.* The nurse who left me the voicemail last night. She's a friend of Liv's, and that means she should know where she lives. I rush back inside to the reception desk to see if someone can help me track her down.

Liv hasn't seen the last of me.

Chapter Five

OLIVIA
Present Day—October

I CLUTCH THE LEATHER STEERING wheel in a death grip, my hands visibly trembling. I try my best to focus on my surroundings as I navigate the chaotic streets, once again thankful for the subway station a half block from my apartment so I don't have to drive very often.

Driving in the city isn't for the faint of heart. We're stuck in bumper-to-bumper traffic during the mid-afternoon rush, the sound of blaring horns and someone shouting obscene profanities coming from off in the distance. The greater population of New York City is out in full force today, oblivious to the fact that my entire life is in shambles.

It reminds me of the long drives I used to take as an undergrad at Cornell when I visited Mac every Saturday morning. I'd travel overnight to avoid traffic, and arrive at the prison right at eight a.m. so I was always the first visitor of the day, and most guards usually gave me extra time with Mac until the mid-morning rush of other visitors.

As we stop at another red light, I turn to check on Mac. He's slumped in his seat with his eyes closed, and I sigh in relief when I hear his raspy, uneven breaths. Thankfully, the nurse on duty gave him another dose of morphine shortly before he was discharged from the hospital, so he shouldn't feel any discomfort for the next few hours.

I know seeing Milo again has taken its toll on Mac, especially since the last time they saw each other in person, Mac was stuck behind plated glass, unable to stop his grief-stricken teenage son from storming out of the prison visiting room. And now, since history repeated itself earlier today when Milo hastily left the hospital room, Mac's barely spoken a word.

Just then, Mac's eyes slowly crack open, and he looks blankly at me.

"Hey there," I say quietly. "We'll only be in the car for a few more minutes, and then you can lie down again, okay?"

He nods absentmindedly.

"I know we haven't talked about what happened at the hospital earlier, but if you want to address the elephant in the room—or I should say, car—let me know." I reach over to pat his leg in a show of comfort.

"Kiddo," he murmurs. "I'm okay, I promise." It takes all his strength to get the words out as he tries to find his bearings. "My son came back to me today. I've prayed for this moment for nearly twenty years. He might harbor a grudge against me for what happened, but it's better than complete indifference. At least I saw him before it was too late."

A single tear drips down his cheek, and I carefully wipe it from his face.

"Mac, he doesn't have all the facts. If you told him your side of the story about what happened the night his mom died, he might feel differently."

With immense effort, Mac shakes his head back and forth. "No, absolutely not."

"Mac, please tell—"

"No," he interrupts me. "And that's final." He seems to find a second wind, needing to get this out. "My son has made up his mind about me, and there is no changing it. Let the past stay in the past, okay?"

Without a doubt, he is the most stubborn person I have ever met—with Milo coming in at a close second. Like father, like son. Of course I would give my heart to the two most hardheaded men in the state of New York.

"Okay, Mac, you win," I huff out. "Besides, I think that's the last time we'll see Milo."

I let out a sigh of relief as I turn left off Lexington Avenue onto 63rd Street, my parents' bowfront Upper East Side brownstone coming into view. It's been fifteen years since I've been back, avoiding it like the plague until now.

I gaze up at the intricate white sandstone building with its stark black window frames, railings, and imposing double-paneled front door. The picturesque house mocks me. No matter how long it remains uninhabited, it stands as a symbol of the illusion of a picture-perfect family living a life of absolute luxury. The reality is much bleaker—a family ravaged by death, abandonment, and regret.

I chew on my lip as I pull into the ground-floor garage, doing my best to squash down the flood of emotions I have from returning to the place I used to call home. I turn the engine off and look over at Mac. He's observing me with an unreadable expression on his face. I'm about to reach for my door handle when he speaks again.

"Kiddo, I want to say something even if you might not want to hear it," he says. "Remember what I said this morning about putting yourself first? I saw the look on Milo's face when he saw you today. He'll be back, and it certainly won't be to see me. When the time comes, you need to be willing to forgive him." He makes the declaration like it's the easiest thing to ask of me. "Milo has become chained to the hatred festering in his heart, and you're the only one who can help him. Don't let the bitterness drown you too." He pauses, reaching over to pat my hand. "You need each other more than you know. Trust me, Liv. It's been nearly twenty years since I lost Jada, and my love for her has only grown. The one bright side of dying is knowing I get to see her again."

Why does Mac feel the need to keep reminding me that he'll be leaving me behind soon?

If Milo does decide to come back, I'll be the one dealing with the brunt of his wrath, whether I deserve it or not. He's the one who left me, and I don't owe him anything. It hardly seems fair that I should be the one to forgive him first if he reappears in our lives. Besides, I don't even want him to come back…Do I?

"Mac, I—"

He gradually lifts his hand to cut me off. "It doesn't warrant a rebuttal. Just promise me. Promise you'll give Milo a second chance if the opportunity presents itself."

"Fine, I promise, but he's not coming back. You heard him earlier. He's washed his hands of us both. He'll disappear for good this time, and we'll all be better off because of it," I reply, wishing I believed what I was saying.

A hoarse cough racks Mac's frail body, leaving him gasping for air. I rub his back until his breathing returns to normal, then I get out of the car and move around to the passenger side.

"Let's get you inside so you can rest. We've pushed your body too far today."

Mac nods feebly in agreement.

As if on cue, the door to the house opens and Jane, a hospice nurse and my dear friend, walks into the garage. Her curly, ear-length red hair hangs like a halo around her head. I'm delighted to see the bright red-and-pink Minnie Mouse scrubs she's wearing today. Most of her patients are kids, and they go crazy for her ever-changing wardrobe of cartoon scrubs.

Jane and I met a few years back while she was caring for one of my terminally ill cancer patients. I was immediately drawn to her compassionate disposition, and we became fast friends despite our age difference. When the hospital staff recommended Mac go on hospice, Jane insisted she help with his care.

"Dr. Dunham, I'm so glad you and Mac got home safely. We just finished setting up in the front parlor and were able to fit the bed right up next to the windows so he can enjoy the sunshine during the day." She smiles over at Mac.

I've asked Jane to call me by my first name countless times, but she refuses. She claims that I've earned my title as a doctor and that I should insist it is used at all times. I completely disagree, but I stopped arguing with her when I realized it was never going to get me anywhere.

It's then that I notice the giant of a man standing beside Jane.

"This is Jeremy, the certified nursing assistant who will stay with Mac at night so you can get some rest."

I arch my eyebrow in confusion. We discussed Jane coming to sit with Mac during the day, but I planned to take the night shifts.

Jane gives me a ghost of a smile as if she can read my mind. "Mac knew you'd insist on managing nights on your own, so he contacted me directly and asked me to find someone else to help with his care. The one stipulation was that I couldn't say anything to you about it. It wasn't easy, especially when we talked this morning."

Mac lets out a hoarse chuckle from the car. I spin around to give him a scolding look. It's no surprise that he went behind my back. He might think I always put him first, but in reality, he's the selfless one. He's constantly thinking of others, no matter the situation.

If only Milo could open his eyes and accept that there is more to Mac than the drunken man he holds responsible for his mom's death.

Jeremy cuts in to introduce himself. "It's a pleasure to meet you both. I'll be here to help in any way that I can." He turns to address Mac directly. "Why don't we get you to bed so you can rest?"

I watch in amazement as Jeremy effortlessly eases Mac out of the car and helps him up the stairs from the garden floor to the parlor. Jane falls in step right behind the two men, watching them like a hawk, ready to swoop in at a moment's notice if needed.

I find myself frozen in the doorway to the house before I can follow them.

When my mom was diagnosed with cancer, my father converted the parlor of the brownstone into a makeshift hospital wing with state-of-the-art equipment. He might not have loved her, but this setup was better than having her in a hospital, where people would gossip. After Mom died, it was never reverted to its original state, and it seemed like the most logical option when deciding where to go after Mac was discharged from the hospital. Now, I can't help but wonder if it was a mistake to bring Mac to my childhood home.

When Mac's most recent prognosis came back as terminal, he insisted we discuss his end-of-life plan. First and foremost, he demanded he be put on hospice when the time came, refusing to let me care for him alone. He also didn't want to spend his last days in my high-rise apartment. He knew it was my happy place, my bit of heaven, where I should be able to grieve in peace and solitude, and he wouldn't let it be tainted.

In theory, I thought my parents' brownstone would be a good solution. A serene place for Mac to spend his final days, but now that we're here, I'm not so sure. The ghosts from my past roam free in this place, but what are a few more somber memories in the grand scheme of things? *Right?*

From what my father's latest assistant told me when I called a few weeks ago, he hasn't stepped foot inside this place since he went back to Paris after Mom passed away. Milo wasn't the only one who abandoned me, but it didn't hurt nearly as much when my father left. I heard he opts to stay at the Ritz-Carlton whenever he's in New York now, but I wouldn't know firsthand since our limited communication is always through his endless Rolodex of assistants.

As I enter the house, the smell of dust mixed with bleach infiltrates my nose. A cleaning crew came by yesterday to prepare the place for our arrival, but even with a proper scrubbing, the musty scent lingers in the air.

When I get to the front parlor, I find Mac resting comfortably in the hospital bed that's been set up at an angle in front of the massive floor-to-ceiling bay windows. Jane is fussing over the array of pillows surrounding his head.

Jeremy walks over to stand next to me. "This place really is incredible, Dr. Dunham." His eyes dart around the room in amazement.

I mumble my agreement.

He's not wrong. This room was designed to impress. A symbol of my father's wealth, status, and accomplishments. Every piece of furniture was handpicked—from the impressive gas-burning fireplace to the massive Arlington gold, baroque mirror hanging above the traditional-style sofa with a custom champagne-wood finish. I have always found the latter to be hideous, but Father insisted it was trendy at the time.

Even the translucid grand piano with a solid wooden body and acrylic top and legs that my father gave to my mom to celebrate their tenth anniversary had been purchased with an ulterior motive. He said it added another element of elegance to the room. Yet now, it's shoved in the corner with a cloth draped across the top to preserve it—for what, I'm unsure.

The room that once symbolized grandiose splendor is now lackluster at best. Over the years, its greatest purpose has been a makeshift hospice for my mom, and now Mac.

I look over as Jane finishes administering Mac's pain medications. Despite his grumblings, I think he appreciates the relief from the constant discomfort he's been in over the past few days.

"Mac, I'll be back first thing in the morning," Jane says as she fluffs up his pillows one more time before grabbing her backpack from the foot of the bed. "In the meantime, you'll have Jeremy here to help you with anything you might need. I think Dr. Dunham needs some rest, don't you agree?" she asks with a chuckle.

Mac lets out a low laugh, winking at me when our eyes meet. I've got to admit, it's a blow to my self-esteem to be told twice in one day that I'm looking run down. Jane's right, though; a good night's sleep in a comfortable bed will do me some good…if only it were possible.

I walk Jane to the front door, and she wraps me in a warm embrace that I gladly welcome.

"Remember, dear, call me if you need anything. Don't worry about the time, okay? Jeremy is a sweetheart, and I can assure you that Mac will be in good hands until I get back in the morning. Now, go and take care of yourself for a change, but don't sleep in too late tomorrow. I have a feeling you might have an unexpected visitor stop by. Good night!"

She walks down the steps before I can ask what she meant by her cryptic visitor comment. I watch as she strides down the street until she's out of sight.

There's a chill in the air, making its way through my thin scrubs, down to my bones. Despite the cold, I tilt my head to look up at the partially blocked night sky, recalling all the times my mom, Milo, and I stargazed together on the rooftop.

I wonder what Milo's doing now. Did he leave the city, or was Mac right? Could he possibly make his way back to me?

I find myself discreetly looking up and down the street, secretly hoping to catch him walking toward the house. I shake my head and shove the silly thought to the back of my mind. He doesn't even know I'm staying here.

Besides, he's never coming back. I need to get that through my head once and for all.

After a few more stolen moments to myself, my stomach starts to rumble. I go back inside, heading straight for the kitchen. I pull a container of homemade chicken noodle soup out of the fridge and heat it up on the stovetop. My dear friend Dante, a chef in Hell's Kitchen and one of the best chefs in the city, insisted on delivering a few meals for Mac and me. After scarfing down two bowls of soup, I head back to the parlor with one for Mac.

Jeremy has made himself right at home, sitting on the impractical sofa he's pulled up next to the fireplace. A small fire is now glowing inside, spreading warmth throughout the room.

I sit on the edge of Mac's bed, careful not to spill the soup I'm holding in my hands.

"Hey, kiddo. Thanks for all this." Mac sluggishly reaches his arm up to gesture around the room. "I would do anything for you, Mac, you know that. Now, on to more important things. Dante had this delicious soup delivered, and we can't let it go to waste. You need to keep up your strength."

He gives me a skeptical look but cooperates regardless. He would never turn down a meal prepared by Dante.

I feed Mac one spoonful at a time, giving him plenty of time to swallow each delicious bite. We've made it halfway through the contents before he shakes his head, indicating he's had enough.

Without hesitation, I set the bowl on the end table before going to grab his worn copy of *The Adventures of Oliver Twist and Sketches by Boz*.

I lie down next to him over the covers and carefully rest my head against his chest, knowing his strength has quickly dwindled. What I wouldn't give for one of his famous bear hugs right now. I know his end is drawing near as he slips away piece by piece, and there's nothing I can do to prevent it.

I open the fragile book as small bits of red leather flake off from the edges. This particular copy has been with Mac since high school. Jada gave it to him as a gift for his sixteenth birthday, and he hasn't parted with it since. Aside from a single photo, this is the only other possession he has to remember her by.

I trace over the beautifully handwritten note on the inside cover like I do every time before I begin to read.

Mac,

You might come from humble beginnings, but your future is entirely up to you. I can't wait to achieve our dreams together. I love you.

Happy birthday!

Jada

Mac has read this book hundreds of times, but that hasn't stopped him from asking me to read a chapter to him every night since he was admitted to the hospital last week. It seems that the tradition will live on now that he's been discharged. I think it's his way of feeling closer to Jada even though she's gone.

I read until Mac's breathing evens out as he drifts off to sleep. I close the book and rest it in my lap as I welcome the sensation of the rise and fall of his chest. A comforting sign that he's still with me—at least for now.

After readjusting the comforter around Mac's feeble body, I tell Jeremy I'm going to bed early before making my way up to my old room on the third floor. I'm ready to drop from exhaustion, but when I get to the top of the stairs, I find myself turning right toward Milo's old room instead of left to mine.

What am I doing?

I reach for the closed door but can't bring myself to open it, knowing that a room frozen in time is waiting for me. The last time I stepped foot inside, I found a perfectly made bed and Milo's cell phone sitting on the nightstand, his most prized picture of his mom gone.

I start to hyperventilate, gasping for air. I think I'm in the midst of another panic attack, and it feels like my lungs are going to collapse.

I immediately sink down to the ground, unable to hold myself up any longer. I firmly press my back against Milo's bedroom door. I tuck my knees into my chest and lie on the cold hardwood floor, silently begging for a reprieve from the undercurrent of grief that I'm drowning in.

As if my body knows that it's surpassed its limit, sheer exhaustion takes over and I drift off to sleep outside Milo's room, just like I did the morning I discovered he had left me behind.

Chapter Six

MILO
Past—Ninth Grade

I BLINK MY EYES REPEATEDLY as I readjust to my surroundings. The overhead lights in the room are off, making it a little easier to see. The stark white walls, scratchy blanket covering my legs, and the monitor's steady beep remind me that I'm still in the hospital. Which means I wasn't having a nightmare…

This is real life.

Ma is really gone.

I vaguely recall someone giving me the news before a nurse poked a needle into my arm as I thrashed around. Whoever else was in the room kept telling me to calm down and promised that everything would be all right. How the hell can anything ever be okay again? My mom is dead, and from what I've gathered, it's my dad's fault. The last thing I remember is that they were arguing on the sidewalk while I waited in the backseat of the car. If I had just stayed awake long enough to make sure Ma got behind the wheel, she'd still be alive.

A burning sensation comes from my arm. As I reach out to investigate, I hear an ethereal voice coming from the other side of the room.

"I wouldn't touch that if I were you. You got the short end of the stick with the nurse on duty. She's a total grouch, so I'd recommend you try to stay on her good side. I doubt she'll be gentle if she has to insert another IV."

I move my gaze to see a girl who looks close to my age sitting in the small alcove next to the grimy window across the room. She's dressed in knee-length jean shorts, a blue-and-white striped crewneck, and dirt-stained white sneakers. A soft glow of sunlight surrounds her silky brown hair, making her look like an angel with a halo around her head.

She slowly stands up from her perch, shifting her weight from one foot to the other. She cautiously approaches me, but she seems nervous, eyeing me like a predator who's about to attack, even though I'm the one trapped in this bed, hooked up to multiple monitors. She stops and stares at the chair situated next to the bed, and then she starts to gnaw on her bottom lip.

Damn, that's cute.

"Are you going to take a seat?" I ask.

"Um, no, I don't think so. I changed my mind." She shuffles backward.

"Why?" I ask with genuine curiosity.

"You accidently hurt my mom the last time she got close to you," the girl says. "She was forgiving because of your circumstances, but there's no way she'd let you come and stay with us if you hurt me. And I would really like it if you came to stay with us…if that's what you want, I mean. I'm sorry about your mom, by the way. I can't imagine what you must be going through." She ends with a whisper.

God, I could listen to this girl ramble for days. I'm intrigued by her. Why would she be concerned for my well-being when she doesn't even know me? I feel an odd sensation in my chest, and I wonder if it's cause for concern. It almost feels like…what did Ma call it? Butterflies, I think it was. Except it feels more like I have a swarm of bats trying to escape. I'm not sure what's happening to me, but I do know that I want this girl to stay. I need to be close to her, but I still haven't figured out why that is.

"What's your name?" I ask, doing my best to keep her from leaving.

"Olivia," she murmurs.

"Hmm." I hate it. It's far too formal, too stiff. "It doesn't suit you. Mind if I call you Liv for short?"

She stares at me, as if contemplating my request before slowly nodding in agreement, perplexed by my mood change since the first time I woke up.

"Great. Would you mind sitting down?" I point to the chair next to the bed. "I'd like to get to know you a little better."

Liv doesn't have a chance to respond before our bubble bursts and a bellow comes from the hallway. The walls in this place are thin, not meant to keep the sound out. You could hear a pin drop three rooms over if you listened close enough.

"What the hell do you mean, you're bringing him home?" a harsh male voice shouts from the hallway. "For Christ's sake, Marie, we're not running a shelter for troubled teens. He hurt you. The scratch marks and bruises on your arms are proof of that. What we should do is call the police. He's a threat to society."

I can only assume the man is referring to me. I've never hurt anyone before, and I certainly didn't mean to cause Marie any harm—I think that's what he called the woman.

I'm now sitting up straight in bed as I listen to the stranger continue his tirade.

"Let him be someone else's problem. If we allow him into our home, he's going to cause trouble. Is that what you want? What if he tries to attack Olivia in the middle of the night? They'd be sharing a bathroom, so it's plausible. You know better than to trust anyone from Camden," he spits out, his voice full of hate. "You've been camped out in this roach-infested hospital for over a week, dragging our daughter along with you. Enough is enough. It's time you both come home where you belong."

I glance over to find Liv's eyes are about to bulge out of her head. From the sound of it, her father thinks I'm a rabid dog that needs to be put down. He assumes I'm a danger to his family simply because of where I grew up and my family's financial status.

I hate the man already.

An angry scoff comes from the hall. "Harrison, what is wrong with you? Milo is just a boy. He lost both of his parents in the span of a day. I don't know if he'll ever see his dad outside of a prison cell again. You might not care, but Jada was a dear friend of mine, and I will not abandon her son," Marie declares. "If you ever make another stereotypical comment about him again, I will ruin you. Do I need to remind you that

I control your whole universe? With a single call, I could take down your entire business...Don't make me do it. Remember our agreement? You stay in your lane, and I'll stay in mine. Now, go back to Paris. You don't want to miss out on making a few extra million today, do you? I need to go back to attend to *my* family. You know, the thing that should matter most."

I'm in awe of Marie's strength and I don't even know the woman. She stood up for me despite the fact that we're total strangers.

"Fine, Marie, have it your way," Harrison snaps. "Go ahead with this crazy, harebrained scheme of yours. Just keep it out of the papers or the press will have a field day, and don't come running to me when it backfires."

I listen as Harrison's heavy footfalls fade away.

Shortly after, the door bursts open. The woman who was by my side when I first woke up, who I can only assume is Marie, is standing at the threshold of the room. She reminds me of a warrior princess who's just come from battle. She's perfectly polished and put together, but isn't afraid to go to bat for those she cares about. I realize that even though I might not be related to her by blood, she'll protect me at all costs.

She eyes Liv and me suspiciously. "Were you eavesdropping on my conversation just now?"

Our deer-in-headlights expressions give us away, and Liv and I nod like bobbleheads, afraid of what would happen if we try to deny it.

Marie comes over and sits down next to my hospital bed, gesturing for Liv to join her.

"Milo, I want to apologize for what my husband said just now," Marie says with sincerity. "Pay him no attention. He's so consumed with success that he's forgotten what's most important. The amount of money a person has, where they live, or how they dress doesn't define them. Your mom taught me it's when we embrace our differences that we are able to form closer relationships."

Her gaze drops down to the ground as she tries to compose herself. I didn't think Ma had any friends, and I wonder why she never reached out to Marie for help when things got difficult with Dad. I know Marie would have come to her aid if she had asked.

I'm shaken out of my thoughts when I feel Marie's soft hand gently touching mine.

"Your mom was my best friend, and I know she'd want to make sure you were taken care of. Liv and I would both be honored if you came to stay with us, for as long as you'd like. Harrison spends most of his time in Paris, and I can assure you he won't be a problem. What do you say? We can't call ourselves The Three Musketeers without you, now can we?"

As I observe Marie, I can see that she is sincere. It doesn't matter that I'm not a little kid anymore—her remark tugs at my heartstrings, though I'd never admit that out loud. Ma used to call our family The Three Musketeers when things were still good at home, and what I wouldn't give to be a part of a family like that again.

I will never be the same, not after losing Ma. There is no coming back from that.

But that doesn't change the fact that I feel safe and secure surrounded by Marie and Liv. They both seem to genuinely care about me—a total stranger.

I can't stop myself from glancing in Liv's direction to see her peering at me, as if she's silently pleading with me to accept her mom's offer, not ready to say goodbye just yet.

I'm not ready to say goodbye either.

"Yeah, all right, I'll come stay with you," I whisper, hoping it's the right decision.

Two Months Later

"Milo, it's good to see you, son. I've missed you."

It's been years since I've spent time with my dad while he was sober. It's strange now, sitting across from him, separated by plated glass, staring blankly ahead at the man in an orange jumpsuit.

I was told that my dad confessed the morning after the accident. He pled guilty to first-degree vehicular manslaughter and was sentenced to fifteen years in prison with the chance of parole. I promised myself right away that I would do everything in my power to ensure he serves out his full sentence.

I'm technically a ward of the state until Marie is granted legal custody, which means when my dad's public defender requested I visit him in prison, I had to go. So, here I am, forced to be in the same room as the man who killed my ma.

Both my parents grew up in foster care, so neither one has any family to speak of. Dad said it was love at first sight when he saw Ma for the first time in history class. He was immediately drawn to her, and he knew within a few short weeks that they belonged together.

He called her his "alluring beauty" with her smooth, dark-brown skin tone, whiskey-colored eyes that sparkled in the moonlight, and her natural curls that he deemed his favorite trait. They had what Ma called a once-in-a-lifetime love, and it was more than enough for them both.

When Ma got pregnant during the summer before her senior year of high school, she had to drop out a few months prior to graduation. That didn't stop her from supporting Dad through every milestone: high school graduation, a move to Florida funded by a college baseball scholarship, and sadly, a tragic accident that ruined his baseball career.

When we were forced to move back to Camden, they both worked themselves to the bone to keep a roof over our heads.

Along the way, though, what we had stopped being enough for my dad, and alcohol became his mistress, his escape from reality.

Sitting in front of him now, my entire body starts to violently shake when I think back to the night of the car accident. The last time I saw Ma alive…

I squinted up as Ma flicked on the small lamp that sat on my rickety bedside table.

"Little Rabbit, wake up. Your father's at Lucky's again. He caused another bar fight, and we can't afford to pay for any more damages. Brett said he's going to have to call the cops if I'm not there in ten minutes."

I groaned as I rolled over to face her. Ma had called me her Little Rabbit ever since I could remember. She said when I was a toddler, I was wary of other people and only ever wanted to sit and cuddle in her lap. She said I reminded her of a rabbit—tender and sweet, but overly cautious.

Although I had forbidden her from using the nickname in public, it didn't stop her from using it when we were at home.

"Ma, what the hell?" I said with frustration. "Why not just leave him there? Dad deserves to deal with the consequences of his actions. Didn't you just get home from work? You should be in bed, not hauling his ass out of the bar again. At this rate, babysitting him will become your full-time job."

"Milo Leland Covell, watch your language," Ma scolded. "Your dad is a part of our family, and we take care of our family…always. Especially when they're going through a rough patch, understand?" She paused, waiting for a reply.

I took a closer look and noticed that Ma's shoulders were slumped, dark circles under her eyes. She looked utterly exhausted. I didn't want to make things any more difficult for her than they already were.

"Sorry, Ma. I'll tone it down. I just don't think we should go get him this time. Besides, why do you need me to go with you? I'm not a kid anymore. I can be left alone, you know."

"I just thought you might be able to help if he gets out of hand, that's all," she said. "Your father is a good man; he's just going through a hard time. I hope you know that we both love you very much."

She didn't waste any more time arguing with me. I watched as she got up from my bed and left the room. I heard the creak of the stairs, the rattle of keys being picked up from out of a dish, and a minute later, the front door slowly opening before closing again.

I heaved a heavy sigh as I threw the worn blue blanket from my body that I used in place of a comforter and grabbed the first pair of sweatpants and hoodie I could find on the floor before chasing after Ma. I knew I shouldn't take out my frustration on her. This was all my dad's fault.

Ma was the kindest and most thoughtful person I knew. Even after a long shift at work, she was always there to greet me when I got home from school and spent time with me until I went to bed. She never complained, and she loved my father unconditionally, regardless of his laundry list of flaws.

I knew Ma was worried that Dad would drink himself to death one of these days, but I was unsure how to stop it.

So, I did the only thing I could by racing down the stairs and heading outside before jumping into the passenger seat of our 1989 Honda Civic— a beater car on its last leg.

Ma looked over at me with a weary smile on her face. "Thanks for coming, Milo. It really means a lot."

"I love you, Ma. Now, let's go get Dad."

As we pulled up to Lucky's, I saw a form slumped up against the brick wall with a beer bottle still clasped tightly in their hand. As we got closer, it wasn't a surprise to find that it was Dad.

Ma pulled up next to the curb, dashing out of the car as soon as she had parked. I watched as she leaned down next to him, speaking softly in his ear. He absentmindedly stroked her hair as she spoke. After a few minutes, she helped him stand up before prying the half-empty bottle from his hand. He slurred his complaint, but couldn't do much aside from sway back and forth.

"Come on, Mac. It's time to go home," Ma said in a soothing voice. "Milo has school in the morning and needs to get back to bed."

Ma threw Dad's arm over her shoulders, just like she had hundreds of times before, and he moved clumsily to the car. Thankfully, he was able to carry most of his own weight.

"Jadaaaa, baby, I missed you," Dad slurred. "You know I love you, don't you?"

Ma smiled up at him even though it didn't seem to reach her eyes.

"Jada, give me the keys, baby. I'm driving."

"Mac Arthur Covell, you are drunk as a skunk. There is no way you are driving, especially not with our son in the car. Now get in the passenger seat. I mean it!" Ma's voice didn't leave any room for argument.

I rolled my eyes. They had the same conversation every time we came to pick Dad up, and Ma always won this particular argument.

I impatiently tapped my foot as they continued to bicker about who was driving. I finally jumped out of the passenger seat and moved to the back, letting out a lazy yawn before lying down on the bench seat. I had an algebra test in the morning and could use some shut-eye. I'm sure Ma wouldn't mind if I slept on the way home. Besides, there was no telling how long it would be until Dad finally got in the car.

I was suddenly jerked awake by the screech of tires and Ma's screams, and within seconds, I was thrown forward, hitting my head on the back of the passenger's seat before blacking out. The last thing I heard was my ma's pleas for help.

During the first few days after waking up from my coma, I blamed myself. If I had stayed awake a few more minutes, I could have made sure my dad got into the passenger seat, and Ma would still be alive. Yet, as the weeks have passed, I have come to the stark realization that there is only one person who deserves the blame: my dad.

I refuse to play along with this charade, tuning out my dad as he's speaking. I stand up from my seat, the chair scraping loudly against the concrete floor.

Not caring what he's is trying to tell me, I cut him off mid-sentence. "Stop talking. I am done listening to you," I say, taking a breath to calm my emotions. "In fact, I never want to see you again."

"Milo, son…please, sit back down and give me a chance to explain." He looks up at me with pleading eyes.

It feels as though a flip has switched inside my brain, and the anger finally bubbles over without a barrier to contain it.

"*No!*" I shout at the top of my lungs. "I am not your son. You're a murderer. If you hadn't been drunk off your ass, we wouldn't have had to come get you, and this never would have happened. I will never forgive you. Do you understand me? *Never!*"

Everyone is staring at us as one of the guards rushes across the room to investigate the commotion.

"Son, please..." my dad whispers, his voice deflated.

"I. Am. Not. Your. Son. Don't ever call me that again. A dad puts his family first, and you stopped doing that a long time ago. And now...now you've killed Ma. I'm so damn tired of your excuses, and nothing you say could ever make up for the hell you've put me through. You and me...we're done. Goodbye, Mac."

He calls out to me, begging me to stop, but I don't give him a second glance. He doesn't deserve my sympathy.

When I get back to the visitors' waiting room, Marie jumps up from her chair. She's dressed in skinny jeans, a perfectly ironed white shirt with ruffles around the neck, and a fringed tweed blazer. I can tell she tried to dress down, but she still looks like she just walked off the cover of a fashion magazine. You'd never guess by looking at her that she's the kindhearted soul who took me in simply because it was the right thing to do.

"You're back too soon. Is everything okay?" Marie chews her bottom lip anxiously—a trait Liv clearly inherited from her.

"Let's get out of here. I hate this place," I say.

I literally drag her by the arm as we make our way out of the building. When we finally get to the parking lot, I let out a breath of relief. A town car is idling at the curb, waiting to take Marie and me back to the city. She opens the door, ushering me inside, but I don't move.

"I don't want to see him again," I announce. "You can't make me. I'll run away before I come back here. I mean it." I focus my gaze on the wired fence beyond Marie, avoiding eye contact, afraid of what her response will be.

"Milo, look at me, please," she says quietly.

When I don't, Marie kneels down on the concrete so we're at eye-level. She's oblivious to the dirt and grime soiling her designer jeans. Her only concern at the moment is me.

"Listen to me, young man." She turns my chin with her hand so I'm forced to look her in the eyes. "Do I think you should give your dad the benefit of the doubt and hear him out? Yes, I do. But you have to make that decision on your own. I will never force you to do anything you don't want to, Milo. You are part of my family now, and I will always have your best interest at heart. Your mom loved you more than life itself, and I will do everything I can to make sure you live a happy life," she whispers into my ear as she squeezes me in a warm embrace.

"Thanks, Marie." I hug her back quickly. "Can we leave now? I really miss Liv."

"Of course. Let's go home, sweetheart."

Home? It's only been six weeks of living with the Dunhams and I hadn't started considering it *home* just yet, but now that I think about it, it fits. As long as that's where Liv is, there's nowhere else I'd rather be.

"Yes, let's go home." I climb into the town car, distancing myself from both the prison walls and the man I vow to hate for the rest of my life.

Chapter Seven

OLIVIA
Present Day—October

I FIND MYSELF STANDING IN the opulent kitchen in my parents' brownstone the next morning. I absentmindedly watch as the Vitamix blends up the ingredients needed to make a strawberry-banana smoothie—Mac's favorite.

I woke up in the middle of the night, still lying on the hardwood floor outside of Milo's old bedroom, my body stiff from sleeping on the unforgiving surface. I dragged myself back to my old room, but after tossing and turning for what felt like hours, I put on my running gear and made the fifteen-mile round-trip down to the Staten Island Ferry and back. I couldn't help but reminisce on the weekends back in high school when Milo and I would run the same route, but instead of coming straight back home, we'd take the ferry to Staten Island and spend the day exploring.

On my way home this morning, I stopped at Grendales Market for some produce. Today's a new day, and I wanted to start it out with a nutritious breakfast for Mac and me.

I look up at the clock on the microwave to see that it's already eight thirty a.m. I'm going to be late if I don't hurry. I'm meeting Dante in Central Park at nine a.m., and he can't stand it when he gets behind schedule.

I turn off the blender and open the lid to the jar, inhaling the scent of fresh strawberries. I evenly distribute the freshly made smoothie into three glasses, downing mine in a few gulps before heading into the front parlor. Jeremy already left for the day, but Jane is just finishing up rubbing Mac's arms and hands with lotion to help prevent muscle atrophy—one of the unfortunate side effects of spending the majority of time lying in the same position.

"Good morning." I smile broadly as I set their two smoothies on the bedside table. "I made you both some breakfast." I point to the drinks. "Mac, I'm heading out to meet Dante. I know you're usually early, and I don't want to keep him waiting just because you can't be there. He already likes you better than me as it is." I plant a kiss on his temple before moving away from his bed. "I'll be back this afternoon, okay?"

He smiles back and gives me a slight nod. He seems to be in high spirits this morning. "Thanks for taking my spot today."

"Anything for you. Besides, I haven't seen Dante in over a month. I miss him." I turn to address Jane as I head out of the room. "If you need me, please don't hesitate to call. I'll have my phone with me the entire time."

"Don't worry about us, dear. We'll be just fine." Jane waves me off. "We're going to read a few chapters of *Oliver Twist* today. Mac was mortified when he learned I've never read the book. And, no, I was told watching the movie doesn't count. Take the time to enjoy a few hours soaking up the last of this gorgeous fall weather. It'll be winter before we know it."

I swallow a lump in my throat, not wanting to think about the seasons changing. With winter comes the knowledge that Mac will no longer be with us, and my heart aches at the thought.

I grab my parka from the coat rack in the entryway on my way out the front door. As I shut it behind me, I come to an abrupt halt when I see Milo leaning against the banister of the stairs, a cigarette hanging loosely in his right hand as he looks toward the street. I watch a puff of smoke escape his lips as he exhales, flicking ash from the tip.

I take a minute to appreciate the man standing before me. From this angle, I have the perfect view of his profile, highlighting his well-defined cheekbones and his eyes, which appear to be a bright, crystal blue this morning. The stench of animosity has dimmed since I saw him yesterday, but not by much. He's wearing light-wash skinny jeans with rips in the knees, a fitted white T-shirt, and a gray wool coat with high-top sneakers. Aside from the stone-cold expression on his face and apparent sour attitude, he looks positively mouthwatering.

"As a medical professional, I have an obligation to caution you that smoking is bad for your health," I say with a wry expression.

Milo turns in my direction. A sadistic chuckle escapes his lips before he presses them into a tight, thin line, unamused by my unsolicited advice regarding his poor health choices.

He flicks another piece of ash off his cigarette before taking another puff. In an act of defiance, he aims his next exhale my way, a cloud of smoke invading my personal space—his way of telling me to mind my own business.

I should be outright enraged by Milo's disrespectful action, especially given my profession and the fact that my own mother died of cancer. Yet I find myself entranced, watching as his lips wrap tightly around it, making me wish my mouth could trade places with the cigarette.

I'm captivated as I watch Milo exhale a ring of smoke. He looks up to meet my eyes, giving me a cocky smirk, knowing the effect he has on me.

"Come on, Liv. You used to think it was sexy as hell when I lit up. Don't tell me you've lost your fascination for bad boys," he taunts. "Or do you prefer the hotshot, lawyer type now that you're all grown up and an entitled doctor?"

I clench my fists, steam coming from my ears. How dare he say that. I chose a career in medicine because I wanted to save lives, not for the prestige that it brings. He knows status and money have never mattered to me and that the mere mention of my privileged upbringing has always been a sore spot.

"That was low, Milo, even for you," I say, stating the obvious. "Why are you here? How did you know where we were staying? You know what, I don't care. If you're not here to apologize to Mac, you can be on your way." I point in the direction of the road.

He dramatically rolls his eyes as he scoffs in disgust. "I'm here because you owe me answers, Liv, and I'm not leaving until I get them. I want to know why my sperm donor is living the lap of luxury"—he points to the brownstone—"when he should be rotting in a prison cell. I want to know why you— of *all* people—are helping him. You damn well know he destroyed my childhood, and when that wasn't enough, he destroyed my life too. How the hell could you go behind my back like this?"

Go behind his back? He's the one who abandoned me without a backward glance or explanation. Who the hell does he think he is, trying to blame me?

Milo tosses his cigarette to the ground before unexpectedly storming toward me. I instinctively lift my arms up, shoving my palms against his chest to keep him from getting too close. His words cut me like a dagger, yet I still crave to lean in close and press my lips against his.

I gaze into his frosty blue eyes, silently pleading with him to show some semblance of remorse so I can make a case for my irrational desires, but all I see is an intense ferocity lingering in their depths.

I take two small steps back to create space between us, bumping into the doorway behind me. I jab a slender finger into his chest, fury swirling deep within my soul.

He wants a fight? I'll give him a fight.

"What is wrong with you?" I spit out. "First off, your *sperm donor* has a name. Mac will always be your father, and shame on you for discounting that relationship. Yes, he's made several lifechanging mistakes in the past, but he's suffered the consequences for all of them. He's dying, Milo, not taking a vacation. I refuse to let you show up on my doorstep and cause him any more unnecessary distress."

I pause, giving myself a minute to consider the next words out of my mouth. I won't sugarcoat the truth any longer. Milo doesn't have a problem speaking his mind, so why should I?

"Second, you forfeited the right to have an opinion on my life choices when you left. Need I remind you of the events leading up to your abrupt departure from my life?" I watch as Milo flinches at my frankness. "Don't try to play the martyr. Enough is enough." I let out a choked cry of anguish, forcing myself to suppress the tears ready to spill from my eyes.

"Mac is the only family I have left, and I'm not going to let you disrespect him, got it?" I'm full-on shouting now, without a care as to who might hear my sudden outburst. I take in a deep breath, gearing up for round two when, suddenly, a dog's barking gets my attention. I jump in alarm, bumping right into Milo's chest.

"Sorry," I mumble, not feeling remorseful at all.

That's when I notice the cutest Dalmatian I've ever seen standing behind Milo. Its tail wags eagerly with a mix of concern and excitement. I'm fascinated by the dog's unique features—one side of its face is black, the other white with a black eye. The rest of its body is a glossy white coat adorned with big black spots.

"His name is Sirius," Milo mutters under his breath.

I blink rapidly as I stare down at the dog standing on his haunches in front of me. Milo named him Sirius, after the brightest star in the sky, the very one I used to compare him to.

"He's perfect. Where did you get him?" I ask, bending down to stroke Sirius's head.

He leans in close, rubbing up against my shoulder, letting me know he's pleased with the affection. All thoughts of telling Milo off are on the back burner for now, my attention zeroed in on the loveable dog in front of me.

"I found him abandoned at one of my construction sites the night after a big rainstorm three years ago. He was huddled up under one of the bulldozers. Thankfully he came out when he heard me nearby, or there's a good chance I would have missed him. He's deaf in his right ear, but it doesn't slow him down any. He never seems to have a problem hearing me when I make mention of a snack, walk, or going outside."

As if on cue, Sirius's ears perk up at hearing what are apparently his three favorite words, proving Milo's point.

I give Sirius one more pat on the head before standing up, exhaling a breath and refocusing on the issue at hand. "Milo, did you really track us down just so you could bully a dying man? If there is a single sympathetic bone in your body, you'll find it in yourself to walk away. To forget your vendetta to exact revenge."

I shuffle my feet from side to side as we stand together in utter silence, afraid of what his response will be.

"You've always known the way I feel about Mac, and yet you still welcomed him into your life with open arms. It felt like my heart was being cut right out of my chest when I watched you care for him yesterday. You were supposed to be mine forever, not his."

"It was never my intention to hurt you, but my decisions don't revolve around you—not anymore," I say quietly.

I have a compulsive urge to touch him, to feel his warmth, and to remind him what it feels like to have someone show you compassion.

I hesitantly wrap my hands around his neck, leaning my head into the crook of his shoulder. He keeps his arms stiffly at his sides, clearly unsure how to react. After what feels like an eternity, his arms finally come around my waist. I let out a gasp, reveling in the feeling of *home* being back in Milo's warm embrace.

"I missed you so much, Liv," he whispers into my hair as he brings his hand up to gently stroke my jawline—a sign of fondness that I thought I'd never experience again.

"I missed you too, Milo. More than you'll ever know," I murmur into his shoulder.

I continue to clutch his neck like he's my lifeline, afraid I'll drown if I let go. My nose is buried in his shirt, soaking in his familiar scent of smoke, cinnamon, and pine. Back in high school, he always carried a stick of Big Red in his pocket for when he needed to freshen his breath. After I stole his gum one too many times, he started carrying around two pieces so we each had our own. I crack a smile, thinking back on the fond memory.

We stand on the threshold of my parents' brownstone, holding each other like our lives depend on it—because in many ways, they do. The ache of heartbreak seems to melt away, the two of us suspended in a bubble of desire and fondness. I take a mental picture, wanting to hold on to this memory as a proper goodbye in case this is the last time I see Milo.

After several minutes, I feel Milo start to pull back. I tilt my head to gaze into his eyes, and I'm pleased to find the animosity has dissipated.

"Liv, I should get going…"

"Please don't leave me," I blurt out, not ready to watch him walk away yet.

"What do you suggest? Because I don't see a way around this conflict." He gestures between the two of us.

"I propose a truce—at least for the next few hours. We haven't seen each other in over fifteen years, and I want some time to catch up. There's just one rule: we don't mention Mac as long as it can be helped. What do you think?" I pause, giving Milo some time to think about what I just said. "Please say yes. I'd like to spend the day with you, and then you can go back to hating me to your heart's content." I beam up at him, encouraging him to accept my peace offering.

At first, I think he's going to shake his head, but it appears as though he's deep in thought, contemplating my proposal.

I'm elated when he finally nods. "Fine, I agree to your truce, but only for today, okay?"

"Perfect. Now let's go. I have somewhere to be and I'm already late."

I'm about to rush down the steps when Milo grabs hold of my wrist. "Go where? What about Sirius? My apartment's in Brooklyn."

He has an apartment in New York? Why hasn't he tried to reach out to me until now?

"Sirius can stay here. Jane, a friend of mine, is here with Mac. She won't mind if he keeps them company for a few hours."

"Jane is here?" He lets out a startling laugh. "She never mentioned it, that sneaky little fox."

"What are you talking about? How do you know Jane?" I ask in confusion.

"She called me a couple of days ago out of the blue. She introduced herself as your friend and said that you were caring for Mac all alone and needed me here. I guess you never shared our full history, or she would have known better than to call me."

A laugh escapes my lips, though I'm not surprised she intervened. I have no clue how she got ahold of Milo's contact information, yet I can't find it in me to be mad. She did the impossible and brought Milo back, and right now, I'm grateful he's here, despite our impending fallout.

"I highly doubt that. It would have given her even more incentive to reach out. She thrives off drama. Just this morning, I caught her streaming *The Real Housewives* on her phone. She didn't even look up when I walked by because she was so invested."

"Liv, I really don't feel comfortable leaving Sirius with *that* man," Milo says, referring to Mac.

"Get over yourself, Milo," I say, annoyed. "He's not going to do anything to your dog. Besides, I thought we were pretending he didn't exist," I remind him.

I turn back to the house without waiting for his reply. As soon as I open the front door, Sirius barrels inside, running past me into the parlor. I turn the corner just in time to watch him jump over Jane's chair, landing haphazardly on Mac's hospital bed. He spins in circles before settling down and plopping his head in Mac's lap, giving his hand a long lick.

"Oh my goodness, where on earth did a dog come from?" Jane shrieks. She jumps up from the chair, the copy of *Oliver Twist* falling from her hands as she prepares to shoo Sirius off the bed.

"Jane, it's okay," I call out from across the room. "His name is Sirius, and he's here to spend time with Mac. A little birdy told me you're responsible for his owner showing up at my doorstep unannounced."

Her head snaps up, a startled expression on her face even though she knows exactly who I'm referring to. She cautiously eyes the giant dog sitting on Mac's bed. "I'm glad that man finally came to his senses. Fine, the dog can stay, just as long as you can vouch for him."

I let out a little chuckle and give her a thumbs-up. I look over to find Mac's face buried in Sirius's fur as he shakily pets behind his ear.

"Well, hello there, sweet boy," Mac rasps out. "You're an energetic guy, aren't you?" He turns to me with a grin.

"He's here to keep you company while I'm gone. It looks like you'll get along swimmingly. I'm really leaving this time. I'm so late; Dante will never let me live this down. Seriously, call the police if I'm not home in a few hours."

I spin around to leave and bump right into Milo's rock-hard chest. I didn't realize he had followed me inside. I look up to see that he's laser-focused on the scene before him with an expression that I can't quite decipher.

After a few seconds, he snaps out of his trance, glaring down at me when he finds me staring at him. He spins around and marches straight out the front door, impatiently tapping his foot while he waits for me to catch up.

"Well, are we going or not?" He points to the watch on his wrist. "We'd best not keep *Dante* waiting." His voice comes out in a mocking tone as he gestures for me to lead the way.

I skip right past him, not giving him an explanation even though I know it's eating him up inside, not knowing who Dante is.

We silently make our way down the block as I try to sneak a peek in his direction every now and then.

I can't believe Milo is back at my side—something I've imagined a million times before, but never thought would become reality. We remain silent as we walk, and I bask in my current tranquil state of mind.

Our time together is limited. Milo's a ticking time bomb, ready to go off at any moment, his bitterness dragging down any hope we have at a long-term reconciliation. Yet, right here, right now, we've committed to a truce, and I'm going to enjoy the peace for as long as I can.

Chapter Eight

MILO
Present Day—October

WHAT THE HELL AM I doing here?

I'm kicking myself for agreeing to go on this unsolicited excursion with Liv. I should be back at the apartment in Brooklyn, nursing a hangover and kicking out a one-night stand I met at one of the hundreds of bars in this godforsaken city. Instead, I spent last night chain-smoking and pacing the hallway, waiting for Jane to get back to me. The infuriating woman made me wait until nearly midnight before calling me back to tell me that Liv was staying at her parents' brownstone.

"I'm so late; Dante's never going to let me live it down."

Liv's words have me on the warpath, my sole motivation for following her. Who the hell is Dante, and why does she care what he thinks? What if this is all a sick joke, a way of her getting back at me? Could Dante be her boyfriend? Or worse, what if they're engaged? Maybe I'll get lucky and he'll pick a fight with me so I can make things interesting.

I can sense Liv's gaze on me. She might think she's being stealthy every time she glances in my direction, but she's not fooling anyone, least of all me.

I notice that she's absentmindedly biting her bottom lip—a sign that she's nervous. What does she have to be anxious about? I'm the one blindly following her to an undisclosed location. She looks like she wants to say something but is doing her best to hold back. I'm not surprised when the silence becomes too much for her.

"If we're calling this a truce, it means we're friends for the rest of the day, right?" she asks innocently. "It makes logical sense—at least to me. Because we were friends…well, I'd say we were more than friends the last time we saw each other in high school considering we had sex. Oh shoot…you know what I'm trying to say. Or I hope you do. I just wanted to get to know you—the grown-up version, I mean."

She huffs in frustration, concerned that she didn't get her point across.

She did.

God, I've missed this side of her. The unfiltered version who says exactly what she thinks, but her brain is running a hundred miles an hour and her mouth can't keep up. I always found it cute as hell and am grateful to discover she never outgrew the habit.

"What would you like to know?" I ask.

"Where did you end up? What do you do for work? Do you have a family of your own?" She can't seem to help the flood of questions flowing from her lips. No doubt she has hundreds swirling around in her head that she's thought of since I showed up at the hospital yesterday.

Hell, I do too. I want to know every detail that I've missed during the last fifteen years, but I know we don't have enough time for that.

"Honestly, Liv, there's not much to tell," I say with a shrug. "I live in Las Vegas—that's where I ended up after I left New York. I'm the CEO of a construction consulting firm I inherited from Pike. He's…well, he and his wife Eloisa are the closest thing I have to family. They took me in when I didn't have anywhere else to go."

Liv's face turns ghostly white and she squeezes her small fists tightly together. She's angry, that's for sure. The problem is, I have no idea what I said wrong, but I'm about to find out.

This woman is infuriating. I forgot how difficult it is to keep up with her constant mood swings.

I'm not surprised when she comes to a sudden stop, not caring that we're in the middle of the goddamn street. I gently tug on her arm and am able to hold on just long enough to drag her up onto the sidewalk before she jerks away from me. Whoever came up with the saying "hell hath no fury like a woman scorned," must be on a first-name basis with Liv.

"How dare you," she seethes.

"Jesus, woman, what the hell did I say that has you so worked up?" I counter.

Doesn't she know I can't read her mind?

"You have *always* had a place to go. *You* made the conscious decision to walk away from this life." She gestures around her. "No one forced you out, not even my father."

She's right. Harrison's intimidation tactics never fazed me in the past, and I knew his threats were horseshit. That doesn't mean I didn't use them to justify my reasons for leaving.

"You didn't even have the decency to tell me why you left. You disappeared into thin air, leaving me behind…" Her voice cracks as she tries to keep her tears at bay. "I'm so glad your life turned out exactly how you wanted it to. It sounds like you finally found a family worth your time, void of the drama and tragedy that plagued us both as teenagers."

Her hands are shaking, and she looks so unsure of herself. I don't like it.

I reach out and grab Liv's delicate hands, clasping them tightly in my own, before looking up to make eye contact with her. I'm only going to say this once, and I need to make sure she's listening.

"You're wrong, Liv."

"Wrong about what?"

"I don't have everything I've ever wanted…I don't have you."

She gapes up at me, taken aback by my unexpected declaration. From her expression alone, I can't tell if she wants to slap me or kiss me. Hell, I didn't mean to say the words out loud. If things had been different, she'd be the person I spent the rest of my life with. I might be the miserable ass who's harboring a grudge, but that doesn't mean I don't want her.

God, I want her more than anything…

Why the hell does everything have to be so damn complicated?

Liv's mouth slowly opens to reply to my confession.

"Olivia, you're late!" a male voice calls out.

I pivot around to identify who's dared to interrupt our private conversation. As I reorient myself, I see we're standing near the entrance of Central Park—one of Liv's favorite places in New York City.

A man jumps out of the back of a food truck parked haphazardly on the curb a few feet away. He's dressed in black jogger shorts, a fitted short-sleeved V-neck, and white tennis shoes.

It's the end of October on the East Coast. How is he not freezing?

He starts jogging over to us, and much to my dismay, Liv meets him halfway.

My eyes nearly pop out of my head as I watch them embrace, and I let out a low growl as he picks up *my* Stardust and twirls her around in a circle. Next, I expect them to break out in song like we're on the set of *Enchanted.* Seriously, when is the flash mob going to show up?

"Dante, I'm so sorry I'm late," Liv says apologetically. "It's so good to see you! It's been far too long." Liv squeals with delight as she caresses his hair. "I love the Locs; it's such a good look on you."

She beams up at him, and I scowl in their direction, waiting for them to notice I'm not pleased with the situation.

Did Liv not get the memo that I'm the only person she's allowed to look at with love and adoration? Who the hell does this man think he is, touching her like that? I swear to God, if they're together, I'm going to lose my shit.

More than you have already? You're being a tad irrational.

Really? It's time for my conscience to take a hike already.

Liv is mine. Even if only for the morning.

"Thanks so much for the food you had delivered yesterday, Dante. Mac loved the soup, and it meant so much after the challenging day I had."

I don't miss the nasty side-eye she gives me, making sure I know she blames me for her crummy day.

"Mac wishes he could be here. If he could have gotten past me, I guarantee he would have found someone to bring him and push him around in a wheelchair." She says solemnly.

Dante's eyes soften, and he looks as if he'd give anything to help make Mac whole again, which naturally pisses me off.

"Liv, I'm so sorry. You know you're not alone, right? You have an entire support system at your side, including me. Everything will be okay, just you wait and see," Dante says as he gives her another hug.

Did he just call her Liv? Hell no. Only I get to call her that.

I'm ready to start a fistfight with this irritating man who's emotionally in tune with Liv. I'm about to go off on him when I feel Liv's soft hand latch on to my elbow, silently urging me not to make a scene.

"Dante, I'd like to introduce you to Milo, Mac's son."

I snap my head to look at her. Why would she call me *that* man's son—in public, no less? I'm guessing because she knows I can't react the way I really want to. Not without Dante thinking I'm a total jackass.

"Hey, man, it's nice to meet you."

Without a thought for his safety, Dante leans in to give me a one-armed hug. I grit my teeth as my control quickly dwindles.

"Mac talks about you all the time. It's great to finally meet you. How's the construction consulting business? I hear you're a big-shot CEO." He gives me a toothy grin.

I'm dumbfounded. Until half an hour ago, Liv didn't know where I'd been all these years, so how did Mac? Better yet, why does he think he has the right to go around talking about me with random strangers, especially those who are trying to make a move on my girl?

Dante doesn't skip a beat when I don't reply. Instead, he rushes over to his food truck like he's in a hurry. He rolls out two carts, each one piled high with sandwiches wrapped in waxed paper, single-serve bags of chips, apples, bottled water, and hand warmers.

"Why don't you guys take the north side of the park, and I'll take the south? We'll meet back here when you're done. You'd better hurry it up, or you'll make me late for my next stop." He winks at Liv before grabbing the cart closest to him and jogging off in the opposite direction.

Liv seizes hold of the other cart, prepared to leave without an explanation. She always was an expert at avoidance.

"Now, wait just a minute." I grab her waist, lifting her up so she's forced to let go of the handle. I take a few steps back before setting her down. "Explain. And don't you dare try to pretend you don't know what I'm referring to."

She mumbles something about me being a giant pain in the butt before folding her arms across her chest, pouting like a kid.

"Cute. Are you about to have a temper tantrum in Central Park? If you are, wait a minute, and I'll go find some popcorn so I can enjoy the show properly," I say with a smirk.

"You're nothing but a big bully, you know that, right?" Liv barks at me. "Dante's a dear friend from college, not that I owe you an explanation. He was in and out of foster homes growing up, which ended with him living on the streets by the time he was sixteen. Against all odds, he graduated high school with a full-ride scholarship to Cornell—that's where we met. He's a literal culinary genius. He's the head chef at a pop-up restaurant in Hell's Kitchen, but he's exploring options for a permanent location."

If I didn't despise the guy for flirting with *my* woman, I'd consider recommending him to Eloisa. She's looking for an experienced chef to open a new restaurant in New York. Too bad Dante's on my hate list.

"Milo, are you even listening to me?"

I snap my head up to find Liv glaring at me as she impatiently taps her foot.

"Yes, sorry. Go on," I encourage her.

"I introduced Dante to Mac when he was released from prison, and they connected instantly—mainly because they both grew up in the system and know how broken it is. A few years back, Dante founded Stop Hunger, a nonprofit that delivers meals to the homeless in the tristate area, and Mac helped him get it off the ground. Dante now has fifteen crews who volunteer, delivering meals every Saturday. The very first route started right here in Central Park. Mac hasn't missed a delivery since Stop Hunger's inception—until he got sick. So, I've taken his place now that he can't come anymore."

"I see," I say, even though I actually don't see and it infuriates me.

How could a man responsible for taking a life be capable of doing something noble? Liv and I agreed not to discuss Mac today, so I won't get into this with her right now. Besides, she owes me answers about her relationship with Dante, and I'm not waiting another minute to find out the truth.

"Let me get this straight. Dante is your *friend*? Because you two seem a little too close to be—how did you put it?—'dear friends?'" I make air quotes when I say the words, dear *friends*.

"You're acting ridiculous, Milo. We haven't seen each other in years, and yet you act like you have a right to inquire about my dating life. It's absurd!"

She grabs the cart and storms off in the direction of the park before suddenly spinning on her heels to face me, nearly knocking right into my chest. Luckily, I stop just in time.

"Actually, you're right. Dante and I aren't just friends."

My body visibly tightens, and I barely hold in an anguished snarl making its way up my throat.

"He is one of my *best* friends, someone who has been by my side during some of the most difficult times in my life. He's been a bit preoccupied lately with his restaurant and the wedding preparations; although, Charles has been taking on most of the planning responsibilities."

"Did you just say wedding? Wait, who is Charles?"

"Hmm? Are you talking to me?" she innocently asks.

"Cut the shit, Liv. Who is Charles?" I say in a demanding tone.

"Dante's fiancé, obviously. Now, are you done trying to have a pissing match with the men in my life? I'd like to get a move on. You're slowing me down, and we have a lot of ground to cover."

I swear this woman is going to be the death of me, and she's only been back in my life for less than twenty-four hours.

"By all means, lead the way."

We spend the next hour handing out food and hand warmers to the homeless. There's a chill in the air, and despite their grumblings, these people appear to be genuinely grateful for a fresh meal.

A handful of groups along our route are expecting us, and multiple people make snarky comments about us being late. Liv is sure to point the blame at me every time someone mentions it, resulting in several scowls directed my way. When she introduces me by name, it seems like most people already know who I am.

I'm angry that Mac would talk about me to strangers when he knows I don't want to be associated with him. I'm so lost in my thoughts that I nearly miss it when we arrive at Turtle Pond. Despite my sour mood, a burst of laughter escapes from my lips.

Liv stops in her tracks, a dubious look on her face. "What's so funny?"

"Really? Look where we are. Does it jog any memories?" I point to the pond.

A look of comprehension registers on her face before her cheeks turn bright pink.

"In case you don't remember, please allow me to refresh your memory. It was the summer before tenth grade. Marie had an extra loaf of bread at home, and you had always wanted to feed the ducks. The next morning, you woke me up at the crack of dawn so we could run here. I'll admit, the sheer joy on your face was very endearing."

She groans and puts her hands to her face. "Milo Leland Covell, I forbid you from saying another word."

I click my tongue in disappointment. "The story's not over, Liv. Now, don't interrupt me again; it's rude. Besides, I wouldn't dare deprive you of reliving the ending to this one. It's a classic," I say with a wink.

"You were so damn determined to make friends with those ducks. You were as giddy as a schoolgirl when they swarmed around you in droves." I pause for effect, watching her glower at me. "You were so busy cooing over the innocent little ducks that you missed the giant goose sneaking up from behind. I'll never forget how he snapped at you, hissing in defiance as he tried to grab the bread from your hands, charging right at you. I admit, I was too busy laughing my ass off in the grass a few feet away to be of any help. You stepped backward to defend yourself from the beast before slipping ass-first into the pond. You were so distraught when the goose snapped up the remainder of the bread, leaving you behind, soaked to the bone."

Liv glares at me with her arms folded across her chest. "Are you done?"

"Sure am," I pipe up. "Thanks for letting me reminisce at your expense. That right there was well worth the trip."

By the time we get back to Dante's food truck, I feel lighter. I haven't laughed that much…in years, I guess. I always did feel the happiest when I was with Liv.

As we approach with the empty cart, Dante grins in our direction. "Hey there! Run into any geese today? Doesn't look like it since your clothes are still dry."

"Not you too!" Liv screeches.

I look between Dante and Liv. "How did—"

"This one got a little tipsy one night in college and spilled a few of her best-kept secrets. She's never been out drinking with me since." He gives Liv a mischievous grin, and she waves us off as she heads toward the truck.

Dante holds out his hand for a fist bump. "Us bros have to stick together, am I right?"

I begrudgingly reach out my hand to reciprocate.

"Hearing the news about Mac's terminal diagnosis has been a trip. Liv might seem like she's doing fine on the outside, but she's barely hanging on by a thread. He's her entire world, man. She doesn't talk about you much, but from what I've gathered, you and Mac don't see eye to eye. I'm glad you were able to put your differences aside so you could be here for Liv."

Don't see eye to eye? That's the understatement of the century.

Dante's wrong, though. I didn't come here for Liv. I want to get my answers and to finish my conversation with Mac, then I'm washing my hands of this messed-up situation.

As we approach the food truck, Liv comes out with two giant paper bags. "More deliveries," she announces, beaming up at me. "Dante, I know you're on a time crunch today, so we've got these. We can't have you missing your own cake-tasting appointment. Charles would never forgive me. Give him all my love, okay?"

"Thanks, babe. You're a lifesaver. I'll stop by later this week to see Mac. Make sure he knows he wasn't missed today," he says with a laugh.

I watch as Liv leans in to kiss his cheek, and I feel my blood boil. I don't care if Dante's got a fiancé waiting at home. Liv belongs to me, and she shouldn't be showing affection to anyone else—end of story.

She's not yours anymore, remember? You made sure of that.

Dante walks off, jumping into the driver's side of his truck before pulling away.

"Milo?" Liv calls out to me.

"What is it?" I jerk my head in her direction.

"You have a weird look on your face—the same look you had in high school when you caught Kenny Franklin asking me out."

"I don't know what you're talking about. I don't have a look. I thought we had more deliveries. Lead the way." I gesture for her to go in front of me so I can follow.

Over the next three hours, I trail Liv through New York City like a lovesick puppy as we deliver food for a charity my estranged father helped create. I'll give it to Liv; she's kept her part of the truce. She only mentions Mac when people ask about his health—which is nearly everyone. He's well-loved in the community it seems.

We're standing on the subway on our way back to the brownstone after the last delivery, and I can't help the smirk that passes my lips as I recall when Liv and I spent Sunday afternoons exploring the city with only ten dollars in our pocket. It became a game of sorts. We'd hop over the turnstiles at the subway to avoid paying for a ticket. It didn't matter that we both had MetroCards—we did it for the thrill.

I take in Liv's appearance and can't believe how stunning she is. Her tight yoga pants mold to her curves nicely, and her hair, pulled back from her face, gives me an unfiltered view of her sparkling green eyes.

As we pull up to our stop, the subway is packed, and I find my chest pressed against Liv's back. I take the opportunity to lean in slowly and breathe softly in her ear. Her entire body goes rigid at the brief contact. Before I can tease her any longer, the train stops abruptly. As we exit, a group of wild teenagers runs past us and, to my horror, bumps right into Liv. She stumbles forward, falling to the ground.

"Watch where you're going!" I shout as the kids run up the stairs without a care in the world.

"Jesus, Liv, are you okay?" I crouch down so I can check on her.

She has a huge hole in the left knee of her leggings, and I carefully lift up each of her limbs to ensure she's not hurt. As I'm examining her, I feel her body start to convulse. I jerk my head up, afraid she's having a seizure. Instead, I find her in the middle of a belly laugh, tears streaming down her face as a snort escapes her nose.

"I can't…it's…so funny…"

"Liv, you were accosted by a group of teenagers. How is that funny?" I ask in a scolding tone, not appreciating her taking the matter lightly.

"Milo…teenagers…that used to be us…"

She's cackling like a hyena, and that's when I burst out in laughter right alongside her. I can't help it; the situation is too bizarre. We're both sitting on the ground in the middle of a filthy subway station, laughing our asses off. It's rush hour, and groups of people are milling around us as another train pulls into the station. I can't imagine what passersby are thinking about the spectacle.

I give Liv a quick side hug, pressing a kiss to her temple. "Damn, I miss laughing with you, Liv."

"I missed this too," she says with a genuine smile.

"Let's get you up before we get trampled by the incoming stampede. That's definitely not the way I want to go."

She lets out another laugh at my remark.

The walk back to the brownstone is a silent one; both of us lost in our own thoughts. What happens now? Will I ever see her again? I still haven't gotten the answers I came for, but right now, that doesn't feel as important as it did this morning. Before I know it, we're standing in front of the imposing building that I once called home.

"Thanks for today. I had a lot of fun. It was really good to see you," Liv says as she shuffles her feet nervously.

Am I prepared to walk away from this woman again? I'm not sure, but I know I need some time to process what happened today. I can sense Liv has something on her mind as she nervously bites her lower lip.

"Go ahead and say whatever you're thinking."

"Have you seen a therapist?" she blurts out.

The question comes out of left field, taking me aback. "Excuse me?"

Where the hell does she get off, asking me a question like that? We've had a great day. Why would she ruin it by asking me questions related to my mental health? It's none of her business. Not to mention it's a sore spot for me and a subject I avoid like the plague.

When I lived with the Dunhams, I refused to get out of the car when Marie drove me to a therapy session a few weeks after Ma died. Any time Eloisa suggests I book an appointment with her therapist, I politely decline. I refuse to sit in a cramped room with a stranger and rehash my traumatic past. I'm doing just fine on my own.

Then why does everyone who cares about you keep suggesting you speak to a professional?

"Milo, there is no shame in talking through your feelings." It's as if Liv can read my mind. "It might not be your scene, but come with me next Tuesday night if you're still in town. I attend group therapy at a local church. It's therapeutic to hear people from all walks of life share how they've overcome the loss of a loved one and the things they do to cope on their difficult days. I think it'll help you start the process of finding the closure that you're searching for."

Did she plan this? To lure me on this outing under false pretenses? To call a truce, show me a good time, and then drop this bomb on me at the last minute? I have no clue what she's trying to accomplish by bringing this up, but it makes me angry. Does she think I'll attend one session and magically find a way to get through the grief that weighs me down?

"You've got some nerve bringing this up. I told you once, and I'll say it again: I will never forgive Mac, and I have no interest in singing 'Kumbaya' with a bunch of random strangers. I'm doing fine on my own," I lash out. "Consider our truce over. Now, can I have my dog back so I can get away from this place?"

Liv's face falls in disappointment, but she quickly masks her reaction. Funny enough, my stomach drops at the thought of never seeing her again. It's interesting…I've only been back in Liv's life for less than twenty-four hours, but I already can't imagine my life without her…not again. This is the main reason I stayed away all these years. I knew if I saw her again, I wouldn't be able to resist her.

I watch as she climbs the steps to the brownstone and slips inside. A few seconds later, Sirius comes running down the steps as Liv slams the door behind him.

Chapter Nine

OLIVIA
Past—Tenth Grade

I LOOK BELOW AT THE incredible view of the City of Love. In all the times I've been to Paris growing up, I've never made it to the Eiffel Tower. Mom and I always come at the end of the summer when Father hosts his annual charity event, a lavish excuse to wine and dine his most valued investors and clients. A tradition that dates back to my grandfather's reign. My mom's been planning these functions since she was my age, and although my father won't admit it, he wouldn't be able to pull it off without her.

For three hundred sixty-four days of the year, Mom lives the life of a middle-class soccer mom. At least as much as one who lives in a multimillion-dollar brownstone on the Upper East Side and has a trust fund the size of a small country can.

She goes to the grocery store, cooks all our meals, helps Milo and me with our homework, and always lends a helping hand to those in need. Since the day I was born, she's put her role as my mom first, and I'll forever be grateful to her for that.

Once a year, she transforms, as if by magic, from a PTA mom to an upper-crust socialite, dripping in diamonds. She emulates the perfect hostess, attentive to every last detail—from the hors d'oeuvres to the vintage of the wine served and the name of every person in attendance. That doesn't stop her from knocking an investor down a notch or two with a crass comeback to an insensitive remark.

As a true advocate for the less fortunate, she meticulously selects the charity featured each year to ensure the money raised goes to those in need instead of lining benefactors' pockets. Her motivation for running the event is strictly selfless. In years past, Father has insisted I attend what the social tabloids call Europe's "social event of the season" to show my face before the drinks start flowing and Mom deems it no longer appropriate for a child.

Thankfully, I've been saved from having to attend this year. Despite my father's disgruntled protests, Milo came to Paris with Mom and me. Father begrudgingly gave in when Mom threatened not to come at all, but only on the condition that Milo stays out of sight. We wouldn't want my father's perfect image tainted by anyone knowing that his family took in a poor boy from Camden, now would we? It doesn't matter what Father thinks. He's spent the majority of the past year working outside the country, so Milo hasn't had to tolerate his hatred very often.

It's funny how my life prior to Milo feels inconsequential, and Mom and I have considered him part of our family since the day he came into our lives.

I remember the night we brought him home after he was finally discharged from the hospital like it was yesterday.

I had always been terrified of thunder and lightning. It was the combination of the two things that frightened me the most. There was something unnerving about a bright flash of light invading a dark room, followed by a deafening boom. I didn't care what Mother Nature said…it wasn't normal, it was utterly traumatizing.

Typically, after the first crack of lightning, I ran like a madman down to Mom's room. However, with Milo staying right down the hall, I didn't want to make a bad first impression and have him think I was a big baby. At fifteen years old, you'd think I could be brave enough to handle a little thunderstorm.

As another clap of thunder echoed throughout my room, I suddenly couldn't care less what Milo thought of me. I ripped the covers off, jumped out of bed, and threw open the door to the bathroom. I was relieved to find the connecting door wide open. As the next bolt of lightning illuminated through the closed curtains, I made a mad dash to his bed.

Without thinking clearly, I jumped in next to Milo, sending up a silent thanks to the heavens that he happened to be lying on the other side of the bed as I threw the covers up over my head.

I was shaking like a leaf, pleading for the storm to quickly subside. After a few minutes, the tempest brewing outside appeared to be in a lull. It was then that it hit me…I had jumped into a literal stranger's bed. Sure, Milo was staying at my family's house, but that didn't give me the right to invade his space. He had recently lost his mom; he could still be volatile. The last thing I wanted to do was upset him. Maybe I could sneak out unnoticed, and in the morning, he would forget that the scaredy-cat from the room next door forced herself into his bed.

I started to inch my way to the edge of the bed when I felt a strong arm band around my waist. With ease, Milo pulled me to his side. We were so close that I could feel the heat radiating off his body. He nuzzled his head into my neck, and I became paralyzed from shock.

He had barely said a word to me in the past week. I thought we had made a connection when we first met and I hoped we could be friends, but after being released from the hospital this afternoon, he had asked to be excused to his room the minute we got home. I knew he was grieving his parents, and I wanted to be there for him during this difficult time, although I really couldn't explain why I felt drawn to him.

"I…I'm so sorry I jumped into your bed. I didn't mean to. I…I was scared and wasn't thinking straight," I stuttered, unsure what to do next.

"I'm glad to know I'm not the only one who's scared shitless during a storm. That was nice of you to come and check on me," he whispered back.

I doubted this boy was afraid of anything, meaning he had gone out of his way to help lessen my embarrassment.

"Um…yeah. You're in a new place, and I figured I should check to make sure you were okay."

He chuckled at my lame attempt of trying to play along.

"Don't worry, Liv. I have a feeling we'll be protecting each other from many more storms in the years to come. Now, try to relax so we can get some sleep."

He couldn't be serious…could he?

There was no way I could stay in his bed overnight. A few moments later, his breathing started to even out, assuring me that he meant what he said. I contemplated sneaking out and returning to my bed, but as the storm continued to brew outside, I assured myself it was only for one night.

It was my last thought as I drifted off to the most peaceful slumber I'd ever had.

Since that first night, I haven't slept in my own bed a single time. Every night after Mom comes into our respective rooms to say good night, I anxiously wait until I hear her make her way to the master bedroom on the floor below before I quietly tiptoe into bed with Milo.

We spend most nights talking about our day, who we want to be when we grow up, and playing a little game we've creatively dubbed The Color Game. It's pretty simple. One of us thinks of an object and tells the other person the object's color, then they have to guess what it is by asking a series of yes or no questions. Oftentimes, we play for hours, lying side by side until we eventually fall asleep.

Most mornings, I wake up with Milo spooning me from behind, but aside from sleeping wrapped in each other's arms each night, we've kept our relationship strictly platonic. There's no denying we've had a soul-deep connection from the day we met, but we're still kids. To make it more complex, Milo lives with my mom and me, and if we started a relationship, I worry it would ruin our dynamic.

We've both avoided the impending conversation—at least until now.

"The view is utterly breathtaking from here. I can't believe I've never made it to the top before!" I marvel at the view below. The Seine effortlessly winds its way through the heart of Paris. From here, I can see a fleet of boats moving smoothly through the water as groups of people stroll along the tree-lined river bank. From this high up, they all look like little ants, and I giggle at the thought of reaching out to pluck one of them off the ground. As I look to the right, I easily spot the Arc de Triomphe. I've determined the sight below is much better than the one we have at my father's penthouse apartment.

"You're right about one thing, Liv," Milo says. "The view from here is unmatched. I'd dare say it's the most beautiful sight I've seen in my entire life."

I turn to him, prepared to tease him about getting sentimental over the scenery, and I'm struck when I find his electric-blue eyes zoned in on me, the surrounding panorama the furthest thing from his mind.

My face flushes with heat as a jolt of electricity shoots straight through my spine. My cheeks have turned pink from embarrassment. Milo has spent enough time with me to see the visible signs that his words have affected me. There might as well be a flashing neon sign pointing my direction that says, "Look at me!"

I can't seem to drag my gaze from Milo, mesmerized as he leans in, gently tucking a piece of stray hair behind my ear. I feel weak at the knees, saying a silent prayer that I don't pass out. That would be humiliating, and there's no chance Milo would ever let me live it down.

Oblivious to the melodramatic breakdown happening in my head, Milo places a gentle kiss on my cheek before whispering in my ear, "You are the most beautiful girl I've ever met, and I've been waiting a long time to say this…"

My mouth goes dry and I can hardly swallow. Seriously, I'm about to faint on the upper deck of the Eiffel Tower in front of the boy who holds my heart.

"I love you, Liv."

I blink rapidly, staring at him in disbelief. Is this a dream? It has to be a dream, right?

I start to sway to and fro before grasping tightly to Milo's arm to avoid tumbling to the ground. I've spent so much time keeping my own feelings under lock and key that I'm unsure how to react to Milo's confession.

I worry that everyone will think we're irresponsible, love-drunk, high school kids without a care for our future.

I'd like to think that Mom would be supportive. She cares about Milo as much as I do, and there's no way she hasn't noticed the crackle of chemistry that buzzes between Milo and me anytime we're in the same room.

My primary concern is what my father would do—namely contact social services. I don't want Milo to be taken away. It's my greatest unspoken fear that one day, I'll wake up, and he'll be gone without so much as a goodbye.

If I reciprocate those three little words, there is no coming back from this. Even if we agree to take things slow, our relationship will never be the same.

Am I okay with that?

I think, at this particular moment, I really am.

I slowly reach for Milo's hand, intertwining our fingers together. Desperate to be near him, I find the courage I need.

I draw in a deep breath as I look him directly in the eyes. "I love you too, Milo, more than you'll ever know."

He presses another peck on my cheek before catching me by surprise when he tilts my chin up slightly, slanting his mouth across mine.

Oh. My. Gosh.

Our lips effortlessly mold together as if we've done this hundreds of times. I feel like I'm floating on a cloud, experiencing what some might call an out-of-body experience. I close my eyes as I take pleasure in the feel of his soft lips pressing against mine. I focus on the steady beating of his heart, bringing my hands up to grip his shoulders. His hands automatically wrap around my waist to keep me anchored as we make out like lovestruck teenagers. I let out a disappointed grumble when Milo pulls away.

"Stardust, open your eyes," he says in a low voice.

I begrudgingly peek up at him, a slight frown on my face to make sure he's aware of my disappointment for cutting our moment short.

"As much as I enjoy kissing you, I'd prefer the next time to be somewhere we won't be interrupted. Your delicious moans should be for my ears only. Besides, it's a little difficult to cover up a hard-on in public."

I burst out laughing at his candidness. Milo doesn't have a filter, and I love his utter honesty, even when it's not always in my best interest to hear his truthful opinion.

"Besides, we'll have plenty of time to make out every night since a *certain* somebody doesn't know how to sleep in her own bed," he teases.

"You're the one who texts me from down the hall when I take too long to come to your room." I playfully slap his arm.

"It's those pesky thunderstorms, Liv. I never know when one will come, and I need you close by, just in case." He winks at me. "What do you say we get a move on? We have a whole city to explore before the day is over."

As Milo starts to walk away, I tug on his hand. "Wait, why did you call me Stardust?"

He smirks, gazing at me affectionately. "The other night while we were all stargazing, your mom gave me a mini-lesson in astrology. She mentioned the particles of matter that fall from the stars to the earth are called stardust. I was intrigued, so I looked it up, and it also refers to something that gives you a magical or charismatic feeling."

I draw in a deep breath as Milo reaches up to caress my cheek with his fingertips.

"You've been a light in my life since I met you, Liv. Somehow, you've eased the pain of losing Ma this past year without even trying. You don't look at me like I'm the charity case with a dead mom and a dad in prison. You see *me*—the real me. You're the reason I have hope for a future, as long as you're in it. To me, that's pure magic. You're my Stardust."

I swallow back a lump in my throat. "I love you, Milo Leland Covell. You're stuck with me, forever and always," I whisper as I wrap my arms around his neck, nestling myself into his warm embrace.

We spend the rest of the day roaming aimlessly through the city with no destination in mind. There's no itinerary or agenda; we're simply living in the moment. It's the end of summer, and a slight chill is in the air. Most of the tourists have gone home, giving us the run of the town without the crowds.

By late afternoon, we're weaving in and out of the streets near Notre Dame, passing by the endless rows of shops selling trinkets, souvenirs, and antiques. I pay them no mind, as there's only one type of shop I'm interested in. I come to a halt when I find what I'm looking for: a run-down store with a sign above it. Le Bookshop.

I let out a gleeful squeal, spinning around to face Milo. "We have to go inside. Please? You can wait out here if you want. I won't be long, I promise."

He lets out a low groan. He's spent countless hours following me around the tristate area as I browse used bookstores. He doesn't have the same interest in them that I do, and that's okay. My affinity for children's books is more than enough for the both of us, even though my ever-growing collection is more for Milo than me.

A few months after he moved in, I remember going into his room one day and finding him inconsolable. He had just found out that all his belongings from his childhood home had either been donated or thrown out, and he never got the chance to go through his things before they were given away.

His mom had collected children's books and inscribed each one with a note to Milo. There had been dozens of books with personal messages from her that were now lost forever.

I spent weeks racking my brain, thinking of a way I could help ease his pain. While we were lying in bed one night, the idea struck me.

The following day, I dragged Milo into a used bookstore in Greenwich Village, where I dug through the children's section until I found a copy of *The Tale of Peter Rabbit*. It had been Milo's favorite book growing up and was the namesake for his childhood nickname, Little Rabbit.

I told Milo I was starting a new tradition.

I wanted to collect kids' books in honor of his mom and write a message inside each one. We'd write about our adventures the day we picked each one out. Secretly, I wanted to collect them for our future children. Even back then, I knew

Milo and I would end up together. It's always been inevitable, and I think he's felt the same way from the beginning too.

I can picture it clearly: Milo sitting in a sturdy rocking chair holding our son—who has dazzling blue eyes and curly hair just like his dad—while I sit on the floor in between Milo's legs, resting my head on his knee as he reads from *The Tale of Peter Rabbit*.

I startle when I hear the bell chime above the bookshop door, pulling me out of my own head and back to the present.

"Liv, are you coming?" Milo's holding open the door, waiting for me to get a move on.

I give him a broad smile and nod at the kid behind the shop desk overflowing with paperwork and books that haven't been shelved yet. He doesn't acknowledge me, more invested in the Nintendo DS he's playing on than selling merchandise to a bookworm like me.

I slip through the stacks, making my way to the back of the shop. It's there that I discover paradise: a room filled with children's books stacked nearly six feet high. I drop to the floor, pulling out each book to read the title. Every so often, I can hear the floorboards creaking outside the room—no doubt Milo impatiently checking in on my efforts. Within a few minutes, I have a small pile that includes *The Winston Companion Readers Primer*, *McGuffey's First Eclectic Reader*, and the French version of *Winnie the Pooh*.

Once I've finished scouring the piles, I slowly stand up to stretch my legs. I scoop up my new treasures and return to the main shop area.

Sure enough, as I exit the children's section, Milo is leaning up against a ladder, looking at me with a seductive smile on his lips. He bends down to brush his lips against mine.

Kissing him will never get old.

"Looks like you were successful in your endeavor. I can't wait to see what dedications you come up with for these books. 'Dear future children, I kissed Milo for the first time today. It was purely magical. He's the most amazing specimen on the planet.'" He says the last part in a high-pitched voice, mimicking my own.

I give him a playful shove. "Wrong. Our first kiss was special to me, and I'm saving that core memory for myself for now."

"I enjoyed our first kiss too, Liv. Here, let me take those for you." Milo grabs the pile of books from my hands and makes his way over to the counter to pay.

When we're together, he insists on buying my things. It doesn't matter if it's a pack of pencils for school, an ice cream cone, or my books. He's been helping our neighbors with yard work despite my mother's protests. He insists that he earns his keep somehow. He doesn't want to be considered a freeloader, no doubt due to comments made by my insensitive father whenever he makes a rare appearance in New York.

After we leave the bookstore, we make our way to the metro. Outside the station's entrance, we pass a man dressed in a three-piece, pinstriped suit, polished black shoes, and a cobalt tie that he's pulled loose. As we get closer, I notice a cigarette hanging loosely from his fingers. In Paris, smoking is considered a fashion statement. As the saying goes, all the cool kids are doing it.

I set foot on the steps to head down into the tunnel, but when I turn back, I find that Milo hasn't followed me. He's stopped near the man smoking, eyeing him curiously, his gaze pinging back and forth between the man's face and the cigarette.

"Would you like a light, my friend?" the stranger asks in a thick French accent. "It makes for an excellent stress reliever, trust me."

The stranger hands his cig to Milo, and without hesitation, he puts it up to his lips, inhaling deeply. He lets out a hacking cough, and the man lets out a deep chuckle.

"No, no. Like this." The man gracefully brings the cigarette to his mouth, as if performing a dance, and lets out a slow and deliberate puff. He hands it back to Milo, who copies the same motion.

"A cigarette virgin no more!" the stranger exclaims as he encourages Milo to take a few more drags before showing him the proper way to drop the butt to the ground and smash it with his heel.

"Au revoir," the man calls out as he walks toward an office building nearby.

As Milo brushes past me to head down to the train station, I call after him, "What was that? You don't smoke."

"Correction, Liv. I *didn't* smoke." He smirks as he comes up to press a kiss on my mouth. The taste of smoke lingers on his lips, and I find I don't mind it. *Not at all.*

Chapter Ten

MILO
Present Day—November

IT'S ALREADY FIVE P.M. ON Tuesday afternoon.

For some unexplained reason, I'm considering Olivia's offer to go to group therapy tonight. I haven't spoken to her since Saturday, after I stormed down the street after our spat like a petulant child.

I shut my laptop after hitting send on one last email to approve a contract for the construction on another apartment building in Bushwick. Sirius and I checked out the site this morning, and I'm confident it'll be another successful venture for Lawson Co.

Five years ago, when Pike asked that I take over as CEO, there was just one catch: I would personally oversee our expansion to the East Coast. Little did I know it would entail opening a second office in New York City.

Our business has grown tenfold since then, but that doesn't mean I don't constantly complain about having to spend a considerable amount of time in this cesspool of a city.

Pike knows that I detest the place, yet somehow, he not only talked me into expanding our business here, but also purchasing an abandoned industrial building in Bay Ridge. I've since converted it into an office building, transforming the top floor into my own private apartment and workspace, similar to my setup back in Las Vegas.

Pike was hesitant at first about my request to have my own workspace away from our headquarters, but it was in his best interest to grant me his approval. He gets to run headquarters however he sees fit without the pressure of being CEO, and I get my privacy while running the company that I've invested my time and energy into for the past fifteen years. It's a win-win for both of us.

Aside from my weekly dinners with Pike and Eloisa, I live a solitary life, and I like it that way. My preferences haven't changed just because I run a multimillion-dollar company.

I stand up and stretch before leaving my home office, making my way down the hall to the living room.

The floor-to-ceiling windows let in a soft glow from the setting sun. A lone brown leather couch sits in the middle of the space, not a single decorative pillow or blanket in sight. A massive TV hangs above the fireplace, and there's a fully stocked dry bar in the corner—the one thing I do frequently utilize, probably more often than I should.

Much to my interior design team's dismay, I refuse to fully furnish or decorate the place since I spend most of my time in my office when I'm in town and eat out for most meals.

I look over to find Sirius snuggled up in his cozy dog bed next to the fireplace, chewing on his plush hedgehog, courtesy of Eloisa. Since I refuse to settle down and have kids, she says he could be the closest thing she ever has to grandchildren, so she insists on spoiling him. Sirius briefly looks up to acknowledge my presence before returning his attention back to his favorite squeak toy.

I walk over to the sliding door leading to the balcony and step outside. I'm immediately greeted with a brisk breeze, the thin white button-up shirt I have on not doing much to keep the cold out. I grab a cigarette from the pack I left on the patio table earlier and light one up before pulling out my phone and dialing Eloisa's number. She picks up on the third ring, no doubt anticipating my call.

"Milo, there you are. I've been waiting to hear from you. How did the walkthrough of the Bushwick property go today?" she asks.

"Hi, Els. It went well. We're projecting a thirty percent profit margin on this one. Pike was thrilled when I told him the news. I'll need his expertise on a few things during the coming months, so I'm not sure how much free time he'll have to help out at the restaurant. I'm sorry."

"What on earth are you apologizing for? This whole semi-retirement business is complete bullshit," she states. "Every time Pike comes to the restaurant, he starts bossing my staff around like he owns the place, and it's driving me crazy. To be honest, it's messing with our sex life, and you know how much we enjoy that."

Eloisa doesn't have a filter, and it's times like this when I wish she did.

"Oh my God. Els, we've talked about this. That's too much information. I don't want to hear about how you get it on with Pike, okay? If you need to keep him out of the house and away from your business, that's all you've got to say."

My mind is scarred from the explicit details she's shared with me over the years. I'll never get over the fact that I know Pike's favorite position in the bedroom.

"Milo, a healthy, intimate relationship is important. You would know that if you stopped sticking your dick in anything that moves," she says point-blank.

"Nope, I'm not touching that comment with a ten-foot pole. Can this conversation be over now?" I plead, needing this discussion to end.

"No, I'm not done talking to you." Of course she's not. "How's Sirius? Are you feeding him enough?"

"I'm doing very well. Thanks for your concern." Sarcasm drips from my voice as I'm not surprised she's more concerned about my dog's well-being than mine.

"Don't worry, Sirius is well fed and enjoying the trip. In fact, that reminds me. We went to the vet a couple weeks ago, and she mentioned he'd gained five pounds since our last visit. You wouldn't know anything about that, would you?"

There's a long pause on the other side of the phone, confirming my suspicions. Sirius hasn't been overfeeding himself, and I knew there was only one person fit to be his accomplice.

"Every time the poor dog comes to my house, he bolts to the kitchen and stands by the cupboard, begging for a treat. How can I deny him with those adorable puppy-dog eyes of his?" Eloisa asks innocently. "You know I'm not strong enough to resist him."

I let out a low chuckle. "That dog has you wrapped around his finger. You know that, right?"

"Yes, he does, and I'm not ashamed to admit it. Besides, he deserves an endless supply of baked goods for having to put up with you, don't you think?"

She has a valid point. However, that doesn't mean we won't be rationing Sirius's snack intake or reducing the number of homemade dog biscuits Eloisa sends home with us from now on.

There's a silent pause on the phone, and I can hear her let out an exasperated sigh. A sign she's shifting gears and preparing to tell me something I might not want to hear.

"Do you want to talk about what happened with Olivia on Saturday?" she inquires.

"No, Els, I don't. Liv made it clear she thinks something is wrong with me. Why else would she suggest I go to therapy? We haven't seen each other in fifteen years, and out of the blue, she wants to address my mental health. Who does that?"

"There's no shame in going to therapy. Take it from someone who's attended weekly sessions since I was fifteen. You've carried a poisonous chip on your shoulder since your mom's death. Seeking help doesn't lessen the hurt you've suffered, but it may help you find solace and peace. There is something healing about talking through your feelings, or in this case, listening to how others have coped with the grief from losing their loved ones." Eloisa lets out a sigh. "Don't squander this opportunity because of your negative opinion of your father; this isn't about him. You owe it to yourself to heal, to find the closure you need in order to move past this chapter of your life."

I grip the phone tightly, suppressing the urge to throw it against the nearest wall.

I take another long drag of my cigarette, desperately needing the nicotine after hearing Eloisa's unfiltered opinion. Since my mom passed, I have flat-out refused to talk to a professional. I've always gotten satisfaction from adding fuel to the hatred I feel for Mac. I don't need to pay someone to tell me my coping mechanisms aren't healthy...I already know.

"Els, you do realize that if you were anyone else, I'd tell you to go straight to hell and mind your own goddamn business?"

"Well, it's a good thing I'm me then, isn't it?" she quips back. "And for heaven's sake, it's time for you to quit smoking. Don't you think Liv's already lost enough people to cancer?"

I pause midway through another puff. Eloisa does have a point, yet I don't miss the irony, knowing Liv didn't mind when I smoked in the past. We both adopted bad habits that day back in Paris when I tried my first cigarette.

"How did you know I was smoking?"

"Let's just call it a motherly inst—" Eloisa abruptly cuts herself off.

She's always been careful never to call herself my mother figure, but we both know the truth. After losing my own mom and then Marie, I never thought I'd have anyone to fill the role again...until I met Eloisa.

"You know I care about you and Pike, right?" I reassure her.

"Yes, I know you do, and we love you so much." She says the words I've never been able to verbalize. "Sweetheart, I have to go. It's a madhouse at the restaurant, and I need to check on the kitchen staff before I head home. I promised Pike I'd be back in time for dinner. He's making spaghetti and meatballs. Thank heavens I had the foresight to teach the man how to make a simple yet traditional Italian dish when we got married. It's nice to come home to a meal that I didn't cook. Please think about what I said about therapy, okay?" she implores.

"I'll think about it, I promise. Tell Pike I'll call him in the morning with an update on the Bushwick project, okay?"

"I will. Bye, sweetheart." The line goes dead, and I'm left alone with my thoughts.

I dispose of the used cigarette butt in an empty beer bottle before heading back inside. I change into dark-wash jeans, a gray hoodie, and black high-tops—what Eloisa has deemed my after-work uniform. Like Olivia, I'm a creature of habit, and when I find something I like, I stick with it.

I head to the entryway, grabbing the lone leash hanging from a hook on the wall.

Sirius scrambles from his cushion in the living room, sprinting down the hall like an Olympian track star finishing their last hundred meters of a race. For a dog with restricted hearing, he doesn't miss a beat, especially when a walk is on the line. When he sees the leash, he starts spinning in circles, letting out short barks of excitement.

I lean down to clip the leash to his collar as he nudges my arm with his snout, his tail rapidly wagging in anticipation.

"Whoa there, boy. It's only a walk." He lets out another joyful yip after hearing his favorite word. "You shouldn't get your hopes up, bud. I'm dropping you off with Mac while I go with Olivia for a little while. He's a very bad man."

Sirius tilts his head to the side and whines before exuberantly licking my face, as if he knows exactly who I'm referring to.

"Traitor," I mumble under my breath.

Even my own dog seems to like Mac, and he's usually a great judge of character. He must be losing his touch.

I debate turning back at least a dozen times, but before I know it, Sirius and I are standing in front of our destination. As I stare up at the imposing brownstone, Eloisa's words play on a loop in my mind.

You owe it to yourself to heal, to find the closure you need in order to move past this chapter of your life.

There's truth in her words, I know that. For the last two decades, I've been trapped in a permanent state of torment, allowing my resentment toward Mac to seep into all aspects of my life. I've never learned how to cope with my past trauma, and over time, my pain and suffering have compounded.

As Sirius and I walk up the stairs, I pause mid-step when I see movement in the large bay windows facing the street. Liv is sitting next to Mac on a hospital bed, similar to the one used when Marie lay in the same spot years ago. Liv's head is resting against Mac's shoulder, and her lips are turned up in a wide grin, as if Mac just said something funny. A dull ache shoots through my chest as I watch her smile up at the man I despise.

I can't do this.

As I'm about to turn around and head back to my apartment, Liv's head shoots up as if she can sense my presence. Her inquisitive gaze bores into me, looking right into my soul, the one filled with hatred and spite that I can't seem to control.

Therapy might not be such a bad idea.

I expect Liv to ignore me and go right back to talking to Mac. Instead, I watch with anticipation as she stands up and disappears from the room. Shortly after, the front door swings open, and she stands on the threshold. I blink a few times as I take Liv in from here. She's dressed in tight black leggings, a chunky gray sweater, boot socks, and a pair of Hunter ankle boots. Even in casual wear, she's a goddamn vision.

I'm gearing up for another round of verbal sparring, picking up where we left off on Saturday. Instead, Liv does the last thing I expect.

"You came! I can't believe it," she shouts enthusiastically before launching into my arms.

Without a second thought, I lean into her warm embrace, instinctively wrapping my arms around her waist. I'm instantly welcomed by the familiar scent of her perfume, combined with a hint of cinnamon. I bury my nose in her hair, committing this grown-up version of her to memory.

I'm jolted from my thoughts when Sirius eagerly shoves past us, forcefully making his way through the door. Sure enough, a few seconds later, he appears in the window, having found his way back to Mac's bed, curled up between the old man's legs, making himself right at home.

I knew he was a traitor.

Liv cautiously pulls back before addressing me. "I was just heading out the door. I'm assuming you're here to go with me?"

"Um…yeah, I guess I am," I say hesitantly.

"Okay. I just need to say goodbye to Mac and tell Jeremy I'm heading out."

I grab hold of her arm before she can move. "Who the hell is—"

She cuts me off before I can finish my sentence. "Jeremy is the nursing assistant who's been helping care for Mac. Honestly, Milo, this jealousy act doesn't suit you, and it's getting on my last nerve."

I let out a gruff grunt of disapproval as she spins around and heads back inside. If the tables were turned and I mentioned another woman, she would be singing a completely different tune. This time around, she didn't offer for me to come inside. She must have decided it's better to keep me away from Mac entirely. Smart woman.

I head down the stairs to wait for Liv on the sidewalk, purposefully avoiding the bay window. When I hear the front door creak open, I find her bounding down the steps coming toward me.

"Sirius was elated to see Mac again, and the feeling was mutual. Thank you for letting him stay, that was sweet of you."

"I'm not sweet, and I didn't do it for Mac. It was merely for convenience's sake," I growl out.

"Regardless, thank you," she says, choosing to ignore my irritable disposition.

We walk in silence for several blocks before turning down 1st Avenue, coming to a stop outside a quaint church. A cross hangs above the front door: Friendship Baptist Church. A lone man sits on the top step of the front entrance.

I freeze in a rare moment of vulnerability. The last time I set foot inside a church was for Marie's funeral.

"Are you coming?" Liv's angelic voice snaps me out of my near-panic.

She's made her way to the side of the building, and as we round the corner, I see a chalkboard easel leaning up against the wall that reads, "Grief Support Group every Tuesday at 7 p.m. All are welcome."

Several other people are heading down a set of stairs leading to the basement entrance, and I hesitantly follow as Liv walks down the steps to join them.

She stops halfway, turning to face me. "It means the world that you're here with me and that you're giving this a chance. Remember, you're here to observe. There's no pressure for you to introduce yourself or share your story."

I give her a curt nod, not able to vocalize my feelings. My heart is about to beat out of my chest, tempting me to storm back up the stairs and head over to the bar we passed a couple of blocks back. I could use a stiff drink right about now. Instead, I follow Liv into a large, open space filled with chairs in the shape of a horseshoe. Off to the side is a table of refreshments, which I assume are for after the meeting.

I'm surprised to find most of the seats are occupied. Liv points out the last two available chairs toward the back of the semicircle. As we sit down, an older woman on the other side of Liv smiles at her and reaches out to pat her arm in silent support.

"I'm so glad you were able to make it tonight, my dear. We missed you last week, and it's nice to see you've brought a friend." She nods in my direction but doesn't address me, which I appreciate.

A balding, middle-aged man stands at the front of the room with a clipboard in hand.

"Welcome, everyone. My name is Mike. Whether you've been here before or this is your first time, I'm glad you've joined us tonight." He looks in my direction, making me think I must be the only one who's never been here before.

So much for keeping a low profile.

"This is a safe space, where you can share your story and express your feelings openly. Everyone in this room has experienced loss in some way, shape, or form. This is a place of acceptance and healing as we explore our grief and our personal experience on how each of us has moved forward to find a place of peace in the midst of turmoil. We have a large group today, so I'm going to open the floor to anyone who wants to share. Remember, it's not a requirement, but we do encourage you to speak up when you're ready."

I spend the next hour and a half captivated by the stories of those who choose to share. It's clear that every person here has suffered through a grave loss and has struggled through the grieving process.

Dean, a retired hedge fund manager from Tribeca, speaks of the loss of his wife two years ago to an unexpected heart attack. They were married for thirty years and had no children. His first priority was his career, his wife's needs coming in second—one of the reasons they never had kids. Now that he's no longer working and spends most of his time alone, he's come to understand how his wife must have felt all of those years. He struggles with the guilt that haunts him, knowing that he'll never be able to make amends.

Alice, a young woman who can't be older than sixteen, talks about her dad, who died of a drug overdose last year. He had been a physically abusive father and husband during the last few years of his life as he slowly let the substances take over. Even though a heavy burden has been lifted since his passing, Alice struggles with inner turmoil, a constant battle between experiencing grief over his loss and feeling relief that he's finally out of her life for good. She wanted to join this support group, a place where people of all ages can come to grieve despite vastly different backgrounds. She mentions that she struggles to connect with kids her age since most don't understand what it feels like to lose a parent.

I look over to see Liv smiling gently at the young woman, and I know she'll befriend her, if she hasn't already.

When we were her age, I always felt out of place. While everyone else was concerned about which party to attend on the weekend or which class to skip, I was battling the overwhelming agony of losing my ma and the embarrassment of having a father in prison.

Liv was different from the other kids.

She was empathetic to my loss, and when her own mom lost her battle with cancer, she entered into the lonely and desolate club that a child should never have to enter.

Before I know it, the session is almost up. I might never admit it out loud, but Liv was right. This was an eye-opening experience. I still don't know if I'll attend therapy in the future, but it made me realize I'm not the only one fighting an internal battle with my grief.

"We have time for one more share. Does anyone else want to go?" Mike asks.

"I do." Liv shakily stands up to face the group.

She's a nervous wreck, which surprises me. I'm sure this isn't the first time she's shared with the group. I wonder if she's worried about how I'll react if she brings up Mac.

"Hi, everyone. I'm Olivia." She gives a little wave. "Most of you have heard from me before and know the basics of my journey through grief. Over the years, coming to this group and attending private therapy sessions has made me realize that grief isn't a one-size-fits-all experience. Every person handles loss differently, and the pain of losing a loved one never disappears. It may stay dormant for a while, but it's always there, ready to make an appearance when you least expect it. Recently, I've had several life-altering events occur that have caused my heartache to come to the surface. I'm forced to watch another person I love die right before my eyes. I thought it would be easier this time around, but I'm finding that in some ways, it's even more difficult."

Liv pauses, and I don't miss her hands trembling at her sides.

"There's a piece of my story I've kept locked away for fifteen years. I thought if I kept it a secret and didn't share it with the world, I could pretend it never happened."

I can't take my eyes off her. I silently will her to look in my direction, so I can give her a comforting smile, but for some reason, she's purposefully avoiding eye contact with me.

"A few months after my mom died, I suffered a miscarriage…"

My brain short-circuits at Liv's confession, but I force myself to continue listening, no matter how difficult it might be.

"At the time, I didn't even know I was pregnant. I woke up in the middle of the night, withering in pain, my clothes soaked in blood. I was all alone." She draws in a deep breath. "At a time when I needed help the most, I didn't have a single person by my side. After I was released from the hospital, I questioned whether life was worth living anymore, especially after I returned home to an empty house. My solitude served as a constant reminder that no one cared if I lived or died. In my darkest moments, I found comfort in the form of a letter from someone unexpected. A person I had been led to believe was evil. Out of desperation, I met this man in person, and even from inside prison walls, he helped me—a stranger—find the courage to survive and build a life beyond the sorrow and agony I had suffered."

The entire room is silent. I'm gasping for air, unable to wrap my mind around what she's just shared. Liv was pregnant…with *our* baby. An innocent child I never had the opportunity to meet. She was all alone during the darkest moments in her life, which is why she reached out to Mac in the first place.

I think I'm going to be sick…I have to get the hell out of here.

Mike starts to speak, but he's drowned out by the shrill buzzing in my head. I can't wait any longer. I jump out of my seat, preparing to make a quick exit.

When I see the refreshment table near the door, I can't hold in my bottled-up emotions any longer. I lift the table on its side, throwing it to the ground. The water pitcher shatters and the box of pastries falls in disarray.

As I fling open the door to leave, I see the group participants staring at me in horror like I'm some kind of monster. I thought this place was supposed to be void of judgment. I guess I was wrong. This was a complete shitshow, and it was a mistake coming here.

Without a second glance, I rush out of the room. My only concern is to get the hell out of that torture chamber.

Chapter Eleven

OLIVIA
Present Day—November

MY MOUTH GAPES OPEN AS I helplessly watch Milo flee from the room, the remnants of his outburst scattered across the floor. All eyes in the room are on me—some filled with pity, others with annoyance—as they wonder why I would bring someone volatile to the group.

In hindsight, I should have told Milo about the baby beforehand. It wasn't fair for him to find out for the first time with a room full of strangers.

While I was talking, I could feel his burning gaze, encouraging me to look in his direction, no doubt sensing that I was nervous. I couldn't face him, though…not if I wanted to get the words out. Seeing his initial reaction when I mentioned the baby would have killed me. Until this moment, aside from the medical staff at the hospital and my father, Mac was the only person who knew about my miscarriage.

I don't hesitate to go after Milo. If I don't chase him now, there's a good chance I might never see him again. For all I know, this will send him right over the edge. I cut Mike off as he's trying to defuse the tension in the room caused by Milo's explosive exit.

"I'm so sorry for the disruption, everyone," I call out over my shoulder as I dash up the stairs.

Who knows if I'll be welcomed back after the scene Milo caused, but I couldn't care less at the moment.

Milo might not know it, but he needs me right now. We need each other. We never got to grieve the loss of our child together, and this might be the only chance we get.

As I make my way to the front of the church, I turn to the left and find Milo already halfway down the block.

"Milo! Milo, please wait!" I shout in his direction, but he doesn't turn around.

I don't think he has a destination in mind; he's simply trying to distance himself from the situation. Or maybe it's me he's trying to get away from.

I sprint to catch up but don't say a word as I fall in step next to him.

After several blocks, Milo abruptly stops and takes a seat on the curb outside a closed barbershop. He rests his arms on his knees and clasps his head with both hands. I sit beside him and lean against his shoulder in solidarity. He doesn't acknowledge me but doesn't push me away either.

I remain silent as I look up to see if I can catch a glimpse of the stars. Even with the pollution and bright lights flooding the city, I'm lucky to find myself in a spot clear of obstructions, providing the perfect view of the magnificent night sky. It feels like it's a sign from my mom, letting me know she's here with Milo and me, that everything will be okay.

"Did you know if the baby was a boy or girl?" Milo's broken voice fills the air.

"A girl," I whisper solemnly.

"Did she have a name?"

"I named her Hope."

"Hope…" Milo says her name like a prayer.

I feel a drop of moisture on my head, and when I glance up, I find tears falling from his face.

I've never seen Milo cry before, and I'm unsure how to handle it. I figure he'd prefer if I don't acknowledge it at all…so I don't. Instead, I give him the answers he's been waiting for.

"When I got home from the hospital, I found a box of letters Mac had written to you. There was one for every week he had been in prison. My mom kept them all. I think she hoped that you'd reconcile with him one day, and she knew you would want to read them if that happened. I picked one at random, and I realized after reading it that I wasn't the only one who was alone in this world."

My voice drops to a whisper. I'm terrified at how Milo might react to the details I'm about to share with him.

"I visited Mac in prison, and even though he didn't know me, he treated me like I mattered. He helped me through the most difficult time of my life, even though he didn't have to. He was the one who convinced me to go to therapy." My voice trembles as I will myself to finish my thought despite the scowl on Milo's face. "He was my anchor on the days I didn't think

I could carry on. He might be your damnation, but he was my salvation."

Milo jolts from his spot on the curb, leaving me shuddering from the loss of his body heat. I follow suit, so we're both standing. He's practically growling, his body vibrating with anger.

"How am I supposed to react, Liv?" he sneers. "I'm grateful you had someone there for you, especially after what you went through. But get it through your head...I will never forgive the bastard. It doesn't matter how many little girls he sits with during their cancer treatment, how many meals he delivers to the homeless, or how many nights he's been your shoulder to cry on. It will never be enough. A thousand good deeds will never make up for the life he took. Why can't you understand that?"

I take a few steps back, shocked by his cold and callous response. It took every ounce of courage I could muster to share the details of my miscarriage tonight. I willingly exposed a part of myself that I'd kept buried since I was seventeen, and Milo doesn't seem to care.

I look at the stranger in front of me, a man I no longer recognize.

The Milo I knew would have cloaked me in a warm embrace as he whispered words of reassurance in my ear. He would have apologized profusely for not being there when I needed him. Most importantly, he would have put his own agenda aside to allow us to grieve together for the loss of our child.

I don't know the person in front of me...Not anymore. I gaze up at Milo, silently begging him to fix this, to right his wrongs before it's too late. My hope quickly dwindles as I watch his posture become rigid, his blue eyes turning glacial and his hands clenching at his sides.

"I have to go," he announces before stomping off toward the brownstone.

I think I'm losing him for good this time, and the last remnants of my shattered heart break into a million little pieces as I watch him leave me behind…again.

I give Milo a head start, needing some space. I drag my feet along one step at a time until I'm standing a couple houses down from the brownstone. I watch from afar as Milo jogs up the steps and swings open the front door.

"Sirius, come. We're going home," he shouts at the top of his lungs, not caring if he's disturbing Mac, or anyone else in the neighborhood for that matter.

Within seconds, the dog comes bounding outside, jumping to greet his owner. Milo doesn't even acknowledge the excited pup. He slams the door shut behind them, marching down the steps. Sirius stops when he sees me, barking in greeting.

"Sirius, I said, come, goddammit," Milo snaps.

Sirius lets out a low whine before his tail drops and he runs to catch up to his master. I stay where I am as I watch the duo disappear from view.

Why is it that Milo's always leaving me behind? It should be the other way around since he's the one who's wronged me time and time again.

As I distraughtly enter the front parlor, I completely lose it when I see Mac, who is sitting up in bed as if he can sense something is wrong.

Jeremy gets up from his seat by the fireplace. "I'll be in the kitchen making hot chocolate. If you need anything, let me know," he says quickly.

As soon as he's gone, the dam breaks and a steady flow of tears streams down my cheeks. I rush to Mac's side and curl up in the fetal position next to him as uncontrollable sobs rack my body.

"Milo…he…he came back…I told him about…the baby. He didn't…he left…he left me again. And now, you're leaving me too. I don't want to be alone." I'm a blubbering mess, unable to form a coherent thought.

Mac gently strokes my hair, giving me the comfort I so desperately need right now. "Kiddo, I'm right here. Everything will be okay, you'll see."

I squeeze my eyelids shut, welcoming the oblivion dragging me under from the countless days of little to no sleep. I embrace the feel of Mac's presence, knowing it won't be long until he's no longer here to comfort me when I need him most.

I jolt awake to the sound of knocking.

I pry my eyelids open to sunrays shining through the curtains and turn over to find Mac still fast asleep. As I sit up, I take a moment to reorient myself. I don't see Jeremy or Jane in the room, so whoever is here must have stepped out for a bit.

Another rapid succession of pounding on the front door has me rushing to the entryway. I send a plea to the universe that it's Milo here to make amends for his outburst last night.

For a brief moment, I'm disappointed when I open the door and it's not Milo standing on the threshold. Instead, I'm greeted by Grace, who has a Cheshire cat grin on her face. Stella stands behind her, appearing to be trying to pull her back from knocking a third time.

I covertly shift my gaze from side to side, hoping I'll see Milo loitering on the street like he was last week, but much to my disappointment, there isn't another person in sight.

"I'm so sorry for the early morning disturbance," Stella pipes up. "We were running errands nearby, and Grace insisted we stop by to see Mac. She was concerned when no one answered the door. I had to remind her that people without kids aren't always up at the butt crack of dawn."

Grace giggles at her mom's use of the word "butt."

"I'm so glad you're here," I say with a smile. "I know Mac will be thrilled to see you both. Please come in, it's freezing out there."

I usher them both inside as Grace flings herself forward, her little hands wrapping around my waist for a hug.

"Dr. Dunham, I missed you so much!" she exclaims with a toothy grin.

"I missed you too." I lean down to give her a proper hug. "This is such a pleasant surprise."

"We went to the hospital yesterday for a checkup, and Grace is in perfect health. Although she burst into tears when they said you were off work, caring for Mac," Stella says. "Thankfully, the nursing staff took pity and gave me your address. I hope you don't mind. Now that I think about it, we should have called first. I'm sorry." Stella glances nervously at the grandiose chandelier hanging above the entryway, no doubt feeling out of place in the extravagant space.

Welcome to the club.

"Please don't apologize. It means so much that you stopped by, and I know it'll make Mac's day to see you both. What do you think, Grace? Should we go say hi?"

She nods enthusiastically as she shucks her rainbow-colored jacket on the ground along with her light-up shoes, making herself right at home.

"Yes! Where is he?" she demands, eager to see her friend.

"He's right through there." I point to the front parlor.

Before she can make a break for it, I grasp her shoulder. "Grace, before you go in, remember that Mac is sick and very weak. I need you to be gentle, okay?"

"That's right, sweetheart. You can hug him as long as you're careful," Stella chimes in.

Grace gives us both a look of utter annoyance. "Did you both forget I've had cancer?" she asks. "I'm the only other person in this house who knows what it feels like to be dying and how much it hurts. I'll be careful, I promise." She might be small, but she sure is fierce. "So…can I see him now, pretty please?" she begs.

"Of course."

"*Mac!*" she shouts gleefully as she catapults herself into the room before coming to a halt by his bedside.

I'm relieved to see he's woken up since their arrival, and he seems to be in good spirits this morning.

"Hey there, Peanut. I didn't know you were coming to see me," Mac croaks out. He pats Grace's head as she cautiously climbs onto the bed next to him, making sure not to jostle him too much.

"Mama said this might be my last chance to see you. I don't understand. How come I get to live, but you don't? It's not fair." Her lips start to quiver.

"Oh, no, this is a happy zone only," Mac says in a serious tone. "There's no room for tears here. You're in remission, and that's cause for celebration! Besides, remember the very important job you promised to help me with?" He lowers his voice to a whisper.

"Looking after Dr. Dunham when you're gone," Grace says enthusiastically.

"Exactly. It makes me so happy to know she'll have you as a friend."

"Mac, you're silly." Grace giggles. "Dr. Dunham's already my friend."

"I'm glad to hear it, Peanut."

"Don't worry, we'll make sure Dr. Dunham is never alone."

"Who's we?"

"Me and the man," Grace says.

"What man?" Mac asks skeptically.

"The man from the hospital. He was in your room the last time we visited. I told him he had to promise to help take care of Dr. Dunham when you're gone, and he did. Don't worry, it's all about teamwork. We've got this." She smiles proudly at her own cleverness.

"That was very smart of you to ask for help," Mac says, slightly hesitating.

We haven't talked about what happened when I was with Milo last night, so I'm sure he's worried about how I might react to hearing Grace mention him.

"I'm starving. All those errands made me hungry. Dr. Dunham, can you make me breakfast?" Grace blurts out, ready to change the subject to something more important—her growling stomach.

"Grace!" Stella chides. "We don't ask to eat at other people's homes without an invitation. It's not polite. You know better."

I let out a lighthearted laugh. "It's okay. Consider yourself invited. I'm starving too. Why don't we order something from the diner around the corner?"

Grace eagerly nods her head in agreement.

We spend the next several hours with Grace and Stella, and Jane joins in when she returns from visiting her other patients. Grace ropes Mac into watching *Frozen* on my laptop, and they snuggle together on his bed throughout the entire movie. I snap a photo to look back on later.

When it's time for them to leave, I watch as Grace reaches out to give Mac one last hug. "I love you always," she whispers.

"I love you too, Peanut," Mac rasps out. "Don't forget our promise."

"I won't," she whispers back.

I wave goodbye as Stella and Grace take off down the street. I feel a slight tug at my heartstrings as I recall countless times when I walked the same street with my mom. What I wouldn't give to have her here with me today. She and Milo's mom must be rolling over in their graves, appalled at the mess Milo and I have made of things. The problem is, I have no idea how I can make any of this right.

I'm about to head inside when I see something white and black in my peripheral vision. It's hurtling straight for me, and I glance over just in time before Sirius jumps into my arms. Thankfully, I'm able to hold myself upright as he licks my cheeks in greeting.

I look up when I hear the beat of feet running across the pavement. Milo is jogging toward me with an exasperated expression. Sirius must have evaded his grasp, too excited to be reunited with his new friend to wait for him.

"Sirius, get down, boy," Milo scolds.

The dog begrudgingly drops down on all fours, looking back and forth between Milo and me.

Why are they here?

Part of me is thrilled to see Milo, but another part is furious that he would show his face again after what happened last night.

"I see the little nuisance has been to visit." He points in the direction Grace and Stella went.

"Her name is Grace," I correct him. "She's a kid with a kind heart who's been through the wringer, so show some respect. Now, if you don't mind, I have more important things to do than spend my day bickering with you. Sirius is welcome to stay if he'd like. You, on the other hand, can leave, because we're done." I sigh in relief when my voice comes out with confidence. "Whatever this thing is between us, consider it null and void. You've got the answers you came for, and now it's time for you to go. I refuse to be your proverbial punching bag any longer. Enough is enough, Milo."

Chapter Twelve

MILO
Past—Eleventh Grade

I WEAVE IN AND OUT of the crowded streets, zooming past City Hall Park.

"Come on, Liv. You're slowing me down! You can go faster than that," I shout over my shoulder.

I wonder if she can even hear me with all the commotion around us, but then I hear an exasperated grunt coming from behind me. She despises talking while she runs, saying it messes with her concentration. So, naturally, when I'm feeling extra competitive, I like to throw random jabs her way since I know it riles her up, hoping that the distraction will give me the advantage I need to stay ahead of her.

Truth be told, between the two of us, there's no question that Liv's the faster runner. She was recruited to be on our school's track team but politely declined. She says if she were to run for sport, it would take all the fun out of it. Harrison was furious when he found out she turned the coach down, chastising her for wasting her talents. He said it would bring prestige to the family if she were to run competitively, but she couldn't care less. In the end, he blamed me, saying I was holding her back, calling me a bad influence. He's not wrong, though in our case, Liv calls all the shots. I'd follow that girl to the ends of the earth if she asked me to.

Liv finds running therapeutic, a dedicated time to clear her head when she's having a rough day or she needs to rid her mind of negative thoughts. She's hoping it'll do the same for me. It doesn't, but I don't have the heart to tell her that.

The honorable parts of my soul were crushed beyond recognition when Ma died. The animosity I feel toward Mac has grown like a fungus over time, a slow decay I've welcomed with open arms. I'd rather stew in my resentment and hate than find a way to overcome it, risking the chance of forgetting his destructive actions stole someone I love.

Despite my shortcomings, Liv reminds me every day that I'm worthy of love, affection, and devotion. She's wrong, but I appreciate her thinking otherwise. I'm a lucky bastard to have her heart, and I'll be damned if I ever let her go.

That's why, even though I prefer to sleep in, I let Liv drag me through Manhattan every Saturday morning. I think back to earlier when I woke up to her straddling me, pressing featherlight kisses along my neck, nose, and lips, telling me it was time to get up. I groaned in protest when I turned to look over at the digital clock on the nightstand to see that it was six a.m. I reached out to give her a kiss of my own when she moved out of reach, scrambling off the bed, announcing that it was time for us to head out on our run.

She's such a little minx, teasing me constantly. I'm slowly going mad from my constant state of sexual frustration, literally counting down the days until I can worship her body the way it deserves.

We've agreed to wait to have sex until we graduate high school. I don't want to cause any problems for Marie since she's my legal guardian, especially since Liv and I live under the same roof. I'm pretty sure Marie knows something is going on between us, but she hasn't said anything about it.

We've been doing our best to be discreet, but when we're alone, I can't help but ravish Liv's pretty little mouth and explore her the best I can without going past second base. I always try to cop a feel below her pajama shorts, but she always slaps my hand away, insisting the best things in life come to those who wait. Seriously, as a teenager with raging hormones, there are only so many times I can jerk myself off in the shower to images of the girl of my dreams before I go mad.

Liv's worth it. The words play on repeat in my head like a broken record. Only two more years, and then she'll be mine—mind, body, and soul.

I confess our early morning runs have grown on me, and despite my grumblings, I look forward to them.

Liv and I have created a special bond derived from running side by side as the wind rushes through our hair. Aside from passersby, it's always been her and me in our own little bubble.

I look up after getting lost in my head to see we're quickly approaching Whitehall Terminal.

Liv comes shooting out of nowhere, pointing frantically at her watch then back up at the building. "The ferry's leaving in two minutes. We're going to miss it if we don't hurry," she says, a hint of urgency in her voice.

I give her a knowing smirk. She's challenging me, a mischievous glint shining in her eyes.

"Last one to the ferry is a rotten egg!" I holler, winking at her before lightly shoving her back a step as I sprint forward.

"Milo, you're such a cheater!" she calls out behind me before bolting forward.

It's so on.

I have to dodge a mom pushing a stroller and dive under a couple's linked hands to stay ahead of Liv. We rush to the ferry entrance, sliding through just as the operator closes the gate. He shouts at us for being reckless as we make our way to the other side of the boat. Liv and I burst out laughing, having the time of our lives.

It's packed, given that it's a Saturday morning, but I don't mind. I've zeroed in on Liv, and there is nowhere else I'd rather be than right here with her by my side.

We find a semi-secluded spot toward the back of the ferry. Liv holds tightly to the railing as I wrap myself around her warm body. I press my nose against her neck, inhaling the scent of her perfume mixed with sweat, making my hormones rage, and I can hardly think straight. God, this girl drives me crazy. I plant soft kisses along the column of her neck, slowly making my way up to the shell of her ear. She lets out a throaty moan as I get close to my destination, leaning her head back against my chest.

"Milo, we're in public. Anyone could see us," she breathlessly whispers.

"You don't enjoy my affection?" I ask in a low, raspy voice. "What about this? Do you like this?" I bite down gently on the tip of her ear, caressing it with my tongue. A shudder ripples through her as her eyes fall shut.

A shit-eating grin is plastered on my face as I witness the effect I have on this gorgeous girl.

"You must really hate my affection," I taunt as I continue my teasing.

She tilts her head back to look up at me, a silent plea to give her more. Who am I to resist when she begs so beautifully with her eyes?

I lean down to brush my tongue against her plush lips before slipping it inside her mouth. She lets out a soft moan as she captures my tongue with hers, giving me as much pleasure as she takes. I groan as she presses her hot body against mine, a jolt of pleasure shooting straight to my groin.

"Get a room!" someone shouts from somewhere nearby.

I don't get a chance to react before Liv snaps back while still wrapped in my arms. "We have one at home, but it's much more fun to kiss in public to get a rise out of people like you."

Her giggles stop short when we both look over to see a big, burly biker charging right at us. It looks like Liv might have offended the wrong person with her comment.

"Come on. I think it's time to go." I pull away from her, reaching down to clasp our hands together as we dart in the opposite direction of the angry man. Liv's laughter echoes around us as we make our escape.

"I love you so damn much," I shout over my shoulder.

I can't wait for the day I can finally be inside you, making you irrevocably mine.

"I love you too," she says with a smirk.

God, I'd burn down the world for this girl. I only hope she knows how much she means to me.

"What the hell are you doing out here?"

I jerk my chin up to see Harrison storming out onto the terrace at the back of the house. He rarely makes his presence known in New York, and when he does, I make myself scarce. I usually stay in my room until he's gone, but I came out back for a short cigarette break to relieve some stress—bad call on my part. I should have known he'd be lying in wait to confront me.

"I'm having a smoke. What the hell does it look like I'm doing?" I say tauntingly. "Or would you prefer I do it inside your precious brownstone?"

If it weren't for Marie and Liv, I would light the place on fire to spite Harrison.

I grit my teeth, holding firmly to the stub in my fingers. I take another puff, breathing right in Harrison's direction to prove that I couldn't care less what he thinks of me.

"Besides, my therapist recommended smoking as a way to cope with the emotional damage I suffered after losing my ma," I say sarcastically.

Harrison is well aware I refuse to see a therapist—one of his many complaints about me.

"You degenerate little shit," he spits out. "You have some nerve, you know that? No wonder there's always a foul smell out here. You're attributing to a reduction in the value of the surrounding properties with your bad habit. I don't need any more gossip circulating about this unfortunate living situation than there already is. I thought Marie would have gotten over her obsession with this little pet project of hers by now, but for some reason, you're still here."

The vein in Harrison's forehead bulges as he spews hateful words in my direction. If that wasn't enough, his lips curl up in a malicious smile, pleased with himself for the way he's treating me. He's on a roll and isn't quite ready to leave me be.

"Don't think for one minute that I'm not aware of you leering at my daughter when you think no one is looking. Mark my words, boy. I will not sit back and let her waste her life with the likes of you."

Is he serious? Does he think a few condescending statements from a man I despise will push me away from Liv? Not a chance in hell.

I want your daughter to have and to hold for the rest of my life. I can't wait for the day I can legally call you my father-in-law so I can laugh in your face.

I file the clever comeback in my mind to use as leverage at a later date.

"Goes to show how little you know, Harrison. Mrs. Wellsford next door can't go more than an hour without a nicotine fix; although, she prefers cigars. We often share a cig when her arthritis acts up, and she can't light up on her own. Mr. Velmour who lives two houses down chain-smokes at least five packs a day as if every day might be his last on God's green earth. Marie is the only person who seems to mind that I smoke, and her primary concern is my health. It's funny…while you've spent most of your time out of the country, conning pompous businessmen out of their millions and sleeping with washed-out whores, I've become an irreplaceable member of this family. I'm not going anywhere. Marie and Olivia are my family now, and nothing you say or do will change that."

His face goes beet red, and for a minute, I think he might physically attack me. Then I remember he wouldn't do anything to mess with his picture-perfect outward appearance. No, he prefers the coward's way, spouting toxic words when we're alone and there are no witnesses.

"You're nothing but a lowlife from the wrong side of the tracks who will never amount to anything. I'll continue to bide my time, waiting for you to show your true colors. There's no doubt that one of these days, you will, and when you do, my wife and daughter will finally see you for the scum you are."

I drop my cigarette to the ground, snuffing it out with the heel of my shoe, doing everything I can to keep my emotions in check. I refuse to admit his last words cut me deep, highlighting my insecurities that Marie and Olivia will realize I'm not worth the trouble.

"Admit it, Harrison. You're deflecting," I state. "You've become a bookend in your own life, and it's eating you alive inside. Marie and Liv don't give a damn about your overflowing wealth or the luxurious lifestyle you live. All they want is to be loved by you, and you've never been able to give them that. Liv would do anything to gain your affection. No matter how often you ignore her or direct your passive-aggressive jabs at her, she still wants your approval. It's not too late to be there for them both. They'll forgive you in a heartbeat for your past transgressions, you know that."

"You have no idea what you're talking about," Harrison barks at me. "Mind your own goddamn business." He spins on his heel and goes back into the house.

I smile sadistically, pleased that my reply had its desired effect. Good riddance. If Harrison can't see what he's missing out on by neglecting his daughter and wife, that's his loss.

I will spend every waking moment for the rest of my life making sure Liv and Marie know how much they mean to me and how grateful I am to them for giving me a chance to be a part of their lives.

Our junior year of high school passes by in a blur.

I couldn't care less about making friends, good grades, or college applications. I have no desire to attend university. The plan is to follow Liv wherever she gets accepted for her undergrad program and find a job in the area. I'm good with my hands and have always had an interest in building things, so I figure I'll apply to a local construction crew or attend a trade college if I find something else that interests me.

Liv has spent the past year working her ass off to perfect her SAT scores, bolstering her GPA, and padding her college applications with extracurricular activities and volunteer work. Her goal is to become a doctor, and I will do everything I can to help make her dream a reality.

Although she doesn't have a particular school in mind, we both agree we want to live somewhere outside of New York. We're ready for a fresh start, away from our absent dads and the reign of judgment that's bound to fall on our heads when the world learns about our relationship. Liv insists we go someplace we've never been, where we can simply be Olivia and Milo, two infatuated college kids madly in love. I might never be able to provide Liv with a mansion or a room full of riches, but I know our home will overflow with love and devotion.

I rush through the front door of the house with a hot pizza box in my hands. We're celebrating the last day of the school year by eating junk food and stargazing up on the roof.

Liv and I decided it's time to tell Marie we're a couple. It's important she knows we're serious. Liv is it for me, and this is a lifetime commitment. It might sound silly coming from a high school kid, but it doesn't make it any less true.

Besides, keeping our affection a secret from Marie has become nearly impossible. Aside from Liv and me, she keeps to herself. Though her and Harrison's marriage has never been one of devotion, my heart breaks for Marie. She says that's what happens when you marry for money and power instead of love. She was right when she said that she, Liv, and I would become like The Three Musketeers. She's provided me with another family—something I thought was impossible—and although our situation is unconventional, I don't give a damn what anyone else thinks.

I climb up to the rooftop terrace and pause mid-step when I see the sight before me.

Liv and Marie are lying side by side on a plush rug, a plethora of blankets and pillows surrounding them, creating a three-sided fort with an unobstructed view of the sky above. It's somewhat foggy tonight, so there aren't many stars visible, but that hasn't deterred them from stargazing anyway.

I'm grateful to have a front-row seat to their close, mother-daughter bond. They were best friends long before I came into the picture, and their relationship has only grown over the years.

There are brief moments when I feel envious that Liv still has her mom. Not a day goes by that I don't think about Ma and how different my life would be if she were still alive. I would give anything to hear her call me her Little Rabbit one last time, or to feel her warm touch as she tenderly strokes my hair while reading to me.

Marie's soothing voice carries across the space as she speaks softly to Liv. "If we were looking up at the sky from the North Pole, the North Star would appear directly overhead. There's not an official South Star, although the constellation Crux, also known as the Southern Cross, points in the direction of the South Pole."

Marie's passion for astronomy is infectious, and I could listen to her talk about the stars for hours.

"I want to do something special for your and Milo's graduation next year, and I think it would be fun to plan a trip to the North Pole to see the northern lights. Or better yet, we could visit Iceland. I've always wanted to go there. What do you think?"

"Mom, that sounds amazing," Liv says, overcome with excitement.

I take the last few steps onto the terrace, making my presence known.

"Milo, you're back!" Liv gleefully calls out, turning to face me. She doesn't move to get up, which means dinner will have to wait.

I set the pizza on the outdoor patio table that's been pushed up against the wall to make room for our stargazing efforts, and then make my way over to lie next to Liv. She's in the middle, sandwiched between her mom and me—her favorite place to be.

Liv calls Marie her North Star and me Sirius—the brightest star in the night sky. She says Marie is there to guide her in the right direction while I light the way, working in tandem to help her safely make it to her destination.

As Marie talks about Orion and the stars that make up the constellation, I discreetly intertwine my fingers with Olivia's. When we're in the same room, I don't feel complete unless we're touching. I need physical contact to remind myself she's real and that she belongs to me.

The three of us lie there for what feels like hours. I commit this night to memory. A rare feeling of complete happiness buzzes through me, and I wish it could last forever.

After we finally scarf down the cold pizza, Marie announces it's time for us to go to bed.

Liv lets out a groan of complaint. "Mom, seriously? We're far too old for a curfew or bedtime."

Marie chuckles at Olivia's attempt to manipulate her into getting what she wants. "Oh, honey, I wasn't born yesterday," Marie says with a chuckle. "I might say good night to you both in your respective rooms, but after I go downstairs, you'll sneak into Milo's room and stay up well past midnight, lying in bed together, telling each other jokes, playing The Color Game, or making out."

Liv's jaw drops as a look of horror crosses her face. "Um...Mom...we..." she can't seem to finish her sentence.

It doesn't surprise me that Marie knows about us. She's much more observant than Liv gives her credit for.

"Livvy, it's okay," Marie reassures. "There's no need to panic. I know you've been sneaking into Milo's bed since the very first night. I also know that you two have been "secretly" dating since we got back from Paris last year. The only reason I've let it slide this long is because I know you're waiting to take your relationship to the next level until you graduate—at least, that's what my motherly instincts are telling me," she says with a wink.

I feel my cheeks turn red, unable to hide my embarrassment. Marie is definitely getting a kick out of our humiliation.

"So...you're okay with me dating your daughter?" The words involuntarily tumble out of my mouth. I'm desperate for Marie's approval, but I'm terrified I won't get it. I have no idea what I would do if she condemned my relationship with Liv.

Marie walks over and wraps me in a hug. "Milo, I would love nothing more than to call you my son-in-law someday. You're a part of our family, and when the time is right, you and Liv will make it official," she says with a genuine smile. "However, that doesn't mean there won't be consequences if I get an inkling that you two are doing anything more than kissing while sleeping in the same bed. As long as you live under my roof, you'll adhere to my rules, got it?" Her tone comes out biting toward the end, making sure she gets her point across.

"Yes, I understand," I quickly reply, not wanting to know what she might do if I were too slow to respond.

Marie beams up at me, satisfied with my answer. She wraps her arms around both Liv and me, squishing us together in one giant bear hug. "I love you both so much." She gives each of us a quick kiss on the forehead before going downstairs. "You'd both better be in your own rooms within the next thirty minutes, or there will be hell to pay," she says with a wink.

"Yes, of course!" Liv and I shout at the same time Marie heads downstairs.

Perfect.

We have thirty minutes. That gives Liv and me plenty of time to make out under the stars—one of our favorite pastimes.

I'm about to turn to Liv and tell her to lie back down on the blankets when I hear a loud thud from the floor below. Liv gives me a petrified look and sprints past me without a second thought.

"Mom!" Liv screams as she rushes down the stairs, me right on her tail.

We see that Marie has fallen down the steps leading to the second floor. Liv gets to her first and drops to her knees. Marie turns to face her, a glossy sheen covering her eyes.

"I'm…I got dizzy and tripped…Livvy, honey, I don't feel so good…" Marie slurs before her head falls back against the floor.

"Milo! Call 911 now!" Liv screeches out in a panic.

I scramble to pull my phone from my pocket. Somehow, after fumbling with the keypad for a few seconds, I finally dial the number.

As the phone rings, I assure myself Marie will be okay— she has to be. I can't lose someone else I love. There's no way I would survive it a second time.

Chapter Thirteen

OLIVIA
Present Day—November

"LIV, YOU DON'T MEAN THAT. You don't really want me to go."

Milo takes a few steps in my direction until he's standing in front of me, leaning in close, our faces mere inches from each other. This close up, I can see the hint of silver surrounding his pupils, making his eyes glisten in the morning light.

He reaches out to intertwine his fingers with mine as a gesture of good faith, but I jerk back, rejecting his touch. I can't do this with him, not today, not after the way he treated me last night.

"You have no right to tell me how I'm feeling. You don't know me anymore. I mean it, I want you to go. In fact, I have a better idea. I'll do the leaving for once."

I spin around and start jogging up the stairs toward the front door. It feels liberating to finally stand up for myself. To be the one to decide when our conversation is over and to admit that I've had enough of Milo's nonsense. The sooner I can create some distance between us, the better.

I'm halfway up the steps when I feel two steel arms wrap tightly around my waist, keeping my arms locked at my sides, making it impossible to break free. I let out a shrill yelp as I'm picked up off the steps like a tiny ant, helplessly hauled back to the sidewalk below. There goes my brilliant plan of ending this argument before it starts. I forgot that Milo always has to have the last word, even when it's at my expense.

Some things never change.

"You'd better not drop me, Milo, or so help me, I'll make you regret it," I shriek out in distress.

He dares to let out a husky laugh, taking pleasure in my discomfort. If I weren't so mad at him, I'd say his dominant, demanding nature was sexy. He always did know how to push my buttons to get the exact reaction he wanted. Curse him for always making things more complicated than they needed to be.

"Trust me, Liv, I've been in my own personal hell for the last twenty years. Your torment would be a welcome reprieve from the misery I've grown accustomed to," he confesses. "I think I'll go ahead and drop you, then we can get on with it. What do you think?"

He effortlessly tips my body to the side so my head is facing downward as he slightly loosens his grip around my waist, giving me the sensation of falling. I scream out, and Sirius barks from somewhere nearby.

At least someone is concerned for my safety.

"Whoa there, you two. Take it easy. I'm only playing," Milo says calmly.

He gently sets me right side up before placing me on the concrete. My feet are thrilled to be reunited with the safe-and-secure ground. Milo turns to Sirius, scratching behind his ear, soothing him with murmured words of comfort, talking low as if he doesn't want me to hear.

"You're such a good guard dog, you know that, boy? Yes, you are. Don't worry, though, I'd never hurt Liv."

Too bad you've already broken that promise a dozen times over.

Within seconds, Sirius is wagging his tail in delight, thrilled with the undivided attention.

It's been a long time since I've heard Milo speak in such a gentle tone, and I miss it.

I miss him.

That doesn't change my disappointment in how things have turned out since he's returned, though. I can't imagine the betrayal he must have felt when he learned I befriended his dad. That doesn't excuse his behavior, though, and my heart aches at how quickly he dismissed my anguish last night.

I glance over to find that Milo is still distracted with Sirius, and I take it as my cue to make another break for it. This time, I don't even get a full step in before Milo's hands circle my midsection again.

"Where do you think you're going? I'm not done talking to you yet," he whispers in my ear.

"This is ridiculous. Let me go!" I yell. "You don't get to dictate when I'm finished with a conversation. Why won't you get that through your thick-headed skull? If you're permitted to throw a tantrum and act like a petulant child whenever you feel the need to end a discussion, then so can I." I stomp my foot down for emphasis—it feels right in the moment.

I try to wriggle out of his strong hold, but it's no use. His grip is too firm, and it's clear that I'm not going anywhere until he agrees to let me go.

Why couldn't I have fallen for the cute, boy-next-door type instead of the brooding A-hole living down the hall?

"Goddamn it, stop being such a pain in the ass and listen to me. I know you're angry, and you have every right to be. That doesn't mean you get to storm off and pretend we don't need to have this conversation."

He's such a hypocrite. He's the one who keeps running, always leaving me behind to clean up his messes.

Not this time.

"Please hear me out. Once I've said my piece, I'll leave, and you'll never hear from me again if that's what you want. Does that sound like a plan?" he asks in a genuine tone.

The idea of watching him walk away a final time puts a bad taste in my mouth. Truth be told, my stomach bottoms out at the mention of him leaving me again. I'm not ready to unpack the reasoning behind the sentiment, I just know that's how I feel.

We might not be on the best of terms, but I admit, I'll miss our verbal sparring matches. Each quip is like our own version of a love note.

I let out a huff of annoyance, doing my best to hide the fact that he's affected me. "It doesn't look like I have a choice, does it? Although, at some point, you'll tire of chasing after me."

"Never," he counters.

"I'll listen, but only if you do something for me."

"And what is that, Liv?"

I don't miss the sultry tone his voice takes on, trying to get a rise out of me.

"Let me go. I need some space."

"Are you sure, Stardust? You used to like it when I was so close." My treasured nickname is spoken with deep affection. "In fact"—one of his hands releases its hold on my hip, bringing it up to the nape of my neck, gently pushing my hair to the side—"if I recall correctly"—he slowly leans down to kiss the shell of my ear, deliberately letting out a slow exhale— "you used to love it."

A ripple of pleasure shoots straight to my core, and despite my best effort to hold it back, a soft moan slips through my lips. My hands mindlessly grip his arm as another low groan escapes my mouth. It seems to set Milo off, and he moves his head down ever so slowly, planting light kisses down the column of my neck.

What am I doing?

Why on earth am I standing in the middle of the street, letting a man I should detest do wicked things to me in public? This has to—

Another brush of Milo's lips against my collarbone makes me lose my train of thought.

"Milo," I breathlessly call out his name, unsure what I'm asking for.

I wonder if he still tastes the same.

As if he can read my mind, he gently grabs my jaw, turning my head so we're gazing into each other's eyes. He leans down and places his mouth on mine, pressing a passionate kiss to my lips. He pulls back slightly as he rests his forehead against mine.

"I can't believe you're real. I've missed you so much," he admits. "There wasn't a day that went by that I didn't think of you, that I didn't crave your touch or long to hear your voice." The blood in my veins turns to ice, his words a dead weight to my forgotten aching chest. I can't believe I let my guard down.

Milo abandoned me all those years ago, and now he wants to play the martyr? To pretend his actions were excusable, like he did nothing wrong? I don't think so.

He doesn't get to storm back into my life seeking retribution, and then flip a one-eighty when it suits him.

I pry Milo's hands off me and launch forward, putting some much-needed space between us. I spin on my heel, afraid he'll try to take hold of me again if given the opportunity. I place both hands in front of me, warning him to keep his distance.

"Liv, what—"

"I need you to stay where you are," I cut him off. "You're going to listen to what I have to say for once—*without* interrupting. You've been so absorbed in your own feelings that you haven't given mine a second thought."

He doesn't move a muscle, likely wondering what's happening since he's never seen me like this before. In high school, I was always willing to back down where he was concerned. Not anymore. I need to get this out before I lose my nerve—or worse, before he touches me again and I lose my train of thought.

"You discarded me. You chose to leave this life behind and never look back. And you decided to come back years later and declare war against Mac and me. Not once did you stop to think about how that would affect me. We could have been civil and talked things through like adults, but that's not how you operate, is it? No, you have to find ways to blame everyone else for your behavior and shortcomings. Well, guess what. I won't stand for it anymore. Mac means the world to me, and I don't care what you think of him. He's the only person who was there to pick up the pieces after you left."

Milo stays silent, respecting my wish not to be interrupted. His shoulders are slumped as he walks over to the bottom step of the stairs and takes a seat. Sirius follows, tenderly nudging Milo's arms to make room between his legs. It's fascinating to watch how in tune he is with his master, knowing when he needs comfort.

I move over to the spot next to Milo, making sure to keep a couple feet of space between us.

He peers over at me, his weary eyes filled with remorse and regret. "I have no excuse for how I treated you last night. I've never been good at expressing how I feel, and it's easier sometimes for me to storm off like a child than to face my problems head-on," he confesses. "I'm not trying to excuse myself, but put yourself in my shoes. You've had fifteen years to process the death of our unborn daughter. I got the news less than twenty-four hours ago, while in a room full of strangers, no less. For you, it might feel like a lifetime ago, but to me, it's happening in real-time." His voice cracks as he does his best to compose himself before continuing. "I stayed up all night thinking about what would have happened if I had stayed. I never would have recovered from another loss so soon after Marie's death. I would have been toxic, corrupting your positive outlook on life in the process. I left to save you from my demons and to avoid snuffing out your bright light. Now that I know about the baby, I'm even more confident I made the right choice to leave when I did."

I let out a shuddery exhale, snapping my head in his direction, his words causing my heart to obliterate to smithereens.

He doesn't regret leaving me behind?

"Are you serious?" I ask, raising my voice in anger. "How can you think I was better off coping with the loss of my mom and our daughter without you? I spent the months after you left completely isolated, without a single person in my corner. Not only did you walk out on me, but my dad did too. The same day, no less, and I haven't seen him since. So, please explain how you can say those hurtful words without batting an eye?" I heave a sigh of relief, grateful for the chance to finally say those words out loud.

"It tears me up inside knowing you had to go through the loss of your mom and our daughter alone. I wish more than anything that I could have been there for you in person," he says with sincerity. "But I know myself. I would have been sucked into a vortex of utter damnation, and you would have suffered far worse than you did. There's no saying what kind of damage I would have caused if I had been here. God, Liv, I'm so sorry. I wish I had been stronger for you." He begs me with his eyes to say something…to do something.

Honestly, I don't know where we go from here. How can we move past something like this? Not to mention the hate that Milo feels for Mac…It's all too much.

"Sorry doesn't cut it. Not this time," I whisper so softly that he has to lean in to hear me. "You weren't the only one who lost one of the most important people in their life. Instead of building a fortress of support around me when my mom died, you completely shut me out. You literally locked your bedroom door and refused to speak to me when we were in the same room. Even then, *I* went out of my way to care for *you*, despite drowning in my own grief. That still wasn't enough for you, though. No, you took my virginity—the last shred of dignity I had left—knowing you wouldn't be there the next morning to console me. So, please excuse me for not showing you any more sympathy." My voice catches at the end as I fight back the tears about to burst like a dam.

"You're so preoccupied with this vendetta against Mac that you've done yourself a disservice in the process. Are you happy with the way your life turned out, Milo?" I ask with sincerity. "Can you honestly say you've lived your life to its fullest? The resentment and anger you've held on to is only hurting you. Yes, your dad made a mistake—a colossal one—but news flash: so have you. So have I, for that matter," I openly admit. "There's no need to rehash the past."

I feel Milo stiffen beside me, seemingly unsure how to respond.

"I can't be your savior, not this time. I will never be happy as long as I put everyone else's needs before my own. I used to think if I loved you enough, you'd heal, learn to forgive, and move forward." My voice is low as I find the courage to finish my thought. "You have to be the one who decides to move on. It's not something I can do for you…I know that now. The only thing I can control in this equation is me. I don't deserve to be trampled on and treated like dirt. I think this is the end for us, Milo. It's time for us to say goodbye...for good this time."

The tears start to fall, and there's nothing I can do to suppress them. I squeeze my eyes closed, desperate to shut out the world around me. Within seconds, I'm snuggled into Milo's embrace. He gently nuzzles his face into my neck, clinging to me tightly. Sobs rack my body, and it's as if he's keeping me together by holding me tight. I'm vaguely aware of a snout resting against my thigh, wanting to help ease my sadness too.

"Liv, don't you get it?" Milo says in a hushed tone so only I can hear. "It doesn't matter how messed up in the head I am. I will always want you," he vows. "I hate to break it to you, but you and me? We'll never be over." He pulls back slightly, reaching out to caress my cheek with his hand, gently stroking his thumb against my jawline.

I let out a choked cry, unable to form an intelligible word as a flood of emotions courses through my body.

"It doesn't matter how many years we're apart, the physical distance between us, or the animosity we feel toward each other. Whether we like it or not, our souls have been intertwined since before we met, an invisible force always pulling us back to each other. Our fates are intricately woven together; one can't be unraveled without the other," Milo admits.

"Remember back in high school when you used to call your mom your North Star, and I was the bright star leading your way?" he asks, not continuing on until I nod. "Well, you've always been my sun. My only source of oxygen, light, and energy. Without you, I've been shrouded in nothing but darkness and my own misfortune. I don't have an answer for how we get through this. I just know that we have to find a way through it together," he declares as he holds me tightly. "You're it for me, Liv. You're my beginning, middle, and end. I can't walk away from you again…"

I don't speak as I lean my head against Milo's shoulder, no fight left in me. I take in the feel of his strong arms wrapped around me as he holds me close, both of us in dire need of a reprieve from the constant turmoil in our lives.

Chapter Fourteen

MILO
Present Day—November

WITH LIV'S BODY PRESSED THIS close to mine, I can almost feel her heart beating through my own chest, as if we're one.

I glance down to find her eyes are closed, and I savor the brief respite from our near-constant bickering. Seeing Liv in a relaxed state calms the conflicting emotions whirling inside me like a hurricane. She's always known how to soothe my aching heart, making the unbearable bearable without even trying.

I miss this. I miss her. I miss the way things were before I forced us to go our separate ways.

When I was young, I was a sociable kid and always had a seat at the popular table in school. After Ma died, though, I shielded myself by creating distance from everyone. Marie and Liv were the only exceptions. They instantly crept their way into my heart. I had no interest in making other friends, especially at a new school. Kids my age didn't understand why I walked around with a permanent scowl and never talked about my family. The only one who tried to understand and showed me unconditional empathy was Liv.

During those lonely, dark years, she was my sole source of sunlight and showed me there was more to life than pain and misery. That it was possible for me to experience a glimpse of happiness…as long as I was with her.

We were two peas in a pod, peanut butter and jelly, the sun and the stars.

When she jumped into my bed during that thunderstorm, she sealed our fate, and we were inseparable until I left her behind.

We've both changed over the years—there's no denying it.

Liv has grown into a confident, fierce, resilient woman who's never lost her positive outlook on life. She took her grief and anguish and somehow turned it into something beautiful. She didn't let Marie's and Hope's deaths define her. Instead, she used them as stepping stones to make a better version of herself, creating a life she deemed worthy of living. Her eternal optimism is contagious, and everyone she comes in contact with is fortunate to bask in her warmth.

Me, on the other hand? I barely recognize the man looking back at me in the mirror. There's no question I've always been a miserable bastard, bathing in bitterness since my mom was taken from me. There was a time I never would have treated Liv with disrespect, let alone made her cry. Sure, we didn't always see eye to eye, but I never raised my voice or snapped at her. She was too important to me.

As the days without Liv multiplied, my heart became hardened until she was no more than a memory placed on the top shelf in the corner of my mind. Even Pike's and Eloisa's kindness and love have never been enough to thaw my ice-encased interior. There's only one person who could ever save me, and that's Liv—much to her dismay.

When I found out Liv was a part of Mac's life, something broke inside me. I was devastated to know she had initiated their friendship and readily welcomed him into her life with open arms. It doesn't matter her reasoning; it still hurts all the same. She's the only person I ever shared my deepest thoughts and fears with.

My first reaction to Liv's betrayal was to break her, destroy her, the way she had done to me when I got the news.

I once worshipped the ground she walked on during the years we were together, and this was how she repaid me?

Although, my original plan was short-lived when I saw her again in person. She was all grown up, those big green eyes doing unexplainable things to me as they sucked me back into her world, leaving me conflicted.

Seriously, how the hell did we get here? Once upon a time, Liv and I were madly in love, vowing to spend the rest of our lives together. In the blink of an eye, we're now full-grown adults, broken and battered, struggling to move past the betrayal and hurt we've caused each other.

I meant it when I told her that a day hadn't gone by when I didn't think of her. I might be a cynical son of a bitch, but that doesn't mean I don't have feelings. I'd argue that I feel more than most. Each loss is amplified by the last, compounding the gaping, concealed wound, which is partly why Liv's disloyalty hurts so much.

We now find ourselves at a turning point, one that doesn't allow for backtracking. It comes down to a single question: are we worth fighting for?

I will never forgive Mac. He'll die knowing that his only child disowned him, hating him for his misdeeds. I'm beginning to realize that Liv never deserved the same treatment, though.

She's right. I'm the one who wronged her first, and if I hadn't erased myself from her life, she would never have gone to Mac, and we wouldn't be in the predicament we now find ourselves in.

I still think she's better off without me, and I'll never apologize for my decision to leave when I did, though I should have handled it better by telling her goodbye. Now that I have her here in my arms, I'm not sure if I'll be able to let her go again, regardless of my irreconcilable emotions.

"Liv," I say quietly so as not to startle her.

She gradually lifts her head from my shoulder, shaken out of her tranquil trance.

Her tear-stained face makes my chest tighten. I gingerly reach out and wipe away the moisture from her cheeks with my thumb. Seeing her like this makes me want to do everything in my power to take away her sorrow.

"What is it? Are you ready to debate some more?" Her question is void of enthusiasm, and her voice is drained of everything but sadness.

I hate it. The only expressions she should ever need to convey are those of joy, pleasure, and hope.

I furrow my brow, contemplating if I should let her go and walk away for good...but I can't bring myself to move.

Everything inside me is telling me to stay like this for a little while longer before reality sets back in.

"I'm sorry. I don't want us to fight. Can I just spend a few more minutes holding you close? Is that all right?" My question seems to surprise her as she gazes up at me in a daze.

She chews on her lower lip as she contemplates my request. Eventually, she shrugs her shoulders, letting out a despondent sigh. "Okay, I'll stay, but if I do, you have to agree to let me go when I'm ready."

I mumble my agreement before pulling her into my chest, refusing to give her a chance to change her mind. We're caught in the moment, suspended between the past and present, where only we exist and everything else is irrelevant. I block out our current situation—the onlookers gawking at us as they pass, Sirius sitting on his haunches nearby, and Mac, who I know is lying in a hospital bed inside, only a few feet away.

Liv is all that matters.

"Can I ask you something?" I ask in a hushed tone.

"What is it?" Liv doesn't move from her place, cradled in my arms.

"Is it hard being back here? At your parents' house, I mean?" I rub her back in soothing circles as I speak. "Don't get me wrong, we made some amazing memories here, but it was never the same after Marie's diagnosis, was it?"

Liv sits up to face me directly. "You're right, it was never the same," she whispers. "I'm haunted by the memory of my mom passing in the same space where I've brought Mac to stay. Every time I walk into the front parlor, I'm forced to relive those awful memories, unable to hit the pause button. Every room holds apparitions that I can't make disappear.

"The day Mac and I came to stay here, I made it as far as the hallway of the third floor. I ended up in a puddle, curled up outside your old bedroom door," she murmurs. "The last time I was in there, you were gone, your things were missing, and you never came back. I haven't been to this house since the day I was discharged from the hospital after losing Hope. I had the housekeeper box up all my things and subleased an apartment in Hell's Kitchen until I went to college in the fall."

I gently grab hold of her hands, placing them in mine, hoping it'll give her the strength she needs to keep going.

"I hate that I've brought Mac back to a place filled with the ghosts from my past. A house that hasn't been a true home since Mom's passing. It feels wrong."

"Why did you bring him here then?"

"As soon as he was diagnosed with terminal cancer, he said that he wouldn't go back to my apartment once he was put on hospice." She notices my confused expression at the mention of her apartment. "When he was released from prison, I asked him to come live with me. We've shared a place ever since. Although he always insisted on paying rent, utilities, and half the grocery bill, I still got the better end of the deal. He always kept the place clean, did the laundry, and had dinner on the table each night."

My whole body stiffens at her latest confession. Not only is Liv caring for Mac while he's ailing, but she's been by his side every step of the way, including playing his loyal advocate and giving him a place to live.

You can't change the past.

Does this new discovery change my feelings for Liv or my desire to want to make things easier for her?

Realizing the answer is no, I force myself to relax, giving her the chance to continue.

"Mac wanted to ensure I had a sanctuary I could return to, filled with nothing but joyful memories. He worried that taking him back to my apartment while he was on his deathbed would poison my perception of the place, and I wouldn't have a safe space to return to when this is all over."

I might detest the man, but in this instance, I agree with his decision.

"They have a unit at the hospital for hospice patients, but it's far too impersonal," Liv admits. "Though, if Mac knew how I felt about being back here"—she gestures at the brownstone—"he'd insist he be admitted immediately. I can't do that to him...I won't. I wish I could have found him a tranquil setting, away from the hustle and bustle of the city. He deserves that much, despite what you think," she says with steel, leaving no room for argument.

I turn toward the deceivingly picture-perfect brownstone with its matte-black shutters and intricate double-paneled vestibule front door.

I might not hold a single ounce of sympathy for Mac, but Liv loves him. And unfortunately, I love Liv. Even the company she keeps can't stop the undeniable pull I feel toward her—something I've tried to keep locked up tight but have always felt.

I have to find a way to lessen her burden and ease her anguish. I can't take away her grief, but I can come up with a solution for helping her escape this mausoleum and find her a place befitting a final farewell. I mentally flip through my

Rolodex of properties and connections in the area where we could stay.

Did I say we?

I'll have to revisit that thought once I have a solid plan in place.

My apartment in Brooklyn isn't equipped with all the necessities. Besides, there's near-constant construction in the area, which would be far from tranquil.

Las Vegas would be the most logical answer, but Mac is in no condition to fly. And a hotel is out of the question...

It hits me like a bolt of lightning.

I know exactly where we can go, and it's only a car ride away, which Mac should be able to handle in his condition.

Did I say we again?

The spot I'm thinking of has been the only place I've found any solace in the last fifteen years, and I visit every year during the week of the anniversary of Ma's death.

Can I really welcome the man I hate into somewhere so important to me?

It's not for him, remember? You're doing this for Liv.

I wonder if she'll go for it.

A few minutes ago, she was ready to walk out of my life for good, and now, I'm about to suggest the complete opposite.

I have nothing to lose, so here goes nothing...

I'm still holding tightly to Liv's hands, gently gliding my fingers across her palm, doing my best to soothe her, hoping if she's in a relaxed state, she'll be more likely to go along with my harebrained idea.

"I have a proposal for you."

She gives me a startled look as she tries to pull her arms away, but I keep them firmly in place. I'm not letting her go until we've finished this discussion.

"Don't panic. It's not that kind of proposal," I say teasingly. "That would require us to go more than five minutes without shouting at each other, but don't worry, we'll get there someday." I give her a wink, hoping it'll help lighten the mood.

"Consider this another truce," I say, using her words from a few days prior. "Els and Pike have always loved upstate New York. They even spent their honeymoon touring towns in the area when they got married. You know, back when dinosaurs roamed the earth."

My attempt at humor gets a snicker from Liv, which I'm taking as a win.

"It's always been an escape for them when life gets too chaotic. A few years ago, while they were taking a scenic drive in the area, they came across a colonial house on a big parcel of land for sale and immediately fell in love with it. They made an offer on it the same day. It's become their sanctuary, and I wouldn't be surprised if they decide to move up there full-time once they are both retired."

Liv's eyes are still glued to mine as she listens intently to every word. I draw in a deep breath, hoping she takes this next part just as well as the first.

"When they purchased the property, they hired a year-round estate manager who lives in the cottage down the hill from the main house. Her name is Roxanne, and she's a dear friend of mine," I say with fondness. "She managed the place with her husband, up until his passing five years ago. When Pike suggested hiring additional help, she told him he could go straight to hell and said she didn't need 'no help.' It can get lonely at times, so she's thrilled when she has visitors."

"Milo, the place sounds lovely, but is there a reason you're telling me all this?"

"I'm suggesting you take Mac there. It's the perfect place for you to say goodbye, away from the city and the ghosts haunting you both." I can feel her tense up, but I press forward. "It's only a five-hour drive, so it's doable to keep him comfortable on the ride there. What do you say?"

She blinks rapidly, her expression far too stoic for my liking. I don't think this is what she expected when I mentioned another truce.

"That's very sweet of you to offer, but I can't accept." Her voice has a finality to it that makes my stomach drop, revolting at her quick dismissal. I thought she'd at least take some time to contemplate my offer.

I don't accept her rejection.

"Why the hell not? The place I just described is exactly what you're looking for," I say with a demanding tone.

"I can't stay at Eloisa and Pike's place. I don't even know them. Besides, transferring Mac to and from the car by myself would be far too difficult. At least here I have Jane and Jeremy to help me. There's no way I'm asking either of them to spend what could end up being several weeks away from their families and other patients."

She still doesn't understand.

"I'm not suggesting you go by yourself…I'm coming with you. I can drive and help you take care of Mac."

Without skipping a beat, Liv bursts out laughing. I must have somehow given her the impression that this is a joke.

It's definitely not.

I grab her chin, tilting her head so she's looking directly at me. "I'm one hundred percent serious right now. We're going to take Mac upstate, where you'll be able to give him the proper farewell you think he deserves in a place you're not uncomfortable staying. Let me just make one thing clear: I'm doing this for you, and you alone."

"You really mean it?" she whispers, her eyes widening in shock.

"Yeah, Liv, I really do," I say as I press a kiss to her forehead.

Chapter Fifteen

OLIVIA
Past—Twelfth Grade

A SENSE OF FOREBODING HAS lurked in the shadows of my mind ever since Mom fell down the stairs this past spring.

At the time, she was rushed to the hospital, but refused testing of any kind. She insisted she felt fine and attributed the fall to not paying attention to where she was going. Over the following months, though, she experienced multiple "absent-minded episodes," as she fondly dubbed them.

During the first week of June, she put her keys in the freezer and couldn't remember where she had misplaced them. It took Milo and me two full weeks to track them down. A few days later, she blacked out while doing the laundry, and I found her lying on the floor in the mudroom with the lights off. She had no recollection of the incident when she woke up.

The final straw occurred over the Fourth of July holiday weekend.

Milo, my mom, and I were celebrating out on the terrace with a full spread of burgers, hot dogs, Jell-O salad, chips, and watermelon. Mom went to whip up a batch of her famous lemonade, and it didn't occur to me that she might need help.

Milo and I heard a loud crash come from inside. When we rushed in, Mom was kneeling on the ground, trying to pick up shards of glass with her bare hands, blood dripping from the cuts that she didn't seem to notice. Her only focus was the Queen Lace crystal pitcher, scattered in pieces around her. That was when I knew something serious was wrong.

It's now August, and Milo and I are supposed to start our senior year of high school next week. However, it's been the furthest thing from my mind as of late.

Mom has been to several specialists over the past month, including a neurologist she's seen twice. It's funny how even with all the power and influence in the world, there's only so much that can be done to put a rush on lab results.

I've been a nervous wreck, barely able to eat or sleep, worried that something else will happen to Mom if I'm not watching her constantly. I've gone as far as waiting for Milo to fall asleep at night before sneaking down to her room, where I lie next to her in bed, watching the rise and fall of her chest.

Today, we're back at the neurologist's office. Milo and I insisted on coming to show our support during this visit.

We're sitting in a windowless room with blank white walls. The only furniture is a sink, cupboards to store medical supplies, a medical examination table, and two hard chairs meant for patients and their families. It's downright depressing.

At least in the pediatrician's office, the walls are filled with bright and cheery safari animals smiling down at you. Here, I feel like I'm about to be carted off to the psych ward. Depending on the news we get today, that very well could be true.

Mom left the room over an hour ago and hasn't returned. She wanted to speak with her doctor in private before sharing any news with us. I'm perched on Milo's lap, my arms wrapped around his neck and my head resting against his shoulder as he gently rubs my back.

"Stardust, trust me, everything is going to be fine. Marie is the strongest person I know. She's a fighter, and whatever it is, she'll get through it," he says with conviction. "She's not going anywhere, I promise."

I can't tell if his words of comfort are meant for himself or me. Milo puts on a good front, but his pinched eyebrows and bulging veins are clear signs of cracks surfacing in his facade.

Ever since Mom's first fall, I've felt him slowly distancing himself, pulling away from me both emotionally and physically. His mind doesn't know how to wrap itself around the thought of losing someone else he loves, let alone someone he considers his mother figure. He's hanging on by a thread most days, and I can't imagine what will happen if we get bad news today.

I send up a silent prayer for a miracle—not only for my mom, but for Milo and me too.

I'm jolted from my thoughts when I find Mom standing in the threshold of the doorway. Her face is stained with tear streaks running down her cheeks. Her clouded hazel eyes hold my gaze, willing me to stay strong for what's coming next.

It seems my prayer came much too late…

I feel Milo's grip tighten around my waist, and there is no doubt in my mind that my entire world is about to turn upside down. Mom's body trembles as she makes her way into the room, shutting the door behind her, giving us privacy. She cautiously crouches down in front of Milo and me, grabbing ahold of our hands.

"Hey there, you two. Why the long faces?" She lets out a little sniffle as she tries to regain her composure. "I'm going to tell you something, and I need you both to be strong for me. No matter the final outcome, you two will always have each other."

I find myself nodding distractedly, not even sure what she just said. I want her to rip the Band-Aid off already and get the devastating news out of the way so we can find a solution to fix it, the three of us together.

The Three Musketeers.

"I've been diagnosed with glioblastoma multiforme, a type of brain cancer," she says as if reciting a line straight out of a textbook. "I've known for a while, but I wanted to wait to say anything until the doctors determined my final prognosis." Fresh tears start forming in her eyes, and I watch them trickle down her face.

"Mom, you're scaring me," I whisper.

My chest starts to tighten, and I panic. It feels as though I can't breathe. I jerk my hand out of hers, leaping from my position on Milo's lap. I start to pace the small room like a caged wild animal before retreating to the far corner and sinking to the ground, willing myself to calm down. I close my eyes, focusing on the steady beat of my own heart, forcing myself back to the present.

"Livvy," Mom says, keeping her distance, knowing I need my space. "There's no easy way to say this. My scans show that I have an inoperable brain tumor. The doctor recommends I start chemotherapy immediately, but the chances of it making a difference are slim to none. If nothing else changes, I have a few weeks to live at most."

I think she's still talking, but I can't hear her above the ringing in my ears.

Brain tumor.

Cancer.

Only weeks to live.

Those vile words play on an endless loop in my head, refusing to leave.

"No!" I jerk back at the sound of Milo's shouts. "This is complete and utter bullshit. Clearly these doctors don't know what they're talking about. When are you getting a second opinion? They got it wrong. You're not dying!" Milo is on a downward spiral, violently shaking his head.

He's in denial...so am I.

"Milo, sweetheart, I've gotten a second opinion. In fact, I've been to five other doctors, and they all say the same thing. I'm so sorry to put you through this again. I would do anything to fix this—you know that I would if I could," Mom says solemnly. She reaches out to touch Milo's shoulder, but he yanks back his arm.

"Don't touch me!" he screams at the top of his lungs. "Stay the hell away...How could you do this to me?"

He mutters nonsense as he swings open the door, storming down the hall. He knows this isn't my mom's fault, and I know he loves her unconditionally. He doesn't know how to cope with the idea of losing her, especially not like this.

Why is this happening to us?

I scramble to stand up, prepared to follow Milo, but Mom shakes her head.

"Give him some time to cool down. He'll come around. You'll see."

She opens her arms out in a silent plea for a hug. Without hesitation, I throw myself in her embrace, breathing in the scent of cherries and linen, filing the moment away to look back on when Mom's not here.

"Livvy, I promise to fight until my last dying breath. I love you and Milo so much, you know that, right? I wish I could make this easier for you both."

"Mom…" I say reverently, cherishing this tender moment between us.

You can't leave me all alone.

How will I survive without you? You've always been the driving force keeping our family together. Father doesn't want anything to do with me, and Milo won't be able to survive losing you. It's not fair. You're supposed to be there to watch me graduate high school, college, and medical school. Who will walk me down the aisle at my wedding if you're not here?

Please don't leave me, Mom. What will I do without my North Star?

I keep those thoughts to myself.

There's no reason to cause her any added stress today. So, instead, I say the five words that I know she needs to hear the most right now.

"I love you, Mom…always."

Mom proves the doctors wrong.

She lives for another four months.

Father makes a surprise appearance a couple days after her official diagnosis and ends up staying at the house while Mom fights her losing battle with cancer.

He still goes into the office every day and keeps his distance from me, but he stops harassing Milo for the most part. They avoid each other like the plague instead of exchanging hateful words whenever they come in contact.

A couple of weeks after Mom starts chemotherapy, it becomes apparent that it's causing her more harm than good, and they immediately stop the treatments.

That doesn't stop her hair from falling out in clumps or spending hours with her head pressed firmly against the toilet seat. She quickly becomes too weak to walk up and down the stairs, so a hospital bed is delivered to the house and placed near the large bay windows in the front parlor. Shortly after her chemo treatments stop, she's put on hospice, and a steady flow of nurses and nursing aides come in to ensure she has the best care twenty-four seven. I helplessly watch as my larger-than-life mom deteriorates before my eyes.

She insists that Milo and I go back to school as planned.

That doesn't stop me from skipping class whenever I can get away with it or sprinting home as soon as the last bell rings. I opt out of all extracurricular activities during the fall semester, wanting to sneak in every last moment I can with Mom.

Milo shuts himself off from me completely after Mom's diagnosis. He spends most of his time in his room, smoking out on the terrace, or disappearing for extended periods without telling anyone where he's going. He rarely visits Mom, and flat-out refuses to acknowledge me when he can help it.

He's gone as far as locking his door at night—a silent slap to the face.

We've slept in the same bed every night since he moved in, so I can't understand why he's doing this to me. Why now, when I need him the most? He promised we would get through this together, and it's turned out to be a lie.

Every night, I crawl in next to Mom on her hospital bed and we talk for hours. Toward the end, I do most of the talking, but it doesn't matter. I'm grateful to spend time with her while she's still alive.

One afternoon, I walk in to find Milo with his head lying on her lap. My mom's strength has mostly dissipated, yet she somehow finds the energy to gently stroke her fingers through his hair, giving him the comfort that he desperately needs.

I tiptoe out of the room and stand in the hallway, out of sight, not wanting to disturb them. I listen as my mom and Milo exchange one of their last conversations.

"I want you to know that I've always considered you my son," she painstakingly rasps. "There's no question your mom sent you to Olivia and me, and I couldn't be more grateful. It brings me peace knowing that Olivia will have you by her side when I'm gone, and that she'll never have to be alone." I can hear her strained breathing as she finds the strength to finish. "Don't let sorrow drag you down. Let your love for Olivia keep you afloat. You'll need each other more than ever once I'm gone."

"You saved my life, Marie, and I'll never be able to repay you. I don't know how I can move on from losing both you and my ma." Milo's response is barely above a whisper.

It makes me wonder what will happen when Mom is finally gone and it's just the two of us.

As the holidays fast approach, Mom's health rapidly declines. I decorate the parlor with a Christmas tree, decorations, and presents so she can enjoy one last holiday with Milo and me.

She passes away on Christmas Eve.

Despite the distance Milo has put between us, we come together that last night to say goodbye.

He carries Mom's fragile frame to the rooftop terrace where I make a fort out of pillows and blankets. He gently lays her down on a soft white duvet, and I rest her head on a pillow. Milo and I lie on either side of her, clutching her hands as we gaze up into the night sky.

No one says a word as I softly hum "Catch a Falling Star" by Perry Como, Mom's favorite song. As she takes her last breath, I rest my cheek against hers, whispering words of love, the last she'll ever hear.

I now know exactly how Milo felt when he lost his mom: nothing will ever be the same.

We are both permanently changed, and I fear there is no coming back from this tragedy.

Chapter Sixteen

MILO
Present Day—November

I WORK WELL INTO THE night, catching up on a few logistics for the Bushwick project so the contract will be ready to sign next week.

Once I finally climb into bed, sleep eludes me, my conversation with Liv from the day prior running rampant through my mind. I toss and turn, debating if I made the right decision to offer to take her and Mac to the house upstate.

I haven't spoken to Mac since the day at the hospital last week. Now, I'm volunteering to help with his care and taking him to a place that Eloisa and Pike consider their home away from home. A place I view as a safe haven and visit every year on the anniversary of Ma's death. I didn't share this information with Liv yesterday because I knew she would never have taken me up on my offer if she had known.

She needs this, and I won't let anything get in the way of that. Her placid expression after accepting my offer made it worth it. I would move heaven and earth to see her that relaxed every day for the rest of my life.

Is it possible for us to have a life together after everything we've been through?

My primary focus has to be on the short-term.

Liv and I will have to deal with the repercussions of our decisions, whether good or bad, at a later date, but I'm treating this as another truce, and I'll do what I can to be on my best behavior. Even after my inner pep talk, I spend the next several hours battling an internal debate, my conflicting emotions waging war against themselves.

I finally give up on rest and am up with the sunrise, much to Sirius's delight. He's always been an early riser, eager to start his day, motivated by the homemade peanut butter dog treat he's rewarded with after our jogs.

Every morning, like clockwork, he sits on his haunches at my bedside, holding his leash between his teeth, waiting for me to get my ass out of bed.

Today is the exception. I'm the one standing by his comfy dog bed, holding out the leash. He lifts his head, confused why I'm hovering over him, but clambers off his mat when he notices I'm wearing my running shoes.

We run through Sunset Park with a breathtaking view of the sunrise, making our way along the Upper New York Bay. Though, my pace has slowed to a jog since high school, Eloisa blames my nasty smoking habit, insisting that my poor lungs can't handle working double time. She's not wrong, but it hasn't stopped me from going through several packs a day as I've been trying to navigate the Liv and Mac situation.

After twelve grueling miles, my head still isn't clear. In fact, I'm more conflicted now, concerned that I've made the wrong decision.

I want Liv in my life—at least for a little while longer—and taking her and Mac upstate guarantees that will happen. The question is, can I really contain my temper while in the same room as the man I hate?

Once we get back to the apartment, Sirius takes off down the hall to the kitchen. When I get there, I find him up on his hind legs, sniffing along each of the cabinets, trying to determine where the snacks are so he can open up the correct cupboard with his nose.

"Sirius, what are you doing? Get down from there," I snap at him. I'm not angry, but he's much more likely not to repeat this behavior if I reprimand him.

He jerks his head back to look up at me, startled by my sudden appearance and being caught in the act.

"This is why I hide your treats in a new place every day, boy. Seriously, you can't wait thirty seconds?"

He starts to bark, demanding to know where his tasty biscuits are hiding. I let out a chuckle. At this point, I've lost all hope of teaching him any manners.

I walk over to the pantry, retrieving the square Tupperware sitting on the top shelf, filled to the brim with homemade dog treats. I break one in half and throw a piece toward Sirius.

Sirius jumps up and catches the snack in his mouth midair. Some days, I question what's in those things. Eloisa has to be putting crack inside because the poor dog is nearly as addicted to these as I am to nicotine.

Once Sirius has finished gulping it down, he licks his chops to ensure he gets every last crumb. Before retreating to his bed, he picks up his hedgehog squeak toy along the way. Aside from our daily runs and occasional outings, he doesn't let the thing out of his sight.

After a cold shower, I pack a bag for the trip upstate, throwing in a couple of sweaters, wool socks, and a hat. It's early November, which means it'll be chilly. I send a silent prayer of gratitude Eloisa's way, glad she insisted I have my closet fully stocked. She said it was ridiculous to haul my things back and forth from Vegas since I stay here so often for business. In this particular instance, I agree with her.

Once I get everything together that Sirius and I might need while we're away, I head to my office to give Pike a quick call before heading out.

I want to get an early start to avoid the mid-morning rush, especially on the Upper East Side, where traffic is always a nightmare. One of the many reasons I'm not fond of the city.

As I hit the call button, I stand near the floor-to-ceiling windows facing the street, watching as people start their day. Some are heading to work, others to the gym, and those with time to spare walk down to the local coffee shop to grab their daily caffeine fix.

The phone only rings twice before Pike picks up, likely expecting my call despite the early morning hour in Vegas.

"Good morning, son. Are you heading out?"

When I first met Pike, I cringed when he would call me son. He was well aware of my severed relationship with my dad, and it always irritated me that he used the particular term of endearment. Recently, I've found that it doesn't bother me much anymore. I don't mind being referred to as Pike's son, although I'm not ready to share that with him just yet.

"Sirius and I were about to leave, but I can cancel if necessary. I'm sure Liv would understand. I stayed up late last night working on the Bushwick contract, and there are still several outstanding tasks that need to be completed before we close the deal next week. We've been working on this one for three years, and I don't want to screw it up because of an irrelevant personal matter."

Part of me hopes Pike will ask me to stay in the city.

Instead, he makes a disgruntled sound, obviously disapproving of my response. "Are you trying to convince me or yourself?" he asks blatantly.

"What do you mean?"

He's always talking in riddles. I wish he'd get straight to the point instead of making me read between the lines.

"You're scared, Milo, and you're deflecting, trying to use work as an excuse not to confront your fears," Pike says with certainty. "Since the day I met you, you have always been transparent about your feelings toward your dad. The hate you feel for him is palpable. So, spending an undetermined amount of time with him in close quarters must be the last thing you want to do. I'm sure you've considered retracting your offer at least a hundred times in the last hour alone, but based on our conversation last night, you're not doing this for Mac. You're doing it for Olivia, giving her the gift of a proper send-off for the man she considers a father figure." There's a short pause on the line as Pike shifts his phone from one ear to the other.

"You might not have talked about Olivia much in the past, but each time you have, your entire face lights up. Even now, knowing what you do, you're willing to put her needs first, and trust me, son, someone that special should be treated with the utmost care."

I step away from the window, sitting down in my office chair, contemplating what Pike said. I don't say a word, but my silence doesn't bother him. Whenever he gives his unsolicited opinion, he's come to expect that I'll listen to what he says, but I won't always reply. This time is no exception.

"Eloisa and I discussed it after we got off the phone with you last night. We've decided to come to New York City for a few weeks." His voice is filled with authority, not leaving me room to argue. "We'll stay in the apartment while you're away, and I'll follow through with this phase of the Bushwick project in person. That way, your full attention can be on Olivia to help her through this difficult time. You'll have your entire life to work, son, but this might very well be your last chance to support Liv in this capacity."

"Pike, I can't ask you to do that," I say. "You made me CEO, trusting me to run the company. What would it look like to our employees and the board if I pawned off our biggest deal to date?"

"Trust me, the only person who will notice is Richard." He chuckles. "The only reason he'll care is so he can hold it over your head. I swear, the two of you act more like squabbling siblings than boss and assistant. You're both going to be in deep shit when Eloisa decides she's ready for me to retire for real. Who will keep you both in check then?" he asks.

"I'm sure you'll find a way to keep tabs on us even then," I say. I'm betting that pigs will learn to fly before Pike officially retires. "Are you sure about coming out here?" I ask hesitantly.

"Son, you'll never have another opportunity to reconnect with Olivia like this again," he says. "If you don't take it, you'll regret it for the rest of your life—I can assure you," he says, unwavering. "Besides, Eloisa wants to look at a property near Hell's Kitchen as the potential site for her new restaurant. So, really, you're doing us a huge favor by letting us crash at your place," he says.

Of course, it all makes sense now.

Pike has several properties in the city he could stay at with a moment's notice. The suggestion to stay at my apartment is all Eloisa's doing—an elaborate scheme to decorate the place and make it feel more like a home. Since the building was completed, she's been trying to convince me to hire an interior designer to spruce up the place.

No doubt, when I get back, I'll be greeted with an excessive amount of wall art, throw pillows, blankets, rugs, and whatever else she can squeeze inside. I know she means well, and if she likes it enough, maybe she'll convince Pike they need to spend more time in New York and I can stay in Vegas.

It's a win-win if you ask me. But then why does the idea have a pit forming in my stomach? This situation with Liv might not be permanent, and I'd do well to remember that.

"Okay, Pike, if you say so. I appreciate you doing this for me," I say with sincerity. "But I swear, if I come back to fuzzy throw pillows on the bed, I'm going to lose my shit."

That earns a laugh from Pike. "You'll have to take it up with Eloisa, son," he says. "I'll admit, she's far too excited to come to the city, which means there's no telling what she has planned."

I groan into my hand, imagining a bright pink comforter on the bed. Thank goodness this isn't my full-time residence or I'd be more concerned.

"Oh, and before I forget," Pike pipes up. "I spoke with Roxanne last night. She's thrilled that you're coming and will have everything ready for your arrival this afternoon. She also told me to mention she'll have an early dinner prepared since she's sure you'll be hungry after the long road trip," he says.

"Thank you so much. I know you and Eloisa usually like to take a trip up there this time of year, and I appreciate you being willing to change your plans so I can do this for Liv." My voice is filled with gratitude.

"Milo, how many times do I have to remind you? We're family, and family looks after each other. Now, stop stalling. Olivia's waiting, and you don't want to get stuck in the early morning rush," he says with finality.

"Okay. Thanks. I'll talk to you soon."

He ends the call before I can stall any longer.

Well, here goes nothing.

After a quick stop to pick up a surprise I plan to give Liv later, Sirius and I drive over to pick up Liv and Mac.

I rented a RAV4 for the occasion. Liv will appreciate the sentiment even though, unfortunately, this model is a few years newer than the one I saw her driving that day at the hospital.

Despite Liv's economic status, she's never approved of showing it off—something she and her mom had in common.

She'll be sorely disappointed to know I have a Veneno Roadster sitting in my garage that I've only driven once.

Unlike Liv, I have no problem spending my money. There's no shame in reaping the rewards of hard work. Besides, I'd argue that I'm more motivated after forking out a large chunk of cash for something I've purchased.

The closer I get to the brownstone, the stronger the urge I have to turn around.

Liv double-crossed you.

She cares more about the bastard who killed your mom than she does you.

Why are you putting your own feelings on the line for hers?

The devil on my shoulder—or in this case, my head—has been very vocal this morning. Ever since I showed up at the hospital and saw Liv there with Mac, there's no stopping the vicious thoughts running rampant in my mind.

I'm damn near hyperventilating by the time I turn onto 63rd Street, and I find myself driving below the speed limit as I approach my destination. However, when I pull up to the house and see Liv standing next to the open garage with a million-dollar smile adorning her face, my uncertainty washes away.

You're doing this for her.

My new mantra plays on repeat in my head.

She's worth it.

I pull into the short driveway and park the car, glancing over to check out Liv. I can't seem to help myself.

She's dressed up more than I've seen in the past week. She's wearing black skinny jeans that mold to her curves perfectly, a white turtleneck, and a light-gray, lapel-neck overcoat that falls to her knees. She's paired the outfit with her signature white sneakers. I adore her for not wearing heels— they've never suited her. To combat the light dusting of snow we got overnight, she completed her ensemble with a beanie, the ends of her glossy locks falling in waves past her shoulders.

I can't wait any longer. I need her in my arms, and I need it now. I jump out of the car, heading straight toward her. I'm a man on a mission and won't stop until I get what I came for.

Once I'm standing in front of her, I gently grab hold of her jaw with my thumb and index finger, leaning in to press a kiss against her sultry lips. I savor the taste of mint that greets me as a soft moan escapes her mouth. It seems she's enjoying this as much as I am.

"Milo, what are you doing?" she gasps.

God, there's no way I'm going to be able to keep my hands off her during this trip. There's no question that she will be miserable at the thought of losing Mac. I want to give her something positive worth remembering too.

"I was giving you a kiss. Is there a problem?" I say in a teasing manner. "I missed you and needed to show you how much."

"You saw me yesterday," she says.

I give her a smirk. "Yes, and that was far too long ago. Now, enough dawdling. Let's get this show on the road."

I'm not sure if she can tell I'm trying to deflect with humor. At any moment, Mac is going to appear at the door leading into the garage, and I don't know if I can manage not to lose my shit when I finally face him again.

Liv grabs two giant suitcases that are leaning against the stairway. I grab them from her, and just as I've finished packing them neatly in the truck, I hear voices coming from the house. I look up to see a giant of a man holding tightly onto Mac, who looks even frailer than he did the last time I saw him.

They stop halfway through the garage as Mac starts wheezing, followed by a heaving cough.

Jesus Christ, at this rate, he's going to die right here in the driveway and Liv will never forgive me since moving him in this condition was my idea.

I jog up the drive to meet them, pushing the man aside. "I've got this," I snap. Annoyed for some reason that the man isn't being more careful with Mac.

I effortlessly scoop Mac up into my arms, alarmed by how light he is. If I had to guess, I'd say he weighs even less than Liv at this point.

I stride toward the RAV4 where Liv's already standing with the back door open, waiting for us. She's beaming up at me, obviously satisfied with my unexpected act of kindness. Sirius is sitting at her side, his tail eagerly wagging when he notices who I'm carrying in my arms.

I bypass them both and get Mac settled inside the car, scooting him up so his back rests on the stack of pillows leaning against the door. Once I'm sure he's comfortable, I grab the wool blanket from Liv and drape it over his legs.

Sirius starts to whine, impatiently waiting for my go-ahead. When I finally nod, he jumps into the backseat and curls up between Mac's legs, laying his head on Mac's stomach—his new favorite resting spot.

"Sirius can come up front with Liv and me if he's a bother back here," I mumble toward the ground, unable to force myself to speak directly to Mac.

"Of course not. We're friends now, aren't we, buddy?" he rasps.

I see out of the corner of my eye that he's feebly lifting his hand out to rub Sirius behind the ear to show his fondness.

I don't grace him with a reply as I shut the door, securing him and Sirius inside. When I turn, I see Jane has joined Liv outside, giving her a big hug.

"Have a safe trip, Dr. Dunham. Let me know when you arrive, okay? If you need anything, call me day or night." She finally pulls back, giving me a stern look when she notices I'm staring in her direction.

"Of course, Jane. Thank you so much. I couldn't have survived the past few days without you and Jeremy," Liv says, full of gratitude.

She turns to Jeremy, giving him her thanks, as well, before he walks to his car parked down the street.

Liv walks over to climb into the car, but before I can follow, Jane grabs ahold of the collar of my shirt, clearly wanting to stay something before she lets me leave.

"You do right by her, or you'll be answering to me, you hear me?" she threatens.

"You have my word," I say, and this time, I mean it. "Thanks for all that you've done for her, and for calling me when you did."

"No need to thank me. Dr. Dunham's been my friend for a while now. I'd do anything for her. Besides, it's not me you should be thanking for that call." Before I can ask who she's referring to, she takes off in the same direction as Jeremy.

Once I get into the driver's seat, I observe Liv as she stares at the brownstone in front of us. She doesn't move an inch, not even when I gently stroke her arm affectionately.

"Are you ready to go?" I ask softly.

"Hmm?" she says absentmindedly. "Oh, yeah, sure. Sorry, I was just thinking about…everything. You have no idea how much this means to me." She gives me a soft smile.

I lean in to whisper in her ear. "Anything for you. I promise by the end of the trip, you'll know that's the truth."

I turn on the ignition and back out into the street as we leave the brownstone for the last time—thank God.

Chapter Seventeen

OLIVIA
Present Day—November

WHEN I SPOKE WITH MAC about Milo's proposal to stay at Pike and Eloisa's house upstate, he said yes without hesitation, and ever since I broke the news, he's had a grin on his face.

It doesn't faze him knowing Milo is only doing this for me. He said it's more than he could have ever asked for just to be in the same room as his son again. I only hope Milo can find it inside himself to put the past aside and offer Mac an olive branch before he passes. If not, Milo will spend the rest of his life regretting not making amends with his dad.

On our way out of the city, I turn around to find Mac asleep. I'm grateful I had the foresight to ask Jane to give him another dose of pain meds right before we left. The main reasons were to guarantee his comfort and ensure he could sleep peacefully on the car ride. Although, I'll admit, I did have an ulterior motive.

For as long as I've known Milo, his emotional state has been unpredictable. He's like a yo-yo, bouncing up and down on its string, temperamental and difficult to control. You're never sure when it might get tangled in on itself, becoming a jumbled mess and a nightmare to unravel.

I'm terrified of what Milo might say to Mac if he were lucid. I figured Milo couldn't do any damage if Mac was unable to have a coherent argument. He prefers his opponent to be able-bodied and capable of dishing out as much as he gives, which is fortunate for Mac due to his drug-induced state of mind.

Mac's light snoring, the buzz of traffic, and the low hum of the radio are the only sounds accompanying me as I assess my current situation.

I'm in the confines of a small SUV with my ex-boyfriend and his terminally ill, estranged father. The same estranged father who I consider my family. We're all driving together upstate to stay in a colonial-style house, essentially turning it into a makeshift hospice for Mac. A final farewell for the man who's been there for me during my darkest days.

Not to mention the sexual tension that has been brewing between Milo and me since I saw him standing in the hallway of the hospital.

Why can't I seem to control myself when he's around?

Between Milo and me, our lives would make a captivating soap opera. The abnormal number of tragic events that have occurred continues to uptick, making me wonder what we ever did to the universe for it to conspire against us. If only Milo were willing, we could team up and stick it to the forces dead set on making our lives a living hell.

Images of Milo and me in battle armor, defending ourselves against Avenger-like villains, play through my head. Without warning, I burst out laughing, an ungraceful snort escaping my nose.

Unfortunately, I've never been good at expressing the proper emotion at the right time. I'm the girl who giggles at funerals, cries when I'm happy, and laughs when I see a dick for the first time—despite being turned on in the moment.

Seriously, what is wrong with me?

I'm just grateful Milo hasn't brought up *that* particular incident yet. To this day, I get embarrassed just thinking about it.

"What's so funny?"

I let out a shriek in between chortles, startled by Milo's intrusion on my version of *Looney Tunes*. He gives me a skeptical look, obliviously concerned for my mental state.

"I'm…it's…" Another laugh escapes my lips as tears run down my cheeks. I slump in my seat, unable to manage my own mobility. I have no control over my bodily functions and am grateful I haven't peed my pants yet.

Now that would be embarrassing.

"Liv, seriously, you're freaking me out. It's time to stop now," Milo says with a smirk. He's getting a kick out of seeing me like this.

"Milo…I…I'm…" I wrap my arms around my waist, my abdomen starting to ache from my unrestrained laughter. My fit continues for several more minutes until I finally compose myself long enough to breathe properly. Once I've managed to resemble a sane person again, I sit up in my chair, wiping away the residual tears from my face.

"You good?" Milo gives me a sideways glance. "The bottled water in the cupholder is for you. It should help you calm down a bit. You're lucky Mac is asleep so only Sirius and I had to witness your nervous breakdown. If someone from work watched you cackle like that, they might be concerned about your ability to care for patients," he teases.

"Jerk," I quip back as I playfully punch him in the arm, careful not to distract him from driving.

"Are you going to tell me what was so funny?" he asks. "Was it my face? Do I have something on my face?" He pretends to rub away the invisible culprit spread across his chin.

"You're such a dork." Something I didn't think I'd ever say again.

I love this playful side of him. I miss it. *I miss us.*

"Honestly, my thoughts were much more dismal than that," I admit.

"Of course. Only you would laugh at something I can only assume is sad and depressing," he says with a grin. "I think it's a gift. You're always cheerful and happy, looking on the bright side, even when things are dark and dreary. It's one of the reasons I love you."

His confession comes out of left field, without any warning.

I whip my head to look at him. "Wh-what did you say?" It feels like the air has been knocked right out of my lungs.

Milo glances over at me. "That's right, Liv. I love you. To tell you the truth, I don't think I've ever stopped," he says with certainty.

"Milo...I...why are you telling me this now?" I screech, unable to control the downward spiral of emotions swirling inside my head.

There's no way I can say those three little words back. The last time I gave Milo Covell my heart, he stomped on it and left without a backward glance. I honestly don't know if I'll ever be able to feel confident saying those three little words to him again. The fear that he's going to walk back out of my life at any minute is always at the forefront of my mind.

"Liv, I'm sorry. I didn't mean to freak you out," Milo says in a calming tone, doing his best to talk me off the ledge. "I don't expect you to say it back. I just thought you should know." He ends in a whisper before focusing his attention back on the road.

There's an awkward silence in the car, and I'm not entirely sure what to say or do next. So, I do what I do best...deflect.

"I was thinking about the irony of our situation," I say, glancing over to make sure Milo's listening. "How it feels like we're on the set of a TV show, waiting for the director to call cut and congratulate us on our Oscar-winning performance. Neither of us deserves the grief and heartache we've experienced, and more than anything, I wish I could take away the suffering you've had to endure."

Milo reaches across the console and brushes his fingers along my jawline. "I don't know how you do it...always putting the needs of others before your own. Like now, for instance, instead of referencing your own grief, your primary concern is for me." Milo drops his hand down to my lap and grabs hold of mine, intertwining our fingers.

Another silence fills the vehicle, and this time, I welcome it. I turn my attention outside to observe the late fall morning. A fresh blanket of snow has left the trees glistening with frost—a reminder that the holidays are right around the corner.

I keep peeking over at Milo from time to time, trying to decipher if this is real, if he's real, or if this is all a beautifully packaged dream, doubling as a nightmare.

Whenever he looks in my direction, I pretend that I'm checking on Mac, who's still fast asleep. Sirius has made himself right at home between Mac's legs, and I love seeing the special bond they've created. I know that on some level it's made Milo more susceptible to being near Mac, knowing that his loyal companion considers him a friend.

After the fifth time stealing a glance, Milo speaks up, clearly aware of my antics. "You really do care about him, don't you?" He nods toward the backseat, referring to Mac.

I let out a humorless laugh, making it clear I'm disappointed with his question. "Isn't that obvious?" I push his hand off my lap, needing some space to get through this conversation. "If you've been paying attention to anything I've said in the past week, you'd see that for yourself."

"I guess it's just hard for me to understand since I don't know the side of Mac that you do," he admits.

"Back in college, despite the challenges Mac faced behind bars, he always came to our Saturday visits with a smile on his face. He intently listened to me ramble about my classes, the subjects I struggled with, and always had a word of advice to get me through a rough week.

"The scar on his face? He got it a few months before he was released from prison. An inmate shanked him with a knife, aiming for Mac's carotid artery, but thankfully, Mac was able to shift his body in the nick of time. He refused to let the doctor call me for several days, knowing I had a big exam that week and didn't want to disrupt my studying. Even in his time of need he put me first."

My heart aches at the memory, remembering how helpless I felt after getting the call that Mac had been hurt. It tore me apart knowing there wasn't anything I could have done to prevent it.

"Every year on the anniversaries of Jada's, Marie's, and Hope's deaths, he's always brought home a candle for us to light in honor of them." I gaze at the backseat, smiling at Mac. "Like I mentioned the other day, he's the one who insisted I go to therapy shortly after Hope died. I wouldn't be this cheerful and happy if it weren't for Mac making sure I got the help I needed when I was at my lowest point. I meant it when I said I owe him my life," I say. "I will be there until his last dying breath, because he would do the same for me."

There's a lengthy silence after my unsolicited speech, and I'm concerned Milo will choose to ignore me for the remainder of the car ride. That's his usual prerogative if he doesn't agree with something or doesn't know how to express how he's feeling. I'm shocked when he opens his mouth, preparing to speak.

"Liv, I'm happy Mac was there for you when you needed him." His voice is filled with sincerity. "I still hate the man, but I'm doing my best to empathize with you.

"When I got to Vegas, I had no place to live, let alone money for my next meal. And then Pike and Eloisa came along. Without any incentive, they offered me a roof over my head, a job, and loyalty, which I didn't deserve. I wouldn't be the man I am today if it weren't for them. So, I can't fault you for finding the same comfort in Mac, because I love the woman you've become, and I know it's partly due to his influence."

The difference is that you chose to be alone. I didn't. You always had a place by my side.

I wish I had the courage to tell him, but I don't. It's not worth rehashing the subject more than we already have.

I heave a sigh, wishing he'd give Mac the benefit of the doubt. "I appreciate that. I only wish you would give Mac a chance to explain himself, to hear his version of the events that took place the night you lost your mom. You'll realize that—"

"Drop it, goddammit," Milo snaps. "Every time we make progress, you drag up the past. I'm here with you both, aren't I? Why isn't that enough for you?" Milo slams his palm against the steering wheel as I jerk back in my seat, shocked at his sudden outburst of frustration.

I turn around, grateful that Mac is still sleeping. I know he'd never tolerate Milo's behavior if he were awake. I spin back to the front, making sure I have Milo's full attention before speaking. "I'll let that outburst slide because I know this is a sensitive subject, but I won't let you treat me that way again. I don't deserve your wrath, no matter what you might think," I say with steel.

"Shit, Stardust…" Milo's voice cracks. He rests his hand on my thigh, gently brushing back and forth with his thumb. I welcome the show of affection, desperate to return to the lighthearted conversation we had mere minutes ago.

"I'm sorry, Liv. I shouldn't have snapped at you. You're absolutely right. I overreacted, I know that. I'm trying to make this work. Can we agree not to talk about the night of the accident again? I know exactly what happened. There's no reason for me to discuss that night ever again, okay?"

I reluctantly nod. There are facts he's missing, truths that need to be shed, but I'll respect Mac's wish not to tell Milo unless he asks. Besides, it's clear that nothing I could say would change Milo's opinion of Mac, and it's not worth another fighting match.

"Do you remember the game we used to play late at night when neither of us could sleep?"

His question surprises me as we shift back to playful banter. A mischievous grin flickers across my face, and I don't hesitate to start a round of The Color Game, just like old times.

"I'm thinking of something white."

He points outside. "If it's snow, I'll never let you live it down. Is it an object?"

"Nope." I emphasize the *P* with a loud pop.

"Does it belong outside?"

"Um…sometimes?" I shrug my shoulders. I swear he asks trick questions to throw me off on purpose.

"What do you mean, *sometimes*?" he taunts. "It either belongs inside or outside. There's no in between. Yes or no answers, remember? For God's sake, you made up the rules, woman."

I let out an unladylike snort, my free hand reaching up to cover my face. He's right, I did make up the game, and somehow, I always find myself breaking the rules anyway.

"Fine, no. Technically, it doesn't belong outside. Satisfied?"

"No, not nearly satisfied enough." He gives me a quick wink as he squeezes my thigh, clearly not referring to the game. "Is it food?"

"Yes."

"Is it a fruit?"

"No."

"There's only one right answer. It's got to be a marshmallow," he says with a triumphant smile.

"Ugh, how do you do that?" I ask, slumping my shoulders in defeat.

"You're far too predictable, Liv—that's how."

"I let you off way too easily. It's your turn. Do your worst," I challenge.

As we drive upstate, Milo and I spend hours playing the same game we made up when we were kids. I revel in seeing him this carefree for a change.

We're still a couple of hours away from our destination when my stomach starts to rumble loudly. My cheeks turn bright red from embarrassment.

"Oh my gosh, please ignore that. I'll be fine until we reach the house."

Milo fervently shakes his head. "Not a chance in hell. We're stopping, and that's final. I know firsthand what happens when your empty stomach goes unfed."

"You're exaggerating. I'm not *that* bad."

Milo barks out a laugh. "Liv, you literally get full-blown hangry, and while I adore your feisty side, I'd prefer to avoid one of your epic meltdowns." He squeezes my thigh again in a teasing grip. "Do I need to remind you of the day we got stuck on Staten Island for the day and both of us had forgotten to bring any money? You didn't eat for a solid ten hours and were an absolute nightmare by the time we got home. I'd prefer to avoid a repeat if you don't mind."

"He's right, Liv." I'm startled when I hear Mac pipe up from the backseat. "You do get cranky when you're hungry. I think it's best to play it safe and get you fed ASAP."

I face the backseat and Mac is now sitting upright, a grin on his face. He gives me a subtle wink when he notices me gaping at him. He's in good spirits, which I'm attributing to the pain meds and the fact that he's in the same space as his son. He doesn't even seem to mind that they're not on speaking terms.

"It's good to hear I'm not the only one who's had to deal with Livzilla. She's absolutely terrifying. Don't you agree, Sirius?" Milo asks his loyal sidekick.

Sirius gives an enthusiastic bark, pleased to be included in our conversation.

"I can't believe you're all ganging up on me. Especially you, Sirius." I reach back to give him a scratch on the head. His tongue sticks out of his mouth as he soaks up the affection. "I'll admit, I might be a *little* hungry, but we have a problem."

"What might that be?" He fakes a shocked expression.

"Mac is in no condition to go into a restaurant, and I don't want him exposed to any unnecessary germs. Maybe we could find a drive-thru. Would that work?"

Milo gives me a disappointed look, clicking his tongue in a show of disapproval. "Liv, Liv, Liv, give me some credit. It's been a while, but I still know you better than you know yourself. Don't worry, I've got us covered."

I raise my eyebrows in confusion as I watch him signal his blinker to get off on the upcoming exit, following the signs to the nearest rest stop.

"Milo, what did you do?" I ask.

"I figured we'd end up in this situation, so I did what any man would do to avoid his woman having a breakdown of epic proportions."

His woman?

"I stopped by one of my favorite delis on the way to pick you up this morning and grabbed a few things for us to eat. I grabbed some strawberries, an assortment of cubed cheese, sliced sourdough bread, honey-baked turkey, Castelvetrano olives, and chocolate-covered raisins."

All my favorites.

"He thinks of everything, doesn't he?" Mac directs his question toward me, acutely aware Milo must have planned this ahead of time, going as far as making a special stop to get all the foods I love most.

"Yes, he really does." I can't keep my eyes off Milo, a big smile on my face.

As we pull into the parking lot of the rest stop, my heart is full of gratitude. Milo and Mac might not be communicating directly with each other, but at least Milo is controlling his temper, which I'm taking as a win. A delicious meal that includes all my favorites is just the icing on the cake.

Chapter Eighteen

MILO
Past—Twelfth Grade

IT'S NEW YEAR'S EVE, AND I'm standing on the back patio in the freezing cold, watching the snow fall from the sky. I can hear the nearby celebrations in the surrounding neighborhood and, off in the distance, the sound of clashing pots and pans as the people of New York welcome in the new year.

For me, it's a bitter day in hell that I wish would finally end.

We buried Marie today, and I felt hollow inside as her casket was lowered down into the cold, frozen ground. I sat next to Liv as she quietly sobbed, mourning the loss of her mom, yet I did nothing to console her. It's been that way ever since we received Marie's diagnosis. Liv and I are two ships passing in the night, unable to find our way back to each other after such a great loss.

I haven't shed a single tear. Resentment and fury thrash around in my mind, with no way to calm the tempest brewing inside.

I'm furious at Marie for not going to the doctor sooner, I despise Liv for making me *feel*, and I loathe Mac for taking Ma away from me in the first place. If it wasn't for him, I would never have met Marie, and the crater-sized hole in my chest wouldn't exist. Most of all, I'm repulsed with myself for thinking I could find happiness and somehow conquer my shortcomings, riding into the sunset with Liv. It was always just an illusion—a convincing mirage, but no less a sham.

Since Ma died, I've felt like a ticking time bomb with an undisclosed countdown. I knew that at the drop of a hat, something would eventually come along and unexpectedly detonate the explosion waiting to combust inside me. My internal timer went off when Marie told us she was dying. Every ounce of control I had built up over the years disintegrated in the blink of an eye.

By the time I got back to the brownstone on the day of Marie's diagnosis, I could no longer contain my anger. I pushed my bedroom door open, snatching the lamp sitting on the nightstand and smashing it against the wall, taking great satisfaction as it shattered across the floor. I impulsively went over to my dresser, yanking off the only picture I had of Ma, ripping it to shreds, desperate to erase all memory of her and the pain her death had caused. It was too late when I realized the damage I had done. The pieces of photo paper lay lifeless on the ground.

That night, I wandered aimlessly through the city, ignoring every call and text from Liv. I returned the next morning to a quiet house.

I had walked into my room to find the remnants of glass had been cleared from the floor, a new lamp sat on the nightstand, and an identical copy of the photo I had destroyed was displayed in a polished silver frame. When my eyes drifted to the bed, I found Liv fast asleep under the covers, hugging my pillow tightly. She had come searching for me, needing comfort after getting the news that her mom was dying, and I hadn't been there for her.

I realized in that moment that if I let her, she would spend the rest of her life picking up my broken pieces without a second thought for her own well-being. I refused to let her lose sight of her hopes and dreams because she was tied to the likes of me. I've kept my distance over the past several months, unsure how I was going to tell her goodbye when the time came.

I'm pulled back to the present when a voice startles me from behind. "Why the hell are you still here?"

I spin around to see Harrison storming out of the house toward me.

He looks like he hasn't slept in days. His eyes are puffy and his blond hair is askew. He's wearing a ratty T-shirt with sweatpants hanging low on his hips. It's the first time I've seen him dressed in anything other than a three-piece Armani suit. He's holding on to the can of beer in his hand like it's his only lifeline.

Marie's diagnosis and subsequent death have taken their toll, affecting him more than he'd ever let on. Although he stayed here in the house during the past few months, he refused to visit her before she passed. The endless regret swims in his eyes, and he'll let those harmful emotions fester and stew, leading to his damnation.

How do I know? Because I'm the same. It's the one thing we have in common.

"Harrison, we *just* buried your wife today," I say with exhaustion. "Can we wait until tomorrow before we're at each other's throats again?"

"No, I don't think so, *son*," he slurs, spitting out the term of endearment, hoping to get a rise out of me. "This is all your fault. You're responsible for Marie's death. If she hadn't taken you in, she'd have been able to put her health first. Instead, she let a lowlife piece of shit into our lives, and look what happened. You killed her, and you'll have to live with that for the rest of your life. How do you think Liv feels? You took away precious time she could have spent with her mom because Marie was so invested in you."

His cruel words cut me like a dagger. He always knows exactly what to say to hit the bullseye and cause me the most pain.

"You're no longer welcome in this house," he seethes. "It's time you take responsibility for your own life and get the hell out of ours. You turned eighteen last week, so it's perfect timing, don't you think? Liv doesn't need you here to hold her back any longer. She deserves better than the likes of you."

It's like Harrison has climbed inside my brain and read my thoughts word for word. Everything he said, I've thought to myself hundreds of times. I've already made up my mind that I have to leave Liv, I just don't know how I am going to be able to look into her innocent green eyes and tell her goodbye. She'll never understand why I have to do this.

"You'd better be gone before I'm back in the morning," Harrison demands before marching back inside.

I stay in place for several minutes until I hear Harrison slam the front door behind him, shaking the entire house.

Once I know he's gone, I snuff out my cigarette with my shoe and somberly make my way inside, up to the third floor.

I pause when I get to Liv's door, knowing she's inside. I draw in a deep breath before quietly opening the door and tiptoeing over to the bed, the mattress dipping as I sit down on the edge. Liv is curled up under the covers, her silky brown locks splayed out around her pillow. Her tear-stained face makes my heart ache, knowing she must have cried herself to sleep after getting home from Marie's funeral.

As if she can sense my presence, her tired eyes flutter open, immediately honing in on me. A look of confusion crosses her face, and she draws her eyebrows up in concern. She cautiously scans the room, trying to find a plausible explanation as to why I'm hovering over her while she sleeps. I rarely come into her room. She always came to me before I started locking her out—both physically and emotionally.

When I made the decision that I was going to leave after Marie passed, I knew I had to take drastic measures. Liv has become too dependent on me, which isn't her typical style, so I did what I had to and started locking my door at night. That way, when I'm gone, she'll be used to sleeping on her own again.

After all the nights of her coming to find me in my room in the past, it's fitting that the last night I'm in this house, I'm the one to come to Liv. To lay myself at her feet and worship her like the goddess she is. No one will ever compare to her; she will always be *my* Stardust.

"Milo, what's wrong? What are you doing in my room?" Liv asks wearily, her voice full of concern.

I lean down to press my nose against her temple, inhaling the smell of vanilla, jasmine, orchid, and cinnamon. Even though I've been ignoring her, that hasn't stopped her from pickpocketing my jackets and stealing my Big Red gum whenever she gets the chance. It's a turn-on, knowing we share the same scent, and I purposely make sure there's always an extra stick of gum for her to take.

My hand absentmindedly strokes Liv's hair. I'm desperate to give her a glimpse of the affection I've deprived her of these past few months.

"I've missed you...I'm so sorry I haven't been there when you've needed me most. I'm a mess. You deserve so much better. I'll never be good enough for you..."

That's why I have to let you go.

The words don't come out, no matter how many times I've practiced saying them in my head.

I slightly pull back, preparing to break the news. To tell her that I'm going away and that we need a clean break. Not because I don't love her, but because she means more to me than life itself. She deserves a carefree existence, filled to the brim with happiness that she'll never get if I stay.

Before I can form my thoughts into a coherent sentence, Liv leans up on her elbow so she's resting on her side. She reaches out to cup my cheek with her delicate hand. "I need you." Her voice comes out so soft that I almost miss it.

"I'm right here." I clasp my hand tightly around hers, keeping her warm palm pressed against my cheek. If she needs me to stay until she falls back asleep, I will. Now that I think about it, maybe it's best to wait until morning to break the news. After all, she buried her mom today and deserves a brief pause from the anguish she's battling.

Liv sits upright, frantically shaking her head, frustrated by my reply. "No, you don't understand. I *need* you…"

She brings my hand to her lips, pressing a featherlight kiss to each of my fingertips as she speaks.

"I need to feel your touch."

Kiss.

"Your skin against mine."

Kiss.

"Your warmth."

Kiss.

"Your lips pressed to mine."

Kiss.

"I need to feel you inside of me."

Kiss.

Her sensual words have me frozen in place. This is a side of Liv I've never experienced. She's always been the voice of reason in our relationship, the one to hold back when I've been on the precipice of giving in to my carnal desires.

"Milo, I can't wait any longer," she confesses. "The pain…it hurts too much. Please take it away, even if it's only for a little while. Give me something good to remember on a day that's been filled with nothing but sorrow. Please, do this for me?" she pleads.

I might not be able to give her a lifetime of happiness, but this is something I can do for her. A brief glimmer of peace that she can replay during the moments she's in the depths of despair, grieving the loss of her mom and my absence.

Sex wasn't on my mind tonight. I planned to give her the proper goodbye she deserved, to explain why I need to get out of New York and why she can't come with me. I can't bring myself to tell her now. Not when she looks so fragile and broken, asking me to give her pleasure only I can provide.

I might be a selfish bastard, but I want this too.

I need this too.

I've waited so long to have Olivia Dunham, wholly and completely, and if this is the only chance I get, I'm not giving that up for anything.

I pull the comforter down to the end of the bed so I have a clear view of Liv. She's wearing one of my old flannel button-ups, which is bunched up around her waist.

God, she looks so damn sexy in my clothes.

As my eyes move down her supple body, I spot a pair of hot-pink cotton briefs I didn't know were part of her wardrobe.

Her pouty lips are slightly parted, begging me for a taste— though I know that one taste won't ever be enough. I won't be able to stop until I've worshipped her entire body, showing her how much she truly means to me.

And then you're going to leave her?

"Liv, are you sure about this?" I ask. "Because my self-control is barely hanging on by a thread." The bulge in my pants is physical proof that I want her more than anything, but only if she agrees. I'd never push her to do something she might regret later.

You don't think she'll regret it once you're gone?

I squeeze my hands tightly into fists at my sides, not allowing myself to reach out and touch her until she gives me a direct answer, knowing that I'll lose all control once I do.

The better part of me hopes she'll come to her senses and tell me to get out, but the remaining part is silently screaming for her to give me the green light already.

Liv is a goddess, my own forbidden fruit that I've desired, lusted after, and waited for since the first time I saw her. Even in the midst of darkness and suffering, she's always been my light, guiding me home, and in this moment, it's no different.

Without a single word, Liv smirks at me, using one of her long, slender legs to seductively shimmy out of her panties, flicking them to the floor with ease. She gets up on her knees, pressing them firmly into the mattress as she reaches up with shaky hands to remove my flannel one button at a time. The suspense is nearly unbearable. I almost heave a sigh of relief when she finally tugs the oversized shirt from her body, tossing it next to her discarded underwear. She peeks up at me through long eyelashes, feigning innocence as if she didn't just perform a private striptease, her body on full display to me for the first time ever.

And the last.

"I want you. Do you…do you want me too?" A hint of vulnerability seeps through as her voice cracks.

God, how did I get so lucky? This girl is the most beautiful creature I've ever seen. *How the hell am I ever going to let her go?*

I take a step back from the bed, observing Liv's flawless body from this vantage point.

"I will always want you—*always*. Don't you ever forget that," I say as I pull my jeans off, tossing them onto the growing pile of clothes on the floor.

I'm starting to breathe heavily and I haven't even made physical contact with her yet.

"That's not very reassuring to hear when you're all the way over there." She crooks her finger, beckoning me to join her, as she bites down hard on her lower lip.

I groan, mesmerized by her unexpected display of self-assurance. It's such a fucking turn-on, and she damn well knows it, playing me like the strings on a violin. She's usually much more reserved, though no less confident, outside of the bedroom. It seems that she enjoys role-playing the part of a seductress, luring me in with a sultry smile and a playful manner.

Don't worry, Liv. I'll make it good for you, I promise.

I yank my T-shirt up over my head as quickly as possible, refusing to be away from her for a second longer. I'm down to my boxers, hastily shaking them off one leg at a time.

"God, I don't know how long I'll be able to last, not after seeing you like this," I confess as I climb back onto the bed, meeting her in the middle.

My own hand trembles slightly as I wrap my arm around her waist, pulling her close. I lean down to hover my mouth over hers, not quite making contact, savoring the sounds of our intermingled breathing starting to pick up pace. I reward her with a soft kiss, and a relaxed moan escapes her mouth.

This is everything. I can't contain myself any longer. I give her one more passionate kiss on the lips before my mouth moves leisurely…

Down.

Peppering kisses along her jaw.

Down.

Nipping her neck with my teeth.

Down.

Caressing her collarbone with my tongue.

Down.

Wrapping my lips around one of her pert breasts.

A jolt of pleasure shoots straight to my groin at the contact. How the hell have I gone this long without tasting her like this? It's fucking nirvana.

I gently glide my tongue across her nipple as she arches her back, forcing my head closer to her chest, exactly where she wants it.

"Milo." My name falls from her lips like a prayer.

What I wouldn't give to hear her call out my name like that every day for the rest of my life.

Then why the hell are you leaving her?

"You like that, Stardust?" I taunt as I alternate between flicking her nipple with my tongue and biting down firmly.

Her hands wind tightly in my hair, tugging as she guides me to what pleases her most. I switch to her other breast, showering it with the same attention, devouring them both like it's my last meal. As I continue to ravish her tits with my mouth, my hands skim down her body, caressing her stomach in small circles.

When I reach her legs, they fall open of their own accord— an invitation for me to explore. My fingertips graze her skin in teasing strokes, and when I get to the apex of her thighs, her breath hitches, a direct link to my dick.

For the love of God.

I draw in a deep breath, summoning every ounce of willpower I have left. This first round is going to be quick. There's only so long I can hold out for my first time.

Remember, her pleasure comes first. She always comes first.

If that were true, you wouldn't be going away.

As I push two fingers inside her, Liv arches off the bed as she screams, "Oh, Milo, that feels so good."

I start teasing her clit with my thumb, and that's when she goes wild. She bucks her hips, pushing me deeper inside. Her eyes fall closed as she chases euphoria. I can't have that…I need to watch her as she falls over the edge.

"Stardust, open your eyes. Let me see you," I say with authority.

Her emerald-green eyes snap open, staring up at me with fondness.

"There you are." I press another kiss to her lips as a reward for doing as I asked.

"Please," she rasps out. Her breathless plea is my undoing.

I continue my assault, biting down on her breast while I plunge a third finger inside her. She screams out as she comes apart. My entire world is tipped on its side as I watch the girl I love experience orgasmic bliss for the first time.

"What's happening to me?" She looks up with a dazed expression.

Holy shit, I'm in heaven.

It's official. There's no way in hell I'm going to last more than a minute once I get inside of her.

I continue dipping my fingers in and out of her as she rides my hand with abandon. "Ride it out. Let it feel good."

She snaps her eyes back to mine as she trembles with unadulterated lust.

Her throaty moans combined with her frenzied pants directed in my ear have me frantically grasping for straws as I try to restrain myself. Before I can embarrass myself in the most important moment of my life up until this point, I rip my mouth away from her breast and pull my fingers out of her.

A low growl escapes Liv's lips. She's not happy with the turn of events.

I know how you feel, Stardust. I never want to stop either.

"Milo, don't leave," Liv says on a whimper. She yanks me back down, a look of sheer panic on her face.

"Don't worry, it's not over yet," I promise. "I need to be inside of you—*now*. This might be short, but I promise to make it last longer next time," I say as I pepper kisses across her cheek.

Don't promise her a next time, you asshole. Not if you're walking away after this.

"Can you lie down for me?" I ask in a husky voice.

"Mhmm," Liv says, nodding eagerly as she scrambles to lie down in the center of the bed. She looks up at me with complete trust and adoration, waiting for my next command.

Of course she is. She trusts you even though she shouldn't.

I shove my negative thoughts aside, focusing solely on how I'm going to worship Liv's lithe body.

I climb over her, hovering as she wraps her legs around my hips. My erection juts out, eager to play. God, just a few more seconds and I'll finally know what it feels like to be inside her.

Liv's eyes widen as she takes me in fully for the first time. She must have been too preoccupied while I was getting undressed to have noticed before. She bites down hard on her lip, unable to take her eyes off me. I grin, thinking it's from the sheer size of me—there's no question I'm well endowed. However, I'm thrown for a loop when Liv starts to chuckle.

What the fuck?

"Are you laughing at my dick? Are you insane?" I growl out.

"I, um…" She slaps her hand over her mouth as another burst of giggles escapes her lips.

"Oh, Stardust, you're in so much trouble." I shake my head in disappointment.

"It's just…it's so…" She lets out another fit of laughter, unable to contain her reaction.

This is unbelievable. I have a perfectly acceptable cock; she'll see that soon enough. It's time I show Liv just how much of a man I really am.

I reach down to grab my shaft, lining it up with her entrance, before pushing into the hilt without warning.

"BIG," Liv screams, her unfinished sentence finally falling from her lips.

That's more like it. There's the reaction I was looking for the first time.

Her laughter completely vanishes and is replaced with a low, keen grunt. I grin from ear to ear, pleased with her response. I lean down, kissing the tip of her nose. "God, I love you, Liv. So much."

If this is what heaven feels like, sign me up for a season pass. I'm never leaving. This feels right. I'm home…Liv's my home.

She looks up at me with pure ecstasy in her eyes. "Move, Milo. Please move," she pleads.

Anything for her.

I slowly start to pump in and out as adrenaline flows through my veins. God, if I had known that sex with Liv would be like this, I would have convinced her to give in years ago. I can't get enough as I reach up to grab her hands, intertwining our fingers as I spread our arms above us. Liv's head is tipped back, her heels digging into the mattress. Heat rushes to my groin at the sight, and I'm not sure how much longer I can last.

"Oh my gosh!" Liv breathes out as I push deeper. Her body is pulling me in, begging me to stay.

"God, you're incredible. I can't hold out much longer." I tilt her chin back, slanting my mouth across hers, slipping my tongue inside to find hers as I thrust back inside of her.

I love you.

I see you.

I'll miss you.

I pull out and thrust back in as I hold back the words I don't have the courage to say out loud.

Holy shit. Her walls constrict around me, and I can't think straight. All I can do is continue to thrust in and out of her, lost in my own pleasure. There's no way I can last when I'm watching her come apart.

"You're so beautiful like this," I heave out.

"Milo," she gasps as she starts to shudder, and that's my undoing.

We find our release together. The world spins out of control, and there's nothing we can do to stop it.

I hold her in my arms as we come back to reality after what felt like heaven on earth. I slowly pull out of her, brushing my lips across her nose before dropping down on the bed next to her.

Liv wraps her body around me like a baby koala, clinging to me tightly. We lie in silence, afraid to burst our carefully constructed bubble.

After a while, Liv starts to shake as sobs rack her body.

"I miss her so much," she wails. "I'll never see her again."

God, I'm such an ass. She just lost her mom, and I took her virginity the same day.

"I'm here, Liv. I'm here. Everything will be okay." I smooth down her hair, gently rubbing her back in a show of comfort.

"Milo, I love you," she whispers before her breathing evens out and she falls asleep within seconds.

I lift her up and place her under the covers before climbing in next to her, just like I used to. Except this time, we're naked.

I inhale her scent one last time before following Liv into a state of oblivion.

I wake up with the sun the next morning. Liv's lying beside me, flat on her back. Her arms splayed across her face with a smile, and I hope she's dreaming of me.

God, she's the most beautiful thing I've ever seen.

I take in a deep breath, knowing what I have to do. I have to leave before she wakes up. There's no way I can do this when she's awake to confront me. I sit up in bed, leaning over to press a gentle kiss against Liv's lips.

"I love you, Stardust. I always will," I whisper with reverence.

As I get up and prepare to leave this house for the last time, I know I'm making the right decision.

Someday, Liv will find a man worthy of her. Someone who will bring her nothing but happiness and joy. Who will always put her needs before his own, no matter the cost.

I only wish that man could be me.

Chapter Nineteen

OLIVIA
Present Day—November

I'M JOSTLED AWAKE BY THE sound of crunching gravel grating against the tires of the SUV. I blink away the grogginess from my nap, lifting my seat so I'm sitting upright. After our spontaneous pit stop for a picnic, Mac and I both got some much-needed shut-eye during the remainder of our drive.

"Welcome back to the land of the living."

I glance over to find Milo grinning at me from the driver's side, amused by my uncharacteristic, docile mood. He knows I can be temperamental when I wake up, and that hasn't changed.

I need another minute to regain my composure, so I give him a half-hearted nod before leaning my head against the headrest. I shift my gaze to the backseat to find that Mac is still fast asleep.

Milo offered to drive the whole way so I could rest, which I appreciated. These past few weeks have been utterly exhausting, and it feels like the heavy load I've had to carry alone has finally been lifted from my shoulders. Milo still won't directly acknowledge Mac, but it's a relief to have him here regardless.

I notice that Sirius has gotten up out of Mac's lap, his face pressed against the glass as he pants in excitement. Based on his reaction, I assume he's been in the area before, which means Milo has too. He never mentioned that when he offered for us to come and stay, which there must be a reason for.

Now that I think about it, I recall him saying he was close friends with Roxanne, the estate manager. The only way he'd know her is if he's been to Pike and Eloisa's property.

"Have you been here before?" I ask.

His entire body stiffens, like he's hesitant to answer.

"Yeah…I have," he admits. "I come up at least once a year by myself, and occasionally with Eloisa and Pike; however, they usually prefer their privacy. In full transparency, they treat the place like it's their annual honeymoon, so no room has been untouched, if you get my meaning."

I wrinkle my nose, trying to block out the mental image that popped into my head despite not knowing what Eloisa and Pike look like.

"Eww, Milo! You're so crude. I didn't need that visual." I playfully slug him right in the bicep like I used to back in high school when he said something inappropriate that I didn't approve of, which was typically every other sentence.

To be fair, I think Pike and Eloisa have the right idea. If Milo and I were alone, visiting under different circumstances, I probably wouldn't mind having our own fun in the secluded house.

Where did that thought come from? There's been sexual tension between us since he's been back, but that was totally out of left field.

Milo and I might have only had sex once, but he's the best I've ever had. No other man I've slept with has been able to fill his shoes—in or out of the bedroom. And based on the heated looks and passionate kisses we've shared in the past few days, it's safe to say sex with the adult version of Milo would be explosive.

Okay, rein it in, Liv.

"In all seriousness, this is their private escape whenever things get too chaotic. Between Eloisa juggling multiple business ventures related to her restaurant and Pike still playing a fundamental role at Lawson Co., their lives can be very stressful. It's been a saving grace to drop off the radar so they can recharge and rekindle their romance. Eloisa always says that coming to stay here has saved their marriage."

From what Milo says, it sounds like Eloisa and Pike typically come here without him.

Does that mean he comes to stay with other women? We haven't discussed our past romantic lives, and I'd prefer to keep it that way if we can help it. We don't need to bring up another controversial topic that would lead to another heated argument.

"You mentioned that you come up at least once a year. When is that?" I ask.

"The anniversary of Ma's death," Milo admits.

"I see," I whisper quietly.

"I came to stay with Eloisa and Pike a few months after they closed on the property. It was the first time in years I felt any semblance of peace, and it became my sanctuary.

Somewhere I could come to mourn and honor Ma and Marie. A place to clear my head when the internal chaos became too much." Milo's voice starts to tremble as he speaks, his hands in a death grip on the steering wheel.

"Roxanne's husband died five years ago, around the same time of year that Ma did. Since then, we've started a tradition where I come up for a few days and we get drunk and reminisce on what she calls 'the good ole days,' when things were much simpler than they are now and our loved ones were still alive." Milo is laser-focused on the road, refusing to look at me while he shares this part of himself that he's kept under lock and key until now. "Roxanne favors Macallan over Jack Daniel's, so we bring our own alcohol to avoid a bar fight in Eloisa's beloved dining room. You might even say our yearly get-together is our own version of group therapy, just with fewer people, which I prefer." He lets out a low chuckle at his own dark humor.

"Milo, I had no idea," I say with regret. "Why didn't you tell me this place is important to you?"

"Because you wouldn't have agreed to come if you had known," he states flatly.

He's right, and I'm mentally kicking myself for not asking these questions before I accepted his selfless offer. The house we're going to stay at is significant to him. A place he comes so he can honor his mom, certainly not somewhere we should bring Mac.

"Turn the car around," I order. "Mac and I can find a hotel to stay in tonight, and in the morning, I'm taking him back to the city. I can't ruin this place for you. I'll be fine staying at the brownstone for a little while longer, I promise." I can't help my rambling as I try and sort out the next steps in my head.

Milo lets out a low growl as he briefly turns to look at me before focusing back on the road. "No."

"Excuse me?"

"Goddammit, woman, you're so infuriating," he says in a raised voice. "I'm doing this all for you...can't you see that? I love you. I want to share my sanctuary with you, to give you the time you need to say goodbye to Mac. Regardless of what happens, we'll both be dealing with the aftermath of these coming weeks for years to come. Why don't we worry about the future once it gets here? After everything I've put you through, please let me do this."

I can't seem to find it in me to continue this argument, nor do I want to.

"Okay. Thank you," I murmur.

I'm sitting on the edge of my seat as we turn onto a private drive. We're greeted by a white fence lining both sides of the road, with fields as far as the eye can see and a dusting of snow covering the ground.

I'm in awe as we drive up to the picturesque colonial home ahead with a gray stone exterior and black shutters. Two massive white pillars frame the glass-paneled front door. It's much bigger than I had envisioned. I imagined we'd be staying in a quaint cottage with the bare necessities. My heart hammers in my chest, even though I feel a sense of peace I haven't felt in years.

We pull through a circular stone drive featuring a fountain in the center, surrounded by a circle of bushes. The landscaping must look absolutely stunning in the spring and summer when the foliage is thriving.

I grin when I see that every window of the house is adorned with an evergreen wreath, accented with red and green berry sprays and pinecones.

This may not be someone's primary residence, but it feels like a real home—more so than my parents' brownstone has since my mom passed. I'm glad that Mac and I will be staying here instead.

As soon as we're parked, the front door swings open and a short woman with long black hair braided down her back comes running down the steps. This must be Roxanne, the estate manager Milo spoke so fondly of. He mentioned that she was in her early seventies, but looking at her now, I wouldn't have guessed she was a day over fifty.

I watch their initial interaction closely as I step out of the SUV. I'm surprised to see Milo rushing over to meet Roxanne at the bottom of the stairs, lifting her into the air as he hugs her.

"Roxanne, it's been too long. It's so good to see you," he says with enthusiasm. "Thanks for accommodating us on such short notice, especially with Thanksgiving only a few weeks away. I hope we're not disrupting any big plans."

"Oh, hush now. Don't be ridiculous." She waves him off with her hand. "You know I haven't had big plans since the 70s. Now those were the days."

Milo lets out a full-on belly laugh, which seems to please Roxanne.

"I sometimes forget why I like you so much," Milo teases. "That is, until I come back to visit."

My mouth drops in shock, losing track of their conversation.

I haven't seen this particular side of Milo since we were teenagers. I'm not sure what happened to my brooding grump, but I love this tender and kind version of him. It's how he treated my mom, and I bet it's similar to how he interacts with Eloisa.

I'd say it's comparable to why I gravitated toward Mac, longing for someone to take the place of my absent father. Even before he left me behind for good, Harrison Dunham was never active in my life, creating a permanent, gaping hole in my heart. It might sound cliché, but Mac has filled a void for me, and I'm grateful to him for that.

"You must be Olivia. It's such a pleasure to meet you, my dear." I'm pulled from my daydreaming by Roxanne's touch as she gives me a warm embrace. "I'm glad you've come to stay."

When she pulls back to get a better look at me, I find she has the kindest eyes, full of warmth and light. I see now why Milo suggested we come here. He knew I would appreciate someone like Roxanne to get me through the next few weeks since I can't have Jane here with me.

He's right, he still knows me better than I know myself, and I'm not sure how I feel about that.

"Thank you. We're very grateful for your hospitality, especially given the circumstances," I say solemnly.

"Of course, my dear." She lowers her head in sadness. "I'm so sorry for what you're going through. I've suffered through a similar loss, and it's never easy. My dear husband, Frank, passed away five years ago. Near the end, he needed total care, which was difficult to watch. I've already told Milo, and I'll tell you the same, I'm here to help however I can."

I'm touched by her words and have to force the tears back, refusing to start crying before we even step inside.

"Thank you," I croak out.

She gives me one last squeeze before turning her attention back to Milo.

"Where on earth is Sirius? I've missed that sweet boy."

Just then, the dog in question comes barreling out of the SUV, jumping straight into Roxanne's arms, giving her a big lick on the cheek in greeting.

"Oh goodness, I've missed you too, boy." She pulls out a dog treat from her coat pocket and holds it out in the palm of her hand. Sirius wastes no time gobbling it up.

I pivot back to face the car and see that Milo already has Mac in his arms and is heading straight for the house. Roxanne jogs ahead to lead the way inside. After licking his lips one last time to make sure no crumbs were missed, Sirius sprints to catch up, and I tail behind, taking in the view.

When I step foot inside the foyer, I'm stunned speechless.

The first thing I see is a grand staircase paired with naturally light, hardwood steps. Cornflower-blue Toile de Jouy wallpaper adorns the walls, matching perfectly with the impeccably detailed crown molding embellishing the ceiling and baseboards.

I understand why Eloisa and Pike instantly fell in love with this place…it's pure magic. The interior is gorgeous, and the calming ambiance would make anyone want to come and stay forever.

As I make my way down the hall toward the sound of Sirius barking, I can't help but take a peek inside the rooms along the way.

To my right is a library with two leather chesterfield couches placed in the middle of the space, and three of the walls are lined with white floor-to-ceiling bookshelves filled to the brim with antique books. A rolling ladder that is attached to the ceiling rests against one of the upper shelves. The wall on the far side of the room is covered in a light blue paisley print, and a three-pane window in the center filters in a ray of sunlight. I've just decided this is my favorite room in the house, even though it's the only one I've seen so far.

Farther down the hall to the left, I pass a formal dining room, the decor giving it a casual feel. The walls are painted a light gray, and a grandfather clock rests in the far corner, its steady ticking echoing quietly in the room. The four-seater solid oak table in the center of the room with black-and-white floral, cushion-backed chairs makes me smile.

Even in this grand space, a functional table was included instead of incorporating something grandiose simply because it would be aesthetically pleasing.

I get to the end of the hall and turn to the right, where I can hear Roxanne talking. I enter a cozy living room with three large windows facing the backyard. There's a dusting of snow, but I can still make out the brick pathway leading to a garden with several fountains placed throughout.

I pause when my gaze flicks to the hospital bed in the room, positioned so the occupant can look outside, similar to the setup at the brownstone.

A square table nearby is neatly lined with Mac's medicines, his copy of *Oliver Twist*, and a water cup with a straw. Mac is lying in bed, surrounded by several plush pillows, his wool blanket covering his legs. Sirius has made himself right at home between Mac's feet, and both are already snoring away.

I look around the room and pause when I see a Christmas tree in the corner decorated with bright lights and red and white ornaments, dozens of neatly wrapped presents underneath. The mantel on the stone fireplace is lined with stockings that read *Milo, Liv, Sirius,* and *Mac.*

There's no question that Milo orchestrated this, creating a similar setup to what I had when my mom was sick all those years ago—a chance to spend one last holiday season with Mac since he most likely won't make it to Christmas.

I don't understand how Milo made this happen overnight, but it means more to me than he'll ever know. He might have been mostly absent when my mom was sick, but he's making an effort now, and I'm not sure how to process that.

My chest tightens, and I can't catch my breath as I rush from the room. I don't want Mac or Roxanne to see me like this.

The gravity of our situation has suddenly hit me, and I can't ward off the looming panic attack creeping in. I get halfway down the hall before I'm too dizzy to move forward.

This can't be happening.

I sink to the ground and bring my legs up close to my chest. The walls are closing in around me, and there is nowhere for me to escape. I find myself rocking back and forth.

No, no, no.

The hurt seeping from my chest won't go away, and it seems there is nothing I can do to stop it now. I can usually detect when a panic attack is coming on, and that's when I do my breathing exercises, but this time, it came out of nowhere, so I wasn't able to prepare.

I squeeze my eyes shut as I try to find an escape from the madness.

"Liv!" I vaguely hear Milo calling out my name, but I'm too far gone to respond.

I can hear myself continuing to chant, "No," repeatedly, but I can't stop myself.

Milo's never seen me in the middle of a panic attack before. They didn't start until after I lost Hope, triggered by the onslaught of multiple traumatic experiences I experienced in rapid succession.

Milo scoops me up in his muscular arms, and I instinctively wrap my hands around his corded neck, desperate to feel him close. I snuggle deep into his chest, embracing the feeling of being wrapped tightly in a safe cocoon.

I recall my therapist telling me that if I ever find myself trapped in the middle of a panic attack, I should use my senses to help ground myself. I've never tried it before, but I'm desperate to escape the sensation of being shut inside a box that's getting smaller and smaller. I take a shuddering breath as I try to focus.

I concentrate on inhaling the scent of cinnamon, pine, and smoke coming from Milo. He hasn't had a cigarette since he picked me up this morning, and the smell is fainter than usual. I listen to the creak of the floorboards as Milo wordlessly climbs up the stairs to the second-floor landing. My ears pick up the squeak of a door as we move through a room, and a faint rustling as I'm gently laid down on something soft. I brush my cheek against the plush material as I'm pulled back into Milo's chest as he spoons me from behind.

I finally get the courage to pry my eyes open and slowly blink, keenly aware that we're lying on a king-sized bed covered with a white down comforter.

Using my senses to reorient myself is starting to work, but I'm still gasping for air and having difficulty regulating my breathing.

"Liv, can you take a deep breath for me?" Milo asks softly. "Like this: Breathe in for one, two, three, four, five. Breathe out for one, two, three, four, five."

Milo guides me through the same exercise that my therapist taught me. I've used it hundreds of times, yet right now, it feels as if it were the first, and I'm grateful for his guidance as he coaches me through one breath at a time.

"You're doing well. Let's do it again," he praises, encouraging me to continue.

I nod as I take another deep breath, counting out loud with Milo. "One, two, three, four, five..."

We repeat the routine several times, and at some point, my breathing finally evens out until I have total control over my body again. I don't move, not ready for Milo to let me go.

"How often do you have panic attacks?" Milo asks from behind.

"Every few months, but not as many as I used to," I admit.

"I'm sorry, Liv." He nuzzles his nose into my neck.

"How did you know what to do?" I ask curiously.

"Pike suffers from panic attacks too. The first time I witnessed him having one, we had just finished up a standard board meeting, nothing out of the ordinary. We were in his office, and he suddenly collapsed to the ground. Thankfully, Richard, my assistant, knew what to do and was able to talk me through how to help him."

"I'm really glad you don't think something is wrong with me."

"I could never think that. We all have our own way of coping with stress, and this is your body's way of managing it. There is no shame in that," he says with sincerity.

"Thank you, Milo. I think I got overwhelmed when I saw the Christmas tree and decorations and remembered that they represent that Mac won't be around much longer."

"Damn. I'm so sorry. I didn't realize it might be a trigger. I just wanted to do something special for you."

"Hey"—I tilt my head back to look at him—"I appreciate the sentiment. It means the world that Mac can experience one last Christmas, and you made that possible. I know you didn't do it for him, but I'm grateful for the gesture regardless."

"Anything for you, Stardust," he says before placing a gentle kiss on my lips. "Now, why don't you close your eyes and get some rest?"

"What about Mac?"

"Roxanne can sit with him for a little while, okay?"

"Okay," I mumble, fighting the urge to fall asleep.

Within seconds, my eyes flutter shut, and I barely hear as Milo gently whispers, "I love you, Liv," in my ear.

I don't say it back, unable to form the words as sleep drags me under.

There's no question that I love him back—I've never stopped. But I can't say those three little words out loud until

I know he's here for the long haul and won't walk away from me again.

I'm so tired of being left alone.

That's the last thought running through my mind as I fall into a peaceful slumber, wrapped tightly in the warmth of Milo's arms.

There's nowhere else I'd rather be.

Chapter Twenty

MILO
Present Day—November

I HOLD TIGHTLY TO LIV as her breathing evens out. Her hands slowly lose their grip on my arms as she finally drifts off to sleep.

I lie next to her for a while, afraid of disrupting her if I move. I forgot how much I'd missed having her next to me. I've had insomnia since I moved to Vegas, and the one variable that has been missing is Liv.

However, right now, sleep is the furthest thing from my mind as I think back to when I found her curled up in the middle of the hallway floor.

I had just gotten back inside from bringing our luggage in from the car and was shocked to find her in that state. She was rocking back and forth with her eyes squeezed shut. I dropped the suitcases I was holding and rushed to her side, knowing from experience that she was having a panic attack.

I feel guilty, knowing I'm partly to blame. I thought it would be a meaningful gesture to decorate the living room for the holidays like Liv did when her mom was sick. When I called Roxanne to see if she could make it happen before we arrived, she was thrilled to lend a helping hand. It hadn't occurred to me it might bring up painful memories for Liv, especially during this time of year.

My head is pounding, and I feel like I was struck by a bus. I slip my arm out from underneath Liv as I slide off the bed. I watch as she rolls over to the empty space I vacated, subconsciously grabbing my pillow, squeezing it to her chest.

Even in her sleep, she's searching for me.

I feel a twinge of guilt, leaving her alone in bed like I did all those years ago.

This time is different.

I'm only going outside for a few minutes.

But what happens when Mac is gone? Where will that leave Liv and me?

Once I'm sure she's still sound asleep, I slip from the room and head downstairs, grabbing my coat hanging on the rack in the corner of the foyer before heading out the front door. It's early evening, but the sun is already setting, causing a frigid chill.

I pull a cigarette from my jacket pocket and light up. The second I let out my first puff, I instantly feel the stress melt away. I savor the sensation of relief after the near-constant turmoil I've battled since returning to New York.

"If you think any harder, your head might explode, and that would be a bitch to clean up."

I turn to find Roxanne stepping out onto the porch. She's wrapped tightly in her black parka, wearing snow boots. She reaches her hand out in my direction, and without a word, I know exactly what she wants. I pull out another cigarette and place it in her palm, giving her a light when she's ready.

The first time we met in person, she caught me having a smoke out here. I braced myself for a long lecture about my life choices, but instead, it turned out we shared the same vice.

"Is Olivia all right?" Roxanne asks, likely curious since she came out of the living room earlier just as I was carrying Liv up the stairs.

"Physically, she'll be fine. I'm more concerned about her emotional state. She's exhausted. It's clear she's worn herself to the bone since Mac's diagnosis, and I don't think she's taken a break since. She's always been the selfless type, taking on the role of caregiver for her loved ones even when she's on her last leg with nothing left to give. She doesn't think I know, but when her mom first got sick, she would sneak down to her room and watch over her throughout the night. It's in her nature to care for others, regardless of her own well-being."

I lean against one of the pillars on the porch, taking another drag of my cigarette as Roxanne silently observes. I've found her to be a great confidant over the years, and I call her regularly since I'm usually only able to make it up here in person once a year.

"I'm conflicted, and there's nothing I can do about it," I tell her. "It still hurts to see how close Liv and Mac are. And now I have to come to terms with the fact that the man I hate is right inside that house." I point in Mac's direction for emphasis. "A house that is special to me. The only reason he's here is because Liv made the choice to include him in her life, and for some reason, I can't watch her suffer any more than she already has. To be honest, I have doubts that we'll be able to move past all this once Mac is gone."

I haven't openly admitted those feelings out loud until now, and I'm relieved to get them off my chest. From the looks of it, Roxanne isn't pleased, a stoic expression on her face.

There's no guessing what's going through her head, though I'm about to find out. She's never hesitated to give me the cold, hard truth, even when I'd prefer she didn't.

"Milo, I like to consider us friends. I'd even say we're besties, like the cool kids say nowadays." I chuckle at her reference. "You know me well enough to appreciate that I'm a straightforward gal. I always call things exactly how I see them. So, let's be honest.

"Take it from someone who's lived well past her prime. When it comes to Olivia, it's time to let bygones be bygones. It's simple—forgive her, and move on." I'm about to argue, but the stern expression on Roxanne's face makes me think twice. "If you're so intent on making a list of the ways she's wronged you, then it's only fair that you make the same list for all the ways you've wronged her. There's no question that your list would be far lengthier than hers."

I've never thought about it that way before. I've been so focused on Liv's betrayal that I forgot I've done the same to her.

"When you arrived in Las Vegas, you were lucky that Pike and Eloise welcomed you with open arms. Yes, you've worked hard for your success, but from day one, you had their unwavering support." Roxanne briefly pauses to take another drag of her cigarette. "Olivia didn't have a single person in her corner after you were gone—*not one*." Disappointment rolls off Roxanne's voice in waves. "Despite that, aside from defending Mac, has Olivia shown any ill will toward you since you came back a few weeks ago?" She tilts her head, examining me as she waits for my admission.

I hesitantly shake my head, ashamed to acknowledge I've treated Liv poorly. However, that's not good enough for Roxanne, who's ready to keep dishing out my well-deserved lecture. I'm beginning to regret my frequent candid conversations with her right about now, knowing she's this comfortable with telling me how shitty of a person I am.

"The woman I met today is a pillar of strength. She has put her entire career on hold to care for an ailing man who's not biologically related to her. She even put aside her own pain and suffering to make sure you're comfortable in this situation, despite her being the one staying in an unfamiliar house, preparing to say goodbye to someone she cares for unconditionally. Hell, if I were in her shoes, I wouldn't be nearly as forgiving. Not when you show up unannounced, ready to throw me to the wolves simply because I've shown compassion to someone you deem unworthy," Roxanne states. "Trust me, she's a gem, and she's going to slip through your fingers if you let her."

I flinch at the sound of that. I don't like it...not one bit.

"It's funny, Milo. During one of our yearly drinking pity parties, I specifically recall you saying Olivia was your only source of sunlight. Tell me, what attributes does she have that made you call her that?" Roxanne pauses for effect but doesn't give me enough time to respond. "If I had to guess, I'd say her kindness, empathy, and affection for those she cares about. Would she be the person you fell in love with if she didn't treat Mac with compassion, or show him the same generosity she showed you when you lived with her and her mom? Olivia saw your father, a man hurting just as much as she was, and wanted to be there for him. You should be celebrating her devotion, not tearing her down because of it. Don't be the reason her light is snuffed out, the thing that makes her who she is. You won't like watching it disappear for good." To emphasize her point, Roxanne drops her cig to the ground, smashing it with the toe of her boot.

"Take it from someone who lost the love of their life," she says somberly. "It's been five long years since Frank passed, and not a day goes by that I don't miss him. He was my rock, my protector, and my soulmate. There will never be another person, career, or amount of money that could ever replace him or take away the void he left behind. Are you ready to lose out on the second chance of your once-in-a-lifetime love because she's a good and caring person? Nothing she has done has been out of malice, spite, or revenge. Can you honestly say the same?"

No, I can't, and I'm ashamed to admit it.

The only reason I came back to New York was to find a way to make both Liv and Mac pay for their wrongdoings. I wouldn't have made the effort if Liv hadn't been a part of the equation.

I was convinced that my anger toward her was justified because she was close to Mac. Even after I found out about the miscarriage, I had a difficult time accepting their relationship. Until now, I've begrudgingly put my feelings aside, convincing myself I was doing Liv a favor.

Roxanne has made me realize that's complete bullshit.

While I've been busy playing the martyr, Liv has put her well-being on the back burner while juggling my temperamental ego and caring for Mac.

I lean against the pillar behind me, feeling like a complete jackass.

"Shit, Roxanne," I mumble. "It's safe to say that you've rightfully put me in my place."

"One last thing for you to think about," she says. "Picture yourself a year from now. Can you envision your life without Olivia?" I open my mouth to speak, but she stops me before I can reply. "There's no need to answer me. It's something you should contemplate over the next few weeks while you're here." Roxanne gives me one last sympathetic smile before walking down the front steps, trudging toward a pathway alongside the house.

"There's a pot of chili on the stove. Make sure Olivia gets some when she wakes up. I'm going to my cottage for a few hours, but I'll be back later tonight," she announces. "Tell Olivia I'll take the night shift and sit with Mac. She needs some rest. Besides, I don't trust you enough to spend an entire night with him. Who knows what you might be tempted to do?"

"Wait. If you're leaving," I call out as she keeps walking, "who's going to sit with Mac until Liv wakes up?"

"You are."

Wait, what?

She moves out of view before I have a chance to respond.

Of course Roxanne would do this to me. That's what I get for sharing my true feelings and confessing I hate the man. Instead of showing me any empathy, she goes out of her way to make sure I'm forced to spend time with him...alone.

Despite the frigid temperature, I stay out on the porch until I can't feel my fingers, doing my best to avoid the inevitable. When I can't stand the cold any longer, I begrudgingly go inside.

I check on Liv first. She's still napping peacefully, curled up against my pillow. I'm tempted to wake her so she can watch after Mac, but as I look down at her features, softened by sleep, I can't bring myself to do it. There's no question I've been a constant thorn in her side this past week. The least I can do is give her some time to rest.

I hesitantly go downstairs and find myself standing at the threshold of the living room where Mac is staying. It's dark, except for the lone lamp on the bedside table and the glow of the Christmas tree in the corner.

I'm relieved to find Mac asleep. Sirius raises his head off Mac's lap to see who dares to disrupt his nap but lies back down without so much as a greeting when he sees that it's me. I'm inconsequential when Mac is in the room.

Go figure my own dog prefers the company of the man I despise. *Everyone* is Team Mac these days.

I take this opportunity to observe him without any disruptions. The few times we've been in the same room since I showed up at the hospital, Liv has been there, and I've either been screaming in his face or ignoring him.

I appreciate the chance to get a better look without being scrutinized. He's facing me, so I have an unobstructed view of his gaunt features. His cheeks are sunken in, his lips are dry from dehydration, and I can hear the crackling pauses between each breath.

He's lying in the middle of the standard-sized hospital bed, but he's so frail that there's at least an extra foot of space on either side of him. The man in front of me can barely lift his head, let alone be a worthy adversary. As I continue to watch him, I determine that when all is said and done, I can't take pleasure in tormenting the dying man before me...not anymore.

Things might have been different when I came back, but now, all I can think about when I look at him is Liv and the grief she's being forced to endure as she watches him deteriorate before her eyes. I would give anything to take away her heartbreak, even if it means having to play nice with Mac until he's gone.

Roxanne is right that Liv has been nothing but selfless, and it's time I take a page out of her playbook. Which means I have to put her first—*without* an ulterior motive.

I'm staring at Mac and realize too late that his eyes have fluttered open. He lets out a hoarse laugh when he sees me standing in the shadowed doorway.

"Have you come to finish me off?" he asks, his voice scratchy from underuse. He tilts his head, trying to get a better look at the man who used to call him dad. "Fair warning: you'd be doing me a favor. Dying from cancer is a bitch. I give it zero out of five stars." He chuckles at his own joke. "If you want to ensure maximum pain and suffering, you might want to hold off on giving me the axe just yet. Or better yet, make those heavenly pain meds disappear. Those are a godsend every four hours, so I suggest you dispose of them if you want me writhing in agony until the bitter end."

I rapidly blink as I stare down at Mac. I'm perplexed by his bleak humor. He's near death's door, in the same room as his estranged son who wishes him nothing but harm, yet he's still cracking jokes.

Who is this man?

I make an impromptu decision and move farther into the room, making myself at home in the fabric lounge chair Roxanne moved next to Mac's side earlier.

As I lean back in my seat, I'm aware of him clocking my every move, unsure how to react to my uncharacteristic behavior. It seems I've unknowingly initiated a silent peace treaty. No doubt I'll have to grapple with the repercussions of that decision later on, but for now, I'm taking this minute-by-minute.

"The house is beautiful, and the Christmas decor is a nice touch," Mac says. I can tell that every word causes him immense pain, but it doesn't stop him from speaking.

"It's all for Liv," I say sternly, not wanting to give him the idea that I'm trying to reconcile. "Her parents' brownstone holds nothing but painful memories, and I wanted her to have a place to come where she could share your last days on this earth in peace. She deserves that."

He doesn't bat an eyelash at my bluntness. He's accepted his fate, and seems anxious to move on.

"You're right, Liv does deserve the very best," he agrees. "Where is she?"

"She wasn't feeling well. I think this was all too much for her," I say, gesturing around the room. "She's resting upstairs, but she'll come to check on you as soon as she wakes up."

I'm not about to tell the ailing old man that Liv had a panic attack. If I did, he'd demand I take him up to console her.

"She carries the weight of the world on her shoulders, Milo," he rasps out. "You have every right to hate me, but please don't take it out on Liv anymore."

I respect him for standing up for Liv the best he can in his condition. "Why do you think I'm here, old man? I'm doing my best to put aside my feelings toward you because that's what Liv wants."

"You love her, don't you?" Mac says confidently.

"I have loved that woman since the first time I saw her," I proudly admit. "She was there the day Marie told me that Ma died. She's the only reason I pushed through when things got hard. I know I've put her through the wringer, but I'm doing my best to make up for it...hence why you're here."

"I'm glad to hear that," he grits out before leaning his head back against his pillow. His eyes start to droop shut.

It seems our short but intense conversation has completely tired him out. It's then that I spot the familiar copy of *Oliver Twist* sitting on the edge of the bedside table.

"You still have this old thing?" I ask as I gently pick it up to investigate.

Mac nods. "Of course I do. Your Ma gave it to me. I'll always cherish it." He looks longingly down at the well-loved novel in my hand.

I clench my teeth at his sentimental reaction. I don't understand how he could treat this replaceable possession with so much care, yet willingly gamble—and lose—with Ma's life. It doesn't make any sense. I want to lash out and demand answers. Or better yet, rip up the book he considers precious while he watches from afar, unable to stop me.

I surprise myself when I don't do any of those things. Instead, I do the most unexpected thing of all: I let the comment slide.

For Liv.

"Would you like me to read you a chapter while we wait for Liv to wake up?" The words feel like sandpaper coming from my mouth, but I force them out anyway.

If I have to spend time with Mac, I might as well do something to distract myself. I'm stunned that I'm sitting in the same room as the man I swore I'd never face again unless it was to exact retribution.

But here we are.

Mac gives me a weary look before nodding.

As I crack open the tattered book, I pause when I see Ma's handwritten note inside the cover.

> *Mac,*
>
> *You might come from humble beginnings, but your future is entirely up to you. I can't wait to achieve our dreams together. I love you.*
>
> *Happy birthday!*
>
> *Jada*

A lone tear makes its way down my face at the realization that Ma once touched this very page. I brush the parchment with my fingertips, imagining her pressing pen to paper as she wrote.

I was devastated when I found out that all the children's books Ma had inscribed to me over the years before her passing had been donated shortly after Mac's arrest. I remember being enraged that I had lost something so meaningful, and yet somehow, this lone book survived, and I can't help but feel thankful for that.

I can understand now why Mac cherishes the book, even if I don't think he deserves the keepsake.

I force myself to flip to the first page, and as I begin to read, I feel a little lighter, knowing I'm holding the same book Ma held years ago, making it possible to feel close to her even though she's passed.

Chapter Twenty-One

OLIVIA
Past—Twelfth Grade

I LET OUT A STIFLED groan as I stretch out my arms and legs, only to discover that my entire body is deliciously sore.

Wait, what?

I throw my hands up to my face in embarrassment.

Oh gosh, now I remember. I had sex with Milo last night.

I. Had. Sex. With. Milo. Last. Night. What is wrong with me?

I practically begged him to have sex with me before *trying* to seduce him with my clumsy attempt at a striptease—it was subpar at best. And let's not forget that I laughed…at his dick. Right as we were about to have sex for the very first time, a moment we had both anticipated for years. I looked him right in the face and literally cackled.

Nice, Olivia. Real nice.

I wonder how loud we were.

What will Mom—wait...Mom...she's gone. Her funeral was yesterday morning. I had sex with my best friend the same day that I laid my mom to rest. What was I thinking?

A flood of guilt rushes through me like a freight train. How could I have been so stupid? Milo and I were supposed to wait to take our relationship to the next level until we graduated high school and moved out. In all the romcoms I've watched, it never turns out well for the couples who sleep together prematurely.

It doesn't help that Milo has been acting as though I don't exist these last few months, and now suddenly we're intimate? Talk about an awkward situation.

Why did I do it?

I was desperate to numb the pain and despair I felt, lying in bed, knowing my mom was gone and that there wasn't anything I could do to bring her back.

I need Milo now more than ever, and I shouldn't have jeopardized our relationship for a brief moment of reprieve. I still can't believe I pleaded with him to sleep with me...

The longer I lie here, the less I regret what we did—as long as Milo feels the same way.

Maybe this can be our outlet, our way of coping with the loss we've suffered. In fact, Milo owes me a repeat—he was that good. I inhale deeply, peeking out between my fingers, afraid of what I'll do if I find him lying next to me, naked. In the past, to avoid jumping each other sooner than planned, it was one of our rules that we always sleep with pajamas on.

I pause when I find the other side of my bed empty, and when I cautiously reach out to touch the mattress, it's ice cold.

I bolt up in bed, reaching for my phone on the nightstand. It's only nine a.m., and I don't have any calls or texts.

Where could he have gone? Maybe he couldn't fall asleep and decided to go back to his room. I don't blame him; I tend to toss and turn at night.

Or worse…what if he's planning to go back to ignoring me?

Not happening.

"Milo," I call out, hoping he can hear me from his room.

No answer.

"Milo," I say a little louder.

Still no response. He must still be asleep.

I climb out of bed, wrapping the comforter around me to keep warm.

I take a quick pit stop in the bathroom on my way to see Milo and am mortified when I find mascara streaks running down my cheeks and my hair shooting out in all directions. No wonder he left me alone in bed. I'm a complete wreck this morning.

I take a minute to wash my face, removing the residual makeup. As I reach up to grab a towel from the hook by the sink to dry off, I pause midway when I notice that Milo's toothbrush is missing from its holder.

That's odd.

Maybe it was old, and he threw it away as a reminder to replace it with a new one.

It might sound logical, but I can't help the nagging voice in my head as I casually walk over to the shower to find his razor missing too. My hands start to shake as I slowly walk toward the closed door to his bedroom. I don't understand why he would shut me out again, not after what we did last night.

"Milo," I say with a shaky voice. "Can we talk?"

All I hear is my own heartbeat, only silence coming from the other side of the door.

I'm trembling as I turn the knob, pleased to discover it's unlocked. I push the door open to find Milo's bed perfectly made, which isn't normal. He *never* makes his own bed. I've always been the one to do it as we're rushing out the door to school each morning.

I march over to his dresser, blinking my eyes in disbelief when I find the empty picture frame sitting in front of me. The replacement photo I had made of his mom after he destroyed the original isn't inside anymore. I flip the frame over, tearing off the back to make sure it didn't somehow get lost. Clearly, I'm not thinking straight.

I rush to his closet. It's still jam-packed full of the clothes Mom purchased for him over the years, but his favorite Vans hoodie is missing.

Am I losing my mind?

I rush over to his nightstand and come to a stop when I see his phone sitting on the surface.

I don't understand. Why would he leave? There's no way he would have left after what we did last night.

Right?

Not after we buried my mom. He, of all people, knows that I need him here with me. I was there for him when his mom died, so naturally, he'd do the same for me.

Wouldn't he?

Maybe he ran out of cigarettes and went out to the bodega down the street to get more. Or wanted some time to cool off and went for a run without me.

I'm in denial as I storm around the room, throwing pillows and clothes haphazardly to the floor, desperate to find a note or any sort of explanation of where he went and when he plans on coming home to me.

The harsh realization hits me like a lightning bolt.

He's never coming home. Last night was his way of saying goodbye.

I wipe away angry tears as I walk out, slamming the door behind me. I crumple to the floor outside his room, my back pressed up against the doorframe as I curl up on the cold, hard ground. My chest feels tight, and I can't breathe.

Please don't let any of this be real.

I rock back and forth, begging for relief from the stone-cold reality that is now my life.

Come back, Milo. I need you.

My silent prayer falls on deaf ears as my eyes fall shut.

"Olivia, what are you doing on the floor? Get up this instant!"

Thinking Milo is back, I'm sorely disappointed when I'm met with my father's beady eyes boring into me. I must have fallen asleep on the floor outside Milo's room. Father's primary concern should be why I was passed out on the ground. Instead, he only cares that I'm sprawled out on the floor in an unladylike fashion.

He's dressed impeccably, sporting a three-piece gray Armani suit, a cobalt tie, and his hair is slicked back in its typical fashion.

He hasn't said a word to me since my mom's funeral, and even then, he only acknowledged me when he dragged me around the funeral home to greet each of his investors, clients, and so-called friends, as if I should have been honored that they made an appearance to pay their respects to Mom.

She hated every single one of them.

Not once has Father asked about my well-being. Not seeming to understand or even care that I've lost my anchor, my North Star, my everything.

Mom was my entire world until Milo came along, and Father knows that. He's ignored me most of my life, except to tell me when I'm doing something he disapproves of.

When he moved back into the house after Mom got sick, I hoped we could reconcile. That his fatherly instincts would finally kick in, and he'd be there for me during this difficult time. I was wrong. You can't teach an old dog new tricks, and Father is set in his ways.

"Father, what's going on? Where are you going?" I ask, noticing the briefcase in his hand.

"I'm going back to Paris. What do you think?" he snaps, rolling his eyes. "Now that your mother is gone, there's no point in me staying around. I've been gone for far too long as it is."

My stomach drops right out from under me.

He can't be serious. I gaze up at him, hoping to find a trace of sympathy, or for him to extend an invitation to stay with him in France. I'm sorely disappointed when all I see is an annoyed expression on his face, clearly put out that this conversation hasn't ended yet.

He's dead serious. He's walking out on me too.

"I don't understand," I say. "Mom's gone. What about Milo and me? We don't graduate until May. You're going to leave us here by ourselves?" The questions flow freely from my mouth, afraid I won't get another chance to ask them.

"Olivia, don't be naive. You'll be eighteen in June...you don't need a babysitter. It's time you learned to take care of yourself, so why not start now?" he asks sincerely.

I'm stunned speechless. He truly believes every word coming out of mouth.

"Besides, that worthless street urchin should be out of your way soon enough."

My mouth drops open in shock at his words. "I'm sorry...what did you just say?"

"I made sure *that* boy knew he was no longer welcome here now that Marie is gone. He's taken advantage of this family enough. When I confronted him yesterday, it seemed like he had already made up his mind to leave—thank God, or I would have had to kick him out onto the street."

Milo knew he was leaving when he came to my room last night? He slept with me even though he knew he wasn't staying?

"Olivia, are you listening to me?" Father barks out. I jerk my head up to focus back on the man towering over me. "I need to leave for the airport so I don't miss my flight."

He turns to leave, but I call out to him with one final plea. "Wait. You knew Milo was leaving, and yet you're still choosing to leave me too? I just lost my mom. Did you think to ask me if I wanted you to stay?" I ask in disbelief.

"Honest to God, Olivia, how can you be so daft?" Father spits out as he paces in front of me like a caged animal. "Do you think I asked to be a father?" he shouts in my face. "Of course I fucking didn't! It was your mother's one stipulation. She agreed to marry me if we had a child. I got control over a billion-dollar company; all she got out of it was *you*." He barks out a laugh. "There's no question I got the better end of the deal. I hate to say it, but you're rather disappointing."

I blink up at him with a hollow expression, waiting to wake up from the nightmare that is my life. Parents don't say these kinds of things to their children, do they? Especially not after said kid has lost their mom and is grieving her loss.

How could Harrison be so cruel? I don't have the heart to call him Father…not after what he said.

"I have to leave now," he snaps at me before starting down the stairs. "Don't worry, Olivia," he calls out. "Your mom left you with a substantial trust fund. You'll never want for anything."

What about a family or love? I'll always want for those things.

"If you happen to need something, call my assistant, and she'll take care of it." He doesn't wait for me to respond. He couldn't care less what I have to say.

I jump at the sound of the front door slamming shut behind him, leaving me all alone once again.

What makes me so unlovable that every single person who means something to me has left me behind?

The days crawl by at a snail's pace, and I find myself trapped in a perpetual state of torment.

I spend my waking hours in a daze, forced to tolerate the constant drone of teachers and the gossipmongers at school. The news about Mom's death and Milo's departure shortly thereafter is now widespread, but I do my best to tune them out.

To avoid confrontation, I spend my lunch hour hiding out in the back stall of the bathroom, a tray full of untouched food on my lap. I avoid eye contact with other students in the halls. I can't stand their looks of pity mixed with curiosity, like I'm a science experiment they can't wait to get their hands on.

Every day that goes by, I fall deeper into the dark hole of depression. My will to live is slowly slipping through my fingers every new day that I'm forced to face alone.

Losing my mom took a heavy toll, a void in my heart that can never be mended. My father leaving me behind for his life in Paris was a reminder that I'm unwanted, unloved, and not worth sticking around for. The final nail in the coffin was when I realized that Milo really isn't coming back.

Even three months later, there are times I'm convinced Milo will decide he's made a terrible mistake and come home to me. Though, in my heart, I know that's not true. There's nothing left for him here but painful memories and his haunted past. If he's found the fresh start he's been searching for, there's no reason to revisit this chapter of his life.

Part of me wants to hate him for what he did.

He knows what it feels like to lose someone, to drown in despair with no chance of escape. Yet, in his darkest moments, he always had my mom and me. I can't comprehend how he could push me aside as if I meant nothing to him, not after he claimed me and vowed to stay by my side no matter what.

It's early April, but there's still a chill in the air as I trudge down the street on my way home from school. I drag myself up the stairs of the brownstone, where I now live alone. When I'm at school, a housekeeper comes to clean and stock the fridge with premade meals, but she's always gone before I get home.

I unlock the front door and stare blankly inside as it creaks open. An empty entryway is the only thing to greet me. I drop my backpack on the ground, stepping over it to climb the stairs. There's no one around to care if I put my things away, so why should I make an effort?

I enter my room, heading straight for the built-in window seat to get a good vantage point of the sky.

I'm surprised to find snow starting to fall gently to the ground, a picture-perfect moment I wish I could share with my mom. She was always my biggest advocate, and if she were here, she'd rush into my room, wrap her arms around me in a warm embrace, and tell me that I'd never be lonely again because she'd always be here with me.

Today is one of those days where I can't find a reason to continue living anymore. There's no one around to care if I get good grades, graduate high school, or become a doctor.

Most importantly, there's no one here to care if I live or die.

I curl up in a ball as I watch the unexpected snow fall, slipping into a restless sleep.

I abruptly wake up with intense cramps in my abdomen. The sharp, white-hot pain shooting through me is pure agony, and I feel something dripping down my legs.

I stumble from my seat to turn the bedside lamp on, reaching between my thighs to investigate. I pull back to find my hand covered in blood. I have no idea what's wrong with me, but I know I need help.

"Milo," I croak out. "Milo, I need you!" I yell a little louder this time, desperate for him to come.

What's taking him so long to respond? Now that I think about it, why am I in my room in the first place? We always sleep in his room, never mine. Something isn't adding up.

"Milo please, something's wrong, I need—" I cut myself off mid-sentence when I remember that he's not here.

No one is.

I'm alone. Utterly and completely alone.

I bend down, bracing myself as another jolt of pain rips through my stomach. I take in a deep breath, forcing myself to think about what to do next.

Realizing I have no car and no one to call, I grab my phone from the nightstand and order a ride share—the only other option I can think of besides calling 911. It's the middle of the night, so I can't imagine it will take long for someone to arrive and take me to the hospital.

I crawl to the closet through the excruciating pain, discarding my pajama pants soaked with blood, replacing them with a clean pair of stretchy sweatpants and a long-sleeved T-shirt Milo didn't take with him. I've gotten into the habit of sleeping in his clothes to help me feel close to him now that he's gone.

I make my way down the two flights of stairs leading to the entryway, slowly and in a great deal of pain, before I make it out the front door, shutting it behind me.

I let out a sigh of relief as my ride pulls up alongside the curb just as I get to the sidewalk. I'm impressed that I made it this far on my own.

I can do this.

After confirming with the middle-aged man that he's my driver, I carefully slide into the backseat to avoid jostling my body, panting heavily as I go.

"You okay, girl?" my driver asks, his voice tinged with concern.

"I'll be fine, but would you mind if we get going? I'm in a bit of a hurry," I say calmly.

The poor man's eyes nearly bug out of his head when he checks his phone and puts two and two together that my destination is the hospital.

I'm about to reassure him that it's not an emergency and he has nothing to worry about when another unrelenting cramp causes me to scream out in agony. I squeeze my eyes shut, doing everything possible to hold back the tears I desperately want to let fall. I'm afraid if the driver sees how much pain I'm in, he'll kick me out of his car and make me wait for an ambulance on the side of a random street in New York City.

I think we're moving, but I can't tell for sure. It sounds like the driver is saying something, but I can't hear him. It feels like I'm in a dark tunnel, and the man's voice is muffled beyond recognition.

I fade in and out of consciousness, slumping down on the seat next to me, my face pressing against the cool leather. I can vaguely hear shouting in the distance, but I can't speak to tell whoever it is to keep it down so I can rest my eyes for a minute.

I find myself falling into a welcome oblivion where my mom isn't dead, my father thinks I'm enough, and Milo is here with me.

Chapter Twenty-Two

MILO
Present Day—December

I'VE BEEN AT THE HOUSE upstate with Liv and Mac for nearly five weeks. The longer we're here, the more the days bleed together.

After witnessing Liv's panic attack and talking with Roxanne, I've come to the stark realization that I can't have one foot in and one foot out anymore. It needs to be all or nothing with Liv. Despite the animosity that lingers when Mac and I are in the same room, I know I've made the right decision. Liv deserves the tranquil farewell she desperately wants with him.

When Marie was sick, I spent most of my time in my room, refusing to watch her slip away. I couldn't cope with the thought of losing her, the residential trauma from Ma's death haunted me. I don't remember who was in and out to help with Marie's care. What I do know for certain is that when Liv wasn't at school, she spent every waking moment at her mom's side, taking on the role of her primary caregiver.

There's no question that I was, and still am, a grade-A asshole.

But the difference now?

When Mac takes his final breath, Liv won't be alone. I'll be there to hold her close as she mourns his loss, to comfort her in the aftermath.

Occasionally, the thought pops into my head that Liv could be the one keeping me together after this is over, but that's complete bullshit. I remind myself that Mac doesn't mean anything to me. He deserves this fate, and I should be happy he'll be gone soon.

So why aren't I then?

As the weeks tick by, we've all been in a perpetual holding pattern. Mac's condition worsens by the day, and there is no telling when will be his last.

During the time we've been here, he's lost the ability to eat by himself, to sit up without assistance, or to speak more than a few words at a time. The more control he loses over bodily functions, the more dependent he becomes. I now see why Liv had hospice coming in as soon as Mac was released from the hospital.

We've quickly fallen into a routine where Liv spends the nights nestled next to Mac in his bed, Sirius curled up at their feet. It's a tight fit, but that doesn't stop them. Liv insists that she stay close enough to monitor Mac's breathing and to be there in case he needs her.

She demands taking the night shift on her own, saying at least one of us should get some rest. However, after tossing and turning during the first couple of nights, I started sneaking downstairs once everyone falls asleep. I camp out in the hallway outside the living room with a pillow and blanket. The need to be close to Liv outweighs a good night's rest.

Every morning, Roxanne comes to the main house to make us breakfast and a big pot of coffee—the primary food group that's kept us all going this past month.

By the time Mac wakes up each morning, I'm waiting at his bedside.

When I discovered his love for Charles Dickens, I got out *The Complete Works of Charles Dickens,* the Gadshill Edition from 1899 that Eloisa stored in the library. Mac and I have since finished reading *Dombey and Son, A Tale of Two Cities,* and are currently making our way through *Great Expectations.*

We avoid any semblance of real conversation, which I appreciate. I'm only there to read to him while Liv gets some rest.

However, Liv must have had the same idea as me because sometimes when I look out into the hall, I catch sight of a sock-clad foot sticking out that looks very similar to hers.

My favorite part of our day is in the early evenings.

While Mac takes his afternoon naps and Roxanne prepares dinner, Liv and I always sneak off to the library and sit together on one of the chesterfield sofas. I lean against the armrest with my legs spread out so Liv can sit against my chest. She reads from the medical journals she found at the bottom of the bookshelves the first week we were here, while I review financial reports and contracts Richard sends me for work.

I treasure each stolen moment of peace with Liv, not knowing how many more we'll have before everything comes crashing down around us.

This afternoon, Liv is determined to switch things up, insisting we go on a jog together. We've both neglected our regular workout routines, and she's craving a sense of normalcy. I was able to keep up with her during our runs back in high school, and I figured we'd both slowed down some as we've gotten older.

I was wrong. *Very wrong.*

"Come on, old man. Can't you keep up?" Liv shouts over her shoulder from up ahead.

Sirius barks in agreement as he stays in step with Liv.

After the first mile, Liv suggested I let her take Sirius's leash, saying that he might appreciate a faster pace than what I was capable of.

She had a good point.

That doesn't mean I didn't give her a nasty scowl before hesitantly handing the leash over. On the other hand, Sirius has been in heaven, savoring the feeling of running in full strides for the first time ever.

We've been going for six miles, and I think I might pass out.

Six. Fucking. Miles.

Has Liv broken a sweat? No.

Have I? Absolutely. I'm sweating like a goddamn pig, even in the middle of winter.

I've been tricked.

"Let's go for a jog," Liv had said.

A jog, my ass.

Let the record show that Liv doesn't jog. She *runs*. Correction: she *sprints*.

While I've gotten slower with age, she's somehow gotten faster. Much faster.

I'm the elderly woman you find power-walking through the mall on a Saturday morning, whereas Liv's a gazelle running through the forest without a care in the world. They don't pair well, especially when the old lady nearly has a heart attack trying to keep up with said gazelle.

I holler when I finally see the house up ahead. The trees along the drive are glistening with ice crystals, and if I wasn't about to cough up a lung, I'd take a moment to appreciate the beautiful scenery in front of me.

I've had quite enough *jogging* for one day. In fact, I've decided there will be no more *jogging* in my future if Liv's invited.

I slow down to a walk as I gulp in the fresh winter air, eager to get inside. I look up to see Liv and Sirius running back to meet me—no doubt coming to brag.

"Hey there, slowpoke. How'd you enjoy your jog?" Liv asks with a smirk on her lips.

"That"—I point to where we came from—"was not a jog. *That* was a goddamn six-mile sprint. If I didn't know any better, I'd say you purposely left me in the dust to prove that you're faster than me."

There's no question that was exactly what she was doing. She's always had a competitive streak, and I forgot how far she'll go to prove her point.

"I didn't *try*, Milo." She brings both hands up to do air quotes. "I am faster—there's no question about it—and Sirius here is my witness. Aren't you, boy?" She bends down to scratch behind his ear as she smirks up at me. "Besides, if you quit smoking, you'll have a better chance of keeping up. You're not getting any younger; it's time you started taking care of yourself," she says in a patronizing tone.

"Excuse me?" I say as I glower in her direction. "You're the one who thinks it's sexy when I smoke. You can't take your eyes off my lips anytime I light up."

It's the truth, and she can't deny it.

"There are plenty of other things you could do that I would find just as sexy." She peruses my body with her eyes, obviously pleased by what she sees. "Besides, you can't force Sirius to jog at a crawl for the rest of his life. The poor thing needs to run at full speed every once in a while."

She looks up at me with a pout on her lips. God, she's sexy as sin when she's tormenting me.

"You're such a smart-ass, Liv. You'd better watch yourself," I say in warning.

Her expression turns wary as she stands up, preparing to back away from me. Before she has a chance, I lunge forward, picking her up and throwing her over my shoulder like a sack of potatoes.

"I'm concerned for your well-being, Liv," I call over my shoulder. "You were running far too fast; I think you need to cool off." I try to mask my voice so she can't sense the grin plastered on my face as I carry her to the snowbank alongside the road a few feet away.

"No! Milo, don't you dare. You put me down this instant," she shrieks, knowing exactly what I have in mind.

Without preamble, I gently toss her back-first into the large pile of snow. She cries out when her body hits the ice-cold snow. That should teach her not to mess with me in the future. Besides, she's got a fleece-lined puffer jacket and thermal leggings on, so she'll survive.

I drop down on top of her, leaning up on my elbows so she has room to breathe.

Liv stares into my eyes with a look of unrestrained lust mixed with shock. It's clear that my closeness turns her on, and I'm glad to know I'm not the only one who's affected. The longer I'm in close quarters with her, the harder it is to restrain myself. I want nothing more than to feel her lithe body pressed against mine without any barriers.

The snow is starting to seep into my jacket sleeves, and, shit, it's cold, but I couldn't care less. The only thing on my mind is Liv. I haven't kissed her since yesterday and am eager to feel her mouth against mine.

I zero in on her plush lips and lean in for a kiss. I'm mere inches away from my target when I'm suddenly pelted with a snowball right to the face.

What the hell?

Before I can gain my bearings, Liv shoves me off of her and I fall back into the snow. As I'm wiping the residual moisture off my face, I see Liv running for her life down the lane toward the house. She lets out her signature cackling laugh, pleased with the prank she pulled. Sirius is right on her tail, turning back to me, letting out a series of sharp barks, warning Liv to hurry up if she wants to make it safely inside before I catch her.

Game on.

I leap up from my place on the ground and sprint toward the house as fast as I can, my screaming lungs long forgotten.

If Liv thinks she's safe, she has another thing coming. I catch her just as she lands on the first step of the porch, wrapping my arms around her before throwing her over my shoulder.

"Milo Leland Covell, stop treating me like cattle!" she screeches as her tiny fists pound furiously against my back.

I pay her no mind as I wave to Roxanne, who's standing on the top step, a cigarette resting between her fingers.

"Good afternoon, Roxanne," I say with a smirk, ignoring the fact that Liv's hanging over my shoulder like a slab of meat. "Do you mind sitting with Mac tonight? I've got to teach this one some manners." I point up at Liv. "She thinks tricking people into going for a six-mile sprint and throwing snowballs in their faces afterward is acceptable behavior. It's appalling if you ask me." I shake my head in mock disappointment.

"Of course. You kids have fun." Roxanne gives me a wink as I stride past her.

I yank the front door open and Sirius slips past me, running down the hall toward his favorite spot at the bottom of Mac's hospital bed.

"Milo! Seriously, let me go," Liv huffs out.

"Shh. You'll wake Mac with all that racket," I tell her. "Besides, I can't put you down. I'm not done with you quite yet."

Without another word, I climb the stairs two at a time, racing to the second-floor master bedroom. The place hasn't gotten much action since we've been here since we both spend most of our nights downstairs.

I can't keep my distance any longer. I'm an addict, desperate for every scrap of attention she'll give me, and the draw I feel toward her is all-consuming.

It's been fifteen miserable years since I've been inside her and felt her body moving in time with my own. There's no guarantee that we'll get another chance to be together undisturbed, so I'm taking advantage of the situation while I can.

As we enter the master bedroom, I slam the door closed behind us. Setting Liv down, I make sure her feet are planted firmly on the ground before letting go. As soon as I release her, she tries to dart past me, but I grab hold of her midsection, pushing her up against the door. I press my hands firmly against the doorframe on either side of her head, trapping her in.

"I told you, Liv, I can't let you go. Not yet," I murmur, pressing my nose against her neck. I inhale her sweet scent, now mixed with sweat and endorphins. "You're irresistible. You always have been," I say with reverence.

"What are you doing?" she whispers, a hint of curiosity in her voice.

"Something I've waited fifteen long years to do again."

I brush my nose tenderly against hers once, twice, a third time. A show of the affection and devotion I feel for her.

I whisper against her lips, so quietly that she has to stay completely still so she doesn't miss my words, "Do you remember what you said to me the night we had sex? When I came into your room to check on you?"

She innocently shakes her head, feigning ignorance. "Refresh my memory," she breathes out.

There's no question she knows exactly what I'm referring to.

"I believe your exact words were, 'I need you.'"

I tip her chin up with my thumb and index finger, making sure I have her undivided attention. "All these years later, the tables have turned. I'm the one pleading with you. I need you more than I need air." I pause, gazing into her mesmerizing green eyes, watching as they blink back at me in shock. "You are my sole source of sunlight, the only thing in my life worth living for. I've waited far too long to bask in your light. I need you, Stardust—all of you."

I wait with bated breath for Liv's reply. The silence is deafening, the fear of the unknown creeping in around me. I won't pressure her to do anything she isn't ready for, but I will be sorely disappointed if she denies me now.

I'm pleasantly surprised when Liv closes the distance between us. She gets on her tippy-toes, slanting her lips across mine with ease. Her tongue slips inside my mouth, exploring as she desperately seeks the pleasure we've both craved all these years. Her hands find their way to my hair, her slender fingers weaving through my curls.

I take hold of her hip, rubbing myself against her like a sex-crazed teenager.

God, I can't get enough. She's the only person who has ever had this kind of effect on me, my drug of choice, making me feel alive and free for the first time in years.

"I need you too, Milo," she whispers quietly.

The longing to be inside of her is overwhelming. I'm desperate to feel her skin against mine. To hear her unfiltered cries as she's in the throes of passion. To see her come undone for me, and me alone.

Now that I know she wants the same thing, there's no reason to waste another minute.

I begrudgingly back away from Liv, and she lets out a growl of disappointment.

"Take it easy, tiger." I chuckle. "I can't do what I want to do with you with clothes on."

I pull my shirt up and over my head before tugging my sweats and boxers off. Without prompting, Liv follows suit, stripping off her athletic gear, our clothes falling into a haphazard pile on the floor.

We're left naked and wanting. Liv slowly lifts her head to face me directly, her vibrant emerald-green eyes sizzling with lust. The energy in the room is electric as we stare at each other, as if to say...

I see you.

I want you.

I *love* you.

We haven't even touched skin to skin yet, but we're both panting heavily with anticipation, hopelessly lost in the moment.

God, Liv's body is exquisite. I want to spend the entire night worshipping her the way she deserves. If I were a gentleman, I would have taken my time, stripping off her clothes piece by piece before guiding her over to the king-sized, four-poster bed, where I'd lay her in the middle, kissing her entire body before making love to her.

Thank God I'm not a gentleman, because I need to be inside her—*now.*

"God, Liv, you're fucking sexy," I say in a hushed tone as I close the distance between us. "I wish I had the patience to savor this moment."

"Shut up and take me already," she demands with a seductive smile.

I don't need to be told twice. I grab hold of her hips and effortlessly lift her into my arms. She automatically wraps her long, sexy legs around my waist, winding her hands around my neck. I take two steps forward so her back is pressed against the wall.

"You're mine. You will *always* be mine," I say with conviction.

I grab ahold of my shaft with my hand, guiding myself inside Liv. She leans her head back, moaning at the welcome intrusion.

"You feel so good," she groans, her fingers desperately clutching the nape of my neck.

As I push inside, I pause to catch my breath, kissing her forehead with a reverence I never thought I was capable of.

Why the hell did I ever leave this woman? God, I'm an idiot.

During our time apart, Liv was always with me. Like a virus, she infiltrated my mind, body, and soul, refusing to leave, even as the years apart ticked by. I was a goddamn fool for thinking I'd be anything but miserable without her by my side.

I very well might still drag her down to the depths of hell with me, but I can guarantee she'll feel immeasurable pleasure while she's there. There's no chance I will be able to walk away from her now, not after tonight.

How the hell did I ever let her go in the first place?

"You're perfect, Liv." I smash my lips against hers, desperate for another taste. "Absolutely perfect."

"I need you to move. Now," she pleads.

"As you wish."

I push in and out in a steady rhythm as we both let out strangled moans. Liv meets me thrust for thrust, relishing in the feeling of me deep inside her.

"Milo, I'm…I'm going to…"

"Let go. I have you."

We find our release together, revealing in the intense bliss, welcoming the feeling with open arms.

"It's always been us, Stardust, you and me," I pant out. "This is how it was always supposed to be."

"Always been us," she agrees in a whisper.

As we come back down from our heightened pleasure, I know for certain that Liv is all that matters. She is my entire world.

I would walk to the ends of the earth for this woman, no questions asked.

As I brush a piece of hair behind her ear, Liv grabs my arm before I can pull back. Her eyes fixed on the tattoo located on the inside of my left wrist. She gives me a perplexed look, trying to make sense of what she's seeing.

I always said I would never get ink because Mac was covered in tattoos, and it was one less similarity I wanted to share with him.

"You got a tattoo of your mom's name?" Liv asks softly, caressing my wrist with her fingers.

"Yeah, I did. It felt right. A way to remember her."

"It's beautiful," Liv says earnestly.

"You're beautiful," I say with reverence. "I love you."

She smiles up at me but doesn't say the words back.

That's okay. I know the truth. She'll say the words out loud when she's ready.

Right now, all I can think about is splaying her on the bed and taking her again, nice and slow. We have a lot of lost time to make up for.

Chapter Twenty-Three

OLIVIA
Present Day—December

I WAKE UP WITH A warm body wrapped around mine.

I tilt my head back to find Milo sound asleep, his arms securely banded around my waist and his face nestled in the crook of my neck. I forgot how much I missed sleeping next to him.

Shortly after the snowball incident last night, Roxanne texted Milo saying that Mac was asleep for the night. She insisted that she stay with him so Milo and I could get some rest and promised to let us know if his condition worsened.

A few hours later, we found dinner waiting outside the bedroom door, confirming my suspicions that Roxanne knew we were doing a lot more than "getting some rest."

I do appreciate the brief reprieve and the chance to rekindle my physical relationship with Milo.

We stayed up until the first rays of dawn passed through the windows this morning, alternating between mind-blowing sex, making out like crazed teenagers, and talking about everything under the sun.

It feels like we're getting to know each other for the first time again, and in many ways, we are. We've spent the last fifteen years apart, and although some things haven't changed, so many others have.

Like the fact that Milo spends every Sunday at Pike and Eloisa's for dinner, is an advocate for water conservation, and considers the cornetto—an Italian version of the croissant—his favorite food. I also learned that he lives in a penthouse apartment with Sirius, which is situated a floor above his office.

He's built an entire life outside of the one we shared in high school, and I can't help but mourn the time we've lost.

I feel Milo stir behind me shortly before he starts planting gentle kisses along my collarbone.

"Good morning, sleepyhead," I breathe out, turning over so we're face-to-face.

"Good morning. I hope you're not too sore this morning," he whispers against my lips as he takes hold of my chin with his thumb and index finger, tilting my head back to press a passionate kiss against my mouth. "I've missed this, waking up next to you."

I've missed this too.

"Mmm, I can think of a few other things I've missed," I say, slipping my tongue between his lips as a soft groan escapes his mouth.

I take a good look at Milo in the morning light. Black curls fall against his forehead, his bronzed skin contrasts perfectly with his vibrant blue eyes, and his chest is on display for me to enjoy. He looks like a model on the set of an underwear photo shoot, and I'm the lucky woman who got to share his bed last night.

I recall a time during our sophomore year of high school when a girl in my algebra class tapped me on the shoulder during a lecture. She wanted to tell me how sorry she was to hear that I had to live in the same house as Milo, the charity case no one wanted.

I wish I could say that I took the high road and didn't let her words affect me, but that wasn't the case. I took a page straight out of my mom's book and clocked the prissy gossipmonger square in the nose, telling her to go to hell.

As far as Milo is concerned, I've never uttered a curse word a day in my life, and I'll take my secret to the grave. In my defense, it was justified. I got suspended for two weeks, and Mom had to foot an astronomical plastic surgery bill, but standing up for the boy I loved was well worth it.

In my opinion, Milo is worth ten times more than any of the privileged businessmen who come from old money, running their global empires with their New York City penthouses and mistresses situated around the world—my father included.

From what Milo has told me, he's earned his seat at the helm of Lawson Co., making it one of the nation's most prestigious construction consulting firms.

He may be plagued by personal demons, but he has integrity, works hard, and loves deeper than anyone I know.

The best part? He's *all* mine—at least for now.

"What time is it?" Milo asks as he pulls back from ravishing my mouth.

"It's almost seven," I reply as I sit up to stretch my arms. "I'm going downstairs to see Mac. I already feel guilty for leaving him last night, and I don't want to miss out on any more time with him. Plus, I'm sure Roxanne is exhausted from spending the night on the couch."

The second the words are out of my mouth, I regret them. I don't want Milo to think last night didn't mean anything to me.

"I'm so sorry. I didn't mean it like that. Gosh, I'm making a mess of the situation, aren't I?" I ask as I throw my hands over my face in embarrassment.

"Hey." He gently pulls my hands back so he can look me in the eye. "It's okay, Liv. I'm not mad. Last night was nothing short of amazing, and I can't wait to do it again, but we're here for Mac. He's your main priority, and that's how it should be." He kisses me one more time and gestures toward the door. "Don't keep him waiting."

I clamber out of bed and throw on the leggings and thermal long-sleeve shirt I wore the day before.

I jog down the stairs, anxious to get to Mac, but I stop dead in my tracks as I round the corner to the living room. I'm shocked to find the man in question sitting up in bed by himself, his copy of *Oliver Twist* open in his lap. Sirius is lying in his usual spot at the foot of the bed.

"Mac, what are you doing?" I ask hesitantly.

"Reading. Is there a problem?" he asks, giving me a perplexed look. "Roxanne went out to grab a few things at the store but said she'd be back within the hour. It looks like it snowed last night." He points out the window. "I'd like to sit out on the patio this morning if that's okay."

My heart warms at his crooked smile.

"Um, yes…yes, we can."

I'm frozen in place, unable to fully comprehend what I'm seeing. Over the past few days, Mac has needed help to eat, sit up, and even turn over. Even forming a simple sentence has become nearly impossible, yet here he is, speaking without a problem.

The "surge" is what we call it at the hospital.

Oftentimes, when a person is close to death, they get a sudden increase of energy and alertness. Many families without experience have false hope that their loved ones are recovering.

Unfortunately, I do know better, which means my time with Mac is coming to an end, much sooner than I hoped. I refuse to miss the precious time that I do have left.

"Let's get you dressed, and then we can go outside. Sound like a good plan?"

Sirius leaps from the bed, barking with joy at hearing one of his favorite words—outside.

"Sure, kiddo, I'd like that." Mac grins.

"Oh, and a hat. We can't forget a hat," Roxanne calls out from the hallway closet. The second she walked through the door and saw what we were doing, she snapped into action.

"That woman is acting like we're taking a trek to the Arctic, not to the back porch," Mac grumbles under his breath. His frail frame is dwarfed by black snow pants, a gray winter coat, and wool socks that Roxanne demanded he wears.

I let out a small laugh at his disapproval. I've missed this side of him so much.

"I heard that," Roxanne shouts from the hallway. "Stop fussing. You'll thank me later when you're warm and toasty instead of freezing your ass off."

"What the hell is going on here?" Milo asks as he walks into the middle of the chaos.

Roxanne pushes past him as she rushes over to shove a beanie over Mac's head.

"Well, well, well...look who finally decided to get out of bed," I say with a smirk.

"Keep it up, Liv. You know what happens when you tease me." He winks.

I don't miss Mac's knowing gaze. His lips turn up in a smile, satisfied at the newest development in my relationship with Milo.

"Mac wanted to spend some time outdoors today," I say, turning to address Milo. "I've already set up a couple of chairs on the back patio. Would you mind carrying Mac out for me?"

"Yeah, sure." Milo shrugs.

My melancholy demeanor makes it evident that something is wrong, but Milo doesn't inquire further.

Once Mac is suitably dressed, according to Roxanne's high standards, Milo gently picks him up from the bed and carries him out back. I've set up two lounge chairs side by side and covered one with a layer of blankets and a pillow so Mac can comfortably rest his head.

"Thanks," he says as Milo sets him down on his designated chair.

I wrap the extra blankets around him and tuck the red scarf—Roxanne's last-minute addition to his outfit—around his chin to keep the bitter cold out.

Once he's settled in, he takes a deep breath, inhaling the fresh winter air. It might be frigid, but the sun is shining above—a contrast from being cooped up inside for weeks on end.

"This is nice, kiddo. Thank you." Mac beams over at me.

"Anything for you, Mac," I say, relaxing in my chair, tucking my knees to my chest to keep myself warm.

I look out to find Milo and Roxanne standing next to one of the snow-covered fountains in the spacious backyard. They each have a cigarette in hand as they talk with each other.

Roxanne has been so helpful these past few weeks. On Thanksgiving, I woke up to the aroma of cinnamon, nutmeg, and vanilla. She surprised us with a full feast of roasted turkey, stuffing, creamy mashed potatoes, candied yams, green bean casserole, rolls, and a homemade pumpkin pie.

She said we couldn't miss out on Mac's last Thanksgiving. We spent the afternoon gathered around his bed as we ate the delicious food Roxanne had prepared.

Milo's dislike of Mac—and the reason for it—hasn't stopped her from treating Mac and me like family, going above and beyond to help care for an ailing man, and I will never forget her generosity. Milo bursts out laughing at something Roxanne said.

"You did that," Mac says hoarsely, nodding toward the pair.

"What do you mean?" I ask.

"You're responsible for the megawatt smile on Milo's face. He hates me, but he's put his personal vendetta aside for you. I'm surprised that you were willing to take my advice."

"And what advice would that be?"

"You forgave him," he states. "No matter how often he's walked away from you or thrown cruel insults your direction, you defended yourself and demanded he treat you right. I'm proud of you for that, and for helping him to become a better man. You made all of this possible." He gestures toward the house. "You brought my son back to me. I can rest peacefully now, knowing that you have each other."

"You are the two most important people in my life, Mac. I'm already losing you...I can't lose Milo too. Not again," I choke out, trying to keep my tears at bay.

"Be patient with him, kiddo. He's going to have a much harder time than you when I'm gone."

Yes, and there's a valid reason why.

"Please talk to him while you're still able to. Don't you want to reconcile before it's too late? I know Milo would want that, and he deserves to know the truth about what happened the night his mom died." My voice takes on a whiny tone, but I can't help it. I need him to listen to me.

"No," Mac says without pause.

"Mac—"

"Olivia, I said no," he scolds. "I'm not spending the limited time I have with my son arguing over the past. Please let it go. For me?" He gives me a hopeful smile, waiting patiently for me to comply.

"You know I can't do that. He deserves to hear the truth."

"You can tell him after I'm gone," Mac suggests.

"He'll never forgive me, not for keeping this from him."

"Yes, he will. He needs you, and there's no way he'll ever let you go again."

"I think you're wrong. Besides, he doesn't need me. He has a new life outside of the one we built together," I tell him honestly.

"So do you, kiddo."

"That's not true."

"Yes, it is. You have so many people who love you and who will be there to support you when I'm gone—that man out there is top of the list." He points to Milo. "Trust me, Liv. I know from experience what it's like to find your soulmate, the one person you can't live without. He let you go once; he won't make that mistake again. You're his everything." He feebly reaches out his hand to hold on to mine.

"I love you, Mac," I say with a sad smile.

"I love you too. You and Milo are my entire world, and I have you to thank for my life these past fifteen years. You made it bearable, even on the most difficult days."

I press a soft kiss against the palm of his hand.

There's so much more that I want to say. To beg him one last time to confide in Milo, and to thank him for saving me when I needed it the most. I consider myself lucky to have been a part of his life, and I will do everything I can to honor his legacy.

We both sit back in our lounge chairs, silently enjoying the fresh air. Once the temperature starts to drop and I can hear Mac's teeth chattering, we go back inside.

I'm not surprised when Milo comes to Mac's bedside and reads to him once he's settled back in bed. I park myself out in the hallway with Roxanne at my side, and she wraps her arm around my shoulders. A silent reminder that I'm not going through this alone.

We listen to Milo's mellow, soulful voice as he reads from *Great Expectations* for hours. We witness a tender moment between the men that I never thought would be possible.

"The agony is exquisite, is it not? A broken heart. You think you will die. But you just keep living. Day after day, after terrible day—"

"Milo," Mac cuts him off from reading.

"Is everything okay?"

"Yes. I don't think I've ever been better," Mac murmurs before letting out a raspy cough. "I've had to live with a broken heart for the past two decades. That's a hell of a long time to be apart from the woman I love. Every unwanted day slipped by without a way for me to stop time from moving forward. I'm going to be reunited with my Jada very soon, and that makes me a happy man."

"There's no doubt that she's waiting impatiently for you on the other side, Mac," Milo says with surety.

He might not mean it, but it's important that he said it anyway. Knowing he is willing to comfort Mac during his last moments means so much to me.

I'm itching to run into the room, but I force myself to stay where I am, giving the two men this time to say goodbye despite the ill feelings between them.

"I want you to have my copy of *Oliver Twist*. It's my most prized possession, and it's yours now," Mac utters hoarsely. "You should have your ma's handwritten word with you always. I only wish I could have given it to you sooner."

"Thank you," Milo murmurs, his voice thick with emotion.

"And you'll take care of Olivia?" Mac asks.

"Always," Milo says without pause.

"Good...that's really good. I want you to know that I will always love you, son," Mac says with conviction.

Milo doesn't throw a tantrum or demand that Mac take the words back. Instead, he smiles at Mac and goes back to reading.

Mac and Milo don't make amends or discuss the past. The estranged father and son simply accept each other where they are in this moment, and that's enough. It has to be, because there's no going back.

Shortly after their conversation, Mac falls into a comatose state. Sirius doesn't leave his side, sensing something is wrong.

By midnight, I fall asleep, curled up at Mac's side, knowing this will be the last time I'm comforted by the unsteady rise and fall of his chest.

I wake up to the sound of the wind howling outside the window and rapidly blink my eyes open to find that it's still the middle of the night. Roxanne must have left the bedside lamp on when she went home, a soft light now illuminating the room.

"Kiddo?" Mac rasps out next to me, barely able to get the single word out.

"Hey there, Mac. What do you need?" I ask, turning to face him.

"I think I'm ready to see Jada now," he whispers, and a ghost of a smile passes his lips.

Tears start to stream down my cheeks. I know this is the end, and I clasp his hands in mine, resting my head against his shoulder.

"I think that's a great idea. She'll be so glad to see you." I gently stroke his cheek as he closes his eyes. "My mom told me once that the sky symbolizes freedom. You're like the sky. It's your turn to be free, to take flight and leave this world. I'll think of you whenever I look up at the starry night sky," I choke out the words as my hands start to quiver. "I will always love you, Mac." My voice cracks at the end, knowing this is the last time I'll say those words to him.

I sense the moment Mac lets out his last breath, a content smile on his face before he slips away.

He's back with Jada now, giving me a sense of peace, but it's not enough.

My soft cries turn to inconsolable sobs as I tremble in agony. I'm suddenly lifted into Milo's strong embrace as he carries me to the couch on the far side of the room. He settles in with me curled on his lap, stroking my hair, whispering words of comfort.

"I'm so sorry, Liv. I'm so sorry that he's gone."

Milo is my only source of strength, holding me together when all I want to do is fall apart, and I love him for that.

This time I won't have to grieve alone.

Chapter Twenty-Four

MILO
Past—Twelfth Grade

I LEAVE THE DUNHAMS' BROWNSTONE filled with a mix of relief and dread. The city is fast asleep, most of its residents dozing off their hangovers and late-night celebrations from welcoming in the new year the night prior.

I shuffle down the steps, looking back at the imposing building standing before me. Now that Marie's gone, I don't belong here anymore.

Liv, my beautiful, selfless Stardust, is much better off without me, and we both know it.

If I had waited until she woke up and been forced to watch her quivering lips and downcast eyes as she begged me not to go, I wouldn't have been able to stand my ground. I would have stayed by her side and eventually dragged her down to a life of misery, just like Mac did to my ma, until neither of us recognized ourselves. I love Liv too much to let history repeat itself.

There is no hope for my darkened soul, encased in bitterness and malicious intent since my ma died, now compounded by Marie's passing.

My sweet Liv, who represents everything that's good in this world, should get the chance to move on. To overcome the loss of her mom, graduate college, and achieve her lifelong dream of becoming a doctor. I refuse to stand in her way. So, I took the coward's way out and slipped out while she was still fast asleep and unable to argue with my choice.

I'm more than ready to leave behind Milo Leland Covell, the charity case from Camden. The poor kid with a dead mom and a dad in prison, who was taken in by a rich family who pitied him.

My past is a landmine of traumatic experiences, but the last four years were sprinkled with fond memories shared with Liv and Marie that have helped ease my grief for a short time. Regardless of the cherished moments, I will always be emotionally damaged, wearing my invisible scars like a badge of honor.

I remain unsympathetic to Mac and crave the aggression I experience when I think of him. I'll never forgive him for his past transgressions, and I will do everything I can to ensure that he suffers for the rest of his life for what he did to Ma...and to me.

If only he had gotten his drinking problem under control and found a better way to cope with his demons, Ma would still be alive. I would never have had come to live with the Dunhams, suffered through the loss of Marie, or walked away from Olivia because I was damaged goods.

Fuck anyone who says I should forgive and forget. It's a crock of shit.

Mac will pay for the suffering he's put me through until the day he dies, and I will ruin anyone who gets in the way of my retribution.

I spend the rest of the morning aimlessly wandering the city, unsure where to go next.

I have no other family to speak of and only a couple hundred bucks in my pocket from a few odd jobs that I did for some of our neighbors before Marie got sick. I'm not naive; I know that won't get me very far.

What the hell am I going to do?

By nightfall, I find myself back in Camden, New Jersey, sitting on the curb across the street from my childhood home.

The place has since been fixed up, barely recognizable from when I lived here. It's still on the wrong side of town, but it looks like an entirely new house now. It's almost...idyllic. The worn siding has gotten a face-lift and a fresh coat of paint. The old, rusted railing that used to lean sideways has been replaced with a sturdy black banister that stands upright. A festive evergreen wreath hangs from the glossy black front door. I watch through the window as a family of four and their Great Pyrenees puppy—most likely a Christmas present for the kids—gather around the dining room table for a New Year's dinner celebration.

A sense of indignation flows through my veins. This was Ma's home. Even in its run-down state, it was her safe haven, a place to call her own after all the years she spent being passed around from one foster home to the next. She deserved the better version, and it breaks my heart she never got it.

As snow starts to fall around me, I get up from the curb, taking in one last glimpse of the remnants of my shattered childhood, knowing that I'll never come back here.

I go to the local bus station and push one hundred eighty dollars toward the cashier at the ticket counter. "How far away can I get with this? I don't care where I end up, just as long as it's not on the East Coast."

The woman gives me a skeptical look but nods in understanding.

When she slides the ticket back to me, I mumble my thanks as I walk toward the bays filled with buses. I anxiously peek down at the ticket to see where I'm headed, and the words "Las Vegas" jump out at me.

I silently board the bus, sitting near the back, away from the other passengers. I'm not in the mood to make small talk with strangers.

I set my backpack next to me, containing the only possessions I own—the last of my money, a toothbrush, a razor, my favorite hoodie, the picture of Ma, and a change of clothes. I might not have much now, but I will make a name for myself someday. I refuse to spend the rest of my life living in poverty or being a rich family's charity case.

I sleep most of the way to Vegas, the events from the last few days catching up to me. I get off at every stop, surveying the area to see if I could imagine living there. By the time I get to Colorado, I've made up my mind that I'm going all the way to Vegas.

As I watch the landscape rush by, I can't help but think of Liv. By now, she knows that I'm gone, and she will have found my phone on the bedside table. She might be angry at first, but in the end, I know she'll be okay. She still has her dad. He might not be much, but I'm sure he'll stay while she adjusts, and in the fall, she'll go off to college.

The idea of her dating some frat boy boils my blood, but I push the thought away. This is what I wanted. To give her the chance to find her happily ever after, and she can't do that if she doesn't move on.

That's why you left, I have to remind myself.

She deserves a well-adjusted man without baggage who can give her the life she deserves—with a white picket fence, two-point-five kids, and the promise of a happy, fulfilled future.

The sun is setting as we make our way onto the Vegas strip. The Greyhound bus pulls up to Caesars Palace, making a special stop for the bachelorette party that boarded in Colorado. I might as well get off here and start exploring the city I now call home, so I grab my bag and follow the group of eager women.

The girls closest to me turn back as they exit, giving me a little wave. I doubt they'd be interested if they knew my wallet was empty. I give them a curt nod before stepping out into the cool night air, glad I had the foresight to put on my hoodie before getting off the bus.

My senses are overloaded as I spin in a circle, in awe of the glitz and glamour of this place, the lights of the city shining bright. It's a stark difference from New York's fast-paced energy, especially with its iconic architecture and sophisticated aristocrats.

I might not have a penny to my name or know where my next meal is coming from, but I know I've found my new home.

Time doesn't seem to exist here, and I aimlessly wander for hours. I roam from one casino to the next, watching visitors from around the world gamble away their life savings, placing bets at the blackjack table, taking their chances with roulette, and making a last-ditch effort to win back their losses at the slot machines.

The aroma of smoke filling the air has my mouth watering, begging for my next nicotine fix. God, what I wouldn't give for a cigarette right about now. Unfortunately, I used the last of my money back in Colorado to buy a shitty breakfast burrito from a gas station. My addiction will have to wait until I find a job.

Eventually, I return to the Strip, observing the street entertainers in extravagant costumes. I can't help but laugh at the parade of drunken patrons who can't seem to walk upright as they chug down alcoholic beverages like pigs at a trough.

As the night wears on, I move in the direction of the residential part of the city. I'm exhausted and ready for some shut-eye, but I need to find a place to rest for the night without raising any suspicions.

After walking several miles, I come across a construction site for a new apartment building.

Off on the far side of the structure, I find an excavator that's unlocked and climb up inside the cab. I'll rest my eyes for a couple of hours and get the hell out of dodge before anyone shows up for work in the morning.

No one will ever know I was here.

With that final thought, I promptly pass out with my head pressed against the glass.

I'm abruptly woken up by something prodding at my ribs. I grunt in annoyance as another jab hits my abdomen.

What the hell?

I jerk upright when I remember where I am, and I have no clue who or what is trying to disrupt my sleep.

The sun is rising over the horizon, but it's still too early for the workers to be here already.

I notice that the cab door is wide open. I closed it before I fell asleep, so the question remains, who's out there waiting to confront me?

I cautiously lean outside to find a middle-aged man with peppered gray hair and a full-grown beard observing me. He's wearing worn work boots, straight-legged Wranglers, and a red-and-black checkered flannel. A long piece of PVC pipe rests in his grasp, clearly the culprit of the residual ache in my side.

"You're trespassing, kid. This is private property," he shouts up at me. "I don't take kindly to being dragged out of bed at the crack of dawn for this." His gravelly voice is firm, but I sense a hint of sympathy.

I blink down at him, trying to decide how to respond. I didn't see a security guard roaming the grounds last night, so there must be sensors or cameras on-site that sent an alert when they detected movement. Shit, what am I going to do if this guy calls the cops? I have no one to call if I'm arrested. I can't spend my newfound freedom behind bars.

The man looks to be in his mid-forties. I'm sure I could outrun him if I have to, but I'll need to get down from here first.

"You're damn lucky one of my foremen didn't find you. They don't appreciate their equipment being tampered with. Come down from there before you break your neck, kid," the stranger hollers up at me.

I'm not a kid. I'm a grown-ass man who can take care of himself.

Rolling my eyes, I grab my backpack off the cab floor, throwing it over my shoulder before effortlessly jumping from the machinery to prove my point.

"The name's Pike," the man grunts in my direction before tossing the PVC pipe onto the ground a few feet away.

Good. At least he's not planning on beating me with the thing.

I cautiously start to back up, hoping he's distracted enough that I can get a head start on my escape.

As I spin on my heel, ready to make a break for it, Pike grabs hold of the handle of my bag, using the leverage to pull me toward him. I could ditch the backpack and make a run for it, but I can't part with the picture of Ma—it's all I have left of her.

"Now wait just a minute. You're not going anywhere until we have a chat," Pike says, leaving no room for argument. "Why were you sleeping out here? You don't look homeless or like you're on drugs, so what's your story?"

He gives my outfit a double take, clearly aware that my clothes are designer, aside from my Vans hoodie. I never asked for this shit. Marie always bought my clothes and insisted that I had the best money could buy. I've always hated people assuming that I was taking advantage of her generosity, when in reality, I would have been content to shop at thrift stores for my wardrobe.

"It's none of your damn business where I'm from, and I don't have a family," I snap back. A flicker of self-loathing flashes in my eyes as the statement slips from my mouth.

What about Liv?

No matter the distance I put between us, she'll always be my family.

"I don't care for your attitude, son. I'm only trying to help you. How about you show me some respect, and I'll do the same for you, okay?" Pike levels with me.

I steel myself at hearing him call me son—an endearment I've long since banished from my vocabulary. I remind myself that he doesn't know about my past and that it's best not to piss off the person who holds my future in his hands.

"Yeah, I understand," I say.

"How old are you, son? And don't you dare lie to me. I'll find out if you do."

"I'm eighteen." I don't mention that my birthday was only a week ago.

"Good. That makes things much easier," Pike says cryptically. He pulls out his phone and starts typing furiously. He looks up briefly to acknowledge me. "You're sure you have nowhere else to go?" he questions.

Dumbfounded, I shake my head and stare at him.

His attention goes back to his phone. Once he's finished, he points at the truck nearby, which I didn't notice before. "Hop in," he orders before getting in the driver's side.

He's a man of few words, so I don't dare ask any more questions.

I can't believe I'm actually considering getting into a stranger's vehicle, but I'm out of options, and it's not like I have anywhere else to go. Besides, aside from his surly demeanor, Pike seems harmless. I can always bail later if I need to.

The F-150 Raptor in custom matte black is still running. When I get in, I'm greeted with a warm leather seat and hot air blowing in my face, bringing life back into my frozen fingertips.

As we leave the construction site, Pike doesn't say a word. We drive in silence as "If You're Going Through Hell" by Rodney Atkins plays through the speakers.

Very fitting.

Pike's focus is on the road as he hums along. He might be rough around the edges, but he seems like a good man under his gruff facade.

Before I know it, we're turning down a paved lane, southern live oaks lining both sides providing a layer of privacy to the ranch-style home that comes into view as we round the bend.

The front yard has been meticulously landscaped, incorporating mulch, gravel, and a variety of cacti. I've never seen anything like it.

"Eloisa calls it a desert landscape design," Pike says as if he can read my mind. "She insists that we do our part to conserve water, which means no grass. In my opinion, it's a much bigger pain in the ass to maintain than watering a lawn, but if it keeps my woman happy, so be it." He gives me a wink as he parks in the driveway. He turns the ignition off and hops out of the truck.

"Who's Eloisa?" I call out as he walks away.

"My wife," he says. "She's inside. It's best if we get a move on; she doesn't like to be kept waiting."

He lets out a low chuckle as he heads to the front door, pausing when he notices that I haven't followed. He lifts his arm in a *come here* motion, which gets my butt in gear.

I clamber from the vehicle, slinging my backpack over my shoulder just in case I have to make a run for it if things get weird. I dash up the porch steps as Pike opens the solid oak front door.

I stop mid-stride when I notice the welcome mat that reads, "Every Family Has a Story—Welcome to Ours."

"Eloisa picked that out," Pike says from the entryway. "The minute she saw the thing in a shop window, she had to have it. She insisted it would make people feel more at home when visiting. I don't think a doormat has that kind of influence, but it made her smile, so here it is."

I have to agree with Eloisa. I already feel like I've received a warm welcome and I haven't even met her yet. It makes it that much easier for me to get the courage to step inside.

As I enter the foyer, I'm greeted with the sweet scent of sugar, butter, and spices. It feels like I've been transported to a street corner in Paris, standing outside one of the bakeries located on every corner.

I take a minute to observe my new surroundings. Off to the right is a study with a large wooden desk, three of the four walls lined with built-in bookshelves, each filled to the brim with books. To the left, I find a dining room with a solid oak kitchen table, a large holiday-themed floral arrangement displayed in the middle. The place is spacious, but the minimal furniture is well-loved. It's a cozy space that could easily feel like home.

We pass through a hallway and a flight of stairs before entering an industrial-grade kitchen, fit for a Michelin-starred chef. All of the appliances are stainless steel, and I'm a bit perplexed when I count not one but three ovens lined up next to the massive wall of sage-green cabinets.

"You poor thing!" a voice coos from behind me.

As I turn around, I'm ambushed by a pair of arms attached to an energetic, short, brown-eyed woman donning a black sheath dress with a pinstriped bib apron covering the front. She gets a good look at me before smiling and pulling me in for a hug. Her positive energy is contagious, and I can't help but grin back, despite my current circumstances.

"Pike told me that he found you sleeping at the Keller site. I'm sure you're exhausted, but let's get you something to eat before we talk about anything else. I didn't know what you liked, so I whipped up a little bit of everything." She gestures to the granite kitchen island overflowing with a fresh batch of what looks like golden brown croissants, crispy bacon, scrambled eggs, a bowl full of fresh berries, and freshly squeezed orange juice.

Her version of "a little bit" is much different than mine.

Eloisa ushers me to a stool next to the counter and encourages me to eat. I hesitantly sit down but don't delay once my stomach rumbles. I grab the empty plate in front of me and pile it high with the feast Eloisa has prepared. I have no idea when I'll have the chance to eat again, so I'm going to take full advantage of this couple's generosity until they determine that I'm no longer worth the trouble.

I stuff one of the pastries in my mouth, moaning with pleasure as the savory, buttery flavor greets my taste buds. "Holy shit, this croissant is so good," I exclaim as I take another bite, unable to control myself.

Eloisa gasps, obviously offended by my comment. I give her a dubious look, unsure what I said wrong. Pike lets out a belly laugh from the other side of the kitchen.

"Pay Eloisa no mind," Pike says. "She's a professionally trained Italian chef, so it's in her blood to defend her country's heritage."

"Oh, I see...what did I say wrong?"

Eloisa clicks her tongue in disappointment and points at the baked good in my hand. "That's called a cornetto. It means 'little horn' in Italian. They call for less butter than a croissant, more sugar, and have egg yolk brushed across the top to make them a perfect golden brown."

"Well, the *cornettos* taste great!" I declare, grabbing another one from the plate.

This gesture placates Eloisa, and she gives me another soft smile.

I spend the next half hour consuming everything in sight. Just as I'm finishing up my third plate of food, Pike comes around the island to sit next to me.

"Eloisa and I talked about it, son, and we'd like you to stay here with us," Pike says.

"I'm sorry, what?" I ask, not quite sure I understand.

"You can stay in the studio apartment above the garage. There's a bedroom and bathroom, but you'll eat all your meals here with us. You'll offend Eloisa if you don't."

I turn around to find Eloisa giving me another one of her warm smiles.

"Tomorrow morning, I'll take you back to the Keller site and you'll work on one of the construction crews. You'll start at the bottom like everyone else. If you so much as step one foot out of line, you'll be out on your ass faster than you can blink, got it?" Pike says matter-of-factly.

I'm confused, and all I can do is stare across at him with my mouth gaping open. He's offering me a place to stay, a job, and delicious food. What's the catch?

"I still don't understand," I admit. "Why would you let someone you just met stay with you? Besides, don't you need permission from your boss before you offer me a job?"

Eloisa lets out a lighthearted chuckle. "Oh, honey, he doesn't need permission from anybody. He is the boss. Pike owns the largest construction consulting firm in Las Vegas. He just hasn't gotten rid of the mountain-man beard or his need to micromanage every project, so it's easy to confuse him with the average construction worker."

"Oh, I see," I say with surprise.

Pike clears his throat to get my attention. I look over to find him watching me with a compassionate expression. "At one point or another, everyone needs a fresh start, son. I don't need to know your past to determine that you're a good kid with a big heart. Eloisa and I have the means to help you get the new beginning I'm assuming you want. You have to decide if you're willing to put in the hard work to make a name for yourself."

My gaze bounces from Eloisa to Pike and back again. Their offer seems genuine, and I like that they're making me work for it instead of giving me a free ride. They expect me to earn my keep and better myself. This is the opportunity I've been searching for, and I'd be crazy not to take it.

"I'll accept your offer on one condition," I say to Pike.

"What is it?" he asks.

"You have to let me pay rent."

Pike seems impressed that I don't want any handouts and that I'm eager to do my part to contribute.

"You have yourself a deal, son," he says, reaching out to shake my hand in agreement.

I smile up at Pike and Eloisa with gratitude. I finally have the clean slate I was searching for. Now, if only I could stop thinking about Liv…

Chapter Twenty-Five

OLIVIA
Present Day—December

WE DRIVE BACK TO THE city in silence, spending the majority of the ride staring out the window at the snow-covered scenery.

Occasionally, I catch myself checking the backseat, a bleak reminder that Mac's gone. In his place, Sirius is lying down with his head resting on one of the pillows, whining every so often. He can sense something is wrong, no doubt wondering what happened to his friend.

Milo keeps his right hand on my thigh as a subtle sign of solidarity. He might have tolerated Mac during the past few weeks, but he never stopped hating the man. I'm not ready to unpack how that makes me feel, or dive into his conflicting emotions. Instead, we both bask in the silence, our short exchanges remaining strictly superficial.

We left the house upstate first thing this morning. Roxanne said we could stay with her as long as we liked, but I politely declined. I couldn't be in the place where Mac had passed only a few hours prior. I was anxious to get back to my apartment, my safe haven. The place where Mac and I had created countless happy memories. It's been nearly two months since I've set foot inside, and I'm desperate for the comfort of familiar surroundings. Mac was right when he suggested we stay somewhere else after he got sick, and now I'm grateful to have a place to go where I can grieve on my own terms.

I've been so absorbed in my thoughts that I don't realize when Milo pulls into the garage of my apartment building. I'm vaguely aware of him calling my name, but it doesn't register that he's speaking to me until I notice my door is open and he's crouched on the ground next to me. He gently strokes my cheek as he patiently waits for me to come back to reality.

When my glazed-over green eyes finally make contact with Milo's brilliant blue ones, he gives me a warm smile.

"There you are. Welcome back," he says tenderly, as if my mere acknowledgment of him were an achievement worthy of praise.

I love him for that—his willingness to support me without casting judgment on how I grieve.

I really wish I were ready to say "I love you" out loud, but I'm not. He needs to hear the whole truth first. I wouldn't be able to survive if I uttered those words, and he still chose to walk away from me afterward.

Milo leans in to gently kiss my forehead before reaching his full height. "What do you say we go inside?" he asks.

I nod, unable to find my voice.

He helps me out of the car, Sirius following closely behind, and I lead the way to the elevator. The ride up to my floor remains somber, and once we're standing outside my apartment door, I'm shaking uncontrollably, unable to get the key in the lock. I sigh, frustrated that I'm struggling with such a simple task.

"Here, let me help," Milo chimes in, tentatively taking the key from my hand and opening the door with ease.

As soon as the door is ajar, Sirius runs inside, eager to explore. I falter in the entryway, cautiously glancing around to find my apartment exactly how I left it.

The hand-painted, stained-glass bowl—filled with Mac's spare change, keychains, and various knickknacks—sits on the console table in the hall next to an overflowing pile of bills.

I admire the pastel floral prints Mac bought from a local street artist hanging proudly on the wall. They were a gift for my birthday last year. He always went out of his way to support his local community, purchasing items from small businesses and local street artists whenever possible. It means the world to have physical proof of his kindness and desire to make a difference in my home.

My chest tightens as I clock a pair of Mac's cross-trainers underneath the table, right where he left them after he took a long walk through Central Park the morning before he was hospitalized.

"Liv, I'm going out to grab your suitcase and Sirius's dog bed. I'll be right back," Milo says before walking out the front door.

I move further into my modern-styled apartment, laughing at the hodgepodge of furniture in the open-concept living area that I fell in love with when I toured the place.

My tuxedo-style white linen couch sits across from the green tweed recliner Mac found at a yard sale in Brooklyn. The vast collection of children's books I've acquired over the years resides in the line of black milk crates resting against the far wall that Mac brought home after finding a dozen in a dumpster near Hell's Kitchen. The wrought iron kitchen table in the dining area is surrounded by the retro red-and-white dining chairs Mac acquired at an estate sale in Midtown.

At first glance, the kitchen is Pinterest board-worthy, but only until you open the cupboards and find the Christmas-themed China set Mac purchased from a thrift store. I remember the day he came home with the set nestled inside a cardboard box, excited to share the treasure he scored.

I moved into my apartment a month before Mac got released from prison. It was important to me that he had a place where he would have a fresh start.

From the moment he moved in, he refused to take a dime from me, not wanting to take advantage of my generosity. He secured a job at the bodega down the street two days after his release and insisted on paying a portion of the rent, providing half the furniture, and buying other household items.

I accepted his terms without complaint. I wasn't surprised when he started bringing home newly acquired trinkets from back alleyways, dumpsters, yard sales, and thrift stores. He had grown up in foster care, and once he was emancipated, he and Jada had to find cheap ways to get the necessities.

Our mismatched possessions were a reminder of the ragtag family Mac and I had become. He was the gruff ex-con and I was the jaded young woman who had found a friendship in the most unlikely of places.

I hear the sound of scratching, followed by a whimper. When I go to investigate, I find Sirius sitting on his haunches, scratching at Mac's closed bedroom door. A lump gets caught in my throat as I open the door, knowing Sirius will be sorely disappointed when he discovers Mac isn't inside.

I crack the door, and he shoves past me, barreling into the room at full speed. I watch as he becomes agitated, turning around in frustration, confused why he can smell Mac but can't find him.

"I'm sorry, Sirius," I murmur. "I miss him too."

I examine the beige walls, twin-sized bed frame, black dresser with missing knobs, and the bright orange metal nightstand.

I sit on the edge of the bed, positioned in the middle of the room. When Mac moved in, I planned to buy a king-sized bed for his room, but he declined, insisting that he needed something smaller or he wouldn't be able to sleep.

You can take the man out of prison, but you can't take the prison habits out of the man.

The photo of Mac, Milo, and Jada on the nightstand catches my attention, set in a simple silver frame.

"I remember that day." Milo's voice startles me.

I look up to find him standing in the threshold of the room, and I'm frozen in place as he comes over to sit beside me.

"I think I was five at the time," he says in a downcast tone. "That picture was taken an hour after Mac surprised Ma with the house he'd bought her. To this day, I can remember how he insisted on blindfolding her on the car ride there, wanting it to be a secret until she saw the place in person." Milo's voice drifts off as he gazes down at the picture longingly. "I won't ever forget Ma's face when she saw the dump for the first time. Based on her reaction, you would have thought Mac had gifted her a mansion in Beverly Hills. It sure wasn't much, but it was ours, and that's what mattered most to Ma—having a home to call her own."

He shuffles his feet from side to side, obviously uncomfortable with revisiting his past.

"I remember Mac promising Ma he was going to fix the place up one room at a time, transform it into her dream home, right down to the white picket fence. That never happened," he says in a disappointed tone. "Shortly after that picture was taken, Mac started drowning his sorrows in a bottle of whiskey, and the last shreds of hope Ma clung to were flushed down the drain."

I study the photograph. Mac sits on a rickety old porch with Jada on the step below, leaning against his burly chest. Her head is tipped back and she's gazing at him with adoration. Mac smiles down at her, his expression filled with love. Milo is resting in Jada's lap, his little arms wrapped around her neck as he looks straight into the camera with piercing blue eyes. The ideal combination of his parents.

Despite the drab setting, they appear deliriously happy— the perfect moment, frozen in time. A stark reminder of Milo's carefree childhood before it was ripped from his grasp far too soon by unfortunate circumstances.

"I can't believe Mac kept it all these years," Milo murmurs.

"Aside from *Oliver Twist*, it was the only possession that he took with him to prison," I say. "Regardless of what you think, Mac loved you and your mom."

I flinch as soon as the words slip from my mouth, bracing for Milo's verbal backlash...but it never comes.

"You're right. He did love us both back then," he admits.

I blink up at Milo, surprised by his response.

A mere month ago, this conversation would have gone very differently. I appreciate him making an effort to be amiable despite his personal feelings toward Mac.

I am doing my best to cherish every precious second I have with Milo. There's an expiration date on our time together, and this calm will eventually come to an end, leaving a raging storm in its wake.

Once Milo finds out the truth—the *real* truth—I'm worried that the relationship we've worked so hard to rebuild will be rocked to its core with no hope of reconciliation.

"Milo?"

"Yeah?"

"Can we get out of here? I think I'd like to take a bath now."

If I sit in Mac's room any longer, I'll become a blubbering mess, and I'd rather spend the last of my energy doing something that will end my day on a lighter note.

A smile crosses his lips when he understands my double meaning of *bath.*

What I want more than anything right now is to be close to Milo, without anything between us—physically or emotionally.

"Of course, Liv. Whatever you need," he says.

Milo scoops me up into his muscular arms, my head resting perfectly in the crook of his shoulder. We leave the room and, as if reading my mind, Milo shuts the door behind us. At some point, I'll have to go through all of Mac's things, but for now, I'd like to keep my head buried in the sand a little longer.

Out of sight, out of mind.

As we make our way down the hall, I notice Sirius has found his dog bed that Milo put next to Mac's old recliner. He's resting on it with his hedgehog squeaker sitting below his chin.

Poor Sirius. Even his favorite toy doesn't seem to hold his interest anymore.

Milo confidently strides through the apartment, locating the master bedroom with ease. When we enter the room, he bypasses the king-sized bed and heads straight for the door leading to the bathroom. He turns the light on before placing me on the white granite countertop, leaning in to gently kiss the tip of my nose.

"Stay right there. I'm going to prepare your bath," he gently orders.

He walks to my freestanding tub, turning on the faucet before pulling a bottle of lavender bubble bath from a nearby shelf and pouring a generous amount into the rising water. He's a natural at this, and I appreciate his desire to care for me.

I can't help but wonder how many other women he's drawn baths for while we were apart.

Did he ever join any of them?

Why does it matter? The past is in the past, and he's here now. I'm the one sharing a bath with him tonight.

Once Milo is satisfied with the temperature of the water, he turns back, his heated gaze zeroing in on me like a lion to a gazelle. I let out a shuddered exhale as he stalks toward me, a man on a mission. I clench my thighs in anticipation, eager for what comes next.

I'm desperate for a break, needing a distraction from the anguish churning inside me, a chance to escape the grief threatening to pull me under.

Milo comes to a stop between my legs. His presence is all-consuming as he towers over me, gazing down with those piercing blue eyes. He places his hands on either side of my hips, and it feels like he can see straight into my soul.

I'm here with you.

You're not alone.

I love you.

The unspoken words reverently pass between us. Knowing that the fierce and sexy man standing before me loves me and has sacrificed so much to be here is such a turn-on.

My tongue absentmindedly brushes across my top lip as I picture him pressing his mouth to mine, worshipping me the way he did the other night. I think back to being shoved against the bedroom door, my legs wrapped tightly around his waist as he thrust into me with abandon. His fingers pressed firmly into my thighs as I threw my head back, enthusiastically shouting his name.

A soft moan escapes my lips when I'm unable to control the memory's effect on my body.

Milo's eyes glisten with understanding as he leans in close, nipping the outer shell of my ear before whispering so softly that I almost miss his words. "Stardust, are you turned on? Are you thinking about what it felt like to have me deep inside you as you shattered apart in ecstasy?"

"Yes." I breathe out the single word as a shiver ripples down my spine.

He stands up straight, a cocky smirk plastered on his face at knowing just how much his presence affects me.

I'm mesmerized as he lifts my right arm, pulling it through the sleeve of my sweatshirt before repeating the same process with my left. He drags the shirt up over my head, tossing it into the corner.

His hands are back on me within seconds as he unclasps my bra. My aching breasts are freed from their confines, begging for relief as I remember the feel of Milo's fingers brushing across the tips in a teasing fashion.

I let out a low growl when he pays them no mind. He lets out a soft chuckle but otherwise ignores my show of frustration as he undresses me.

He gently grabs my wrists, tugging me up to a standing position. He effortlessly pops open the button of my jeans, pulling each pant leg down until they pool around my ankles. He traces his fingers up my thighs until he gets to my panties, dragging them down my legs. I'm going to lose my mind if he doesn't give me more—and soon. I can't stand the clinical way he's undressing me when what I really want him to do is tear my clothes off and grind against me while we both chase our pleasure.

I'm desperate to feel his gentle caress as he worships every inch of my body. It's only been two days since we had sex, and I'll go crazy if it doesn't happen again tonight. If I had known the adult version of Milo Covell was this good in bed, I would have jumped him weeks ago. He's the only thing that can numb my grief and despair.

Right now, I find myself at Milo's mercy, an addict to his touch, his taste, his affection. I need him like I need my next breath. At this moment, I would do just about anything for him to show my body the attention it craves.

I'm relieved when he kneels on the rug in front of me, and I think this is it…the moment he'll finally give me what I've been waiting for.

I'm captivated as he trails kisses from my knee to my inner thigh. He pauses as he gets close to my center, blowing out a soft puff of air. The sensation has me letting out a keen whimper, a shock wave of pleasure going straight to my core.

"Milo, please," I call out, pleading for him to move a few inches closer to give me the release that I want. That I *need.*

"Shh, Stardust. We're going to take a bath, remember?" he taunts me.

I let out a low snarl when he pulls away from me. What does he think he's doing? I might die of overstimulation if he leaves me like this for much longer. I lean forward, yearning to close the distance he's trying to put between us.

"Easy there, my little minx," Milo teases as he softly grasps my shoulders and pushes me back down on the counter.

He bends down to pull my bottoms from around my ankles, one at a time. Now that I'm completely naked, Milo looks at me from head to toe, taking in every inch of me.

He's still fully dressed, which is entirely unfair. If I had it my way, his clothes would be long gone and he would take me right here, right now. Unfortunately, he doesn't appear to be in any hurry. In fact, he seems to be enjoying my suffering a little too much. Doesn't he know that patience isn't one of my virtues?

"The water's ready," Milo announces, lifting me into his arms as if I weigh nothing.

He gently deposits me into the piping hot water, and I welcome the accompanying sting, letting the heat soak through my tense muscles. The smell of lavender envelopes the room with a sense of tranquility.

I snap my head up when I catch Milo *finally* stripping out of his clothes.

I'm entranced as he pulls his sweater up over his head, offering me a front-row seat to his bronzed, well-defined abs, leading down to his V-line. I bite my lip in anticipation as I lean over the edge of the tub, enjoying the private striptease Milo is gracing me with.

I can't seem to drag my eyes away as he pulls his pants down, leaving him in a pair of black boxers. I know exactly what he's packing underneath, and I'm eager for him to remove them.

I want to do more than watch.

He gives me a giant grin as he steps out of his underwear, his cock proudly jutting out.

I don't think I'll ever get used to seeing him like this. *Naked and all mine.*

"Like what you see, Liv?" he asks proudly.

He reaches over to turn the faucet off before climbing into the tub behind me, careful not to splash any water on the floor. He settles in, wrapping each of his muscular legs around mine. His corded arms circle my waist as he pulls me into his chest until I'm cocooned inside his strong embrace.

I absentmindedly bring my hand down to his wrist, tracing the cursive tattoo of his mom's name. *Jada.*

"I've been thinking about getting a similar one on my right wrist," I say quietly.

"Of your mom's name?"

"Sort of...I want to get her initials, alongside Hope's and Mac's..." I pause, preparing for his outrage. "Please don't be angry with me, not while we're getting along so well."

I tilt my head back to see his face, afraid of what I'll find. I brace for his cruel remarks and I scold myself for saying that out loud. Undoubtedly, he'll be furious at my desire to honor Mac in the same way he honored his mom.

I'm shocked when all I see is a look of utter devotion.

"Stardust, I'm not angry."

"You're not?"

"No, I'm not. If that is the best way to remember those you've loved and lost, I support you one hundred percent. If you'll let me, I'd like to be there when you get your first tattoo."

"Promise you're not mad?"

"I promise." His voice drops to a low, seductive tone.

Every muscle in my body tenses as Milo's lips graze my shoulder. He presses featherlight kisses against each freckle, the brush of his mouth causing me to quiver with excitement. Without warning, he bites down softly against my skin before caressing the same area with his tongue.

A soft cry escapes my lips as he repeats the process several times, biting down before soothing the tender area.

"I need more, please," I cry out.

"Anything for you," Milo whispers in my ear.

His hands find their way out of the water to caress my needy, heavy breasts. He continues his assault with his mouth, making his way up past my collarbone as he firmly kneads each breast, adding extra pressure when I let out a low groan. A scorching heat builds between my thighs that already has me begging for release.

As his callous fingers pinch the dusky peaks of my nipples, I arch back, relishing in the delicious sensation. Without hesitation, he bends down to capture one of the tips in his mouth. My breathing becomes erratic, and I'm unable to think clearly.

"Mmm," I hum in appreciation.

He drops one of his hands down into the water, moving skillfully to the apex of my thighs. Two of his thick fingers find their way to my opening, plunging inside.

"Oh, Milo," I exclaim, unable to control my reaction.

"That's it, Stardust. Call my name out as I worship this perfect body of yours. I'm here to please you, to serve you, to love you. Let me make you feel good, baby," Milo says as he pushes a third finger inside of me, furiously moving them in and out in a steady motion.

I'm hovering on the precipice, about to fall over the edge. My moans, mingled with Milo's heavy breathing, have me writhing in the water. He presses his thumb against my clit, providing me with immense pleasure.

"Let go, Liv," he murmurs in my ear.

His words are my undoing. I throw my head back as I'm carried away into orgasmic bliss. I'm floating on a cloud, free of all my worries and cares. The only thing that matters is being here in this moment with Milo.

I rest against his chest as he skates his fingers up and down my arms, helping me come down from my euphoric state.

"I need you inside me," I whisper softly. I can't wait any longer.

Without hesitation, he pushes up out of the tub, water splashing across the tiled floor. He helps me out of the bath, leading me to sit on the countertop.

"You're absolutely stunning. I will never tire of seeing you like this, wanton and naked."

Please let that be true. I would give anything for us to spend the rest of our lives together, making up a collection of memories just like this one.

Milo steps between my legs, pushing inside of me in one deep thrust. I bring my hands up to grip his shoulders, digging my nails into his skin as he begins to thrust and in out of me in a frenzy. I let out a low groan, relishing the feeling of being so full.

"Please don't stop," I pant out.

"Never, Stardust. Never," Milo vows.

He picks up his pace, moving in time with our matching heartbeats. A look of lust-filled appreciation is on his face, sending his silent words through me each time he thrusts.

Thrust.

You are mine.

Thrust.

You belong to me and me alone.

Thrust.

You are my home.

Thrust.

I will love you always, Stardust.

"Holy shit," he calls out as I cling to him. "Liv, I can't hold on much longer." He lifts up on the balls of his feet, giving himself the extra height he needs to plunge in deeper, allowing me to feel every single inch of him.

"Milo, that feels incredible," I cry out as I gasp for air.

He drops his head against my shoulder, putting all his energy into driving home.

This is what life would have been like if he had stayed all those years ago. This is what life *could* look like if we're able to move on from the past.

I really want to make this work.

Milo roars out in triumph as he finishes inside of me.

"God, you're incredible, you know that?" he murmurs as he plants a soft kiss against my nose.

"I'd like to do that again," I say matter-of-factly.

"Sure, baby, we can do that as many times as you want." He grins down at me like a Cheshire cat, pleased with my request. He lifts me off the counter and carries me into the bedroom for round two.

Later that night, I fall asleep nestled against Milo's chest, Sirius lying at the foot of my bed. This feels real. A family to call my own.

You have to tell him the truth, the thought creeps into my head as I drift off to sleep.

Chapter Twenty-Six

MILO
Present Day—December

I'M NOT COMPLAINING, BUT LIV has been insatiable in the days leading up to Mac's wake. It feels as if we're desperate to make up for fifteen years' worth of lost time. Unsure what a future together might look like, or if we even have one. Instead of talking through our feelings, we've been using sex as our primary means of communication—another silent truce to avoid any serious conversations until after the wake.

On Tuesday, Liv joined me in the shower, where I took her fast and hard from behind. After our morning stroll through Central Park on Wednesday, we didn't even get past the hallway before I was ripping off her clothes and rutting into her against the wall. Yesterday, I woke up in the middle of the night to her riding me like a professional cowgirl, a shimmer of moonlight shining over her exquisitely naked body like a spotlight.

This morning, though, things were different. I made love to her nice and slow, taking my time with gentle kisses and softly spoken words of affection, showing her just how much she means to me.

She's been battling a mix of grief, lust, and love over the past few days as she tries to grapple with Mac's death. When I'm around, Liv does a good job of masking her suffering. When I leave the apartment, though, all bets are off. There have been multiple times that I've returned from helping Pike with the Bushwick project to find Liv curled up on Mac's bed, clutching one of his pillows as she silently sobs. I know she's petrified of showing me her true emotions, worried that it'll set me off.

If only she knew the truth…

Every day since Mac passed, the hate and resentment that took residence in my heart for the last two decades has slowly started to fade. My every waking moment is no longer consumed with thoughts of revenge or payback. Those feelings have since been replaced with desire, devotion, and adoration for Liv. She's all I care about.

My own personal source of sunlight.

I'm ready to put the past behind us.

I will never forget what Mac did, but he's gone now, and I can't afford to spend another second dwelling in the past on something that I can't control, not if I want to keep Liv. There's no question in my mind that I want to keep her.

Forever.

There isn't a scenario in which Liv and I don't spend the rest of our lives together, preferably fucking like rabbits every chance we get and having babies. Lots and lots of babies—soon, if I have any say.

That escalated quickly.

By the time we're preparing for the wake on Friday afternoon, I'm anxious to get it over with. To put this chapter behind us and move forward once and for all.

I put on a suit and tie and watch as Liv changes into the bell-sleeved, chiffon sheath dress Mac purchased for her the day after receiving his terminal diagnosis. He knew Liv would be grieving and wanted to give her one last gift to remember him by. How do I know? Because it's the same thing I would have done. It seems that Mac and I were much more similar than I care to admit.

When we arrive, it's a mere ten minutes before the crowd starts to gather, and Liv is lost in a sea of mourners coming to pay their respects. She insisted that we hold a wake instead of a funeral, wanting something more personal since Mac had been cremated.

I'm not surprised to see the version of Mac that Liv knew was a well-respected man. I feel a dull ache in my chest, though, as a reminder that I never had the opportunity to know this side of him.

Because he took away that choice before you ever could.

The majority of people here don't know who I am, all of them under the impression that Liv is Mac's only family present.

That's how you wanted it, remember?

"Milo, hey, man. It's good to see you again."

I turn to my right to find Dante walking toward me, where I'm doing my best to avoid the masses.

"Hey, Dante. I'm glad to see a familiar face," I say. Now that Liv and I are together, I don't mind so much that they're friends.

"I wish it were under better circumstances." His voice is apologetic. "Charles wishes he could have been here to pay his respects, but he's out of town for work. He sends his condolences to you and Liv."

"Thanks. I know it means a lot to Liv to have you here," I reply with sincerity.

"Of course. Anything for her—she knows that. Mac was a great man, a pillar of the community, and he will be dearly missed. Not a day will go by that I won't think of him."

"I'm really glad that Liv has you in her corner, Dante. I want you to know that."

"I'm the lucky one. Speaking of which, I'm going to go see if I can find her so I can pay my respects. See you around, man." He gives me a slight nod before going to search for Liv.

Up until a few weeks ago, that conversation, hearing someone praise Mac and put him on a pedestal, would have sent me into a blind rage. Now? I'm grateful to him for facilitating the long-lasting friendship that Liv has forged with Dante. To ensure she would have someone who'd be there for her, no matter what.

However, if Dante wasn't engaged to a man, it'd be a completely different story. I'm the only straight man she'll ever need in her life. I'm keeping her all to myself, cutting out any and all competition before they ever have a chance.

Liv is mine now—end of story.

"Hi, mister!"

Oh no.

I scan the room, looking for a quick escape, but before I can make my move, Grace comes out of nowhere, launching herself at me. She's dressed in a frilly dress that must have come straight from a vintage *Rainbow Brite* collection, paired with her signature light-up shoes that look like they haven't had a break in hours.

Without hesitation, she wraps her tiny body around my leg, giving me her version of a hug. When I finally acknowledge her, she crooks her finger, gesturing for me to bend down so she can tell me something.

I lean over so we're at eye-level and ask, "Where's your mom, little girl?"

"Right over there." She points across the room, where Stella is talking to a couple other women dressed in scrubs. I assume they're Liv's coworkers who've come straight from their shift at the hospital.

When Stella sees me stooped down next to her daughter, she gives a hesitant wave, her stone-cold stare a warning not to mess with Grace—*or else.* How can such a tiny woman be so terrifying?

"What do you want? I'm busy," I say, hoping the little nuisance will get the memo and go find someone else to terrorize.

"No, you're not," she states matter-of-factly. "You've been hiding in this corner since Mama and I got here. I've been watching you."

Okay then. That's not creepy at all.

"Yes, I'm busy hiding out. Now, what do you want?" I snap. *Why won't this little girl leave me alone?*

"Did you keep your promise?" she asks innocently.

"What promise?"

Grace scowls at me, clearly infuriated that I'm not giving her the answer she came for. "At the hospital, you promised you'd look after Dr. Dunham so she wouldn't be by herself when Mac was gone. She's so sad, and I think she needs more friends to help make her happy. Can you help me? I really don't like seeing her so upset," she says as her lips start to quiver.

Great. I wonder what Stella will do to me if her daughter suddenly bursts into tears in my presence.

"Hey now, little girl," I say in a soothing voice, doing my best to calm her down. "Like you said before, we're a team. Do you think I'd ever let my team down?"

She hesitantly shakes her head.

"Dr. Dunham and I are very good friends, and I promise that I'll do everything in my power to make sure she's happy again."

Grace's frown turns into a smile as she nods enthusiastically.

For some odd reason, I want to keep that smile on her face. It's clear she's a good kid who cares about Liv as much as I do, which I appreciate. I can only think of one appropriate response that's good enough for this occasion.

I rest my hands on her shoulders, making sure I have her undivided attention. "You've made Mac proud, Peanut. Real proud."

Her eyes widen with delight when I call her by the nickname Mac used at the hospital the day I returned to New York.

Without warning, Grace jumps into my arms, her little hands holding tightly to my neck as she hugs me. I awkwardly pat her on the back, not sure what else to do. Eventually, she gets tired of my lack of enthusiasm before letting go.

"Does that mean we're friends?" she asks innocently.

"What?"

"If we're both friends with Dr. Dunham, that makes us friends too, right?" She looks at me with a hopeful expression.

"Sure, kid, we're friends," I mutter.

"Yay!" She claps her hands with joy. "I'm going to go tell Mama that I have a new friend. See you later, mister," she shouts over her shoulder as she runs off into the crowd, bursting into a fit of giggles as she goes, obviously not remembering that we're at a wake.

No wonder she and Liv get along so well. They both laugh like mad scientists at the most inappropriate times.

As I stand up, I find Liv walking toward me, coming from the opposite direction of where Grace just ran off.

"I'm glad to see you made a new friend today," she teases.

"Friends or not, that little girl is a nuisance."

Liv raises her eyebrow. "Really, Milo?"

"Fine. She might be growing on me, but only just a tiny bit," I grind out.

"Before you know it, we'll be planning playdates for the two of you and you'll be indoctrinated into the wonderful world of *Frozen*." She laughs, no doubt at an image of Grace and me sitting in front of a TV, wearing tiaras and belting out "Let It Go."

"Are you done?" I ask in a serious tone.

"I guess." She pouts. "It's just so fun to torment you." She wraps her slender arms around my waist, leaning her head against my shoulder. "Thanks for being here today. I know this can't be easy for you, and it means everything to me to have your support."

"Anything for you, Liv." I pause, catching myself before I say *I love you.* I've avoided the dreaded L-word these last few days because she still hasn't said it back, tensing up each time I do. I know she'll say it when she's ready, but I'd rather avoid any more uncomfortable conversations for the time being.

"Milo!"

I grin when I see Eloisa pushing her way through the crowd, waving at me enthusiastically. Pike trails behind her, a stern look on his face. I think he may be the only person who dislikes crowds more than I do. I honestly have no idea how either of us have successfully run a multimillion-dollar business with our lack of people skills. Yet, somehow, between the two of us, we've made it work.

Liv steps off to the side as Eloisa marches right up to hug me, squeezing me tightly.

I've decided from here on out, aside from Liv, I'm banning all physical contact. I've had enough touching today to last me a lifetime.

"I've missed you so much!" Eloisa exclaims, her gaze shifting to Liv every few seconds.

Pike gives my shoulder a grip, his show of a greeting. It seems I'm not the only one wanting to avoid unnecessary physical contact.

"I missed you too, Els," I say.

I texted her every day while Liv and I were away, but kept the calls to a minimum. I've never gone this long without seeing her in person, and I didn't realize how much I'd miss her until now.

"Are you going to introduce us to the beautiful woman standing next to you, son?" Pike asks.

Liv's eyebrows shoot up when Pike calls me son. She seems even more perplexed when I don't snap at him for using that particular moniker.

"Yes, of course." I beam with pride, stepping away from Eloisa to pull Liv to my side. "Pike and Els, I'd like you to meet my Liv."

Yes, she's mine, and I want everyone to know it.

"I'm so glad to finally meet you both," Liv says politely, giving Pike and Eloisa a shy smile.

Without any warning, Eloisa moves in, kissing Liv on both cheeks before giving her a tight embrace. I should have warned Liv that she's a hugger.

"I already know that we're going to be good friends," Eloisa says with certainty. "It makes me so happy to see that you and Milo have finally found your way back to each other. He's much more tolerable now that you're back in his life."

Liv's cheeks turn beet red, giving away her embarrassment that Eloisa and Pike know of our past history. She's quick to recover, though, not missing a beat.

"I'm the lucky one," Liv says. "I want you and Pike to know how much it means to me that you opened your house upstate to Mac and me. I will never be able to repay you for your kindness."

"Of course, my dear, anything for you. You're family now, and we take care of our own," Eloisa states in a kind tone.

Liv gives Els and Pike a broad smile as a lone tear slips down her cheek.

There's no question that Eloisa's words affected her. Liv's been worried she'd be all alone when Mac died, and I think she is starting to see just how untrue that is. Liv has an entire support system at her beck and call. A network of family and friends, ready to rally around her when she needs them most.

There are moments I wish that I were the only person she needed. Now that I have her back, I don't want to share her. If it were up to me, we'd spend the next six months secluded from everyone else, making up for lost time without distraction.

"Come on, Eloisa. We've taken up enough of Liv's time tonight. There will be plenty of time for us to get together soon." Pike gives a wink in my direction. "It was nice to meet you, Liv. Keep this one in check, will you?" He points over at me while giving Liv a big grin.

"I'll do my best," she calls out as he and Eloisa walk off toward the exit.

"You're a miracle worker," I tell Liv.

"Why do you say that?"

"The only person Pike ever willingly smiles at is Els."

"He just likes me more than you," she says with satisfaction. "I have a few more people I need to thank for coming. I'll be back soon, and then we can go home." She presses a kiss against my cheek before disappearing into the crowd.

Home.

I like the sound of that. I might hate New York, but I think I'd be willing to follow Liv anywhere as long as we were together.

I find a chair in the corner of the room and take a seat while I wait for Liv to finish.

It's dark outside by the time the last of the mourners leave. Liv finally makes her way over to me, and as she approaches, I can tell she's utterly exhausted.

I pat the chair next to mine, encouraging her to take a seat.

All I want to do is get her home and run her a hot bath before we curl up in bed. I've blocked out my schedule tomorrow so we can have the entire day to ourselves without any disruptions.

Before we can leave the funeral home, though, I need to tell her how I feel about the Mac situation. That I'm finally ready to put it to rest once and for all so that we can move forward together.

"Liv," I say as I reach out to clasp both of her small, delicate hands in mine, rubbing her palms with my thumbs.

"Yes?" She gives me an expectant look.

"I want you to know that I appreciate you asking me to come today...I mean it."

"You do?" She looks surprised.

"Yes, I do. Is it hard to attend the wake of the man responsible for Ma's death? Sure. But that doesn't change the fact that you mean the world to me, and I would do anything for you," I say with conviction. "I'm ready to put the past behind us, Liv."

"What are you saying?" Her voice is barely above a whisper.

"I want a life with you. I don't want the ghosts of our past to haunt us anymore. Don't you agree?"

I expect Liv to jump for joy and finally declare her love for me, but she doesn't do either of those things. Instead, she seems conflicted, her eyes wide, like a deer in headlights. I don't get it. I thought she would be eager to move on from all this, even more than I am.

I'm shocked when she pulls her hands from mine, settling them into her own lap.

"I can't do this anymore," she says quietly.

"What do you mean you can't do this anymore?" I demand.

There is no way I'm letting her break up with me. Hell, are we even officially together? I don't give a damn. She's mine, and she'll have to deal with the consequences of that, because I'm not letting her go.

"Milo, there's something I need to tell you."

"Why are you acting so strange? You can tell me anything...you know that, right?"

Why is she doubting me after everything we've been through? Haven't I proven to her that I'll put her first, no matter what?

"I need to tell you something about the accident, the night that your mom passed away." She grimaces, knowing damn well how I'm going to react.

I shoot up from my chair, spinning back to face her. Why did she have to bring this up today? We've been doing so well. Why the hell would she ruin that? We're at Mac's wake, for God's sake.

"For the love of God, Liv. Didn't you hear what I just said?" I shout in frustration. "I'm finally ready to put the past behind us, and that includes rehashing the horrific details of what happened to my ma. Why can't you drop this?"

Liv is suddenly fuming with anger, steam practically coming out of her ears. She jumps from her seat so she's standing right in front of me. She may be shorter than me, but there's no denying she's just as fierce as I am.

"I'm sick and tired of you burying your head in the sand. For once in your life, stop being a stubborn pain in my ass!" she screams in my face.

I finally understand the severity of this conversation. Liv never swears. Not when her mom passed, not when I showed up unannounced at the hospital a couple of months ago, and not during the dozens of arguments we've had sense since then. She's always kept herself in check...until now.

"Well, it looks like you're not giving me a choice on whether I want to hear you out or not. What the hell do you have to say that is worth causing a catastrophic fight between us?" My voice is low as I do my best to maintain the peace.

She looks me dead in the eye, preparing herself for whatever she's about to say.

"Mac wasn't driving the car that night," she says in a dry tone.

I feel the blood drain from my face. I'm ice cold, unable to process the words that just came out of Liv's mouth.

"What. The. Fuck. Did. You. Just. Say. To. Me?" I take my time in getting each word out as I try to wrap my head around the ramifications of the bomb she just dropped.

I clench my fists at my sides, my jaw rigid with tension. She slowly takes two steps back, legitimately afraid of me.

"Both your parents were ejected from the vehicle, and the first responders on the scene couldn't determine who had been driving. The morning after the accident, Mac woke up hungover and handcuffed to his hospital bed while an officer shouted in his face, telling him that he was responsible for killing his wife. From what Mac has told me, it sounds like they were relentless. He couldn't remember what had happened, so he confessed under pressure. By the time he recovered his memory, he'd already pled guilty, so there was nothing his public defender could do to overturn the decision.

"The attorney I hired during Mac's parole process was able to dig up an old police report stating that your mom had been driving the night of the accident. There's no telling why the prosecution never mentioned it, or if they even knew the document existed, but it was enough, along with Mac's good behavior, to convince the parole board to grant him early release.

"Mac made me promise not to tell you unless you asked me specifically. He wanted you to come to him willingly, ready to reconcile. He didn't think you'd believe him otherwise."

For some reason, Liv thinks she's safe to come near me and she slowly reaches out to touch my arm. I can only assume it's in a pathetic show of comfort, but I recoil at the thought of her touch.

"Don't fucking touch me," I bellow out. "Do you realize what you've done?"

Mere minutes ago, I was ready to declare my undying devotion to this woman, to tell her I would follow her to the ends of the earth. Now, I can't even stand the sight of her.

"Milo, you have every right to be upset, but it wasn't my truth to tell," she admits. "I'm not sorry for honoring Mac's request. There were plenty of times when I told you to talk to him, to listen to his side of the story, and you flat-out refused. That's on you."

"Are you serious? Do you hear yourself?" I roll my eyes, trying to understand how she can't see how wrong she is. "You've known about this since I came back here for answers. You sat by as I spewed hateful words at a dying man when you could have been the one to help mend our relationship before it was too late. If you had told me the truth, I would have been able to make amends with my dad while he was still alive. You stole that opportunity from me."

I need to get away from here before I spiral any more out of control. I need to get out of this city. Now.

"Let me guess, Liv. You wanted Mac's love and affection all to yourself. You wouldn't have been able to stand it if my dad had forgiven me, because then he would have stopped loving you. You were nothing but an imitation, a replacement when he couldn't have me in his life."

I've hit an all-time low. If I were in my right mind, I wouldn't say these cruel things, but I'm not. I'm a train wreck, and I'm taking Liv down right along with me like I always knew I would.

"You're nothing but a goddamn liar," I spit out, my voice filled with hatred. "You made me think I was the only one in need of forgiveness, but that wasn't the case, was it?"

It's a rhetorical question. I don't want her to answer me.

"We're finished, Olivia, do you hear me?" I say, void of all emotion. Her full name coming from my mouth is a warning not to provoke me any further.

"Milo, please…" Tears stream down her cheeks as she pleads with me to understand. To somehow accept that she's been lying to me all this time.

It's over. The damage is done. Mac is dead, and I'll never be able to ask for his forgiveness for how I treated him when he was never to blame for any of this. Ma's death was nothing more than a tragic accident.

The last thing I see before storming out the front door of the building is Liv dropping down to her knees in despair. I can't find it within myself to go back and offer her comfort. Not after the irrevocable damage she's caused us both.

We're broken beyond repair, and I fear there's no coming back from this…for either of us.

Chapter Twenty-Seven

OLIVIA
Past—Twelfth Grade

"I DON'T UNDERSTAND. CAN YOU repeat that, please?" I ask.

After I passed out in the back of the Uber, I was rushed to the emergency room. Luckily, my driver had only been a block from the hospital when I collapsed, so he was able to quickly get me the medical attention I needed.

I woke up to a crabby nurse poking and prodding my arm, scolding me for being an irresponsible kid and not calling 911. I spent over two hours listening to her drone on about how inconvenient it was that I was a minor, because she couldn't get ahold of my father and I didn't have anyone else for her to call.

I'm sorry that me being all alone during a medical emergency is a problem for you, Gladys.

Before I could go on a full rampage, the ER doctor on call, Dr. Montgomery, arrived to deliver news that had me gasping for air.

"You lost the baby. Olivia, I can't begin to express how sorry I am for your loss," he says with regret.

I can't seem to clearly comprehend his words. My fast-paced breathing and startled expression finally clue him in that I didn't know I was pregnant in the first place. He slowly reaches out to pat me on the shoulder in a show of compassion, but it doesn't bring me any comfort.

"Olivia, you had a miscarriage tonight. That's why you were bleeding and had pain in your abdomen," he tries to explain in a gentle tone. "I want you to know, this isn't your fault. These things happen sometimes, and there is nothing you could have done differently to change the outcome. It's important you remember that."

I nod in agreement, still not sure what's going on.

"We've had a difficult time reaching your dad. Are you sure there isn't anyone else you can call to come and sit with you? You need all the support you can get right now," Dr. Montgomery says.

"No, there's no one to call," I croak out.

I know the man is only trying to help, and it's not his fault the only people I love are gone. The last thing I want is to be left by myself without anyone here to console me after being told I just lost my unborn baby. A baby I hadn't even known existed until now.

The worst part is that both Milo and my father made the conscious decision to abandon me. They could have been here if they wanted to be. Mom didn't have the same choice, but I know she'd be by my side if she could.

"Is there anything I can do to help you process this?" Dr. Montgomery asks.

"I'm sorry. I'm just…I'm trying to wrap my head around the fact that I was pregnant. I only had sex once, and that was three months ago, and I haven't had any symptoms. Wouldn't I have known if I was pregnant?"

Now that I think back to the past few weeks, I *had* been overly tired and feeling nauseous throughout the day, but I just figured it was related to the depression.

I hear a stifled snort coming from the corner of the room where Gladys is standing. I glance over at her just in time to catch the tail end of her rolling her eyes. I might have been naive to think having unprotected sex one time wouldn't lead to pregnancy, but that doesn't give her the right to judge me for it. I was just told that I lost my baby. You'd think that would earn me some semblance of kindness. I guess not.

I was going to be a mother, and now, my baby's gone.

The thought sends me into a tailspin and my chest constricts, making it difficult for me to breathe. My heart aches for the loss of a life that I didn't even know existed until now.

I can't seem to wrap my head around the idea that Milo and I were going to be parents. A baby, a little bundle of joy, to love, protect, and cherish for the rest of our lives.

Of course we had talked about having a family someday during our countless conversations about our future, but that was before our world came crashing down. Maybe he would have stayed if he had known…if I had carried the baby full-term. Now, that hope has been slashed, and I'm forced to carry this burden alone.

"Every woman's pregnancy is different. Some get morning sickness within a few weeks, whereas others don't notice any symptoms until much later. You were only twelve weeks along, so it was still very early. Like I said, there was nothing you could have done to prevent this, Olivia. It wasn't your fault. I truly am sorry for your loss."

I numbly nod like a bobblehead as a single tear trickles down my face. My new reality sets in, and all I'm left with is a forsaken place where I've been tossed by the wayside, forced to grapple with the loss of both my mom and child all on my own.

Is this kind of life even worth living for?

The question slithers into my mind like a poisonous serpent on the hunt as Dr. Montgomery and Gladys shuffle out of the room, shutting the door behind them, leaving me alone with my toxic thoughts.

The next morning, I return home to my family's empty brownstone.

My father never called to check in on me, even after the hospital staff left both him and his assistant several messages.

He wouldn't even notice if I wasn't here anymore. I doubt he'd even care if I simply…disappeared from his life for good.

I find myself standing in my mom's bathroom, staring down at the bottle of heavy-dose painkillers she was prescribed when she got sick.

I inhale deeply as the smell of cherries and linen hits my nose, expecting to turn around to find my mom rummaging in her closet for a sweater before heading downstairs for breakfast.

I would give anything to be with her again. To hear her voice, feel her embrace, and tell her how much I loved her.

I absentmindedly pick up the bottle, turning it around in my hand, the pills clanking against the container. I wonder what it might feel like to take a few, to fall into a void of nonexistence, where I don't have to *feel* anymore. I'm just so tired. Maybe there's a reason I came into my mom's room today. Maybe I was supposed to find these, a way I could be with her again...*and Hope.*

I amble, unrushed, into my mom's closet, not quite sure what I'm doing.

I don't think I'm suicidal. At least, I haven't thought much about ending my life. I'm just having a hard time imagining my life past this moment, unsure what the future holds without a family to share it with.

I collapse to the floor, mindlessly looking at the endless racks of clothes on the wall. I tilt my head back when I see something shiny peeking out through a pair of jeans. I crawl over to investigate, pushing back the pants to discover a large tin storage box with a painting of the stars scattered across the lid.

The pill bottle slips through my fingers, crashing to the floor. I ignore the commotion as I pry open the box to reveal hundreds of letters, all addressed to Milo. I sort through the pile, and upon closer inspection, I discover they're from Mac.

He's been writing to Milo from prison, one letter every week according to the dates on the envelopes. If Milo had known these had been delivered to the house, he would have torn them to pieces the minute each one arrived. It makes sense that my thoughtful mom would preserve them, keeping them hidden, waiting for the right time to give them to Milo. Unfortunately, the time never came, and now, it never will.

I grab one of the letters at random and tear it open, hoping to find *something* inside, although I have no idea what.

Dear Milo,

Not a day goes by that I don't think of you and that fateful night that your ma was taken from us.

There are many things that I would change if I could go back, the most important being that I would have fought for you. For a life beyond this prison cell and the chance to rebuild our family. There's no denying that I had a role in your ma's death, but there is more to the story than you know. I only wish you could find it in your heart to listen to what I have to say and be willing to forgive me for my shortcomings.

Marie visited me last week. It was the first time we'd met in person. Your ma had talked about her fondly, and when I was arrested, I'd called Marie, knowing she would give you the life I no longer could.

She came to tell me that she was diagnosed with an inoperable brain tumor. She was beside herself with anguish, unsure how to break the news to you and Olivia. Especially knowing that you've already been through so much suffering.

I told her that the best thing she can do is to be honest, open, and transparent with you both. To use the rest of the time she has on this earth to cherish, love, and hold you close.

Life is meant to be lived to the fullest. To hold sacred every second of every day because you never know when it will be your last.

Take it from someone who squandered his chance at happiness, blind to what was right in front of me. Simply because my life didn't turn out the way I'd hoped it would...

All I can ask from you, son, is that you don't let this experience negatively define your life. Don't let the loss of your ma or Marie break your spirit. You're stronger than that. You deserve to live, to flourish, to thrive. A lifetime of happy memories are ahead of you if you let them in. Never stop fighting to find joy.

I will always be here for you with open arms, and you will always be my son. I pray that we will be reunited one day.

I love you,

Mac

These words might have been written for Milo, but I know I was meant to read them today.

I've been so consumed with myself these past few months that it never occurred to me to reach out to Mac. He's just as alone as I am—even more so, it would seem. I doubt anyone notified him that my mom passed away or that Milo is in the wind.

I pull my phone from my pocket, knowing what I have to do. It's crazy, but I'm desperate. I only hope Mac will be able to help me. I'm not exactly sure how, I just know I have to see him...today.

I shake as I hand over my ID to the prison guard, nervously biting down on my lip. My internet search was successful in providing detailed information on what to expect when visiting someone in prison. I even found a blog post listing out what you should wear. I got a little carried away and showed up wearing baggy sweatpants and an oversized sweater, my hair is pulled back into a short ponytail, and I didn't put on a lick of makeup.

"You're not on the approved visitors list," the stoic man behind the desk snaps at me.

"You don't understand. I really need to see Mac Covell. It's urgent. It'll only take a few minutes," I insist. I didn't come all this way for nothing.

"That's not how it works around here. You can't just waltz into a prison and demand to see an inmate. What's your relationship to Mac anyway? You his kid?"

I'm not sure how to answer that. If I say no, my chances of getting in are nonexistent. "Uh...sort of. It's complicated."

I shuffle my feet back and forth as my nerves get the best of me.

"It's always complicated." He lets out a humorless laugh. "Look, kid, I really can't let you in. You're not on the list, and I'm not putting my ass on the line by bending the rules for a minor without a parent present."

I squeeze my hands into fists at my sides, my fingernails digging into my palms. I'm doing my best to control my frustration, knowing it won't do me any good if I go off on the guard.

"What's your name?" I ask innocently.

He looks back at me in surprise but hesitantly replies, "John. My name is John."

"It's a pleasure to officially meet you, John. My name's Olivia, but you already know that." I point down at my ID, which he's still holding between his grimy fingers. "I know your policy states that I need to be on the visitors list, and I understand that. I'm only asking that you make this exception once. I really need to talk to Mac."

He starts to shake his head, but I'm not ready to give up.

"Please just listen to me." My voice is raised as I throw my hands up in the air. This is not going how I planned it at all. I inhale through my nose, forcing myself to regain my composure, calmly bringing my arms back down to my sides.

"I'm going to be honest with you, John. I'm not in a good place. I was just released from the hospital after having a miscarriage. I lost my baby, and Mac lost his grandchild. Please don't make me put that in writing. He might be in prison, but he's still human. He deserves to hear this news in person, don't you think?" I keep my back ramrod straight as I stare directly into John's eyes, silently pleading with him to take pity on me.

John looks down at the computer in front of him and back at my ID, repeating the process several times before letting out a heavy sigh. "Look, I'm really sorry for your loss. My sister had a miscarriage a few years back and went through a rough patch for a while there. I'll let you through this one time, but if you're not added to the list, you won't be allowed in next time, got it?"

I nod enthusiastically. "Thank you so much."

There won't be a next time. I don't plan on seeing Mac again after this, but John doesn't need to know that.

I wait for what feels like forever and nearly fall out of my chair when one of the guards barks out, "Olivia Dunham, you're up."

I stand up on shaky legs and follow another guard down a low-lit hallway. He leads me into a crowded room with inmates and their visitors.

There are at least a dozen metal tables scattered across the room, each one bolted to the floor. I stop mid-stride when I suddenly realize that I have no idea what Mac looks like. Since the only time Milo visited four years ago, we haven't talked about Mac very often and I've never seen a photo of him.

I'm keenly aware of a loud creak coming from the other side of the room. I look up at the gate being opened and watch as another prisoner is being ushered through by a guard. I let out a small gasp when I see that he's a near replica of Milo. The key differences being his pale skin tone, tattoos covering his bulging arms, and his muscular build.

I find myself intimidated by the big, burly man stalking toward me. What if he tells me to get lost? Or worse, what if he truly is a bad person? What was I thinking, showing up here? Have I really stooped that low that I visit prisoners now?

I'm prepared to turn around and ask the guard to get me out of here, but before I can make a move, Mac is standing right in front of me. He arches an eyebrow, silently questioning who I am and why I asked to visit him.

I'm overcome with emotion, and my upper lip starts to quiver as unwelcome tears trickle down my face.

Without thinking, I launch myself at Mac, wrapping my arms around his giant waist, needing some form of human contact—something I've been deprived of for months. Sobs continue to rack my body as one of his muscular arms awkwardly makes its way around my shoulders, trying to give me the comfort I'm searching for.

"Hey there, kiddo. Whatever's bothering you, it's going to be okay. It can't be as bad as being locked up in here, can it?" he says.

I let out a choked laugh in between my blubbering. "I'm sorry…I…I know we're not supposed to make physical contact. I just…I really needed a hug."

He squeezes me tight before pulling back. "It's okay. I really needed that hug too," he whispers softly in my ear.

After he lets me go, he walks around the table to take a seat at the other end. A guard approaches to cuff the chain around Mac's ankles to the metal table, not saying a word about the scene that just took place, which I appreciate.

"You must be Olivia, Marie's daughter," Mac states.

I look at him with wide eyes as I nod. "Yeah, I, um…well, I came across one of your letters to Milo. The one where you mentioned that she came to visit. I didn't read it on purpose, though. I mean, yeah, I saw that it was addressed to Milo from you, but I just…I needed to know what you had to say to him."

"Is Milo here with you?" His eyes shimmer with hope as he turns toward the visitors' entrance.

I slump my shoulders. He couldn't care less about me. Why would I ever think differently? He doesn't even know me. Of course he'd ask for Milo. I shouldn't be hurt by his reaction, but for some reason, I am.

"No, Milo isn't here," I confess. "Look, I'm really sorry I bothered you. This was all a big mistake. I should get going." I bolt up from my chair and it scrapes loudly across the floor. Nearly everyone in the room turns to stare at me.

"Kiddo," Mac says to get my attention.

"Hmm?" I gaze back down to find him intently watching me.

"Can you sit back down?" he asks. "It's clear you came here for a reason, so why don't we talk for a few minutes?"

I let out a half-hearted chuckle before awkwardly plopping back down in my chair.

I spend the next hour pouring out my heart and soul to a total stranger. I tell Mac about my mom, her lost battle with cancer, and the years I spent with Milo. Finally, after shedding more tears, I share the news about my baby. I'm shocked when he cries right alongside me, and we take a moment to grieve together for the baby neither of us will ever have the chance to meet.

By the time our visit comes to an end, I feel more at peace than I have since losing Mom all those months ago.

When I turn to leave, Mac stops me. "Olivia, I want you to know that you have so much to live for. A beautiful life awaits you, if you're willing to work for it. Don't let what happened to you define the rest of your life. I'd really like it if you decided to come back to see me next week." He flashes a smile before he's escorted out of the room.

Mac Covell unknowingly saved my life today, and I will do whatever I can to show him how grateful I am for his selfless act of kindness.

Chapter Twenty-Eight

MILO
Present Day—April

I GLARE DOWN AT THE cigarette pressed firmly between my fingers. I've been contemplating lighting up for the past hour, but for some reason, I can't bring myself to do it. Since returning to Vegas four months ago, I've lost the urge to smoke altogether.

I might not be a part of Liv's life anymore, but my conscience has been tormenting me around the clock, reminding me that she's already lost Marie and my dad to cancer.

In spite of the declaration I made as I left Mac's wake, I don't think she deserves to lose anyone else she cares about to the merciless disease. Even me, her piece-of-shit ex-boyfriend, the man who walked out on her *twice* and told her that we were finished.

I'm a real keeper.

Needless to say, I've been in a foul mood ever since.

Without smoking—the one stress reliever that's never failed me—I've had to resort to chewing several packs of Big Red a day. It's not nearly as satisfying as a cigarette, but I begrudgingly admit it's done wonders for my health. I'm already back to running at full speed.

During the week, I pour myself into work, resulting in business doing better than ever, even though I've refused to set foot back in New York since the wake.

I spend my weekend nights roaming the casinos on the Strip, in search of someone who piques my interest. I'm desperate to find a woman down for a one-night stand, someone to get my mind off Liv and the way we left things. Over the months, I've come in contact with hundreds of beautiful women, yet I haven't taken a single one to bed.

Zip, zero, nada.

Before Liv came back into my life, I was never satisfied, rotating through women like they were the ice cream flavor of the day. Desperate to sate my ever-growing sexual appetite. However, now that I know what I've been missing, both my brain and my dick are on strike, in agreement that only Liv could ever fully satisfy them.

Aside from my late-night excursions, I've become a hermit for all intents and purposes, even skipping out on my weekly dinners with Pike and Eloisa, avoiding them at all costs. I've gone as far as using Richard as the go-between to pass on all work-related communications between Pike and me.

After storming out of the funeral home, I returned to my Brooklyn apartment to give Pike and Eloisa the full rundown of my conversation with Liv. They didn't agree with how I handled things, especially Eloisa. She was furious and demanded I make things right with Liv. I refused, and since then, avoidance has become my new normal.

I feel a soft nudge against my free hand and look down to find Sirius has come out to the balcony, pressing his head against my hand, asking for a scratch behind the ear.

Since Mac died, Sirius has been moping around. Even his favorite hedgehog and its new companion that Eloisa gifted him have been neglected these past few months. He doesn't seem to understand that Mac is gone for good, so he's confused why we can't visit him.

Oftentimes, he'll stand by the front door and whine, not satisfied when I take him out for our morning run. It always seems like he's searching for something that he can never find.

Me too, bud. Me too.

We ran out of Eloisa's homemade dog treats over a month ago, another reason he's unhappy with me.

I've hit an all-time low where even my own dog hates me. I bend down to oblige him, to show my appreciation for the scrap of attention he's willing to give me today.

"Hey there, boy. I've missed you."

His tail wags happily as he leans into my touch.

Why does it seem like everyone is on Liv's side? Hell, I'm the one who's been wronged. She knew long before I marched into Mac's hospital room that he was never responsible for Ma's death. She listened to me spew hateful words toward him countless times during the time we spent together and never said a damn thing.

Would I have listened?

That's not the point. She should have told me.

Sure, she made subtle comments about me needing to be more willing to hear Mac's side of the story and to be open to putting the past behind me. The problem is, she never shied away from putting me in my place before, so nothing should have stopped her from telling me the truth.

I don't give a shit if Mac made her promise not to say a word. She shouldn't have listened. She deprived Mac and me of any chance of reconciliation before it was too late. Now, I'll never be able to make amends.

Every night since Liv spilled the truth, sleep has eluded me.

I'm haunted by the last words Mac spoke to me. *"I will always love you, son."*

Even on his deathbed, he put me first. He knew the truth would eventually come out and that I would need those six precious words, the same words I'd refused to let him say to me in the past. He died thinking that his only child hated him, but that didn't deter him from giving me a final gift in the form of a father's unconditional love.

It's far too late to make amends with my dad, but I will spend the rest of my life honoring his legacy.

If that were true, you'd forgive Liv and beg her to take you back.

I'm shaken from my thoughts when I hear a knock at the front door. I can count on one hand the number of people who have access to my penthouse, and I'm avoiding them all. Plus, it's far too early in the morning to be considered a reasonable hour to show up on someone's doorstep unannounced. That fact alone gives me a good guess as to who it is, and I'm proven right when I open the door and am greeted by Pike's glowering demeanor.

"What are you doing here?" I ask, feigning ignorance.

From the look of disdain on his face, he's here for a confrontation, one I'd like to avoid if I can help it. It seems Pike has other ideas as he storms right into my apartment without an invitation. I cautiously close the door, preparing for the fallout about to ensue.

"Really, son?" Pike says in a patronizing tone. "You're going to play it like that? Are you seriously going to pretend like you haven't been ignoring your family for months? The people who love you the most? Eloisa has been beside herself with worry, petrified you might disappear for good or never speak to her again."

Guilt eats at me as I picture Eloisa in distress. She's called me hundreds of times since I got back to Vegas, but I've ignored every single one.

"Now, I can tolerate you giving me the cold shoulder, but I refuse to let you further disrespect the woman I love," Pike declares, his eyes swimming with ire. "If you recall, Eloisa welcomed you into our home with open arms in spite of your piss-poor attitude. That woman has stood by the sidelines for the last fifteen years, cheering you on every step of the way. Do you honestly think I would have promoted you to CEO when I did if it wasn't for her advocating on your behalf?"

I jerk back at his callous tone, unaware he had reservations about stepping down at Lawson Co.

"Eloisa has always believed in you, son, even on the days you've rejected her affection. She's never asked to replace your ma. All she's ever wanted is your love." Pike pauses to clear his throat. "After several agonizing attempts at getting pregnant with no explanation for why we couldn't conceive, she pleaded with God to bring her a child. It didn't matter their age, what they looked like, or their background. She simply wanted someone besides me to love. From the moment I found you asleep at the construction site, curled up like a lost lion cub with nowhere to go, I knew her prayers had been answered. Despite your forlorn attitude, you brought new life into our home, and I'd even go so far as to say you saved our marriage. You brought my Eloisa back to me."

Pike gives me a small smile as he nervously taps his foot on the hardwood floor, preparing himself to continue.

"That doesn't excuse your recent behavior. Don't think for a minute that I'll let you continue to take your self-loathing out on Eloisa. I won't allow it. I understand you're in misery, but it's about damn time you got a wake-up call, son." Pike's voice hardens as he stands stiffly in front of me. "I'm telling you now, if you don't get your head out of your ass, you will lose everything good in your life, including Liv."

His harsh words make me flinch, and the thought of never seeing Liv again rubs me the wrong way.

"Son, are you willing to lose Liv over this? The way I see it, you've both wronged each other, but at the end of the day, you have to ask yourself if your love is strong enough to move forward."

I don't move a muscle as I allow Pike's words to sink in. An ache forms in my chest at the thought of Eloisa thinking I don't care about her. She's one of the most important people in my life. She gladly welcomed me into her home and treated me like her own son. It doesn't matter that I carry a chip on my shoulder the size of a boulder, Pike and Eloisa love me unconditionally.

I square my shoulders and find the courage to look Pike directly in the eye. A real man should be able to admit when he's wronged someone—something I'm still learning at the ripe old age of thirty-three.

"Pike, I owe you and Els my life," I say with warmth. "I will forever be grateful for the gift you gave me—a place to start fresh and to be myself. I know you only want what's best for me, and you might think it's Liv, but honestly? I don't think I can forgive her…not this time." A lump forms in my throat, and I fight back the unshed tears I've been holding back for months. Grown-ass men don't cry.

"How am I supposed to move on knowing Ma's death was a terrible accident that couldn't have been prevented and I've spent more than half my life blaming my dad? I'm enraged he didn't fight harder for me. He should never have confessed to a crime he didn't commit in the first place, and even then, he should have done more to clear his name, to make his way home to me, but he never did. It hurts to know he trusted Liv with the truth, but not me. He readily accepted that I would always hate him, so much so that he didn't put any effort into making amends. Tell me, Pike, how do I get past something like that? How do I look Liv in the eye—the one person who was supposed to have my back, no matter what—and forgive her for taking away my last chance at making things right with my dad?" My voice cracks toward the end of my admission, my composure smashed to smithereens.

I sag against the entryway wall as tears fall down my face. So much for being a grown-ass man who doesn't cry. I've never broken down in front of Pike before. Hell, the only three people who've ever seen me like this are Ma, Marie, and Liv.

I'm stunned when Pike drops down next to me and throws his arm around my shoulders, making it easy for me to rest against him as I fall to pieces. The heavy weight of my burdens has finally become too much for me to bear on my own. Neither of us moves as the pain, resentment, and anguish I've held pent up inside of me for the last two decades washes away.

Pike remains a steady presence, a pillar of support and devotion. After a while, he clears his throat, breaking the silence.

"Milo, if you're unwilling to forgive Liv, then you're going to have to cut me out of your life too," he states.

"What do you mean?" I ask skeptically.

"A few months after you came to live with us, I visited your dad in prison. I knew if I had a son of my own, I would want peace of mind by knowing he was alive and well. During the first visit, Mac didn't say much. He wanted me to spend the entire hour telling him about your time with Eloisa and me and your new life in Vegas."

My breath hitches in surprise at this confession. I had no idea he had done that. There were a few times he left town for an undisclosed work trip, but I never imagined it was to meet with my dad.

"He was so proud of you. I visited every year until he was released. He told me the truth about your ma's accident the last time I saw him. He begged me not to say a word. To this day, I've never even told Eloisa." Pike keeps his eyes downcast as he talks. "He wanted you to come to him on your own terms, Milo. He knew that if he told you too soon, you wouldn't believe the truth.

"Son, I didn't maliciously withhold information, and neither did Liv. We only respected your dad's wishes. The person who loved you the most and thought he was making the choice that was best for you. I'm not saying it was the right decision, simply that Liv and I chose to honor that." Pike shifts uncomfortably next to me.

I lift my head from his shoulder, resting it against the wall. I close my eyes as I think through my options. I can choose to be outraged at Pike for going behind my back and not admitting he met with my dad for years. Part of me wants to do just that. However, a bigger part knows that he did it with the best intentions, and I can't fault him for looking out for me.

Liv had good intentions too.

I know that, but her betrayal feels different.

"Milo, it's time," Pike declares. I keep my eyes squeezed shut as he speaks. "It's time to seize your happily ever after, son. There's no denying that Olivia is your soulmate. You've left her twice now, and I have no doubt that she'll move on eventually. She is a beautiful woman with a kind heart. Any man would be lucky to have her. If you wait any longer, someone else will sweep her off her feet. They'll get married and have a family, and by then, it'll be too late. You'll never have another chance to get her back. You've already squandered your second chance. The third strike, and you're out. She's your sun, Milo. Isn't that worth fighting for?"

My eyes pop open, and I glance over at Pike.

Liv with someone else? That's ridiculous. She's mine. She will always be mine.

"What if we can't get past this? What if she can't forgive me? The last time I saw her, I said some things that I will never be able to take back," I confess.

"Milo, you're human," Pike says. "We all make mistakes. It's time you learn from yours and make things right. Go and get your woman back, son. It's about damn time we're all part of the same family, don't you think?" he asks with a grin.

As he stands up to leave, I follow suit, murmuring the words that I've never been able to say out loud before.

"Pike, I want you to know…I love you. You really did save me the day we met. You taught me how to be a man, how to work hard, and how to treat a woman right. You and Els will always hold a special place in my heart. I know Ma sent you both to me, just like she did with Marie and Liv."

Pike gives me a pat on the back, a heartwarming smile on his face. "I love you too, son. Now, please make up with Els so I can get my wife back."

"Sure thing. I'll head over to the house in a little bit, but I need to make a few calls first."

He nods before heading toward the front door.

I'm not sure how, but I know I need to fix things with Liv. Whatever happens, I have to do everything in my power to keep her in my life *permanently*.

"Oh, I almost forgot." Pike turns back to me, holding out a plain white envelope. "This was delivered to the house a couple of weeks after Mac passed. I was planning to give it to you after the wake, but you decided that was a good time to shut me out," he says with a wink.

I silently reach out and take the envelope. I immediately recognize Mac's penmanship as the same that was on the letter delivered to my office last year. As soon as Pike walks out the door, I slam it shut before tearing open the envelope, desperate to read Mac's words…his final goodbye.

Milo,

From the moment your ma and I found out we were expecting you, our entire world changed for the better. We were two kids from the wrong side of the tracks without any family and not a penny to our name. That didn't stop the boundless love we felt for each other and for you.

I remember holding you in my arms for the first time. You were screaming at the top of your lungs with bright red cheeks and a patch of curly black hair on top of your head. You were perfect. I made a promise that day to love and protect you always.

I've made countless mistakes in my lifetime; however, my biggest regret is breaking that promise. Somewhere along the way, I lost sight of what was most important in my life, and it cost me you and your ma. The day I lost Jada is the day I lost a piece of myself, and I no longer felt worthy to be your father.

When I woke up the morning after the accident, I couldn't remember what had happened, and by the time I did, it was far too late. I had confessed, and there was no backtracking. The one thing I did right was call

Marie. I knew she had been a dear friend of your ma's, and it gave me peace of mind to know that she would take good care of you when I couldn't and would love you as her own child.

The day you came to the prison to see me, I had planned to tell you the truth about what happened the night of the accident. By that point, though, you had already made up your mind that I was responsible, and I knew you wouldn't believe anything else. It nearly broke me when you announced to the entire room that I was no longer your dad. However, I understood why you did it, and if I had been in your shoes, I would have done the exact same thing.

Not a day has gone by since then that I haven't thought of you.

When I met Olivia for the first time, she was a mere shell of herself. In some ways, she reminded me of myself after I lost your ma. She needed guidance and direction more than anything. I couldn't do much from inside the prison walls I was trapped in, but the one thing I could do was be there for her.

From the moment I saw her, I knew she was special, and that she was important to you. I made a new promise that day: to be there for Liv until the day you came back for her and realized that your life wasn't worth living without her by your side.

Over the last fifteen years, she has been a beacon of light in an otherwise bleak world. She's like the sun, always lifting me out of the darkness when I'm at my lowest point.

When I found out I had terminal cancer, I knew I had to intervene. You and Liv were always meant to be together. All you needed was a little nudge in the right direction to help you reunite. That was why I asked Jane to contact you. I knew if she mentioned Liv's name, you'd come running, your feelings toward me be damned. I knew you'd be furious with Liv at first, but like I predicted, your anger was short-lived.

Just like Jada was my soulmate, Liv is yours, and there's no force on earth that can keep you two apart. Take it from someone who lost his better half far too early: life isn't worth living without her by your side. No matter your reservations, let them go and worship Liv the way she deserves.

If I know her like I think I do, she told you the truth about the night of the car accident at the earliest opportunity after my passing. I made her vow not to tell you until after I was gone because I wanted you to come to me on your own. In the end, I got what I wanted most. To be surrounded by my family as I took my last breath. You, Liv, and Sirius all close by, in a peaceful and serene setting. I died knowing those I loved most were with me at the end, and that's more than I could have ever asked for.

Liv has found a way to forgive you for your mistakes. It's damn time you returned the favor. Move on from the past once and for all and live life to its fullest—not just for yourself, but for Liv too, and the beautiful family you'll create together.

Please tell Pike and Eloisa I will forever be grateful to them for taking you in and loving you like their own. Both them and Marie gave you the life I never could.

It might be selfish of me, but it brings a smile to my face knowing that I will be with your ma again very soon. I can't wait to see her angelic face, to run my fingers through her hair, and to tell her how much I've missed her.

Don't spend another minute feeling remorse for me. My life didn't turn out the way I thought it would, but I had a good run. Jada and I will be rooting for you and Liv on the other side.

I am so proud of you, and I am honored to call you my son.

Mac

As I finish reading the letter, I can't help but feel overwhelmed by the peace surrounding me. I sense my parent's presence nearby, offering their love and support from the other side, just like Dad said in his letter.

From the moment I met Liv, fate has played a part in our destiny, pushing us toward each other even when we've desperately tried to pull ourselves apart. I know now with certainty that I need Liv in my life, *to have and to hold.*

The question is, how the hell am I going to get her back?

Chapter Twenty-Nine

OLIVIA
Present Day—April

SPRING IS IN THE AIR as I step out of the hospital after a grueling eighteen-hour shift. Mid-April means the birds are chirping, and the perennials in the garden beds along the front of the entrance are starting to bloom. To me, they symbolize a new beginning, a chance to start fresh—my personal motto as of late.

Every time I exit through the main doors after work, I find myself looking up, expecting to see Milo jogging toward me from his spot on the park bench across the street like he did the day he unexpectedly stormed back into my life. Even when he was seeking revenge, he still cared. He denied it at the time, but I like to think I know his intentions better than he does, just like he knows me better than I know myself.

At least, I used to know him best—before he walked out on me a second time.

Under his rough exterior, he's always had a heart of gold, loyal to the end to those he loves.

I never told him I saw him that afternoon, a few minutes before he came to help Mac. I had gone outside to get the car and spotted him across the street, shocked that he hadn't left yet. I had been held hostage by his presence as I watched him wrap his lips around the cigarette resting between his fingers, reverted back to years ago of him doing the same thing as we strolled through Central Park. His broody demeanor was evident as he spoke on the phone, no doubt recapping the situation that had just occurred with Mac and me.

Whenever I think back to the day of Mac's wake, I can't help but wonder if there was anything I could have done to prevent Milo from leaving me again. No matter how often I play the scene in my mind, I come to the same conclusion: he was never going to stay. There isn't a single scenario in which he would have taken the news of his dad's innocence well. Not after spending two decades loathing the man and wishing he were dead, only to discover once he was gone that the reason behind his resentment had been ill-informed.

Milo's anger toward me was justified, and I wasn't surprised by his behavior when I told him the truth. In fact, he reacted just as I'd predicted he would. The only difference being that in my mind, I was naïve enough to think that after he had time to process the truth, he would come back to me. I'd hoped that the good times we shared would outweigh the bad, and he'd decide that, despite everything, he couldn't live without me.

However, as the days pass by, I'm beginning to think this is a repeat of when he left me back in high school. It's more difficult this time, knowing that he walked away because of something I did. At the time, I thought I was doing the right thing by honoring Mac's wishes, but I see now that if I had told Milo sooner, I could have prevented so much heartbreak and pain.

It's too late to change the past now, though.

Milo holds me single-handedly responsible for taking away his last chance to restore his relationship with Mac, and I don't think he has it in his heart to forgive me…not for this.

The last words Milo said before leaving me alone on the floor of the funeral home play on a loop every night as I lie in bed…*We're finished Olivia, do you hear me?*

The way I see it, Milo and I have both made monumental mistakes that have changed the course of our lives. Without a way to alter the past, all we can do now is move forward and start anew.

I hope that Milo is a part of my new beginning, but I know in my heart that even if he isn't, I'll be okay.

My heartache will mend, and the grief will eventually fade. Mac taught me that even in the darkest of storms, there will always be a rainbow at the end, a silver lining worth searching for, and this situation isn't any different.

Even in death, the man is still looking out for me. In the months since his passing, I've discovered he left me with two unexpected gifts and the chance to turn over a new leaf.

The first gift was a devoted support system, a family forged through friendships and unlikely connections. It's something I'd thought I would lose once Mac was gone, but he made sure that didn't happen. I'm surround by a group of people who have rallied around me and have been there to buoy me up when I'm at my lowest and need a shoulder to cry on.

Even though I have been friends with Dante since college, Mac was the one who created a lasting kinship with him, taking the time to connect over a similar upbringing. Mac was an advocate and supporter of Stop Hunger and volunteered his time every Saturday, without fail. Over the years, their strong bond transferred to my own close friendship with both Dante and his fiancé, Charles.

Now that Mac is gone, I've stepped into his shoes, volunteering alongside Dante each Saturday. He's even asked me to be the best person in his upcoming August wedding that will take place in Central Park—an ode to his humble beginnings.

As Grace's doctor, I was merely doing my job. Mac made the effort to provide companionship in the form of sitting with her during her treatments. He went as far as making sure Stella always had enough money to get by so she could spend her time caring for her ailing daughter. I was simply a bystander who benefited from their friendship. Since the wake, though, Grace and Stella stop by my apartment at least once a week to order Chinese takeout and watch *Frozen*.

Even my friendship with Jane grew stronger when Mac came into the equation. Since his passing, we talk nearly every day and go to lunch together on Tuesdays.

If Mac had never intervened, Milo would never have shown up at the hospital all those months ago, and in turn, I would never have been introduced to Eloisa. I was confused when she called me a week after Mac's wake. When I first answered the phone, I was prepared for her to scream and yell at me, condemning me for how I'd handled things with Milo.

I was relieved when that wasn't the case.

She called to send her condolences and see how I was doing. There was no finger-pointing or judgment regarding the situation with Milo. In fact, she didn't mention his name a single time during our first conversation. She seemed to genuinely care about my well-being in the aftermath of losing Mac.

Since our first call, we've spoken at least once a day. She's become a light in my life, the mother figure that I've been missing since my own mom passed away more than fifteen years ago.

The second gift was technically from Milo, yet it was Mac who had brought us back together, so he gets the credit. It's a priceless treasure I never dreamed of having again in this lifetime, a promise of a better future coming with it. I can't help but think my mom and Jada had a hand in this surprise from up above.

This particular gift I'm keeping to myself for a little while longer so I can bask in the afterglow of the news that has forever changed my life as I know it.

I rush down the street, weaving in and out of the throng of people heading home from work. If I hurry, I might still be able to make it on time. Just as I turn the corner, my phone starts to ring. I dig around in my purse, shoving past my wallet, favorite lip gloss, and a pack of Big Red I couldn't resist buying at the convenience store last week.

Luckily, I'm able to fish my cell out in the nick of time, grinning when I see Eloisa's name on the screen. I'm surprised she waited this long to call me today.

"Eloisa, hi! You called at the perfect time. I just finished my shift." I pant as I pick up my pace.

"I'm so glad I caught you. I hadn't heard from you today and was starting to get worried."

Milo wasn't joking when he lovingly referred to her as a mama bear. She's fiercely loyal and protective, and oftentimes, when she's concerned for our safety, her anxiety gets the best of her. Her overprotective inclinations might bother some, but I welcome them with open arms. It's a reprieve from going so long without a maternal figure.

"I got caught up with a new patient or I would have called sooner. What are you up to?"

"I'm testing a new recipe for my ribollita today and can't quite get the spices right this time around." She sighs in frustration. "I'm at home, hiding from the new general manager of Eloisa's Place. She insisted I spend the entire morning recording videos of me preparing some of our most popular dishes so she can post them to TikTok. I don't understand why anyone would want to watch me cook or how it's relevant to the business. Back in my day, good food spoke for itself, and you didn't need a viral video to get people to come to your restaurant."

"Eloisa, weren't you the one who recruited this new manager?" I inquire.

"Yes, I was. Who is more capable of selecting the best candidate for the position than me? She might have been the most logical choice, but that doesn't mean I can't sneak away from time to time when I need a break from her domineering personality."

I let out a bark of laughter, not able to help myself. "Oh, Eloisa, it sounds like you might have finally met your match."

"You have no idea," she mumbles.

I'm glad she finally hired some additional help. Her business has rapidly grown over the last few years. People come from all over the world for a chance to eat at Eloisa's Place in Vegas. It's grown so popular that she's opening a new location in New York this fall, which Dante will be heading up after he gets back from his honeymoon.

I was shocked to find out a couple months ago that Milo had mentioned Dante's name to Eloisa, suggesting he'd be an excellent addition to her team in New York. Within a few short weeks, Dante received a generous job offer he couldn't pass up. Eloisa even included a yearly donation to Stop Hunger as part of his benefits package.

"In honor of Mac, and to keep the good cause going," she told me when I asked her about it.

"You know, I've never been to your flagship restaurant. I guess I'll have to wait until your New York location opens up. Dante and Milo have both told me I'm missing out on your phenomenal Italian cooking—" I abruptly cut myself off when I realize I said Milo's name, but it doesn't seem to faze her.

"I have a better idea. Why don't you take a few days off work and come to Las Vegas? Like I always say, my food is best served in my kitchen, where it's made with love. We could go to a show on the Strip and spend a day at the spa, and I could give you a personal tour of the restaurant. What do you say?" Her voice is bubbling over with excitement, and it breaks my heart to have to turn her down.

"I would like nothing more than to come for a visit, but it's not a good idea." I hope I sound convincing. "You're Milo's family, his safe haven. I refuse to encroach on his territory without discussing it with him first."

Eloisa clicks her tongue in disappointment. "That's enough of your nonsense. You are just as much a part of this family as Milo is, do you hear me?" she says with sincerity. "You're a breath of fresh air after I've been stuck with Pike and Milo for the last fifteen years. I can only handle two sulky, broody men who only know how to grunt out a response for so long. If Milo has a problem with you being a part of my life, he'll have to take it up with me. Though, something tells me he'll come around soon enough."

"It's been four months, Eloisa…"

"Don't give up on him just yet, all right?"

We've never talked about my relationship—or lack thereof—with Milo. I'm not sure why Eloisa suddenly wants to talk about it now, but I don't inquire further. When I glance up, I find my destination is coming up on the right.

"Hey, I'm so sorry, but I have to go. I'm at Giovanni's, and I know better than to keep him waiting any longer than I already have," I say quickly.

"Giovanni's? You're at a restaurant? I thought you had group therapy tonight. Why aren't you there? Who are you meeting?" Her voice unexpectedly turns panicked.

I can't figure out why she's suddenly so interested in my therapy session. Sure, she's nosy, but she doesn't typically ask about that part of my life. I wonder what set off her anxiety today.

"Yeah, I had a last-minute change of plans and have to skip therapy tonight, though believe me, I'd rather be there than here. I'd rather be anywhere but here. I'm so sorry, but I'm already late, so I really need to go. I'll call you tomorrow."

"Oh, okay. Yes, call me back as soon as you can. Goodbye, dear."

As I navigate my way to the hostess station, the woman behind the desk gives me a disapproving look.

I'm dressed in my navy-blue scrubs, white tennis shoes, and a black winter coat. When I got the call to come here, I had planned to go home and change beforehand, but I got caught up preparing a new patient's treatment plan.

This place might be considered a fine-dining experience, but I've always detested those who judge a person based on their appearance without any context. I'm not here to impress anyone, and I couldn't care less about how this particular woman feels about what I'm wearing.

"I'm sorry, but we're completely booked out for the next three months," the hostess snaps at me. She avoids eye contact, dismissing me without a second thought.

"That's quite all right. I'm here to meet someone, and I can assure you, *he* has reservations," I snip back, infuriated with her lack of respect simply because she doesn't think I have deep pockets.

She lets out a heavy sigh, finally glancing up from the tablet in her hand. "Who are you meeting?"

"Harrison Dunham."

A name well respected in the business district, one that has the hostess dropping the stylus she's holding to the ground.

My father has business ventures all over the world, Giovanni's being one of them. He'll invest in pretty much anything if he deems it lavish enough. From the opulent marble floor to the massive crystal chandelier hanging in the lobby, I'd say this place is right up his alley.

"Of course, you must be Olivia," the woman stammers. "Mr. Dunham is waiting for you. Follow me right this way."

Her change in demeanor is spectacular now that she thinks I'm someone of importance. She doesn't know it, but the truth is that I'm of no significance to Harrison. To him, my only purpose is to serve as a trivial pawn in his quest for world domination.

I silently observe the hostess as we make our way through the luxurious space. From a distance, she's gorgeous, with her slender frame, large breasts, and pouty lips. But up close, I can see the clumps in her fake eyelashes, the dark brown roots of her seemingly platinum-blonde hair, and the streak down the back of her left leg from a poorly done spray tan. A mere imitation of the grace and beauty my mother once had.

Her artificial features won't stop my father from taking her to bed tonight. In fact, if she plays her cards right, she just might become lucky wife number seven. According to Father's assistant, there's a vacancy available.

We make our way up a flight of stairs to a private dining room. It's completely empty except for a single table near the floor-to-ceiling windows where I spot my father leaning back in his chair. There's an empty plate of food and a glass of scotch sitting in front of him.

It seems he couldn't wait for me to start his meal, but it doesn't matter. I don't plan to be here long enough to eat a four-course meal anyway.

The last time I saw my father in person, he was leaving for Paris the day after my mom's funeral.

I wish I could say he's grown a potbelly, has a receding hairline, or has lost his sense of fashion. Unfortunately, he hasn't aged a day, still has a full head of blond hair, and looks impeccable in his favored feather-gray Armani suit.

He doesn't lift his eyes from his phone as I approach the table. I watch as he furiously types away with a scowl on his face. Probably in the middle of an urgent business deal worth millions that can't possibly wait until after he's met with his only child who he hasn't seen in over a decade.

Some things never change.

I was skeptical when I got a call from his assistant, insisting I meet with him this evening. I almost didn't come, but I'll admit, my curiosity got the best of me. Now that I'm here, though, I'm beginning to think it was a mistake. The man of the hour doesn't even have the decency to acknowledge my presence.

I wave the hostess off, curtly dismissing her, and can't help but grin at the frown on her face as she walks off when my father doesn't pay her any mind.

I drag my chair out from under the table before sitting down, making as much noise as possible. When that doesn't get Harrison's attention, I try a different approach.

"Father, it's good to see you," I say dispassionately.

He snaps his head up as if surprised to find me sitting across from him. "There you are," he barks. "It seems your lack of time management skills has held strong after all these years."

I guess we're skipping straight past the pleasantries today and getting right down to the insults.

He hasn't changed a bit.

My patience is wearing thin, and I've only just sat down. I can't imagine sitting through the entire dinner like this. *I don't plan on finding out.* As soon as I figure out what he wants, I'm getting out of here.

"You're the one who requested my presence, which means you need something from me. I don't think throwing shade is the best way to get what you want, is it?" I ask in a patronizing tone.

Harrison lets out an aggravated sigh, folding his arms across his chest in a show of dominance. "I wanted to inform you that I've sold the brownstone as I have no further use for it. You have until next Wednesday to get anything out that you want to keep. Everything else will be sold at an estate sale."

He doesn't blink or show any emotion over selling my childhood home. I find it odd since he was the one who insisted my mom move there when I was born, and he was the one who chose every piece of decor, transforming the place into a mausoleum that never quite felt like home. As a kid, I was forced to tiptoe from room to room, petrified that I would break something of significance and face my father's wrath if I did.

I'm actually relieved to hear he's finally getting rid of the place, because I have no desire to ever step foot inside again. I'm about to tell him as much when it occurs to me that can't be the only reason he dragged me here. He didn't even have the courtesy to call me back when I had my miscarriage. There's no way he'd change his tune simply to notify me he was selling my childhood home.

"That's not the real reason I'm here, is it?"

"You're not as dense as you look. I'm impressed," he drawls.

There he goes again with the subtle jabs. As I observe him, I can see sweat on his brow and his right hand is twitching. He's nervous. Whatever he has to tell me must be important.

"There is one other thing I've been meaning to discuss with you."

I roll my eyes at his theatrics. Aside from this dinner, I have no idea when he would have planned on mentioning this "other thing" considering we haven't talked in fifteen years.

"When your grandfather passed, he made me the acting CEO of Kingsman & Reed, but he gave your mother fifty-one percent ownership. She and I came to a little understanding: she stayed out of the company's business, and I steered clear of you. It was a win-win in my book, though if it were up to me, I would have shipped you off to boarding school the day you turned ten."

"Can you please get to the point?" I snip. I'm tired of his attempts to aggravate me and would like to get out of this stuffy restaurant sooner rather than later.

Harrison lets out a loud gulp as he fidgets with his cobalt tie. "When your mom passed, the majority ownership of the company was transferred to you…"

My ears perk up, and I'm suddenly not so eager to leave.

"You were only seventeen then, but you've never showed any interest in the business. For years, I've been able to keep the board satisfied, telling them you didn't want an active role in the day-to-day operations. There wasn't an issue until a few months ago when we had to bring on two new board members." He pauses, avoiding direct eye contact. "They're demanding you either sign over ownership to me, or take a more active role in the business."

My lips slowly upturn into a satisfied grin. I hold the fate of my father's precious company in the palm of my hand. For once, I have all the power in this relationship, and justice has never felt so sweet.

I stare daggers at him while I take a long sip of the water the waiter must have put on the table for me before I arrived. I didn't realize how parched I had been from practically jogging here. Once I finish swallowing, I slowly set my glass back down on the table, circling the rim with the tip of my finger, contemplating my next move.

"Father, are you happy?" I ask.

"Excuse me?" he shoots back.

"I asked if you're happy," I repeat, slower this time. "Are you satisfied with the way your life turned out? Does swimming in your billions bring you joy? I heard through the grapevine that your divorce papers to wife number six have been inked. Lucky girl just made a killing. What'd you give this one? A Lamborghini and a cool twenty million?"

I watch as Harrison grinds his teeth—wanting to throttle me, no doubt. Unfortunately for him, he has to play nice, at least for now. I rest my elbows on the table, leaning in closer as if about to share a well-kept secret.

"Did you know I used to worship the ground you walked on? I spent my entire childhood vying for your attention, foolishly thinking you'd pick me over your extravagant lifestyle one day. Boy, was I wrong.

"The only thing you ever did right was when you made it possible for me to have a real family: Mom, Milo, and me—The Three Musketeers. If you had actually been present in my life, Milo would never have come to live with us, so in reality, I owe you one."

"I hope you haven't let that degenerate troublemaker back into your life. You should know better. No doubt he's somehow got wind of your inheritance and wants to swoop in and take it for himself," he seethes.

I bark out a laugh. "Milo has his own money; he doesn't need any of mine. Unlike you, he's earned every penny he's made. In my eyes, he is ten times the man you will ever be." I narrow in on the stack of papers my father has tried to keep out of view by hiding them under his arm. "Give me the paperwork, please." I nod toward the pile.

He hesitantly slides it over, unsure what exactly I'm about to do. Good. I'm glad I'm unpredictable. It makes it all the more satisfying watching him flounder like a fish.

"I don't want your company, Harrison," I admit.

He seems surprised by my reaction.

"I'll have my lawyer look over the contract, and if everything is in order, I'll sign over my rights to the fifty-one percent. Kingsman & Reed will legally be yours." I pick up the documents and put them in my purse hung on the back of my chair.

Some might call me crazy for giving in so easily, but I disagree. My mom left me enough money to last several lifetimes, but I'd trade it all to have her here with me. No amount of wealth will ever bring her back or buy me a new family. I want more in life than ownership of a poisonous dynasty that will only succeed in dragging me down to the depths of misery.

I turn to face my father for the very last time. "When you're all alone on your deathbed, I want you to remember this exact moment. When your daughter lost the last ounce of respect she was holding on to for you. Consider any hope of a reconciliation with me at a later date null and void. I hope you and your money are very happy together."

I give him a sad little smile before sliding out of my chair and tightening my coat around me.

The last thing I see as I walk out of the room is Harrison's eyes widening when he takes in my full appearance for the first time tonight...and it's not because of my lack of formal attire.

I don't falter or try to explain myself. I don't owe him a single thing.

And just like that, I leave both my father and the last of my childhood trauma behind without a second glance.

Chapter Thirty

MILO
Present Day—April

AFTER READING MAC'S LETTER FOR the fifth time in a row, I know what I need to do to make this right. It's simple.

I have to make Liv my wife. Anything less than spending every last minute of every single day with her until the day I die will never be enough.

I need all of her. Her sexy body. Her brilliant mind. Her kind soul.

In return, she'll have all of me. My everlasting love. My undying devotion. My endless groveling.

I will do whatever it takes to make up for my past transgressions and for walking out on her the way that I did…twice.

There's no doubt that Liv is getting the short end of the stick, but it doesn't matter. We were destined as soulmates long before either of us took our first breath. There is nothing that can stop me from binding us together for eternity.

In order to make that happen, she has to forgive me.

As Eloisa always says when training a new chef, "You have to learn to crawl before you can sprint."

First things first, I need to find Liv. I have to make her see that we belong together once and for all, and demand that we never leave each other's sides again.

Look at me, being willing to compromise. Although I wouldn't be against locking her up in my penthouse if she were into that sort of thing.

After my epiphany, I call Richard, demanding that he book me on the earliest available flight to LaGuardia Airport. He makes it clear that he expects a substantial raise if I expect him to put up with my ill-tempered behavior any longer. I tell him that he's fired before promptly hanging up on him.

The joke's on me.

There's no doubt a sizable bonus will discreetly find its way into his bank account by the end of the week, courtesy of Pike. Without fail, when I get back from my trip, Richard will be at the office to greet me with a steaming cup of black coffee and a stick of Big Red as if nothing happened the week prior.

Our working relationship only functions properly when I consistently threaten to sack him at least once a day, and in turn, he receives a monetary incentive from Pike for putting up with my cranky ass. I don't know how we'll survive once Pike decides to retire for real.

On my way to the airport, I stop by to see Pike and Eloisa to make amends. When I greet her, Eloisa slaps me upside the head before pulling me in for a giant bear hug. She is a blubbering mess when I tell her I love her for the first time, saying she'll always cherish the moment. When she mentions that she has been talking to Liv every day, I tell her to call Liv this afternoon, like she always does, but not to mention that I'm coming to see her. This plan has to go perfectly, and I refuse to let anything get in my way of making things right.

I don't want to take Sirius with me and leave him alone in my Brooklyn apartment while I go see Liv, so he stays behind with Eloisa and Pike. If he had it his way, he'd live with them permanently anyway, where he gets double the dog treats, endless cuddles, and a vast collection of new toys. I predict by the time I get back, his beloved hedgehogs will have a full array of squeaky companions that will be coming home to live with us.

If things go well, Liv will be coming home to live with us too.

My flight ends up being delayed three times and I'm forced to sit in coach, where the legroom is nonexistent and I'm practically sharing a seat with the passengers next to me.

Have I mentioned that I have to sit in the middle seat— my worst nightmare come to life? Between the woman to my left coughing throughout the entire flight, the man hogging the armrest to my right, and the baby screaming in the seat behind me, I nearly have a nervous breakdown. My eardrums are ready to burst by the time we land.

As soon as I get off the plane, I call and leave Richard a lengthy voicemail with some choice words thrown in. At least he had the foresight to ignore my call. I make it clear that he knows he's really fired this time and tell him that no amount of groveling to Pike will save him now.

We both know that's a lie, though, because Pike was probably the one who suggested that he book me a middle seat in economy, knowing that it would drive me insane. A way to give me a taste of my own medicine. He's one of the few people who knows just how far my distaste for crowds and people really goes.

After the plane debacle, I find myself in a taxi, stuck in bumper-to-bumper traffic in the middle of Manhattan. Can't a guy catch a break, especially when he's doing his very best to win back his girl?

Apparently not. It's clear that the universe is conspiring against me.

Do you blame it? You're a total ass.

I hate New York City. The only good thing about it is that Liv's here. Once I convince her to come back to Las Vegas with me, I swear I'm never setting foot in this town again. I'll hire someone to manage Lawson's New York office—or better yet, Pike can take it on while Eloisa is here setting up the new restaurant. To be honest, I haven't really thought about the logistics. What if Liv doesn't want to leave her job? Or worse, what if she asks me to move back here?

I'd do it in a heartbeat. I'd move back to this cesspool, no questions asked.

Hell, I'd move to the North Pole if she asked me to, just as long as we're together.

I look up at the clock again as I impatiently tap my foot against the floorboard. I had this brilliant plan to show up to Liv's group therapy session and share my story. At the end, I'd confess my undying love for her. She'd instantly forgive me, and we'd ride off into the sunset, preferably in a direction that took us away from this rat-infested city. However, that well thought-out plan is unraveling before my eyes as I watch the seconds tick by. I was sure that a taxi would be the fastest way to my destination, but at this point, the train would have been a better bet.

The first time I went to therapy with Liv, she made it clear that they close the doors at seven on the dot to avoid any distractions during the duration of the session. I take another hopeless glance at the clock to see that it's already ten to seven. At the rate we're moving, I don't have a chance of getting there on time.

Screw this.

I grab my backpack sitting on the seat next to me, throw my car door open, and jump out. The driver turns around in his seat, shouting profanities at me, but I don't listen to a word he says.

"Sorry, man. I have someplace to be, and I can't be late. Thanks for the ride, I left you a generous tip," I holler as I toss a wad of cash on the seat before slamming the door shut behind me.

I dash down the street toward the church Liv took me to the last time. I don't dare pull my phone out to check the time, afraid of losing precious seconds I can't afford to waste. My only focus is to run as fast as my legs can carry me.

Thank God I stopped smoking so I can sprint again, or this plan might have ended up with me in the hospital from a collapsed lung.

I run past the front of the church, round the corner, and rush down the stairs. As I get to the bottom step, I see Mike, the grief counselor, shutting the door. Without a second thought, I shove my hand through the crack to keep it from closing.

"Wait, please! You have to let me in," I beg.

He gives me a skeptical look as if to remind me what happened the last time I was allowed inside. It wasn't my finest moment.

"Listen, I swear I won't cause any trouble this time. I had just received some devastating news when I was here last, and I didn't think before I reacted. But I did have my assistant make a generous donation to compensate for the damage that I caused. That has to count for something, right?" I question, my hand still wedged between the door and the frame.

Mike looks me dead in the eye, a calculating expression on his face. "Five thousand dollars."

"Excuse me?"

"You want in? You'll have to donate another five grand to the church."

"Are you crazy?" I shout in distress. "This is a free support group. You can't—"

He shoves my hand out of the way, ready to slam the door in my face if I don't give him what he wants.

"Okay, okay, fine." I put my hands up in surrender. "Count me in for another donation."

I pull out my phone and immediately text Richard with instructions to wire five grand to Friendship Baptist Church. A few seconds later, a text confirms that it's done, followed by a second message asking how economy class treated me.

I knew he messed with the seating arrangement on my flight.

I hold up my phone to Mike's face, showing him the bank transfer receipt.

"Consider my contribution complete. Now, will you please let me in?" I ask, reeking of desperation.

ANN EINERSON

Mike gives me a wide grin when he sees that I did indeed send the money. He seems very pleased with his negotiation tactics, but I'm not amused as I make my way into the room.

I'm welcomed by a semicircle full of people glaring up at me, none of whom look pleased that I was allowed inside. I must have left a lasting impression when I was here a few months ago. As I move further into the room, my stomach drops when I don't see Liv. I jerk my head from side to side, making sure that I didn't miss her somehow.

How the hell is this possible? She told me she hasn't missed a session in years, except for when Mac was sick.

This can't be happening.

I turn back around to look at Mike and find a gloating smirk on his face. He knew that I came here for Liv and that she wasn't here *before* he gave me an ultimatum. Holy shit, the man conned me, the sneaky bastard. I have to give him credit, though. It's no easy feat, convincing someone to hand over a cool five grand without question.

At least it's tax deductible.

"Everyone, take a seat. It's time to get started." He looks directly at me, silently threatening me if I dare make another scene.

Unfriendly stares come at me from all directions as I quickly make my way to the last empty chair in the back.

Is this my penance for all the shit I've put Liv through? There's no other explanation for how things have turned out. I've played dozens of versions of this day in my head, and not one of them involved Liv not showing up to her group therapy session tonight. Now I'm stuck in a room full of people who are silently planning my demise, and I have to spend the next ninety minutes with them.

I shouldn't be surprised this is how things ended up.

I listen as the members of the session share their thoughts, time dragging on as I try to think of a new plan. My gaze doesn't leave the door, willing Liv to appear with a valid excuse as to why she's late.

Before I know it, Mike is announcing that there's only time for one more share. No one makes a move to stand up, and it's so quiet that you could hear a pin drop.

Meanwhile, an internal battle plays out in my head.

If I get up and speak, the meeting will end, and I can go find Liv.

Do you really want to pour out your heart to a room of strangers who hate you?

I came intending to share with the group.

That was when you thought Liv would be here to hear what you had to say.

Fuck it. I don't have time for this.

I bolt up from my chair, the legs scratching loudly against the tiled floor. I swear the lady next to me flinches as I stand.

Seriously? I'm not that scary, unless you count terrorizing a table full of refreshments. Then I'm guilty as charged.

"Hi, everyone. My name is Milo, and I come in peace." I lift my hand up in an awkward wave, but no one laughs or even cracks a smile.

Tough crowd. Or maybe I really am just that socially inept.

"I'd like to apologize for overreacting when I was here a few months ago. It was inexcusable, and not something I'm proud of. I've spent more than half my life telling myself that I was wronged by the world, always playing the victim. Every time something went wrong, I used it as an excuse to lash out. I allowed the animosity and hate that I felt to live rent-free in my mind, refusing to admit I had a problem or might need some help. Truth be told, grief's a bitch."

There are a few soft gasps from around the room in response to my crass language. I make a mental note to tell Liv that I think it's time she finds a new support group. These people are getting on my last nerve.

"It's like I'm driving down a foggy, unmarked road without a map or directions. There are giant potholes along the way, but I don't know their exact coordinates or instructions on how to avoid them. It's the same with grief. There are days when I think I've finally gotten past the worst of the pain, the anguish of losing some of the most important people in my life. Then, when I least expect it, something triggers me, and I'm bulldozed with uncontrollable rage." I pause, debating whether to cut my losses now or finish my thought.

"I convinced myself a long time ago that I was better off on my own. I went as far as shutting out the person who meant the most to me, petrified of spreading my dark disposition to her. The truth is, I really don't give a shit anymore. I can't live without her." *I won't.* "I was shrouded in darkness for so long that I forgot what it felt like to be bathed in the sunlight until she came back into my life, and now I'm addicted."

Once I finish, I realize that my hands are trembling from nerves. I can't believe I did that. I notice the lady next to me has changed her tune and is nodding in agreement. I'm glad she doesn't think I'm a total nutcase anymore.

I'm surprised at how good it feels to have said those words out loud.

I have no plans to make group therapy a regular occurrence, but I think I'll schedule an individual session with a therapist. I know taking care of my mental health is an important part of the process in making up with Liv long-term.

I don't wait for Mike to wrap up or for the meeting to officially adjourn. I walk right out the door—leaving the snack table untouched this time, much to everyone's relief.

As I climb the stairs, my phone starts to vibrate in my pocket. I immediately answer when I see that it's Eloisa. She knows where I am, so this must be important.

"Hey, is everything okay? I'm sorry I didn't call earlier. My flight got delayed, and I was trying to make—"

She cuts me off, her voice filled with sheer panic. "Milo, stop talking. I need you to listen to me. It's an emergency!" She's breathing heavily, and I'm concerned that she's going to have a full-blown anxiety attack if she doesn't calm down.

I take in a deep breath, forcing myself to keep my composure. Eloisa is notorious for overreacting to situations, so I refuse to panic until I know there's actually something to worry about.

"Whoa, Els, calm down. What's the matter?"

"I just got off the phone with Olivia. She's at Giovanni's!" she shrieks into the phone as if I should know what that means.

"I don't understand what you're saying. What's Giovanni's?"

She lets out an exasperated sigh, clearly annoyed that I'm slowing this conversation down. "Olivia is on a date at Giovanni's."

Did she just say date?

"It's one of the most expensive restaurants in the city. She skipped therapy for this, so that must mean something. She never skips therapy. Milo, you have to find her. She can't move on, not when you two were so close to getting back together. You were supposed to get married and give me grandbabies!" she screams hysterically.

The only thing I can register is that Liv's on a date…with another man. *What the hell?* My hands turn clammy, my stomach churning at the thought of someone else's hands on her. It's been over four months, but it didn't occur to me that she might move on this fast. I figured she'd be focused on dealing with her grief over losing Mac and getting back into the swing of work.

"Are you sure she's on a date? Is there any chance you might have misinterpreted what she said?" I ask, needing to be certain.

"I'm sure! She said she had to hang up because she was meeting 'him' at Giovanni's. Who else could she have been referring to? I already called Dante and confirmed that he didn't have plans to see her tonight."

Of course she did. This woman will stop at nothing to get the truth. At least her version of it, that is.

"Els, it'll be okay. I'm headed to the restaurant now. I'm sure it's nothing." The knot in my stomach tightens, afraid of what I'll find when I get there.

"Call me *the* minute you have any news," she pleads.

"I will, I promise."

She hangs up, no doubt going to find Pike so she can give him a play-by-play of our conversation.

I pull up Giovanni's on Google Maps. Overwhelming anxiety ripples through me as I rush through the crowded streets. When I arrive, both the sidewalk and entrance of the building are swarming with people waiting to get inside. I rudely shove past, making my way to the hostess stand. I can't wait any longer to find out the truth. If I've really lost my chance of being with Liv, I need to know now.

The blonde behind the desk plasters on a fake smile when she sees me approach.

"Excuse me. I'm looking for someone," I announce. "Her name's Olivia. Olivia Dunham. She has shoulder-length brown hair and green eyes. Is she here?"

"Olivia? Are you sure?" the woman stutters.

"Positive. I was told she would be here."

"Sorry. She left five minutes ago," she deadpans, not happy that I'm inquiring about Liv. "You don't need her to have a good time. Want to grab a drink after my shift ends in an hour? I'm free all night." Her flirty tone is off-putting, and I can smell her desperation from here.

"No, thanks. I'm married," I state.

Her eyes bulge out of her head. She has a confused expression on her face when she looks down and sees my empty ring finger. It won't be that way for long if I have any say in the matter. Even if Liv was on a date, I've already decided that I'm not letting her go without a fight. All I need to do is find her.

"Do you know which way Olivia went when she left?"

"How would I know? I'm not her keeper," the woman sneers at me, obviously done with the niceties now that she knows I'm unavailable.

I sigh in frustration as I storm out of the restaurant.

Now what? Maybe I can catch her before she makes it back to her apartment. Although I have no idea which way she would have gone. I rush off in the direction of her building, hoping I'll spot her along the way, but despite my best efforts, I don't. By the time I get to her apartment, I find that the doorman is gone for the night, and I can't get inside without a passkey.

"Dammit!" I shout out at the top of my lungs. "Can't a man catch a fucking break?" I mumble to myself.

I throw my fists against the brick wall, leaning my head forward in defeat. Maybe this is a sign from the universe, telling me that Liv and I don't belong together, and no matter how hard we try, we're not meant to be.

I'm about to walk away when I hear an angelic voice to my right.

"What did that poor wall ever do to you?"

Liv.

Chapter Thirty-One

OLIVIA
Present Day—April

MILO SNAPS HIS HEAD IN my direction, letting out a sigh of relief when he sees that it's me standing next to him.

His hair is tousled, his brilliant blue eyes shine with emotion, and his clothes are disheveled. He looks worse for wear, and it's obvious that he's had one heck of a day.

So have I.

"Milo, what are you doing here?" I ask, annoyed.

Not only did I not know he was back in town, but I'm exhausted from the confrontation with my father. The last thing I want to do right now is go another round with Milo.

"Where were you?" he barks, his tumultuous mood in full force.

"I was out. What's it to you?" I bite back.

He's out of his mind if he thinks he can show up here after four months of silence and we'll pretend like he didn't tell me we were finished the last time we were together.

While I admit he had every right to be angry with me for withholding information, that only extends to a certain period of time. It definitely doesn't excuse him for walking away without being willing to talk things through first. He can't storm off every time things get challenging and expect me to wait around for him to come back when it suits him.

I want Milo in my life, but I'm not willing to sacrifice my own happiness for him…not again.

"I came all the way from Vegas to see you. I had an elaborate plan that started with showing up at your group therapy session, but that didn't work out as I had hoped considering you weren't even there…" he explains, speaking as if he can't get the words out fast enough. "And then after sitting through the session anyway, Eloisa called me in a panic, telling me you were on a date."

"A date?" I ask. "Oh, Eloisa…" I shake my head in mock disappointment. It's no wonder she was agitated during our call earlier. "Milo, that's the furthest thing from the truth. I told her I was running late to meet someone, but I never said it was a date."

"Who were you with?" he asks.

I release a sigh, looking down at my nails, making it clear that I'm in no hurry to give him an answer. It will do him good to sweat it out, to consider the possibility that I've moved on.

Milo lets out a grunt, clearly displeased with my attempt at deflecting his question.

"Who. Were. You. With. Liv?" he demands.

This man is infuriating.

"If you must know, I was meeting with my father," I retort. "We had a few items of business we needed to hash out."

"So you really weren't on a date?"

"No, I wasn't, but I don't see how it's any of your concern who I spend my time with," I say, exasperated.

"Thank God," he murmurs under his breath. "That's bullshit, and you know it. You will always be my primary concern," he says.

"You weren't worried about my well-being when you left me alone at Mac's wake," I say. "You've had plenty of opportunities to reach out since then. Why now?" I fold my arms across my chest, letting him know that I'm not backing down without answers.

"Why?" he asks with a perplexed look. "You've consumed my thoughts for the past four months, and not a minute has gone by that I haven't thought of you," he confesses. "I was angry when you shared the truth about my dad, but I should never have left things the way I did. I had no right to play judge and jury, or to treat you the way that I have."

"I should have told you sooner." I drop my head in remorse, not wanting to face him. "It haunts me knowing I was part of the reason you never reconciled with Mac. He thought he was doing the right thing by not telling you what really happened the night of the accident, and I couldn't convince him otherwise. I should have ignored his wishes and told you anyway…and now it's too late, and for that, I'm so sorry."

I can feel Milo staring at me, but I can't bring myself to look at him yet. I'm stunned when he cups my cheek, gently caressing my jaw with his thumb, and brings my gaze to his. His eyes reflect the remorse in my own.

"Hearing you say that means a lot to me. However, you withheld the truth out of love and respect for the man you admired," Milo recognizes. "Mac was the only person in your corner. He earned your trust and loyalty—things I lost when I walked away from you. I don't fault you for honoring his wishes…not anymore. I've screwed up repeatedly over the past fifteen years, and I have no one to blame but myself for the suffering I've caused you."

"Milo—" I start.

"Liv, please let me finish," he interjects, pressing a featherlight kiss against my temple. "I'm so fucking sorry. I may not be able to rewrite the past, but the least I can do is give you the overdue apology you deserve." He draws in a slow breath. "I'm sorry for shutting you out when Marie got sick. I'm sorry for breaking my promise to stand by your side no matter what. I'm sorry for not being there to comfort you when you suffered through the loss of our daughter. I'm sorry for everything I said when I found out Mac was in your life. I'm sorry for blaming you for things outside of your control.

"And most importantly, I'm so sorry for not treating you like the goddess you are. You should be worshipped, cherished, and adored, and I've done a piss poor job of showing you that. I wouldn't blame you if you chose to walk away and never speak to me again." He starts to tremble, and I give him a small smile, encouraging him to finish. "I came here to tell you that I love you…to *remind* you that I love you. There hasn't been a single day during the past fifteen years where I haven't. I'm ready to put the past behind us and start over. I don't want to spend another second without you…please don't make me."

I'm speechless. His apology is unexpected, yet it means everything to me. In the past, I would have immediately accepted it and moved on. This time, though, I need to be sure that he's ready to commit. To fight for us when times get tough.

"What's stopping you from leaving me the next time we go through a rough patch, or I do something you disagree with?" I voice my concerns out loud.

He drops his head, clearly dejected by the facts of our past that led to my question in the first place. He raises his gaze to meet mine and clutches my hands in his, looking equal parts sincere and worried that I'll disappear if he lets me go.

"Unless you tell me to piss off, I'm not going anywhere. When I think about my future, you're all I can see. I need you more than I need my next breath. Please tell me you feel the same way, that there's a way for us to move past this…together," he says, faltering at the end of his plea.

"If you would take two seconds to really *look* at me, you'd see that you're the only man I have a future with, and that no matter what I do, I'll never be able to escape you," I tell him.

"What the hell are you talking about? God, Liv. You're all I see," he exclaims.

I glare up at him, urging him to finally take a full perusal of my body. I watch as he refocuses his gaze, taking in each of my features, one at a time.

My eyes, shining with emotion, pleading with him to make things right.

My hair, waiting for him to run his fingers through it as we make love.

My lips, begging for him to take a taste.

My breasts pressed up against my scrub top, aching to be touched and caressed.

My swollen stomach…

I memorize the exact moment Milo does a double take.

"Liv…" he croaks out, his eyes glued to my belly. He's unable to look away, and I'm worried his brain might short-circuit. "You're—"

"Pregnant with your baby?" I state the obvious. "Yes, I am."

I received the news last month. Just like my first pregnancy, I didn't experience any symptoms during my first trimester, so I was shocked when I found out. I've already scheduled a few days off work and was planning to fly to Las Vegas this coming weekend to tell Milo. It was a conversation that needed to happen in person, but I wanted it to be on my terms. I knew Eloisa would have spilled the beans if I'd told her, so I chose to keep the news to myself up until now.

I refuse to let this baby be a pawn in the drawn-out battle Milo and I have been fighting. The circumstances may not be ideal, but I will never take the unforeseen second chance at becoming a mother for granted. It's all I've ever wanted.

I watch as Milo peels his eyes away from my abdomen and gapes down at me.

"He's our rainbow baby, our fresh start," I whisper reverently.

"He?" Milo croaks out. "We're going to have a son?"

I nod rapidly, a broad smile spread across my face.

Milo sinks to his knees in the middle of the filthy, rat-infested sidewalk. I watch in awe as he tenderly places his large hands on my firm stomach—physical proof that we're going to be parents. He presses his cheek against my abdomen, soaking in the knowledge that our son is growing safely inside.

"Liv…" Milo whispers as tears stream down his cheeks. "I can't change the past, neither of us can. All I can do is beg you to give me the chance to make it up to you. Hell, even if I have to live on the Upper East Side of Manhattan, I'll do it with a shit-eating grin if I'm by your side. As long as I have you and our son, that's all I need."

Knowing how much he hates New York City, it's saying a lot that he'd live here for me.

"I make a vow, right here, right now, that I will do everything I can to shower you and our son with love, affection, and adoration for as long as I live. By the time we're old and gray, you'll wish I hadn't.

I let out a coarse laugh, taking a moment to contemplate my options.

Milo and I are at a crossroads, and the ball is in my court. It comes down to a single choice. We can forgive each other for the wrongs we've inflicted on each other, or we can choose to forget. To walk away and live our separate lives, always second-guessing our decision.

I look down at the man kneeling in front of me, the same man who's spent the past two decades allowing bitterness and resentment to consume him because of the choices his parents made. I refuse to allow our son to carry a similar burden because of the choices Milo and I make.

I'm overcome with peace as I come to my decision.

I choose forgiveness. To spend the rest of my life striving to achieve true happiness, because I've experienced what happens when I don't. Despite the pain and hurt that Milo has caused me, he's also been my greatest source of joy.

I silently place my hands over his as we feel our son kick for the first time.

"I love you, Milo Leland Covell," I murmur. My heart thumps loudly as I finally speak those three little words.

"I love you, Liv. I love you both," Milo says in a hushed tone as he softly kisses my swollen belly.

Every event in our lives has led to this exact moment. Our fates were intertwined long before we met, and our souls were always meant to find their way back to each other.

I gaze into the night sky as I think of my mom, Mac, and Jada. I will forever be grateful to them for the role they played in making this possible.

Milo and I have finally been liberated from the shackles of our past, ready to move on to a brighter future...together.

Ready to forgive by putting the past behind us once and for all.

Ready to forget our time apart, the hurtful words spoken in anger, and the crippling pain.

Ready to create new memories with each other, our son, and our found family.

Epilogue

OLIVIA
Present Day—January

I REST MY HEAD AGAINST Milo's thigh as he gently runs his fingers through my hair. I'm mesmerized by the sound of his gentle tone, filling me with warmth as he reads from the copy of *The Tale of Peter Rabbit* that Eloisa gifted us the day we told her she was going to be a grandma. She sobbed uncontrollably when we broke the news, and then spent the entire next day shopping for our little star.

In typical Pike fashion, he simply patted Milo on the back, saying, "It's about damn time."

There wasn't a question in my mind that he would be the best grandpa to our son.

From my spot on the floor, I look up at Milo seated in the light-gray rocking chair in the corner of the nursery. He's holding the book he's reading with one hand and cradling our three-month-old son, Malcolm Mario Covell, in his other arm.

I knew from the moment I found out I was expecting that I wanted to name him after the two people who had the biggest impact on my life while I was growing up and who were responsible for bringing Milo and me together—Mac and my mom.

Malcolm's soft brown curls fall against his forehead, his piercing blue eyes glued to his father's face, his tiny fists clenched against his chest as he listens to Milo's calming voice. He's the spitting image of his father, and it warms my heart. He's perfect, and he's all ours.

A few weeks after Milo and I reconciled, I moved to Las Vegas and was able to secure an attending position at a top ranked hospital in the area.

I look around the once-empty spare bedroom in Milo's penthouse that we've since converted into a nursery. The wall behind Malcolm's crib is painted black with white decals scattered across, depicting the constellations and the moon in the upper-right corner. A solar system mobile hangs above the crib that plays "Twinkle, Twinkle, Little Star."

On the far side of the room are the floor-to-ceiling bookshelves Pike built for us. They're already more than halfway filled with the children's books I've collected over the years—a hobby I never gave up, even after Milo left all those years ago. I like to think I subconsciously always knew Milo and I would find our way back to each other, and that's why I never stopped.

The top shelf is filled with the books I found in Mac's bedroom closet when I finally had the courage to go through his things. Most were vintage children's books he had found at local thrift stores and various yard sales in Manhattan over the years. Inside each cover is a handwritten message addressed to his grandkids. Milo and I both shed tears when we found these treasures, and we will always cherish them.

Sirius is curled up in his dog bed next to the rocking chair. From the second we brought Malcolm home from the hospital, he found his new best friend and never leaves the baby's side. He still finds time to cuddle with his ever-growing collection of hedgehog toys that we can't seem to keep under control. Eloisa won't stop buying him the dang things, saying she doesn't want him to feel left out now that we have Malcolm.

Our son has only been in our lives for three short months, yet my life before him seems obsolete now that our family is whole. From the minute I held our tiny bundle of joy in my arms for the first time, I knew he was the missing puzzle piece we never knew we needed to close the final gap between Milo and me.

I climb off the ground as Milo lays Malcolm in his crib. We look down as he fusses for a few minutes before settling down. I feel nothing but peace as I watch the steady rise and fall of his chest, comforted in knowing that all is right in our world.

Milo wraps his arms around me from behind, pressing a tender kiss against my temple.

"I love you, Liv," he whispers reverently as he looks down lovingly at our son.

"I love you too, Milo. Forever and always."

Thank you for reading my debut novel, *Forgive or Forget Me*. It means so much that you took the time to read this book from beginning to end, and I hope you enjoyed it. If you did, please consider leaving an honest review on your preferred platform of choice. It's the best compliment I can receive as an author.

If you're not ready to say goodbye, you can read Mac and Jada's heartbreaking yet enduring love story in my free novella, *Our Tattered Souls*, which can be found on my website: AnnEinerson.com

Acknowledgments

TO MY READERS—FOR GIVING my debut novel a chance. It takes a high degree of trust to sit down and read a book from beginning to end by an author you've never heard of before. Thank you for loving *Forgive or Forget Me* as much as I do and for being my inspiration to finish the writing process. I sincerely appreciate every review, post, and comment promoting my book.

To Sandea—For believing in me from day one and for listening to my constant harebrained ideas, no matter the time of day. Most importantly, thank you for putting up with Milo's crass language; he wouldn't have been the same without it.

To Brooke—For being the first to welcome me into the Bookstagram community and saving the day at the eleventh hour. You helped transform *Forgive or Forget Me* from words on a page into an imperfectly perfect love story worth telling.

To Jovana and Sam—Thank you for meticulously reviewing my manuscript and for pushing me to become a better writer in the process. My debut novel wouldn't have been possible without you both.

To Ashleigh, Brittni, and Salma—For guiding me through the publishing process, helping me every step of the way, and making the release of my debut novel a success.

To Nicole—For bringing *Forgive or Forget Me* to life through its cover and for your patience as we worked toward the best representation for this book. It's absolute perfection.

To Tre, Meghan, Shae, Melissa, and Viola—Your honest, detailed, and candid feedback drove me to create a version of this book I didn't even know existed.

To Roxan and Randy—You taught me to believe in myself and to reach for the stars, no matter the distance. I love you both, always.

To Kyler—Thank you for supporting my insane work schedule, for tolerating the endless amounts of takeout and piles of laundry that accrued in the months leading up to this book's launch, and for helping to make my dream of becoming a published author come true.

About the Author

ANN EINERSON IS THE AUTHOR of imperfect love stories that will tug at your heartstrings, keeping you invested until the very last page.

Her strong-willed heroines aren't afraid to take on their moody men when they need to be put in their place. Each of Ann's novels feature a found family, an ode to her love of travel and incorporates a roller coaster of emotions so get your tissues ready.

She keeps an ample supply of sticky notes on hand to jot down the stories that live rent-free in her mind.

When she's not writing, Ann enjoys spoiling her pet chickens, listening to her dysfunctional playlists, and going for late-night runs on the treadmill. She lives in Michigan with her husband.

Keep in Touch with Ann Einerson

Website: www.anneinerson.com

Newsletter: www.anneinerson.com/newsletter-signup

Instagram: www.instagram.com/authoranneinerson

TikTok: www.tiktok.com/@authoranneinerson

Amazon: www.amazon.com/author/anneinerson

Goodreads:
www.goodreads.com/author/show/29752171.Ann_Einerson